THE SLAYER

NADINE LAPIERRE

Frisson

THE SLAYER Copyright © 2011 by Nadine LaPierre

First Printing 2011
Printed in the United States of America

Frisson Books
ISBN-13: 978-0986866807
ISBN-10: 0986866806

DEDICATION

This book is dedicated to all the women who serve and protect with courage and honor in police forces around the world.
And to my grandmother.

ACKNOWLEDGMENTS

I owe the authenticity and foundation of this book to my confidential sources in the RCMP who very generously shared their time, knowledge, and experiences with me. They not only provided me with a thorough understanding of the RCMP, HRP, integrated major crime investigations, and overall police procedures, but with a true understanding of what it's like for female officers serving proudly and expertly in a male dominated Force. I will be eternally grateful.

To the "Newfie Mountie" who shattered my stereotype of female police officers, your compassionate and patient demeanor coating your robust interior is the perfect combination. Most of all, you taught me that integrity is the backbone of any great officer—which you most certainly are.

To Corporal H., if anything ever happens to me I want you on the case! Your superb skills, unshakable core, and dedication to your profession is impressive beyond words. Cst. Renaud aspires to your caliber.

I also owe a debt of gratitude to my source at the Public Prosecution Service. Your ability to explain legalese to me like I'm a five-year-old got me through some complex plotting.

I'd also like to thank "the girls" at the medical examiner's office who share my warped sense of humor. Thanks for everything, especially the "Fried Day" afternoon laughs.

To Ronda Gouchie, a friend with almost two decades experience as a vet tech and animal rescuer, thanks for answering my questions and providing me with much of the information behind the "murder weapon" and veterinary procedures. Glad you had as much faith in my writing as in my matchmaking. *Congrats on the marriage!*

I must also thank Norma Serrato, whose bookshelves are stocked with more lesfic than most public libraries, and whose passion for reading first connected us, but incredible kindness and wonderful humor gave me a lifelong friend. "I'm not a reviewer," she'd always say, but her opinions were always on the mark.

Thanks also goes out to romance author Janet Albert who was very generous in sharing her learned wisdom from the publishing world, and in providing me with tips that helped improve this book.

As the saying goes, "Last but not least…"

I must thank *you*, the reader. With so many books vying for your attention, I appreciate you giving mine a read.

From the bottom of my heart, *thank you* all.

❧ Prologue ❧

Eighteen Months Ago…

It was another uncomfortable, early October night when Tucker C. Hill shifted his weight so he could pull more of his thinning, tattered, blanket around him. His worn cardboard mattress was so damp it squished audibly underneath his movements. He didn't feel it though. He was fortunate enough to have easy access to large, plastic garbage bags courtesy of the park, which was his temporary—least he hoped it was temporary—home.

Sadness and shame overcame Tucker. He'd really hit rock bottom all right. He'd been sleeping on it for about five months.

What had unfortunately become a necessary tradition for many in Cape Breton, Nova Scotia, Tucker had no choice but to leave his beloved isle if he wanted steady work at a decent wage. He'd regularly make the temporary move to Halifax—Nova Scotia's largest and capital city—and work for as long as it took to complete a job, then go back home with some money in his pocket and Employment Insurance benefits he could rely on if he had to wait a few weeks or months till the next job rolled around.

He tried to get whatever work he could back home, but there just wasn't any. Most of Cape Breton was rural, and unless you owned a tourist shop or bed and breakfast along the famed and beautiful Cabot Trail, not a whole lot of work was available.

Little did Tucker know though his first day on the job as a drywaller at Casino Halifax, that he was standing in the very place that would end up contributing to his demise.

It was all fun and games at first—quite literally. So many fancy slot machines, black jack and poker tables. But it wasn't long before Tucker was regularly losing his hard-earned pay to the casino. He eventually maxed out his credit cards and lost his truck by defaulting on the payments one too many times. Then, just when he thought things were really bad, he got laid off from his job.

He did receive some employment insurance benefits, but he was so desperate to win back all he'd lost, he'd receive his two-week cheque on Thursday and be broke by Sunday with no money left for food, rent, or anything else.

He owed seven months' rent when he arrived home from the casino one morning to find a new lock on his apartment door and a sheriff's Order of Eviction announcing in bold, black lettering that he was now homeless.

While most of the homeless congregated or slept in the downtown core under bright lights near the hustle and bustle of city nightlife, Tucker felt safer sleeping in Hemlock Ravine Park. While it was surrounded by numerous homes that edged most of it, the park was not patrolled, very quiet, and rarely visited after dark.

Most of the summer he'd felt fairly warm and cozy in his burrow. To anyone standing a mere few feet away, all the exterior of his shelter appeared to be was a large mound of forest debris passers-by would surmise was left over from Hurricane Juan, a category two hurricane's direct hit with Halifax, which had occurred a few years earlier.

Halifax had been hit hard by the unusual occurrence of a hurricane. The city's centralized location along the Atlantic coast of Nova Scotia made it susceptible to rain and windstorms—even as the rest of Canada and much of the northern U.S. states were getting snow—but it also made the threat of hurricanes quite miniscule.

As they require warm water to develop and sustain them, hurricanes tend to weaken considerably over cold waters such as the North Atlantic. Although not uncommon for them to trek their way up the eastern seaboard, they were almost always down-graded to much lesser storm status by the time they reached Halifax. Then again there's always the exception—every hundred or so years—and Hurricane Juan was this century's exception.

It had decimated most of the city's parks, having mowed down more than half of the parks' trees, many of which had towered there for more than two centuries.

Haligonians wondered why so many strong, healthy trees had been toppled or ripped out of the earth altogether. Experts were quick to point out that the city of Halifax basically sits on a huge rock that juts out into the Atlantic Ocean. The few feet of soil that rests on top of this bedrock is too shallow to support the deep root systems that most hardwood trees require to withstand extraordinarily high winds.

Yep, Tucker Hill had himself a fairly nice spot—a well-concealed den of forest-debris near the park's romantic heart-shaped pond.

According to a sign at one of the park's entrances, the pond was built by a young Prince Edward—future father of Queen Victoria—in 1794, for his French mistress Julie St. Laurent. More than two hundred years later, much of the estate was a city-owned park called Hemlock Ravine—a park that now sat smack dab in the middle of wooded suburbia.

The approaching sound of squeaking wheels turned Tucker's attention away from his thoughts. He wasn't sure what time it was, but it was definitely late.

He opened his eyes and listened. He couldn't see anything from the interior of his surprisingly roomy dome-shaped den, as most of it was covered in black plastic garbage bags pieced and held together with black duct tape he'd bought with the few dollars he hadn't gambled or drank away that summer. His entryway was in the opposite direction of the pond and faced an almost vertical sheer of rocky hillside. His abode was so well constructed and so well disguised as just a heap of forest debris, he was actually quite proud of it.

The single set of footsteps wheeling something were coming closer. Tucker didn't move, but he listened. He heard the rotating squeal accompanied by rustling feet stop less than a minute after they started. He could hear some sort of sounds, but couldn't make out what they were. He continued to listen.

He heard a splash. Followed by a second one. This one clanged a bit.

Probably somebody dumping their garbage, he thought. Then he wondered if it might be anything that could be of use to him.

The pond was fairly shallow. Two or three feet in most places. Tucker knew, however, that what little moonlight there was tonight would not be able to penetrate the thick fog that had rolled in. He would not be able to see a thing even if it was in front of his face.

He decided to wait for the sun to come up and burn away the fog before he investigated.

∽ 1 ∾

Danielle Renaud's waist began to vibrate as she waited in line at a popular fair trade café for her favorite cup of organic chai tea. She hated to lose her place in line, but her occupation demanded absolute discretion.

She answered her cell phone and greeted the caller with an abrupt, "Just a moment, please," then made her way to the far corner of the café where a small but private ladies' room was located. As she closed and locked the door behind her, she put the phone back up to her ear.

"Constable Renaud here." It sounded like, *Ray-no ear*, her French Canadian accent quite prominent.

"Danielle, it's Robert." Robert was Danielle's boss at the Halifax detachment of the RCMP. "Halifax Regional wants to borrow you for an assignment. I've been given the details, but I'll let you get them from the horse's mouth. You're to meet Staff Sergeant John Kline in Special Investigations at HRP headquarters at nine a.m."

Danielle didn't have time to reply as Robert repeated, "Nine a.m., you got that?"

"Yes, I got tha—"

"Don't be late!" Robert followed that up with a loud click of the receiver.

Excitement rode its way up from Danielle's stomach to her throat. She'd been working in General Investigations for five years but had been applying for positions in the Special Investigations Section and Major Crimes Unit for the past two years.

Most homicides, missing persons, and major cold cases in Halifax were handled by the integrated Major Crimes Unit. Meaning, the teams were made up of both Royal Canadian Mounted Police and Halifax Regional Police officers.

While the RCMP had offices and operations across Canada, with an extremely strong national network any RCMP detachment could rely on, HRP was the local city police and knew its own backyard better than anyone.

Danielle looked at her watch. It was 8:20 a.m. Gottingen Street, where HRP headquarters was located, was just five minutes away.

She lowered the toilet seat and sat down on it, cradling her cell phone in both hands and smiling at it. She pressed the R *Work* icon and started tapping her feet, revealing her excited impatience as the phone rang on the other end.

"Halifax Medical Center, Andrea speaking."

"Hi Andrea, it's Danielle. Rachel doesn't have any patients yet, does she?"

"Not till nine. I'll put you through."

Dr. Rachel Matthews answered her direct line with a sense of urgency. "Dannie?"

Even though Danielle *hated* that nickname and Rachel knew it but kept using it anyway, it could not erase Danielle's elation at this very moment. "I've been assigned to Special Investigations!"

"Excuse me?"

Danielle deliberately slowed down her speech. "I'm on my way to Halifax Regional Police headquarters to be briefed on an S.I. assignment. Special Investigations, Rachel! I am so excited!"

"You mean nobody's died, or the condo hasn't burned down?" There was just a slight pause before Rachel admonished her. "I've told you never to disturb me at work unless it's an absolute emergency. You scared the hell out of me, Dannie. I thought something was wrong."

Danielle felt as though she'd been stabbed in the stomach. Not only could she feel all of her excitement and butterflies fly out of her, but everything else that might have been pleasant or even normal had been rudely displaced by the most sour and sickening feeling. She was so dismayed she couldn't even talk. She just lowered her head and looked at the floor.

Two minutes ago she'd been flying high. Now, all she felt was extremely let down and thoroughly…disgusted. Yet again her partner of three and a half years did not have any interest, passion, or support, for her—or her career.

"Hell-looo." Rachel's impatience and annoyance were even more pronounced.

Dejected, Danielle's resignation to the situation was clear. "I don't know why I even bothered to phone you."

"Oh, don't start—"

"Forget it, Rachel. Thanks for the support. Bye."

Danielle hung up so fast she wasn't sure if her words had even had a chance to come out first. She leaned back against the toilet tank and closed her eyes in defeat. She felt like staying there all day, wallowing in her sudden misery, but she knew she needed to pull herself together. She didn't have time to analyze why Rachel's behavior was increasingly insensitive and hurtful. She needed to focus on her job and career at the moment, and that's what she would do.

She washed away the few tears she had not been able to hold back before exiting the washroom. She didn't get back in line for tea, since her appetite for anything pleasant vanished when Rachel had deflated her, but she sat down and stared out a window for a few moments, trying to set aside her sorrow and regain the excitement she'd felt before she called Rachel.

As Danielle sat with her own thoughts, she did not notice a woman sitting with a pen and blueberry tea in hand, observing her. When Danielle left a few minutes later, the woman re-read what she had been so inspired to write.

For reasons as mysterious as the heavens
You have touched me

I did not know you, do not know you, may never know you
But as I journeyed these seas of transparent faces
I encountered yours
Which reflected back to me such substance and inspiration

Your presence in the vastness of this universe
Did not go unnoticed by me

Know that I ask nothing of you
For you have already given me such a rare and precious gift

It cannot be bought, traded, or sold
And it will remain with me forever

You have touched me

❧ 2 ❧

Staff Sergeant John Kline, head of the Cold Case Unit, sat at his desk surrounded by piles of various thicknesses of file folders, reports, and an assortment of other paperwork. Although his face was usually obscured by the tall stacks that surrounded him, he made sure to clear the front of his desk this morning so he could have a visually direct one-on-one with his next appointment.

When she walked in at exactly 9:00 a.m. he was taken aback. Constable Marie Danielle Renaud, thirty-four years of age, had a photo attached to her personnel file that matched the RCMP identification she carried on the opposite side of her badge, but it in no way accurately depicted the woman standing before him. In the flesh, Constable Renaud was simply... *stunning.*

She had tropical blue eyes, a shade of blue Kline had never seen outside the pages of a magazine. Her hair, naturally blond, had strands of caramel and tan, almost the same color of her skin. John had seen and admired many blondes in his fifty-two years, but most of them—the natural ones that is—had very fair skin. Renaud's natural skin tone, however, was that of a perfect tan.

Her face was so remarkably beautiful, with radiant skin and incredibly high cheek bones that framed and reflected the most beautiful eyes John Kline had ever seen. She appeared much taller than her recorded height of five foot six, and the way she carried herself made it apparent she felt very comfortable and secure about who—*and what*—she was.

She adhered to the force's dress code for plainclothes officers: business attire and long hair pulled back so as not to obscure the face. But her clothing fit her athletic body so perfectly even a plain white blouse with matching brown jacket and pants looked elegant on her. In his experience, someone *like her* didn't usually come in this type of packaging.

Some things were not officially politically correct to ask, but knowing unofficial details about certain officers was common, necessary even. It's why Constable Renaud had been selected for this assignment in the first place. She'd been highly recommended when he had—off the record—made inquiries looking for an experienced female investigator who was gay. Or was that lesbian? Or two-spirited, or some other term he hadn't yet heard of but should learn before he got into hot water over for not using.

Christ, keeping up with the latest technologies is tough enough, but this politically correct lingo is even worse.

"Staff Sergeant Kline, I'm Constable Renaud."

"Nice to meet you, Renaud." Kline stretched across his desk and shook Danielle's hand.

"Thanks, I'm very happy to be here."

Kline didn't respond to that, and Danielle didn't think he'd even heard her. She got the impression something was weighing awfully heavily on his mind. "Do you remember the Buchanan case? Happened about a year and a half ago, body found in Hemlock Ravine Park."

"Yes, of course," Danielle replied. "Halifax has its share of homicides, but they're usually domestics or drug related. That one was unusual—for Halifax."

"What do you know about it?"

"Not a whole lot, just what I read in the papers. She was a single woman, registered nurse if I recall, with no known ties to drugs or organized crime."

"That's not entirely true, but I'll fill you in on that later. What else do you know?"

"I remember the press made a really big deal about the fact she'd been found in a heart-shaped pond."

"Yes, dumping the body there might have been significant to her assailant, but it might have also been just purely coincidental."

"Dumping? So she was killed elsewhere? I don't think a cause of death was ever released, was it?"

"We never released it, not even to the family. I know it must be hard on them not knowing, but we can't reveal too much to anyone, not even grieving parents, when it's still an open case." Kline picked up a pen and started rolling it in his fingers. "It was never made public, but we know she was killed in her own home and her body dumped in the park shortly thereafter. A jogger spotted her in the pond about seventy-thirty in the morning. Medical examiner put the time of death between midnight and four a.m. That pond might have been chosen for a specific reason, or it might just be our perp lives near the park and simply found it convenient."

"Do you have any suspects?"

"Wish I could say yes, but the answer is no. Homicide spent well over a year investigating this case. Interviewed everybody and their dog, from staff at the hospital where she worked, to the hundred or so residents who live around the park, and her family, neighbors, friends, current and former lovers—those that we could find. We haven't got much more than stabs in the dark at persons of interest, let alone a suspect."

"Not even unofficially?"

Staff Sergeant Kline adjusted himself in his seat, revealing some discomfort that shouldn't be there for a seasoned officer in his fifties now in charge of an entire unit. "I'm thinking we need a different perspective, Renaud. Maybe come at it from a totally different angle. What has become clear from the investigation so far is that the decedent was, uh, well, I don't know the correct word for it these days, but she was a lady who liked the ladies—if you get my drift."

Danielle now knew why Kline seemed so suddenly out of his element. She let him go on without commenting.

"The only possible lead we've got so far—and it's a remote one at that—is in regards to her social life. It seems she was somewhat of a player. There's a long string of jilted lovers, and that's the closest we've got to any kind of possible motive, so I thought maybe someone with your, uh, knowledge and experience…" Kline flipped a page from what appeared to be Danielle's personnel file. "I see here you were with the military for seven years, military police for most of it. Left to join the RCMP. Spent five years in Québec. One year of that in General Investigations sometimes involving Montreal's municipal police force. Quite a good training ground up there. Lots of drugs, gangs, organized crime. Might not have been directly involved in those investigations, but even the trickling down would have exposed you to enough of it."

"I've seen my share of the shadier side of life," Danielle remarked.

"You transferred here to Halifax from Québec four years ago and remained in General Investigations?"

"Yes, that's right."

Kline appeared to be studying Danielle as he asked his next question. "Have you not had any interest in moving up to Special Investigations?"

Danielle could feel the instant heat rise from her gut, past her throat, and up to her forehead as she tried to conceal her anger. She *had* wanted, *kept* wanting Special Investigations and Major Crimes since transferring to Halifax, but the brass kept stalling, saying there were no openings. She didn't know if this was true or if they were just jerking her around, but every few months for more than two years now she had tried and tried again to move into Special Investigations, and each and every time, she'd been denied it. Surely those requests were in her personnel file. Was Kline just testing her to see how she'd react to the question?

The tropical blue in Danielle's eyes flashed a hint of darker steel, but she kept her cool and responded very diplomatically. "I've been expressing interest in Major Crimes and Special Investigations for a while, but there were no openings."

Danielle saw Kline's eyes leave her face and look back down at the information he had in front of him. He closed her personnel file and tossed it onto a pile sitting on a chair behind him before saying what was on his mind. "I'm going to cut right to the chase, Renaud. I'm thinking this Buchanan woman had a lot more secrets than we've been able to extract. As it usually is, her family and friends think she was as pure and sweet as honey, but you and I both know how even the most innocent looking people often have deep, dark secrets loved ones either don't know or don't want to tell. And Buchanan definitely had her secrets. Her family and close friends say she wasn't involved in drugs, but we found a home-grown marijuana operation in her home. It was very small mind you, but I don't know very many nurses who spend their evenings trying to turn marijuana into hash oil.

"Everyone we've spoken to has been wearing a muzzle in that department, so I need somebody to take another crack at it. And here's the cutting to the chase part. I need that person to be…" Staff Sergeant Kline said it matter of factly, but Danielle could see the uneasiness in his demeanor. "A lady who likes the ladies also. Somebody out there knows something, and I'm hoping you with your…specialized knowledge in that area, might be able to unearth what we're missing."

Danielle wanted this assignment more than anything, even if she wasn't pleased with how she was getting it. "I've wanted to join Special Investigations for quite a while now. I'd love the opportunity to investigate a homicide." She wanted to add, "Even if the only reason you're offering it to me is because I'm gay. Or is that, 'a lady who likes the ladies'?" But didn't.

"Just so you understand, Renaud. This is a cold case, no longer homicide. Homicide has done all it can, and now the Cold Case Unit is just wanting a fresh set of eyes to look at everything from a different perspective. It's only a temporary assignment. Officially you're still a GIS member with the same title and salary. We're just going to borrow you for a while."

Danielle's heart sank somewhat at the word "temporary", but she was used to having to work hard to prove herself, to having to be twice as good and work twice as hard to earn the same respect as her male counterparts. But Danielle felt doubly cursed when it came to her profession, because she was also always having to tear down the perception that her attractiveness meant she couldn't possibly be a great police officer. So far she'd been able to debunk that perception. She just wished she didn't have to do so *again*.

Kline picked up a heavy file folder box and headed to the door. "I'll take this first box to your desk, then introduce you to the rest of the unit."

"You mean I start today?" Danielle followed as Kline walked silently around twisting and turning corridors until he reached an empty cubicle. He dropped the box onto a light grey desk.

"You're starting right now."

⅋ 3 ⅋

Sitting at her new desk and keen to get started on her very first homicide—even if it was a cold one, which by now had such a very slim chance of getting solved, unless the killer suddenly became a born-again Christian and decided to confess—Danielle lifted the cover of the box labeled "1 of 8" and grabbed the first file.

The inside cover had a photograph of the deceased—taken prior to her death and provided by a family member—and a single page stapled underneath, which listed her particulars: name, gender, date of death, date of birth, age, and residential address at time of death.

Every page—and there were lots of them—had a case file number written in the top right-hand corner. It struck Danielle as very sad that someone's life had ended up becoming just a sum of information collected and filed by number.

According to the first two pages of this particular file number's chronicle, the decedent had been a single, thirty-six-year-old registered nurse who lived alone in her own home when her lifeless body was found floating in a city park's heart-shaped pond by an early morning jogger on the fifth of October.

Danielle's eyes searched for the information she was most interested in. When she found it, she was puzzled by it. *Cause of death: Polydrug intoxication. Ethanol, cannabis, ketamine hydrochloride. Manner of death: Homicide. Harmed by person or persons unknown.*

Danielle had never worked in the drug unit, but her required first four years of performing general duties just outside of Montreal had made her familiar with too many drugs she would have otherwise never heard of. Ketamine hydrochloride was one of them. And like all street drugs, it was given a more colorful name by its users: *Special K.*

Danielle re-read the passage that troubled her, this time out loud. "Cause of death, polydrug intoxication. Ethanol, cannabis, ketamine hydrochloride."

She was mystified. According to the cause of death, the woman simply had a few drinks, smoked a few joints, and probably snorted some *Special K.*

Sounds more like accidental death during some heavy duty partying, Danielle thought, *so why was it determined a homicide?*

"She had more than four times the lethal dose in powdered form in her throat and lungs, small amounts in nasal cavities, trace amounts in her stomach," Dr. Martin Petersen said quite matter of factly.

Danielle knew from responding to too many calls from partiers that drugs and alcohol were a lethal combination, often causing respiratory failure and cardiac arrest. "How do you know it wasn't accidental? Maybe just partied more than she should have?"

Dr. Peterson looked up from his notes on file number 14683. He was Nova Scotia's Chief Medical Examiner and affectionately known by local law enforcement as "Doctor Death". While he was not the only medical examiner in the province, all deaths occurring from non-natural causes were his domain. He was superb at what he did—which was very fortunate for the province of Nova Scotia—but there was something very eerie about the man: he absolutely *loved* his job. Never in a zillion years could Danielle ever get excited at the prospect of opening up a corpse, but Doctor Death was passionate about it.

"She was already incapacitated or in a drug-induced stupor when someone shoved a straw down her throat and blew twenty grams of ketamine hydrochloride powder into her. The straw left striations on the uvula, soft palette, pharynx, and esophagus."

Danielle's immediate response was on her lips before she even had time to formulate it in her head. If she had allowed herself time to think, she might not have even asked the question. "Any chance the perpetrator left his—or her—DNA in the throat or lungs? Maybe some molecules from their breath?" Danielle didn't know if she was watching way too much television or just grasping at straws herself.

"I am impressed, Constable." Dr. Peterson lifted his finger like a professor about to teach an important lesson to an eager student. "Exhaled breath condensate was first discovered as an identifiable human bodily fluid in 1980—though most of the research has been quite recent—but unfortunately..."

Of course it was too good to be true. "Here comes the bad news?"

"The research on EBC DNA is so new and controversial, even if we could isolate and tag a perpetrator's EBC DNA, it would never hold up in court. I'm no lawyer, but I can tell you the science of extracting EBC DNA just isn't established enough. It's not used in any forensic labs today, so I would think that any legal case based on it would shrink faster than O.J. Simpson's blood-soaked leather glove."

Danielle was not deterred, however. "It might not hold up in court, but we could still identify the perpetrator based on their EBC DNA, right?"

Exhilaration was building inside Danielle at the mere thought. Even if that piece of evidence couldn't be used in court, determining the identity of Buchanan's killer would impress the socks off the entire unit, and maybe even the Chief. She could barely contain her excitement.

"Did you swab for it?" Then Danielle's pragmatic thinking kicked in and her excitement faded as the probability began to sink in. "Did you keep any...?" Danielle sank into a chair she was standing near. She spoke very slowly now, because she was afraid to hear the reply after her sentence would be finished. "Please tell me you did swab her throat for DNA, or at least kept tissue samples in case any new technology was developed in the future?" Danielle's legs were going numb.

"Hey, what do you take me for? Some inept amateur?" Dr. Peterson smiled, then flipped through some pages before reporting, "Larynx swab, cheek swab, uvula swab, lung tissue, esophagus tissue, tongue tissue. They, along with a few dozen other samples from the deceased, are sitting in storage at the crime lab." Dr. Peterson got up from his desk and waved several sheets of paper in the air. "A copy of this was already forwarded to Homicide, but I'll make you another one."

When Dr. Peterson returned he handed Danielle a copy of his forensics log, shook her hand, and wished her good luck, giving Danielle the impression that he knew exactly where she was headed next.

As Danielle drove from Spring Garden Road to Oxford Street, she mulled over the type of drug used to kill file number 14683. She had never patrolled the streets of Halifax, had transferred directly into General Investigations as a plainclothes investigator, but her impression was that ketamine wasn't very common in Halifax. She didn't know a whole lot about it, but she did know ketamine was a cat sedative. She had investigated many break-ins, and out of several hundred, only a handful of them had occurred at veterinary clinics. It just wasn't a high-frequency crime. Then again, pharmacies rarely got broken into. The security and preventative measures in place these days made it a very rare occurrence, yet oxycodone and hydro-morphone were still major problems on the streets of Halifax. Perhaps ketamine was too and she just wasn't aware of it.

When she hit a red light, Danielle pulled a small, silver device out of her pocket. She pushed a button and said into it, "Get the scoop on street-level ketamine use and distribution in Halifax."

Danielle kept thinking as she drove, and when she got to the next red light, she pressed the button on her digital recorder again. "Look up any break-ins at vet clinics or thefts of ketamine in the year prior to Buchanan's death." Whether a long shot or not, Danielle prided herself in being thorough.

Danielle arrived at her destination shortly before noon. Though it was more commonly known among her peers simply as the crime lab, its official name was Forensics Laboratory Services, and few Haligonians probably even knew what that brick building housed.

Just as she was exiting her newly assigned vehicle with a copy of the forensics log in hand, Danielle felt her phone vibrate. She looked at the display and saw it was Rachel.

"Hello."

"Hi, it's me, Rachel."

"I know." Danielle couldn't find it in herself to state anything other than the obvious.

"I'm sorry about earlier. I was just trying to gear up for the day, and you caught me off guard."

Danielle didn't know what to say, so she said nothing.

"Why don't we go out for sushi this evening to celebrate?"

"Sushi?" Danielle was stunned because she knew Rachel hated sushi. Rachel further amazed Danielle by displaying an extremely unusual willingness to compromise.

"They make vegetarian sushi don't they? And those steamed soy beans you often bring home, I like those too."

"Yes, they do have many vegetarian choices, but are you sure you're okay with watching me eat raw fish?"

"Let's just say the fact that I'm willing to watch you eat raw fish is how sorry I am for this morning."

Danielle managed a thin smile. She was still very hurt, but she was also moved by Rachel's effort—as she had so often been when Rachel did make an effort to try—something which occurred less and less lately. "Okay, how about Dikura's on Dresden?"

"Sure. My last patient is scheduled for four-fifty. Does six o'clock work for you?"

"Six is good."

"Okay, see you then."

Danielle didn't bother saying good bye. She just stared at the phone for a moment before putting it back in its case attached to her belt.

Two weeks after Danielle and Rachel started dating, Danielle suggested they be just friends. Rachel was determined, however. She was the type of woman who knew what she wanted, went after what she wanted, was used to getting what she wanted, and what she had wanted was Danielle.

Every time Danielle tried to express they weren't really right for each other, Rachel would turn on the charm, and Danielle would succumb. Danielle had often thought Rachel should have gone into law, not medicine. She had a gift for making an argument and convincing anyone of anything.

But had Rachel really convinced Danielle they were meant to be together? Or had Danielle just played along, wishing it so badly, she told herself it was so? Such analysis was unpleasant for Danielle, so she responded as she so often did when it came to her personal life and feelings. She shoved it all away and concentrated on her work.

The security guard at the crime lab's reception area required Danielle to sign in as well as produce her badge and photo identification. She didn't have an appointment to see anyone in particular, but she asked to speak with the person in charge of the DNA Analysis Section.

The older gentleman pointed to a sign near a corridor and said, "You'll have to turn your cell phone off and any other devices that transmit signals. Interferes with some of the equipment," he explained.

Danielle knew cell phone use was discouraged in hospitals but wasn't aware it affected some of the equipment at the crime lab as well. While Danielle had investigated countless crimes in her four years in Halifax, general investigations were primarily residential break and enters, robberies, and stolen vehicles. This was her first time at the crime lab, her first special investigation, and her very first homicide—cold or not.

Danielle was reminded of the celebratory dinner this evening. It might be nice to sit with Rachel and celebrate, have something pleasant between them for a change.

A young woman's head appeared in a slightly opened door marked "Authorized Personnel Only".

"Constable Renaud, if you'd like to come this way."

Danielle and her escort made small talk until they reached a brightly lit room filled with equipment. There were three figures in the room, all wearing white lab coats, latex gloves, and identification attached to their lapels.

"Melissa, this is Constable Renaud." The young woman turned to Danielle and said, "This is Melissa Lambert, our senior DNA technician. She'll be able to answer any questions you have."

Danielle thanked her escort, then waited for her to leave before addressing the DNA tech. "I'd like to know if you've tested any of these samples for EBC DNA." She pointed to a series of highlighted file numbers on her forensics log.

"EBC DNA?" Melissa Lambert looked straight into Danielle's lagoon-blue eyes and seemed perplexed.

"Yes. Exhaled breath condensate." Danielle's response contained only a hint of implied ignorance on the technician's part.

"I know what it is, but we don't do that."

"Why not?"

"As far as I know, outside of some limited health studies aimed at detecting lung cancer sooner, no one does it. That technology's never been used to identify an individual if that's what you're getting at."

"That is what I'm getting at. Why not?"

Melissa Lambert stared at Danielle as though trying to decide whether to engage in this conversation or not.

"Why not, what?" Melissa asked with some stoniness.

Danielle let out an impatient sigh and said, "Why isn't it used to identify individuals? DNA is DNA isn't it, no matter if it's blood, semen, saliva, or breath?"

Melissa Lambert stared Danielle down making Danielle think Melissa might be readying for a showdown, when she suddenly relented.

"It's a very promising technology. I've read some interesting case studies, but the collection process of exhaled breath condensate is so cumbersome the chances of extracting DNA from something someone breathed on are less than slim to none." Melissa inspected the polish on her nails. "Sorry."

"Have you ever tried?" Danielle was like a dog with a bone and was not going to let go until that bone disintegrated into irretrievable powder.

"Well, no, but—"

"But what?" Danielle didn't like telling people how to do their jobs, but this was her first—and possibly only—shot at solving a murder, and she was not going to leave any stone unturned. "Can't you at least pull the samples, test them for someone else's DNA? That *is* what you do, isn't it?"

Melissa Lambert's eyeglasses flared as though beams had just been shot out of her eyes. She stood in place for a very long, drawn-out moment before pivoting on one foot and walking over to a computer. As her fingers danced over a keyboard, she crustily reported her findings. "We did test her saliva and swabs taken from the inside of her mouth to see if it contained anyone else's bodily fluids."

"Is that *all* you tested?" Rather than wait for a reply, Danielle demanded, "I want you to test her esophagus and lungs for any DNA that might not be hers."

Melissa's body tensed, and her response was in a frosty monotone. "You'll have to put in a formal request for DNA analysis to be conducted on those tissues." And then supplemented that quite sarcastically with, "You know…*required* protocol for forensic requests."

Danielle felt an embarrassing heat pour over her cheeks. She'd never submitted a forensic request before, but she'd been an officer long enough to know that procedures and protocols documenting everything were the norm. She should have known better.

"And just so you know, we can't collect EBC DNA specifically, but we'll look for the presence of any foreign DNA if that's what you specify in your request."

"I'll have the request submitted by two o'clock this afternoon," Danielle informed Melissa, then began to walk away.

"Officer Renaud!"

Danielle wanted to correct her by saying, "That's *Constable* to you," but didn't want to escalate the tension that already existed between them. "Yes?"

"May I ask you something?"

"What is it?"

"I'm just curious. You asked about exhaled breath condensate, which is very…well, it's definitely outside-the-box thinking, but you haven't asked about what DNA we might have extracted from the carving on her face."

Danielle's face went as white as Melissa Lambert's lab coat, then quickly turned a hot terracotta, which then deepened to a more scarlet shade by the time Melissa Lambert spoke again.

"You didn't know about her face?" Melissa snickered.

Danielle just stared at her.

"You *are* investigating the Buchanan case aren't you? That *is* what you do, isn't it?"

Danielle spun around and stomped out, down the corridor, toward reception. She didn't sign out. She went straight for the door and hit the steel bar so hard with both hands, it swung violently ahead of her as she exited.

Danielle was back at HRP headquarters sitting in her new office. She could not believe she had been so remiss in her review of the evidence documented in the files now covering her desk.

When she retraced her earlier actions, she now recognized her inexperience. She had jumped the gun and raced over to the medical examiner's office, then to the crime lab at the first question that popped into her head. She should have just kept reviewing, taking notes as she read *everything*, before running off and making a fool of herself.

Never again would she allow herself to be blindsided like that. She did it to herself; she was well aware of that. But she made a resolution right then and there, that she would never, ever go seeking information again so inadequately prepared.

By the end of the day, Danielle's eyes were dry and burning. She'd read so much her eyes felt like there was sand in them. From the secondary crime scene report—where Buchanan's body was found, not where she was killed—she learned that the decedent had been found fully clothed, but without shoes or a jacket, and that there were no signs of physical trauma or sexual assault—if you didn't take into account her face.

The first note Danielle made was regarding Buchanan's wallet. Though clearly a woman's wallet, longer and thicker with more compartments than a man's, it was found stuffed into the back pocket of her jeans. *Not even ladies who like the ladies shove these types of wallets into their back pockets*, thought Danielle. *Her assailant must have stuffed it into her pocket for a reason.*

She sat there for a time, thinking, and rubbed her eyes. After giving it further thought, she came to the conclusion that the person who dumped Buchanan's body must have wanted her found quickly because she was placed in a shallow pond and there was no attempt to weigh her down, leaving her visibly exposed.

Her subsequent notes referenced four short strips of grey duct tape found on the ground near the concrete edge of the pond: to find out if the duct tape was used on the victim's body, and to see if it was tested for any DNA. Since many people use their teeth to tear off strips of duct tape, Danielle thought it at least a possibility that the killer may have left some saliva on it.

Danielle then picked up the last file pertaining to the secondary crime scene: the photographic evidence. The source of her recently learned lesson appeared when she flipped over the fourth photograph.

Kristina Ann Buchanan, who in life had been a vibrant, attractive woman with a very pretty face and eyes, now appeared lifeless, discolored, and grossly bloated with a very clear and open gash that swirled around her once beautiful face into the shape of a very distinctive letter "S".

Her eyes, which looked an attractive light green in a photo taken recently before her death, no longer looked like eyes at all but ghastly dark almond shapes where eyes should be.

A close-up showed how the carving started on the left side of her forehead, crossed over to the right, then sliced through her right eyebrow and right eye before changing direction across her nose and continued along her left cheek, curving back around her mouth, just under her bottom lip, then ended where her right dimple would have been—were she still alive and smiling. But she wasn't.

"Don't forget to go home."

Danielle raised her eyes to the voice coming from the opening in her cubicle that served as an open door. She couldn't remember his first name but knew she'd been introduced to Constable Sparks earlier that morning.

"Is it four o'clock already?"

Sparks looked at Danielle with eyes that looked like they belonged to a father who caught his young daughter still awake at midnight. "It's going on seven."

Danielle jumped up from her chair. "Seven? Oh my God!"

"It's easy to lose track of time in this line of work, but be mindful of work-life balance and all that. Go home and relax, get a good night's sleep. You'll be better off coming in fresh in the morning." Constable Sparks gave Danielle a quick salute before disappearing from view.

Danielle gathered the files spread across her desk and hurriedly tossed them into whatever empty drawers she could find. She pulled her cell phone out to call Rachel and that's when she noticed it was off. She'd been so upset when she left the lab she hadn't remembered to turn it back on. Instead of checking for any missed messages, she pressed the familiar icon.

Rachel picked up on the first ring and was her expected cheery self. She answered with, "Where the hell are you?"

"I'm sorry! I lost track of time. I had no idea it was so late."

"I've been calling your cell for the past hour! Why didn't you answer? I couldn't call your office, you didn't give me your new number."

"I don't even know my new number, yet. I was at the crime lab, and I had to turn my cell phone off, then I forgot to turn it back on."

"Do you know how embarrassing it was for me to sit in that restaurant all by myself? Not to mention, you know how much I hate fish, let alone fish that's still stinking raw, and I sat in that stinky fish gut of a restaurant watching plate after plate of rank, raw flesh parade past me, just for you, and you stood me up!"

"I didn't mean to. I was head first in the files of my first homicide and just lost track of time. Surely you can understand that, Rachel. I didn't stand you up on purpose, and you know it."

"I'm home now, and I am not going back out. Pick yourself something up, or don't eat at all—I don't care what you do. I'll be in the tub relaxing, so don't disturb me when you come in."

Relief swept over Danielle when Rachel followed that up by hanging up. It used to upset Danielle when she disappointed Rachel. But for far too long now, Rachel seemed to always be disappointed. Or angry. Or stressed. Or ticked off about something or other, and Danielle felt increasingly worn out by Rachel's rants and negative responses to everything.

Danielle didn't have much of an appetite, but she didn't like skipping meals, so she stopped at the grocery store where she picked up some ready-made sushi before heading home.

Making sure her personal vehicle—a metallic green Jeep Liberty—was locked up and secure in its assigned parking spot in the basement of her building, Danielle rode the elevator to the top floor condo she lived in with Rachel.

They didn't co-own the condo. Rachel had purchased it on her own, and Danielle had been okay with that. They had always kept separate finances. Both were established in their careers when they'd met: Danielle a Royal Canadian Mounted Police officer and Rachel a family physician. Though she'd resisted moving in with Rachel, Danielle finally relented after Rachel bought the condo a year ago. To be financially fair, Danielle paid Rachel a monthly rent.

She considered yelling "I'm home" when she arrived, but she had been warned not to disturb Rachel's evening ritual. After removing her shoes, she made her way to the kitchen where she dropped her grocery store purchase on a counter, then exited again before walking across gleaming hardwood floors into a sparsely furnished bedroom.

Danielle removed her identification and badge from an inside pocket of her suit jacket. When she'd had this suit tailored, she'd specified two interior pockets on each side. Having been frustrated by the lack of practical, inside pockets in women's suits, she began to bring her jackets to a tailor to have pockets sewn inside them. It irritated Danielle that men's suits had more pockets than bubble wrap, yet women were lucky to find suits with any pockets at all.

She continued her after-work routine by unbuckling her leather belt, releasing a handcuff carrier and two holsters as she pulled the belt away. One holster contained her cell phone, the other, a nine-millimeter Smith and Wesson she kept concealed under her jacket near her right hip. After locking her gun and ammunition in a small, fireproof safe that sat on the closet floor, Danielle exchanged her suit pants for a pair of blue jeans.

Danielle touched the fabric of one of her favorite suits and thought of Rachel. Danielle hadn't always dressed so nicely. Before she'd met Rachel, her closet was filled with more casual clothing. Unlike Rachel, who had grown up in Toronto in a very well-to-do neighborhood and had always been concerned with fashion, Danielle had been raised in a rural area of Québec where clothing was more practical than fashionable. But after Rachel convinced her to have not just pockets sewn in but to get an entire suit tailored, Danielle was hooked. She now owned more than a dozen of them and felt they were worth every penny. Though Danielle did carry a small secret about her suits. Although they were custom-made, with fine fabrics cut perfectly to fit, all but one had cost just a fraction of what they should have.

Truth was, Danielle's aunt back home was a very talented seamstress. Danielle paid for the fabric and sewing supplies and insisted on paying her aunt a sum for her time, but her aunt had always refused to accept. Danielle felt very guilty about that however, knowing how much her first suit had cost, so she surprised her aunt and uncle one Christmas with an all-expenses-paid trip to Florida. They had enjoyed themselves so much, it was now an unspoken barter. Her Tante (Aunt) Isabelle would present her with a new suit almost every time she visited, perhaps three or four times a year, and every Christmas her aunt would receive two tickets to a warm, sunny destination scheduled for Québec's coldest weeks of the year.

Danielle closed the closet door quietly before leaving the bedroom and going back to the kitchen. The bathroom door was still closed. She walked past softly, knowing it was best to let sleeping dogs lie.

She pulled a stool up to the counter, not wanting to sit at the dining room table by herself. She felt so lonely. She considered turning on the television for company, but she didn't want to risk infuriating Rachel further. *It shouldn't be like this*, she thought.

Danielle reached for the cordless phone resting on the counter she was sitting at. She pressed speed dial number two, then put the phone to her ear.

Lillian Marsh was sitting in the sewing room of her lakefront home hand sewing teal blue feathers on to a dress. Her pulse quickened in anticipation when the phone rang, but she felt a slight disappointment when she saw the display. It's not that she didn't want to talk to the person who was calling, she was just disappointed it wasn't a particular somebody else.

Lilly answered the phone in her usual pleasant voice.

"Hello."

"Hi, Lilly."

"Hey, you. What's new?"

"Lots and nothing."

"Okay, fill me in on the lots part."

"I started on my first homicide today—a cold case."

"Oh my God, Danielle! Congratulations!"

"Thanks."

"What's wrong? I thought you were dying to move into Major Crimes."

"It's not that. I'm thrilled about the assignment. It's just—"

"Oh. Rachel? What's happened now?"

"Just the usual. She's pissed at me, so I'm eating alone while she soaks in the tub."

"Again? What did you get her for her birthday, a deluxe shower head? The plumbing's getting it more often than you do." Lilly's laughter abruptly ceased and her voice turned apologetic. "I'm sorry, I didn't mean to—"

"It's okay, Lilly." Danielle had let slip a few times how her sex life with Rachel was less than satisfying, so the joke was appropriate. And sadly, probably true.

"How's your dress coming along?" Danielle wanted to change the subject to something more uplifting.

"Oh, it's beautiful, Danielle. You should see it."

"I will. I'm going to that powwow no matter what."

"Is Rachel coming with you?"

"I don't care if she does or not. I'm definitely going." Danielle almost added how she was tired of living like this but knew it would spark Lilly into trying to open up a heart-to-heart with her, and Danielle was too drained for that tonight.

Danielle heard the bathroom door open, then the bedroom door close. She considered hanging up but knew Rachel wouldn't talk to her even if she did—Rachel was an expert user of the silent treatment—so Danielle stayed on the phone.

"Danielle, I know it's none of my business, but—"

Danielle cut her off because they'd had this conversation too many times. "I know, Lilly. It's just—"

"Just a sec, I have a beep." Without waiting for approval, Lilly left Danielle waiting on the line. Danielle wasn't a fan of call waiting. She never answered a beep if she was already on the phone, and she didn't care to be put on hold while others answered another call either. Lilly was back in just a few seconds though. "Danielle, can I call you back?"

"Uh, sure."

"Okay, thanks. I'll call you back in about a half hour."

Danielle wondered who was more important than she was, then realized she was feeling sorry for herself. She decided to call the one person she knew would be so thrilled to talk to her, that even if God Himself came calling, she'd tell Him *He'd* have to wait.

"Allo, Grandmère!" Danielle greeted her grandmother in a happy voice. After asking how she was and getting the typical list of minor ailments, then chit-chatting about the weather, Danielle confirmed she would indeed be arriving in four days for the long, Easter weekend. They talked for a few more minutes, mostly idle gossip Danielle knew her grandmother would excitedly repeat when she sat across from her in person, then ended the conversation with a, "See you Friday."

After hanging up, Danielle figured she might as well go to the bathroom and collect the items she knew would be there. She picked up Rachel's wine glass and empty wine bottle from the side of the tub and retrieved the wet bath towel from the floor, hanging it up to dry. She had just finished rinsing the wine glass and putting it in the dishwasher when the phone rang again.

"Hi, me again. Sorry to cut our conversation short earlier."

"It's okay, gave me a chance to call my grandmother. You're sure you don't want to go home for the long weekend?"

Lilly was from Ugpi'ganjig First Nation, which showed up on the far northeastern region of most provincial New Brunswick maps as Eel River. It was located on the New Brunswick side of the Bay of Chaleur and was along the way to Sainte Maria Goretti, a small village in the Gaspé region of Québec where Danielle grew up.

"No, I want to stay here. I'm really looking forward to some days off to finish my dress and practice my dance."

Danielle pictured Lilly in full ceremonial dress, moving her body according to her Mi'kmaq ancestral tradition. The first time she saw Lilly dance at a powwow Danielle had been swept away by the power and beauty of the dance, and the dancers themselves. Lilly was commanding when she was standing in a courtroom wearing her Crown attorney's black robe over her barrister's jacket and large, white lapels prominently displayed at the neck, but she was mesmerizing when she danced.

Ever since Danielle saw Lilly dancing, she saw her in a different light. One that made Danielle a bit uncomfortable at times, realizing when she watched her good friend dance, how it sometimes made her mouth water.

"Lilly, are you free for lunch tomorrow? I could give you the rest of my news then."

"I am, actually. I do have to be in court for two o'clock though, so why don't we meet at Emborio's around noon?"

Danielle and Lilly said their goodnights, then Danielle prepared for bed. When she entered the bedroom, all the lights were off. Since she knew better than to turn one on, she removed her clothes in the dark, placed them in her own hamper, then very carefully opened a top dresser drawer and removed what she recognized by touch as being a nightshirt. She then quietly slipped under the covers on her side of the bed and sighed deeply before closing her eyes and hoping sleep would soon come.

❧ 5 ❧

When Lilly sat down for lunch her chicken souvlaki and Greek salad were already sitting in front of her.

"I thought I'd save us some time by ordering for you," Danielle explained.

"Thanks. How much do I owe you?"

"Just buy me a drink sometime."

"Deal." Lilly leaned across the table. "Now tell me about your promotion!"

"It's not a promotion per se." Danielle then filled her in on the details of her new, temporary assignment. She omitted the embarrassing lesson she'd learned on her first day but told Lilly which case she was working on.

"I remember that. Don't think they ever had any suspects—not officially anyway. Anybody looking good for it?"

"No."

"No?" Lilly knew that often in crimes where no arrests were made, police still had a good idea who committed the crime, they just needed more time to collect the evidence. Normally they had somebody in mind, at least. "Nobody at all?"

"I've been reading reports and statements all morning, and I've barely made a dent in the pile. It's going to take me the rest of the week, if not all of next week too, to go through them all. But if an entire team of experienced homicide investigators couldn't come up with any suspects, I doubt I'll be able to either."

"Maybe something new will crop up, you never know."

"One thing I do know, I'll sure be ready for a five-day break at the end of this week," Danielle said as she rubbed her temple.

"Oh, that's right. You're taking Tuesday off, too. You must be looking forward to going home."

"It'll be nice to see Grandmère. I've been worried about her since that scare a couple months ago."

Danielle's eighty-four-year-old grandmother had been hospitalized after falling in the kitchen. She hadn't hurt herself during the fall, but she hadn't been able to get herself back up after she fell. Danielle's uncle had found his mother on the floor and called 911. Two days later he called Danielle and told her she should come home, that they couldn't get her grandmother's blood pressure up, nor did they know what was causing it to stay so low. Two days after that, her blood pressure suddenly stabilized, and she was released, good as new. Danielle hadn't seen her since, so was looking forward to seeing for herself how she was doing.

"Is Rachel going with you?" Lilly ran her fingers through her long, dark hair. It was so straight and shiny, it looked like fine strands of ebony glass.

"She's supposed to. She should be talking to me again by Friday." Danielle then relayed the series of events that led to this latest "incident" in her relationship.

Lilly's voice softened. "You're not happy, are you?"

Danielle looked into Lilly's very dark brown eyes. They were so dark they were almost indistinguishable from her pupils. She studied Lilly's face for a moment. If she hadn't already been with Rachel when she and Lilly met, maybe…

Danielle noticed Lilly's eyes dart to the far corner of the diner. Something—or someone—had caught her attention. Danielle looked over and saw a woman who appeared to be in her twenties putting on a striking three-quarter length black leather jacket. The woman then placed an eye-catching black leather beret on her head, taming the long, dark, curly hair that obscured her face from Danielle's view.

Lilly watched the petite woman leave the busy diner with a female companion, then turned her body so she could continue her surveillance of them through the window as they walked down the street. Lilly, who normally did not people watch, was clearly preoccupied with the woman.

"Does that woman have anything to do with your hearing this afternoon?" Danielle asked.

"No."

Lilly didn't say another word about the matter, but Danielle sensed the woman was still on Lilly's mind even after Lilly returned her attention back to their conversation. Danielle tried to extract any information she could by casually commenting on the woman's jacket, but Lilly didn't respond. Lilly was disclosing nothing, and for some reason Danielle didn't understand, that bothered her tremendously.

When she got back from lunch, Danielle logged into Versadex and PROS, two law enforcement databases, which stored digital copies of all reports, statements, and evidence gathered in investigations. She initiated a search for any break and enters containing the keywords "veterinary" or "ketamine" during the year prior to Buchanan's death. Luckily for Danielle, Halifax wasn't as bad as the press sensationalized it to be. There were only two results, and only one had reported a theft of ketamine. She printed off everything pertaining to that case and made a call while waiting for the printer to finish.

She dialed an internal number for the drug unit and, after explaining what information she was seeking, was told she should speak to a Sergeant Carvery. Three minutes later Danielle was one floor above, sitting across from him.

"What's the scoop on ketamine use in Halifax?" Danielle didn't like wasting time with small talk. She asked two more questions before Sergeant Carvery could answer the first. "Is it easy to get? Is it popular?"

"It's not the most popular drug of choice out there, but it does exist. It's more prevalent at nightclubs, raves, stuff like that."

Danielle continued listening to Sergeant Carvery while she wrote herself a note to check the clubs for any possible involvement between Buchanan and the club-drug scene.

"Then there's always the addict who's willing to try anything, and the occasional sexual predator who uses it to render his victims defenseless. Those cases are not as common, because ketamine does have a bitter taste, but if GHB isn't available, ketamine works pretty much the same. Except people don't pass out on ketamine, they just can't move.

"Regular users are generally split into two groups. The younger kids, teens to thirties who hit the dance clubs, and then those who just love trippin' out."

"What exactly do you mean by tripping out?" Danielle had an idea of course, but wanted details.

"The upside of ketamine is that it's both a stimulant and a hallucinogenic. Even though it's an anesthetic, it doesn't act like most anesthetics in that most lower blood pressure and cause the heart to slow down. Ketamine actually raises blood pressure and stimulates respiration. When you add a racing heart to hallucinations, you get what we call trippin' out.

"Now you're too young to have been around during the sixties and seventies, but the romantic notion of hallucinogenic drugs of that day still holds strong for a lot of kids today. They think if they do some *Special K* that their lives are going to turn into some slick music video for an hour or two." Sergeant Carvery spit out his gum, then posed a question. "How does ketamine fit into the case you're investigating?"

Danielle replied as though she were talking to a civilian, not a senior officer. "I can't really disclose that." She then rested her pencil on a note she'd made just a minute earlier and said, "Getting back to something you mentioned, you said that people don't pass out on ketamine, that they just can't move. Can you expand on that?"

"Ketamine is an anesthetic meant to be used only on animals— cats mostly—and there's a big difference between a cat and a human. Most amounts users take, it just causes hallucinations and—"

Danielle interrupted Sergeant Carvery to clarify a thought that entered her head. "When the hallucinations start, do users run and flail all over the place?"

Carvery didn't complete his interrupted sentence, he answered Danielle's question instead. "No, quite the contrary. They hallucinate all right, but as I was saying, they can't physically react to what they see and hear."

"You mean, they're paralyzed? They're hallucinating but they can't move in response to those hallucinations?"

"Right on."

"My God, that sounds more like a nightmare to me. Can't see that being pleasant at all. Sounds like a trip all right, a trip to hell."

"At least with ketamine they can't jump off their balconies thinking they're going on some magic carpet ride. You weren't around for the good old days of PCP. Those trips often ended in a splatter on the sidewalk."

Danielle was glad she didn't work as a paramedic. She didn't think she'd have much compassion for people who were so stupid as to try these drugs in the first place. "How easy is it to get your hands on ketamine in Halifax? Actually, how easy would it have been about a year and a half ago?"

"I'd say nothing much if anything has changed since then. Pretty much all street-level ketamine comes from thefts at veterinary clinics, or shipments to clinics intercepted and stolen."

Danielle thought about it not being a popular first drug of choice. "What drugs are most popular in Halifax?"

"Cocaine is always popular and—"

"Could ketamine be mistaken for cocaine?"

Sergeant Carvery's Tootsie Roll colored skin darkened as tension filled the lines of his face, but he just twiddled his thumbs. Slowly. "Sure it can. In powdered form it looks exactly like cocaine, and it gets snorted the same way. It could be mistaken for heroin too, for those who like to shoot up—"

"Shoot up? How do they turn it into a liquid? Mix it with saline?" During her first few years in the RCMP, Danielle had occasionally responded to calls from upset citizens finding needles and empty vials of saline discarded at the park by some junkie.

"No, it's the other way around. Ketamine originally comes in liquid form, and actually that's the only form of it that's legal. It is illegal for anyone, including legitimate pharmaceutical companies, to sell or distribute ketamine in powdered or tablet form, because it has no legitimate use as a powder or tablet."

"It's sold in tablets too?"

"On the streets it is. Often they'll mix ketamine with other drugs and sell it in tablet form as ecstasy. It's definitely not ecstasy, but lots of inexperienced or first-time users will think it is. The ketamine in those tablets is pretty low though, so they don't lose complete motor control. Usually they're just in a stupor tripping out on the hallucinations."

"Can the average Joe make ketamine at home? Or at least one with a chemistry degree?"

"Nah. It's not popular enough, and it's too hard to make. I can tell you that all ketamine hitting the streets is produced by legitimate pharmaceutical companies. Shipments might get diverted, stolen, or vet clinics might get broken into, but it always starts off as a liquid intended to be used at a veterinary hospital. It's the users or dealers who turn it into powder or tablets, and that's illegal."

"How do they turn it into powder? And why? I mean, is it only because they like to snort it, or does it change its properties when it gets turned into a powder?"

"The how, well that's easy. All they have to do is allow the liquid to evaporate, then scrape the crystals off, grind it into a powder. A ten milliliter vial, at the highest concentration it's sold in, will result in a thousand milligrams of powder."

Danielle craned her head forward. "Are you serious?. My God, with a return like that, I'm surprised there aren't dealers on every block."

"It's not that the amount is increased by drying it, it's just a lot easier for users to measure dosages when it's in powdered form. Plus, a lot of people don't like needles, so they prefer to snort the stuff instead."

"You said it's sold in vials. Can the general public buy it from an online pharmacy or pharmaceutical company?"

"No, it's regulated. Not as heavily as narcotics mind you, but you do have to have a legitimate, licensed veterinary clinic or animal shelter to order it from the pharmaceutical companies, and regular pharmacies don't carry ketamine. It's not used to treat any human diseases, so it's not generally available at regular pharmacies."

"Is it only sold in ten milliliter vials?"

"Up to fifty. Fifty milliliters is the largest vial available, but the fifties are only at a ten milligram per milliliter concentration. A fifty milliliter vial would work out to five hundred milligrams of powder, while a ten milliliter vial, at a concentration of one hundred milligrams per milliliter, will produce a thousand milligrams of powder."

"How much does it cost for a usual hit of ketamine on the streets?"

"About twenty bucks for fifty milligrams."

"Then anybody who would have, let's say, twenty grams of powder, chances are they're a dealer, right?"

"Twenty grams? Absolutely. That's twenty thousand milligrams, remember. Just fifty milligrams is about two lines if you snort it. Two lines is a trip across town maybe. Four gets you into outer space. So twenty grams…" Sergeant Carvery let out a low whistle before finishing his sentence. "Now that's a *lot*."

Danielle lifted her finger, motioning to Sergeant Carvery to pause for a moment. She did some calculations in her head then wrote: *Would have taken twenty 10 ml vials, or forty 50 ml vials to produce 20 grams of powder. If purchased or packaged for sale in 50 mg bags, 20 grams would be 400 bags.*

Danielle stopped writing to ask, "What size would a fifty milligram bag of ketamine be?"

"Quite small. Maybe an inch wide and a quarter inch tall."

"So, even though twenty grams of powder sounds like a lot, a bag containing that amount wouldn't be very large, would it?"

"Not much bigger than a sandwich bag. Certainly easy enough to hide."

Danielle made a note about that and then asked, "If someone wanted to slip ketamine into somebody without their knowledge, how could it be done?"

"Lots of ways, really. Liquid or powder, lots of pervs put it in a drink, but it would have to be a drink with strong flavors to disguise it because ketamine has a bitter taste. It has no smell, but it doesn't taste very good."

"How long before it would start to take effect?"

"If they snort it, maybe five to fifteen minutes before the hallucinations start. Soon after that it causes extreme nausea, heavy duty vomiting sometimes, depending on the dose."

Danielle wrote: *Check if there was any vomit at the scene and if tested for DNA/identity of depositor.*

Sergeant Carvery continued talking as Danielle took notes. "They'd know something wasn't right fairly quickly. If they injected it thinking it was heroin, they wouldn't even have time to finish injecting before they keeled over in a paralytic state. If it was put in a—"

"How long does the paralysis last?"

"Depends on the amount of ketamine and what form it's in, but average dose of fifty milligrams of powder, maybe half an hour. Do you want to know how soon it takes effect if it's slipped into a drink?"

Danielle felt her face flush. "Sorry. I just have one of these minds that jumps ahead sometimes."

Sergeant Carvery, about twenty years her senior, offered her some fatherly advice. "Renaud, running through the bases and getting a homerun doesn't happen in homicide. You jump over a base, and next thing you know, you're told you're out and game's over. No chance for a re-do.

"You've got a really good head for investigative work, I can tell just by the questions you ask. But pace yourself. You're better off taking the time to dot your I's and cross your T's than to have a judge toss all of your hard work out the window. I worked homicide for a few years, I can tell you it's different.

"You've got to stop thinking of yourself as an investigator, and start thinking of yourself as a hunter. A hunter who's looking for the animal who's taken a human life—no matter who, or what, that person was. Anybody who takes a life is an animal in one form or another. Either they're sick, or they're evil, and one way or another, they need capturing and put in a cage where they belong.

"So you have to think like a hunter, Renaud. You can't rush it. You have to sniff your animal out, track him down, and even when you know exactly where he is, you have to make sure your net has no holes in it before you cast it. One hole and he's gone for good.

Remember that. You have to take your time, Renaud. It takes a lot of patience, but you'll get your perp, and you'll develop better skills and instincts if you do."

Danielle's face was a shade darker than it had been. "I'm a little eager, I guess. I do appreciate your advice, Sergeant Carvery." She genuinely did.

Sergeant Carvery opened his top drawer and took out some gum, which he offered to Danielle, but she declined. He popped two squares into his mouth and talked as he chewed. "Okay, Ketamine slipped into somebody's drink, guess that's where we were." Carvery placed his hands behind his head and delved right back into the subject as if there had been no interruptions. "Because the liquid is that much more potent, it's that much more dangerous. If too large a dose is put in a drink after somebody's already had a few, it'll cause cardiac arrest. If they're lucky enough to be partying next door to a hospital with a crack medical team...but chances are, they're a goner."

Carvery's earlier advice was still resonating in Danielle's ears, so she took a moment to review her notes and make sure she wasn't skipping over anything before she left. When she finished, she had just one more question for Sergeant Carvery.

"Is there a great demand for hash oil in Halifax?"

"Not much. There's more money in growing really good bud these days, since it's not worth the extra work and mess of turning it into oil. Most don't go through the effort anymore."

Feeling she had covered all her bases, Danielle now wanted to review what she'd learned from Sergeant Carvery. "Just to make sure I've got this right, the only legal form of ketamine is liquid. It's users or dealers who turn it into powder or tablets. In small dosages it causes hallucinations and nausea, and in larger doses, will cause severe vomiting, increased blood pressure, increased heart rate, and cause temporary paralysis.

"It can be lethal when mixed with alcohol, causing respiratory and cardiac arrest. It has no smell, but tastes bitter, which can be disguised in strong tasting drinks, and it can be easily passed off as cocaine, ecstasy tablets, or heroin."

Danielle jotted down another thought into her notebook: *Check if any needle marks were found on KB and if polydrug intoxication means resp/cardiac arrest.* She then asked Sergeant Carvery, "Have I missed anything?"

"Nope."

When Danielle arrived home shortly after five o'clock she was surprised to see Rachel setting the dining room table.

"Hi!" Rachel's melodic greeting stretched out like a pop singer's intro. "Perfect timing. I've got dinner ready."

Danielle's mind flashed to Bette Midler in the *Stepford Wives* remake. As Danielle was now all too accustomed to, this was Rachel's flip side. Which meant Rachel was now acting as if nothing ever happened, and Danielle was to play along.

"You're home early," Danielle said.

"My last patient was at four, so I decided to come home early for a change."

"Rather than go for a massage, or shopping, or dinner with colleagues?" Danielle's sarcasm embodied several distinct layers of bitterness.

If Rachel noticed Danielle's bitterness, she didn't let on. "I picked us up a couple of pizzas from Morrie's Feast," she proclaimed.

Danielle loved their pizza, and usually when Rachel was thoughtful like this, it disarmed Danielle—even charmed her. But this time was different. Rachel appeared so transparent to Danielle now, she could envision every move Rachel would make, even before Rachel set it into motion.

Rachel removed the personal-sized pizzas from their boxes and put them onto plates. She went to the kitchen and returned with a bottle of sangria. As she poured a single glass of it, she said to Danielle, who was now headed to the bedroom to change, "I picked up a bottle of sangria too, since I don't think you've had it in a while."

Danielle loved sangria, but Rachel thought it was the "welfare version" of red wine, so would never allow it to be served when they had guests or were out to dinner. Unlike Rachel, Danielle didn't enjoy drinking alone, so she rarely got to enjoy it. When Danielle heard Rachel say she also picked up a bottle of sangria, she thought she should enter Rachel into a vacuum cleaner contest. She'd win top prize for sucking up tonight for sure.

Danielle returned from the bedroom with her previously pulled back hair now loosely resting on her shoulders. Not straight, not curly, it had just enough body and bounce to flatter and accentuate her femininity. She wore black jeans and a long-sleeved blue shirt, which deepened even further the color of her stunning blue eyes. The cotton-spandex blend adhered to her body like a second skin, drawing Rachel's eyes to Danielle's full breasts and athletic body.

Rachel smiled at the sight of Danielle's physical appearance. She was never more proud of having Danielle as her partner than when they attended a function or went to dinner with Rachel's friends or colleagues. Danielle was the most attractive lesbian Rachel had ever seen, and had one of the sexiest French accents Rachel had ever heard. Rachel thought Danielle did have a very slight masculinity about her, but it was more boyish than masculine.

Rachel felt her own sexuality was very fluid. Unlike Danielle, she'd had relationships with both men and women, and was attracted to both. She had never ruled out relationships with women, but she never ruled out relationships with men either. Danielle, however, considered herself one hundred percent lesbian.

When they'd first met—in the lesbian erotica section of a bookstore, no less—Rachel had first been struck by Danielle's physical beauty. It was Ingrid Bergman meets Star Trek's Seven of Nine, meets Venus de Milo, meets Jodie Foster, all rolled into one. And yet, she was none of them. She was simply herself.

Danielle had so many distinctive, physically attractive features, she frequently took people's breath away, and it was during those moments that Rachel was just so full of pride that Danielle belonged to her.

"You look very nice." Rachel looked at Danielle like a prostitute trying to entice a john for anything that had nothing to do with love.

"Thanks. You too." Danielle imagined herself making the ritualistic Catholic sign of the cross as her way of asking God for forgiveness for this little white lie. Truth was, Danielle no longer found Rachel attractive under any circumstances. And she only realized that for the first time in three and a half years, at this very moment.

When they'd first met she was attracted to Rachel. Rachel was shorter at five-foot-four, but carried herself as though she were six feet tall. She had no problems plowing through anything—or anyone—ever. She had a confidence that only existed within those so privileged, they'd never experienced want, need, or desire, as these had always been fulfilled.

Unfortunately for Danielle, she'd learned this too late about Rachel. But it had been so beyond Danielle's realm of understanding, so implausible, that it had taken her a very long time to realize that it wasn't just a humorous put-on, that there really truly existed in this world, people who were so privileged that they had no concept of anything other than acquisition. And that was what Danielle finally realized she was to Rachel: just another acquisition.

For the first time since meeting Rachel, Danielle now saw the reality when she looked at her. Rachel's hair was white. So white, it resembled the mane of an Angora cat spiked up with gel. Her skin was equally white. Creamy, without a single freckle or blemish.

It was this background of pure white, in a part of the world where faces were usually in shades of cream, beige and various browns, which made Rachel stand out. Her brown eyes, like two chocolate Oreo cookies floating in a bowl of milk, leapt out and drew attention to anyone who glanced in her direction.

She was well read, intelligent, and very well traveled. She'd been to New Zealand, Africa, all over the States and Europe, and even to Hawaii and Japan. Coming from rural Québec, and having never traveled outside of North America—except for France—this had impressed Danielle.

In the beginning Danielle had enjoyed Rachel's company and razor-sharp wit. Her comebacks were either disarming or engaging, and often both. Rachel could have verbally sparred with Joan Rivers and won. Even people who disliked Rachel couldn't help but be entertained by this undeniable gift.

"So you finally captured the brass ring you had your eye on," Rachel said to Danielle.

It was ironic to Danielle now that Rachel had been the first person she called when she got the news of her new assignment. Now, less than forty-eight hours later, Rachel was the last person she felt like sharing her news or anything else with. Is it possible for feelings to change so quickly? Or had Danielle just run out of steam when it came to dealing with the same old, same old, different event, same result?

Danielle looked at her pizza. She used to be well rounded like that. But Rachel had taken so many slices out of her, she felt tonight like there was nothing left of her but an empty box. The very last thin slice had been taken from her yesterday.

"Are you going to tell me about your new job or what?" Rachel was clearly annoyed again.

Danielle had learned Rachel's upbeat attitude never lasted very long, because deep down it really didn't exist in her to begin with. It had only been there during the seduction. Once Rachel knew she had Danielle's emotional commitment, Rachel had stopped putting any effort into hiding her impatience, irritability and cynicism.

Danielle knew she wasn't "in love" with Rachel, but she had grown accustomed to her, and their life together. Though it felt lately like they were growing more and more apart. But Danielle's Catholic upbringing had taught her that once you partnered with someone, you stuck it through, for better or for worse.

Perhaps this chance to sit down and share would bring some closeness back, so Danielle told Rachel how she really felt about the assignment. "It's just a temporary assignment. And it's not technically a homicide, since it's a cold case. Might be their way of making it look like they gave me a shot, knowing there's no chance of me succeeding, so they can get me to stop hounding them for a permanent spot in Special Investigations."

"It's all politics, Dannie. Just go along and play their game, pass go, and collect your money. That's what I do."

The second Danielle heard Rachel call her "Dannie" she felt her stomach muscles tighten, refusing entry to any further food or drink. Danielle had normally never liked to rock the boat, but she was really fed up. Danielle came forward so abruptly, the sangria in her glass swayed.

"Rachel, *why* do you call me Dannie, when you know I hate it? I positively despise it, and you know it. Tell me why. *Why* are you so disrespectful to me? I don't call you Ray, which you despise, so why the *hell* do you call me Dannie?"

Rachel was stunned. In their three and a half years together, she had never heard Danielle swear. Danielle wasn't religious per se, but her early strict French-Catholic upbringing had certainly played a part in shaping who she was. Even though she heard it all around her every day at work, Danielle simply never used curse words. "Hell," in this context, was one of them.

"Because I'm an Icelandic princess, and rules don't apply to me?" Rachel guffawed heartily, albeit nervously. Rachel's comebacks had always successfully gotten her out of hot water in the past, but she could feel the steam still rising.

Danielle stared at the blood-red color of her sangria, as it seemed an appropriate color for what she was feeling at the moment, but she said nothing in response to Rachel's failed attempt to use humor to put her in her place.

"Hey, I thought we established this going on four years ago," Rachel quipped, "I exist to be served, and you exist to serve me." Rachel's brown eyes popped out from the white canvas that surrounded them. Even the large grin she exhibited as she spoke contained pale lips and blanched teeth that blended into that bland background.

Danielle got up from the table, picked up her plate and wine glass, then entered the kitchen. She noticed Rachel watching her as she tossed her pizza in the organics green bin, then poured her sangria down the drain. Danielle didn't rinse or put her glass in the dishwasher as she normally would. There was a loud clank as she just let it fall from her fingers into the sink.

Rachel continued to eat her pizza and drink her cabernet sauvignon as Danielle returned from brushing her teeth and sat on the sofa in front of the television. She turned it on and started flipping through channels.

Rachel rotated in Danielle's direction, thinking she'd break the very chilly ice by saying something pleasant. It was a tried and true method for Rachel to bring up a whole other topic Danielle loved and felt passionately about. It always defused Danielle and elicited a warm response, effectively melting the frostiness.

"I checked the schedule earlier, and there's a great suspense movie coming on at eight. Do you want to watch it with me?" Rachel didn't care for such movies, but knew Danielle loved them. Rachel knew this would work for sure.

Danielle's only response was to pitch the remote onto the coffee table and march expressionless past Rachel as she made her way to the entrance. She opened the closet and grabbed a flattering suede leather coat that was cinched at the waist. She zippered it up then pulled tight on the strings so that it followed the curves of her shape. She slipped her feet into a pair of casual but stylish leather shoes before simply opening the door…and marching out.

7

Danielle didn't know where she was headed when she left the condo, she just started driving. But half an hour later she found herself knocking on the door of a beautiful lakefront cedar log home she felt very much at home in.

"Danielle!" Lilly was predictably surprised by Danielle's unannounced appearance.

"Hi, Lilly. I was just in the area…" Danielle's voice broke on her last word.

"Everything okay?"

Danielle sighed deeply. Sighing was one of her mannerisms. "I don't know how much more I can take, Lilly. Honestly." She kicked off her shoes while removing her jacket, then hung it on a coat rack in the entrance. Danielle passed Lilly as she automatically made her way to the eat-in kitchen where she and Lilly often talked as they drank tea or shared a bottle of wine. When she stepped in, she stopped in her tracks.

"Um, Danielle, this is Nathalie." Lilly pronounced the name as though it were French: *Nat-alee.*

Danielle stared at the petite woman with long, curly, dark brown hair. "I'm sorry, I didn't realize…" Danielle turned to leave as quickly as she had appeared.

"Please don't go on my account," the woman said without a hint of French in her accent. She held out her hand and said, "Glad to finally meet you, Danielle. Lilly's told me lots about you."

"Wish I could say the same about you," is what Danielle wanted to say. But didn't. Instead, she shook Nathalie's hand and said, "I love your jacket."

Nathalie looked perplexed.

"Didn't we see you at lunchtime today, at Emborio's? You were wearing a black leather jacket and a matching leather beret," Danielle explained.

Nathalie glanced quizzically at Lilly. Lilly appeared to be embarrassed in response, as though she were ten years old, and been caught spying.

"Yes, I was there today, with my agent," Nathalie replied.

"Oh, your agent." Lilly nodded, then smiled

"Yes, Vicki's my agent. I never told you that?"

Danielle studied the woman even more since noticing Lilly's considerable relief that Nathalie's companion had been business, not pleasure. "What type of agent do you have?" Danielle asked. "Are you an actress?"

Nathalie rolled her very round eyes. "God, no. I'm a writer—"

Lilly beamed as she interjected, "A *song* writer. You know that new song that's out, Sammi Tyler sings it? It's called 'I'll be Over You.'"

Danielle drew a blank.

Lilly sang a few bars of the chorus: "I'll be over you when I am six feet under."

"If you don't listen to country, you've probably never heard it." Nathalie said dismissively.

"Sorry, country's not really my thing," Danielle admitted.

"It's not mine either, actually. To tell the truth, I usually can't stand country and western music." Nathalie laughed so authentically, it made Danielle laugh too.

"You don't like country music?" Lilly's eyes showed disbelief. "How can you not like country music? And how could you write such a great country song if you don't like it?"

"Hey, I'm entitled to my Johnny Cash moments. Some songs just go naturally with a forty ouncer of whiskey and a pack of cigarettes— whether you drink or smoke or not." Nathalie laughed again, with ease. Her smile dissolved when she added, "It was just one of those songs that fit the genre." She shrugged and smiled feebly. "And it's selling well."

"*Very* well." Lilly opened her eyes wider in Danielle's direction as she said so.

"Don't listen to her," Nathalie said to Danielle. "She's got stars in her eyes. I blew sparkles off her dress and some of them landed in her eye earlier." Nathalie's smile was firm this time.

Lilly picked up a dress and held it up for Danielle to see. "What do you think?"

Danielle was looking at an exquisite aboriginal jingle dress. "Oh my God, Lilly. It is absolutely dazzling. Wow, what a great job. I *love* the shells." Danielle was touching small black shells, with interior swirls of silver pearl interspersed with metallic greens, blues, and purples. "These mussel shells are incredible, Lilly, and they tie in perfectly with your animal totem."

"That was Nathalie's idea. She's very creative." Lilly said, as she smiled at Nathalie.

"Listen to this." Nathalie stood next to Danielle and started shaking an arm of the dress. The beads and shells sent sounds through the air similar to a wooden wind chime. Danielle smiled as her mood was lifted by the melodic clatter.

"How did you do that?" Danielle's face displayed wonder and delight.

Lilly continued to beam with pride as she held the dress while Nathalie pointed to one of the small, heavy stone beads dangling between two mussel shells. As the dress moved, each and every bead collided with the shells, creating a symphony of stirring tones and melodies. Danielle's hand stayed in position, even though Nathalie's had taken territory over the area, as she described the workmanship.

"Is this the dress you're going to be doing your solo in, Lilly?" Danielle was still smiling in amazement.

"Yes, it is. It's beautiful, isn't it?"

"It sure is." Danielle let go of the dress and looked at Nathalie. "You did a fabulous job with the shells."

Nathalie looked away as soon as Danielle made eye contact. "I should get going, Lilly. I need to make a business call to Vancouver and it'll soon be four-thirty their time." Vancouver was in the Pacific time zone, four hours behind Halifax. Nathalie walked past Danielle without saying goodbye or looking in her direction at all.

"Oh, okay." Lilly looked disappointed as she followed Nathalie into the hallway that also served as an entrance.
"Thanks for coming over and helping with my dress, Nathalie. It's so beautiful. I can't wait to for you to see me dancing in it."

"I'm really looking forward to it. It'll be my first powwow," Nathalie said as she put on her coat. "The other day someone said to me they thought powwow was an odd word for a celebration. I asked her if she thought the word ceilidh was any better."

Lilly laughed. A Cape Breton ceilidh was no different than a Mi'kmaq powwow. Which was also no different than an African kwanzaa or an American spring break, as they all meant the same thing: *Party on!*

Lilly's excitement and anticipation came through in her voice. "Oh you'll love it, Nathalie. The dancing, the singing, the campfires, the sleeping under the stars…"

Danielle's stomach tensed for the second time tonight. She pretended to top up her tea, but was really trying to get a glimpse through the stained glass mirror that hung near Lilly's hall. She couldn't get the view she wanted though, so she listened intently instead, being on alert for the sounds of lips meeting to say goodbye. All she heard though, after Lilly and Nathalie's conversation about the powwow, was a few hushed words she couldn't make out, followed by the door closing.

"Nathalie's going to the powwow?" Danielle's question was out before Lilly's foot hit the kitchen floor.

"Yes, I invited her."

"You seem quite taken with her. How did you meet?" Danielle then mockingly slapped Lilly as she added, "And why didn't you tell me?"

Lilly smiled as though she were smitten and suddenly shy about it. "I don't know. I guess I wasn't sure—I'm still not sure. She's not usually the type I go for."

"No, she's not your type at all." Lilly was five-nine, and usually went for women as tall, or taller, than she was, so it was a great surprise to Danielle that Nathalie—who was probably barely five-one or two—would even turn Lilly's head.

"I met her at one of my dance classes. And as I got to know her, I found I really liked her—a lot. She's so funny, creative, intelligent, thoughtful—"

"Gee, I'm all that and I've never turned your head!" Danielle's face reddened, and she suddenly wished she hadn't said that. Rachel's method of injecting humor at unexpected times was not as successful when Danielle attempted it. She'd been joking—she thought—but she felt a hint of seriousness and uncomfortability surrounding it. Danielle quickly changed the subject. "Is Nathalie French? You pronounced her name the French way but she doesn't have an accent."

"I don't think she is," Lilly replied. "You didn't tell me what happened. Did you and Rachel have another fight?"

Danielle released another of her signature sighs as she leaned her back against Lilly's kitchen counter and grabbed its edge with both hands. "I think I've reached my limit, Lilly."

Neither of them said anything for a moment, then Danielle told her what she thought about her trip home with Rachel. "This long weekend is going to either make us or break us, Lilly. I can feel it."

Lilly reached over and put her hand on Danielle's upper back, giving it a couple of rubs as she said, "I hope it works out for you."

Danielle turned abruptly and flung an arm around Lilly, pulling her close. Before Lilly could respond though, Danielle let go. "I should go." Danielle picked up her still full teacup and poured it down the drain. She then gave Lilly a tap on the shoulder and headed for the door.

Lilly waited an hour or so till she figured Nathalie would be finished with her business call before phoning her.

After Lilly gave Nathalie a brief history of Danielle's relationship with Rachel, Nathalie asked, "Does Danielle know how you feel about Rachel?"

"Yes and no. She was already with Rachel when we met, so I didn't feel it was my place to say anything. As we got closer I tried asking her why she was with Rachel, but she always changed the subject or said she didn't want to talk about it." Lilly could not have emphasized her next sentence more. "God, I hope they break up."

"Break up? I thought you told her you hoped things would work out for her and Rachel."

"I didn't say 'her *and* Rachel.' I just said 'her.' Meaning, things working out for Danielle, would be her and Rachel breaking up."

"I don't know whether to laugh or be appalled," Nathalie said in response. Then she laughed. "I thought I was good with words, but you're exceptionally gifted—at manipulating their meaning at least."

"I'll take that as a compliment," Lilly responded. "Just as a defense lawyer doesn't need to know what I'm really aiming at, Danielle doesn't need to either. At least, not while she's too blind to see what's right in front of her."

"And what's right in front of her?"

"The obvious. Hey, not to change the subject or anything, but Danielle asked if you were French because of how your name is pronounced. I told her I didn't think so."

"No," replied Nathalie, "I'm not French. My grandparents were though, so maybe that's why my mother pronounced it that way. It stuck. Danielle looks nothing like I imagined, by the way."

"Oh, no? What did you imagine her to look like?"

"Well…" Nathalie seemed very hesitant to reply.

"Let me guess. You didn't expect her to be so attractive or so feminine." Being tall, slender and quite attractive herself, Lilly was used to attention, but it was nothing compared to the attention

Danielle often got, which is why Lilly never understood why Danielle stayed with Rachel. Danielle could easily find someone else—if she wanted to.

"It's just, you kept saying she was a cop, and used to be in the military, and used to play soccer and hockey. You can't blame me for thinking butch."

Lilly laughed. "Yes, I know. But you of all people, Nathalie, I didn't think you'd stereotype."

"Okay, okay. Guilty as charged. So what sentence might you be recommending, Madam Prosecutor?"

"Hmmmm…I think I'd be more apt to recommend community service as a first offense."

"And what type of community service would that be? Offering buzz cuts to the butches for a charitable donation?" Nathalie giggled.

"You are so bad!"

"And you love it, admit it."

"Yes, I do love it. There's lots I love about you," Lilly said quite seriously.

"Lilly, I—" Nathalie stopped in mid-sentence.

"What?"

"Nothing. Never mind."

"What? What were you going to say?"

"Nothing. Really. Forget I said anything."

"Oh, come on. Tell me what you were going to say. I won't bite. Yet," Lilly added playfully.

There was only silence on the other end.

Lilly wouldn't normally be so delicate in expressing her interest. Pussy-footing around wasn't her style. She was very attractive, very confident, and had never been turned down, so rejection wasn't anything she feared. Lilly was cognizant of Nathalie's reluctance, however. Even if she didn't understand it, she was well aware of it, and tried her best to be sensitive toward it. "Nathalie, I can tell you've been hurt. You laugh and joke a lot, but I see a sadness in you. I know you value your privacy, but if you ever want to talk…"

Nathalie remained silent.

Lilly decided to go for it. "Nathalie, I'm interested in you. I'd like to ask you out. On a date." The long silence that ensued reminded Lilly of a reluctant witness. Success wasn't going to come easily this time. So she thought.

"Okay, why don't you come over here Friday night? I'll cook you dinner," Nathalie said.

"Wow, you surprised me with that one."

"Did I?"

"Well, you took an awfully long time to answer, so I was expecting to be turned down."

"I doubt anyone's ever turned you down, Lilly."

"Well, I was starting to think you'd be the first."

"Are you disappointed I'm not? I could rescind—"

"Don't you dare!"

Nathalie giggled.

"Would you like me to bring red or white wine?" Lilly asked.

"How about Apricot beer? That would go better with what I'm planning to make."

"And what is that?"

"I'd rather surprise you."

"Are you as good a cook as you are a songwriter?"

"Some things I'm even better at," Nathalie blurted.

"Oooh, I can't wait to find that out," Lilly said flirtatiously. Lilly hoped Nathalie would continue the flirtatious talk, but she didn't.

"Lilly, I have to go. I'll talk to you later in the week, okay?"

"Oh—" Lilly didn't get a chance to complete her sentence. The conversation was already over because Nathalie had hung up.

8

Danielle returned to the condo shortly after 9:00 p.m. Not surprisingly, Rachel was already in bed. Danielle went to the bathroom and returned with Rachel's empty wine bottle and wine glass, both of which she placed on the kitchen counter without rinsing. Her own wine glass, which she'd dropped into the sink earlier, was still sitting there.

Danielle looked at their bedroom door. It was open about six inches. She stared at it.

Danielle hated fighting. She really did. She wished she could just walk into her bedroom, enter her bed, and make love to the woman lying in it. But she couldn't, because she could not longer drum up any desire for Rachel.

"If you're not in bed by nine-thirty, you can sleep on the sofa!"

Danielle could tell Rachel had shouted that from bed.

At 9:31 Rachel poked her head out from the bedroom door and looked across the hallway at Danielle, who was leaned against a kitchen counter. Rachel's angry face matched the hostility in her voice as she informed Danielle of her punishment. "I'm going to bed and locking the bedroom door." Rachel then shut the door hard and locked it just as she said she would.

Danielle stared at the door for a moment, and a tear fell from her eye. Followed by another. And another, until Danielle went to the bathroom to wash them away. She then sat on the bathroom floor and brought her knees up, cradling them. The tears returned.

She thought of her mother…and wondered if she would have ever gotten involved with Rachel if her mother had been there for her when she needed her most.

Danielle walked over to the sink and washed her face again. She then went to the kitchen, opened a lower cupboard door, and retrieved a bottle of Geneva gin. When Danielle opened the bottle, she could smell Juniper trees. To Danielle, it smelled like home.

She poured a generous amount into a tall glass, then opened the same cupboard door and reached far in to grab a bottle of lime soda. She tipped the two-liter bottle until her glass was almost full to the top. She took a sip and made a grimace. She considered pouring half of it out and topping it up with only lime soda but instead she brought the glass back up to her lips and gulped half of it down before lowering the glass back onto the counter. She shuddered.

She then poured more lime soda into it, and tasted. Now this was the taste she remembered and enjoyed. Though like her mother, only occasionally.

Danielle remembered she hadn't had a chance to enjoy a celebratory drink yesterday. She therefore tucked the soda under her left arm, picked up her drink and bottle of gin, then carried all three to the living room where she deposited them on the coffee table before plunking herself down on the burgundy leather sofa.

When Danielle reached the bottom of her second glass of gin, she realized she had to go to the bathroom. When she got up, she was a little unsteady, but wasn't drunk. Yet. She was just on her way, is all.

As she passed the kitchen, she spied Rachel's empty wine bottle and wine glass from the corner of her eye. They were still sitting on the counter, where Danielle had placed them earlier. Had she not done so, they'd still be in the bathroom.

Then, as if struck by the most brilliant of ideas, Danielle stopped, then twirled herself around as though grooving to the sounds of a 1970's disco tune. She danced her way to the counter and seductively performed a lap dance, teasing the wine bottle and wine glass before eventually pouncing and capturing them. She then boogied her way to the bathroom, each move getting a bit wobblier as she went.

She raised the wine bottle up to a light centered on the bathroom ceiling. She saw a few millimeters of wine left in the bottle, and perhaps a drop or two left in the glass. That was enough put her plan into action, she thought.

Danielle half hummed and half sang a seventies classic, "You kin ring ma belllll hmmmm, ring ma bell. You kin kiss ma aaa..." as she eked out the last drops of red wine resting in the bottle. She continued to sing and hum as she saw the drops splash and coagulate onto the white marble ledge of the tub. She then carefully positioned the wine glass dead center of the red stain, and ground it in a few times, making sure that when the rim dried, it would leave its greatest impact when it was finally removed in the morning—or whenever Rachel would give in and pick up after herself.

Danielle then put the bottle back where she'd originally found it, lying on its side on the floor next to the tub, and also pulled the still damp bath towel back to its original position—in a heap on the floor.

For good measure, she stepped on the towel and sang a few bars of "The Twist" as she performed the moves that went along with it.

Her bladder reminded her she needed to use the bathroom so she stopped doing the twist and relieved herself before washing her hands and going back to the living room for a refill.

୫୦ଓଷ

Danielle was swimming. The water was like a womb, so warm and buoyant, so soothing. The pressure of the sea gave all of her muscles a deep massage as she allowed herself to submerge to the ocean floor.

She opened her eyes and looked into the distance where she felt a presence calling. She passed a whale as she swam toward glittering pearls of green and blue. They rested on mounds of crushed mussel shells, with colors that swished and surged with each breath she took. Colors so vibrant, they enthralled.

Danielle felt a touch. Her face, neck, breasts, hands, all were felt by the same one touch. Danielle allowed the heavy swirling of seawater against her body to slowly rotate and wrap her deeper into that touch. She caught a glimpse of a stained glass mirror as she felt a caress on her cheek, then across her lips. She felt so loved.

A mermaid began to sing a lullaby. There were no words, but Danielle knew the melody was French. Three hockey sticks appeared and slowly danced to the mermaid's haunting, soulful melody.

Danielle felt love press into her, then wrap itself around her and take the shape of a sushi roll. She brought her hand up to caress the cheek of the mermaid whose deep green, leathery skin now wrapped itself around her, holding Danielle close and safe.

The mermaid's face was indistinguishable, but her long dark hair danced with the currents of the water. Danielle felt her body press against the mermaid's, as her leathery sushi wrap kept them joined as one. Their arms were pinned against each other now, with their hands clasped, as Danielle caressed the mermaid's hand, tracing a letter 'L' which raised from the back of it.

Danielle looked into the mermaid's eyes, wanting, needing to connect with her. Flecks of dark green reflected from the mermaid's skin, into two dark pools where eyes should be. Danielle stared deeper into them, calling the eyes to come to life. Two blazing sunbursts flashed through the center of both pools. Danielle knew she loved this woman and wanted her kiss more than anything.

Danielle opened her mouth to accept the mermaid's pink, loving gift into herself, but as she did, she heard Rachel's voice shouting.

"It's seven o'clock! Danielle! It's seven o'clock! I'm assuming you'll want to shower and clean up before you go into work, unless you plan on calling in sick, and the way you smell, you probably should."

Danielle opened her eyes and saw a half bottle of Geneva gin sitting on the coffee table, next to an empty bottle of club soda and half glass of what she assumed was left of her last drink. She was so thirsty her tongue stuck to the roof of her mouth.

"I'm leaving for work. Make sure your mess is cleaned up by the time I get home tonight, and if you've spilled anything on the sofa, you'll owe me six thousand dollars."

Danielle's head vibrated as the door slammed. Minutes later, she made her way to the kitchen with eyes still closed. She opened them only long enough to select a glass and fill it with water. She didn't open them again until she had filled and drank the entire contents twice. Her mouth tasted like she'd sucked on juniper tree sap all night. And indirectly, she supposed she had.

She went to the bathroom and scrubbed her teeth and tongue. When she stuck out her tongue, she remembered her dream. Deciding she had no time for dream analysis, she jumped in the shower.

The warmth of the hot water brought her dream back to the forefront. She had felt so loved in that dream, and that feeling still lingered within her as she wrapped a fresh bath towel around herself and entered the bedroom.

She fell onto her side of the bed and closed her eyes. The soft, plush towel wrapped around her took her back to her dream yet again. She got up, retrieved her cell phone and dialed a number.

"This is Constable Renaud. I'll be out in the field this morning, so if anyone needs to get in touch with me, they can reach me on my cell."

Danielle discarded the towel and slipped under the covers. Feeling somewhat rehydrated and clean, she drifted off into a comfortable sleep for a couple of hours.

At ten-thirty a.m. Danielle was standing inside the Victoria Veterinary Hospital where she showed her RCMP identification and requested the names of all staff who had been working there when the clinic was broken into.

After receiving a list that contained nine names, Danielle asked if she could speak to each of them. Fortunately, there were only two who were no longer there or not at work. One had taken a job at another clinic, and the other was currently on maternity leave. She'd contact them later.

Danielle got pretty much the same story from everyone, with only minor changes in details as they pertained to specific duties each had been performing or had been responsible for.

Just a month prior to Buchanan's death, their clinic had been broken into. Although neither the safe nor any of the cabinets were forced open, ten vials of Ketaset—a brand of ketamine hydrochloride—were thought to be missing.

Danielle was just about to interview the sixth person on the list when a dark-haired woman entered, not with an animal, but with an infant. She approached Danielle.

"Hi, I'm Lucy. Lucy Miller."

Danielle glanced at her list and saw she was the woman on maternity leave. "Oh. How did you—"

"Shelly called me. Said you had questions for everybody who was working here when we got broken into. I had to stop in to pick up some forms anyway, so I figured this was just as good a time as any." The baby began to fuss a bit, so she placed a pacifier in his mouth.

"Okay, well why don't we talk now, so you don't have to wait." Danielle walked back into the small examination room the manager suggested she use, and Lucy Miller followed.

"I thought everything was settled about the break-in. I mean, nothing was actually stolen. We did have a break-in, but they didn't get anything. They couldn't get inside the safe or the cabinets where we keep the drugs. We make sure they're locked up every night."

"So why were ten vials of Ketaset reported missing?" Danielle knew what was in the report. She just wanted to make sure that nineteen months later, details matched. If it all happened the way it was stated in the police report, then they should. Otherwise... Danielle was well aware that sometimes time thinned out the veil people threw over certain things.

"It was just a mistake. The person who was covering for me while I was on vacation wasn't used to doing inventory. At first she thought some vials were missing, but they weren't. When I came back I straightened it all out. You can check. Our manager called the police back and told them nothing was missing after all."

Danielle had indeed noted their reason for closing the file, but she wanted to cover all the bases. "This is simply routine. I'm just following up on a recent similar break-in, wondering if they're related." It was more prudent to fib than to reveal her real reason for checking into it again.

Lucy Miller's previously tense face relaxed.

"You said you were responsible for inventory. How much ketamine do you normally order each month?"

"Depends. Sometimes we only have a few surgeries in a week, sometimes a lot more."

"On average?"

"On average, maybe two or three vials of Ketaset per week."

"And what size vials do you order?"

"Mostly fifty milliliter." Lucy paused, then added, "Except in the past I've had to order vials of ten milliliters as well during our peak season."

"When's your peak season?"

Lucy Miller placed her baby on her knee and started bouncing it up and down in a controlled trembling motion. If the baby weren't sitting there, Danielle would think Lucy Miller was nervous as hell. "Summer and early fall," Lucy replied.

"Ten milliliter vials contain more Ketaset than the fifty milliliter ones, don't they?"

Lucy seemed surprised by Danielle's awareness of this fact. "Yes, they do. We usually only order those during our peak season, though."

"Is Ketaset the only brand of ketamine hydrochloride you order, or do you use other brands as well?"

"We only use Ketaset here because we get a discount from the manufacturer."

"Okay, Ms. Miller. If I need to get in touch with you I'll contact you, but I think I've got everything I need. Like you said, nothing was stolen after all, so I don't think we need to look into this any further."

Lucy Miller gave a brief, nervous smile. She picked up her baby and walked toward the door. As she passed reception she waved her baby's cute little hand in their direction and said in a baby's voice, "Bye-bye."

Danielle didn't know if Lucy Miller had just forgotten or what, but noticed Lucy hadn't picked up any forms before leaving. Danielle thought about this for a moment, then turned to a woman at reception and asked, "When is the cat spaying and neutering season?"

"Pardon me?"

"When do most cats get fixed? Is summer and early fall their season to go into heat?"

The vet tech gave Danielle a puzzled look. "There is no season. All female cats can go into heat at any time, year round, as long as they're not pregnant. And the males, well, they're males. They're ready, willing and able anytime. Choosing when to neuter or spay after a cat has sexually matured, only depends on when an owner decides to do it."

Danielle asked if she could speak with the manager again. She entered his office and was there for about twenty minutes. When she left, she was holding copies of three years worth of their monthly drug inventory and all invoices for purchases of ketamine hydrochloride.

When Danielle got inside her vehicle she said into her recorder, "Check to see if various brands of ketamine contain any other substances or preservatives unique to them that other brands might not have, then check if the crime lab found or tested for those— might pinpoint the brand used."

Danielle spent the next two days reading, reading, and reading even more. She avoided the whole situation with Rachel by bringing home files to read as well. As Rachel soaked in the tub or holed up in the bedroom, Danielle sat quietly in the living room reading as much as she could on the Buchanan case. She told herself she would be taking the long weekend off, that at four o'clock Thursday, until 8:00 a.m. Wednesday morning, she would be off the clock. Danielle promised herself she wouldn't even think about work. But of course she did.

❧ 9 ❧

On Thursday morning Danielle called Lilly and arranged for them to meet on the waterfront for a walk at noon. Danielle, who normally ran four or five times a week, had only gotten two days in so far, so she decided to go for a run around eleven o'clock. The walk with Lilly would be a good cool down.

"You put me to shame with your aerobic prowess, with all that swimming and running," Lilly said as Danielle stretched to cool down.

"You're in great shape too, Lilly. Emphasis on the shape." Danielle smiled coyly.

"I wouldn't have this shape if I didn't enjoy dancing so much, because it's about the only exercise I get."

"You don't just enjoy it, Lilly. You're very dedicated. Even with all the hours you put in at work, you still put in what—ten, fifteen hours a week sometimes, dancing?"

Lilly shrugged. "It's how I unwind."

Danielle began to walk and motioned for Lilly to join her. "Speaking of unwind, what are your plans for the weekend?" Danielle was curious if Lilly was planning on seeing Nathalie, but didn't want to be direct about it.

"Just going to relax. Practice my dance and finish my dress."

"Is Nathalie still helping you with that?"

"Yes. We're going to have dinner tomorrow night, then work on my dress on Saturday."

Danielle wondered if that meant she planned on them being together all weekend, but didn't ask. "Which restaurant are you going to? That African place on Quinpool you like so much?"

"No, she hates spicy food. She's invited me to her place for a home-cooked meal." Lilly spoke with admiration as she said, "She's dropped some things off to me a few times. She's a fabulous cook."

"Yes, she seems fabulous at a lot of things."

Lilly stopped in mid-step. "What's that supposed to mean?"

Danielle was taken aback by Lilly's response. "Uh…nothing. I wasn't being sarcastic." Was she? "I just meant, she's a talented composer and lyricist, and she designed a gorgeous dress, and now you tell me she's also a great cook." Danielle held her breath as she waited for Lilly's reaction to her attempt to smooth any feathers she might have ruffled with her comment. Danielle was relieved when Lilly started walking and talking again.

"You know, it really irritates me that the only people they pay to represent Nova Scotia on this waterfront are the Scottish bagpipers. Especially when you know the history of this province, that this land belonged to the Mi'kmaq when the French first arrived, and that Black Loyalists also played a very strong part in shaping what Nova Scotia is today. If they want a true representation of this province, they should have Mi'kmaq dancers on the boardwalk, and definitely something dedicated to black history. I know I'd much rather be able to buy authentic French Acadian or Mi'kmaq wares than those boring, overpriced trinkets you can find anywhere." Lilly was pointing to one of the harborside shanties that covered much of the waterfront. "And the bagpipes—"

"Out in the middle of the harbor?" Danielle laughed, though she was probably quite serious about where she would prefer them to be. "Your dinner with Nathalie, is it a date?" she then asked nonchalantly.

Lilly produced a radiant smile. "Yes, it is. I'm really excited about it. I've never been to her place before, so I'm really looking forward to it—and the date itself, of course."

"How long have you known her?"

"Seven or eight months. We met last fall."

Danielle was stunned. "You met her last fall, and I had to stumble on to her at your house in order to find out about her?"

Lilly looked surprised by Danielle's reaction, but before she could respond, Danielle flashed her a playful smile and asked, "Why so secretive about her? Is she a criminal you decided to bed instead of prosecute?"

Lilly didn't smile back, but seemed rather defensive as she replied, "I wasn't being secretive. She's just very private, and I didn't want her to think I was only interested in her because of her success."

"Well, you didn't have to mention that part to me. You could have just said, 'Hey, I met somebody I'm interested in and her name is Nathalie.'"

"I know how it seems, Danielle, but you don't understand. We met in early September, but it took me forever to even get her to go for a coffee with me. It was well after Christmas before she even let me have her phone number."

"Likes playing hard to get, does she?"

"No, it's not that. I think she's just been really hurt."

"Who hasn't?"

"There's something more to it than that. I'm normally so good at reading people—victims, abusers, criminals. With Nathalie, I know there's something really...troubling, but I just don't know what it is."

"Ah, so that's what draws you to her—the mystery of it all."

"I hadn't really thought about it, but you're right. Nathalie's definitely mysterious, and that intrigues me."

"Where does she live?"

"She has a place up on Maynard. It has three rental units. She rents out two of them and stays in one. She has a cottage down the Valley too, spends most of the summer there I guess."

Danielle's favorite beach was in the Annapolis Valley. She swam at Blomidon Beach as often as she could because the Minas Basin, with its rich, red, clay cliffs, reminded her of home and was one of the warmest salt water beaches in Nova Scotia—which often wasn't very warm at all.

"How serious are you about her?" Danielle asked.

"I don't know. I like her a lot. An awful lot. But there's just so much about her I don't know. She certainly keeps everything close to her chest."

"Do you think she's hiding something? You know you could run her name through JEINS." Danielle was referring to the Nova Scotia Department of Justice's database of all legal proceedings, civil and criminal.

"I already did," Lilly confessed. "But I didn't find anything. Not that I expected anything anyway. I really get the feeling that what she's mysterious about is deeply personal. I'm probably just being overly suspicious."

"You're a prosecutor—you're trained to be suspicious."

"And you're not, Constable?"

"Touché. Guess it comes with the territory. You know, she might just still be hung up on an ex."

"That might be it. Maybe she's on the rebound."

Danielle was dying to know if Lilly was planning on spending the night—or entire weekend—with Nathalie. But since the subtle approach didn't work, she decided to come right out and ask—in the most casual manner she could. "You hoping to get lucky? I hear rebound sex is pretty great." Danielle grinned.

"Well then, I guess you'll have something to look forward to when you and Rachel break up."

It was Danielle who stopped abruptly this time. Lilly turned toward Danielle, but lowered her gaze to the weathered wood beneath her feet and shoved her hands in her coat pockets. "Sorry. I meant to say 'if', not 'when.'"

Danielle sighed. "It's okay," she said to Lilly. *But was it?*

Both walked wordlessly together until they reached the corner of Sackville and Granville streets. They wished each other a good long weekend and briefly hugged before turning and heading in opposite directions.

Near the end of her work day, Danielle did a mental briefing of everything she now knew about Kristina Ann Buchanan, and how she died.

Earlier in the evening of October fourth, Buchanan picked up her ex-boyfriend Maurice Coultier, and her friend and coworker Gillian Stevens, then drove them to her place. All three drank beer and shared a few joints.

Because Kristina lived a half hour from the city and they were drinking, Maurice and Gillian were then picked up by Maurice's brother, Joseph, then dropped off at Gillian's apartment in the city.

Neighbors corroborated the time they arrived, and said they heard them partying till about 2:00 a.m. One neighbor said he banged on the door and woke them up around 4:00 a.m. because in their drunken state they had forgotten Gillian's cat outside, and he'd been meowing incessantly to get back in. The neighbor identified Maurice Coultier as the man who answered the door.

Urine and blood samples submitted the next afternoon confirmed their inebriated status the night before, and so that, combined with neighbors' witness accounts, eliminated them as suspects.

The picture painted by family, friends, acquaintances, neighbors and coworkers of Kristina Buchanan was the typical rose colored version that followed anyone's death. It somewhat annoyed Danielle whenever Mr. or Ms. X, who could have been the nastiest of people when alive, suddenly became all sunshine and roses upon their death. Danielle wondered if eighteen months had been long enough for the sunshine and roses to fade in the eyes of Buchanan's friends and family.

At exactly 4:00 p.m. on Thursday, Danielle left work and headed for home. When she arrived Rachel wasn't home yet, but Danielle expected her at any moment. She started packing right away. She pulled two suitcases out of the storage closet and brought them to the bedroom. She knew better than to open Rachel's dresser even if it was to pack for her, so she just left Rachel's suitcase open on the bed.

After her own suitcase was packed, Danielle sat down on the bed next to Rachel's empty one. Her stomach tightened again.

Maybe Rachel shouldn't be coming with me after all. Maybe Rachel and I need some time apart.

Rachel didn't enjoy Danielle's hometown, which was really just a very small village, at the best of times. Bringing her along after a week of tension and fighting might not be a good idea at all.

At six o'clock Danielle dialed Rachel's cell, but there was no answer. By eight Danielle had left two messages, neither of which had been returned. Danielle wasn't worried though. She was used to Rachel punishing her when she didn't do exactly as Rachel wanted—or expected.

Rachel walked in shortly after eight, laden with shopping bags. She had obviously treated herself to some retail therapy. *Qu'elle surprise.* Rachel didn't remove her shoes, just made her way to the bedroom where she sorted her purchases.

Rachel then came out of the bedroom with her suitcase zippered up but clearly empty. She didn't acknowledge Danielle as she placed the suitcase back in the storage closet. Danielle didn't react. She watched Rachel return to the bedroom, then waited a few minutes before going in.

"I take it you've decided not to come home with me."

"Why would I go for an eight hour drive with someone who's not talking to me?"

"I'm not *not* talking to you. I've just been..." Danielle really didn't want to be wasting her time and energy on this conversation, but she tried to communicate how she'd been feeling. "You weren't exactly supportive when I told you my news on Monday. I was really excited about finally getting into Special Investigations, but you just jumped down my throat when I tried to tell you about it."

"First of all, I've told you not to call me at work when you know I've got patients scheduled. And secondly, you're the one who stood *me* up. I went along, to treat you to something I find disgusting, and *you're* the one who didn't appreciate it. All you were thinking about was your new assignment—which is really just a joke by the way—so I don't feel bad that I didn't celebrate it with you. *You're* the one who should feel bad. *You're* the one who left me sitting there, in a restaurant I can't stand, while you were too self-absorbed to even think about me. *You're* the self-centered, selfish one."

Danielle couldn't stomach this for one more second. "I'm not going to fight with you, Rachel. If you don't want to come, fine."

Danielle returned to the living room and looked over her trip's checklist. Waterproof paper and floral wire were the only two items not crossed out. She looked at her watch, then hurried out the door.

Rather than drive three blocks, then have to look for a parking spot, Danielle just ran the few uphill blocks to the art supply store. It took her just a couple of minutes, giving her almost twenty to peruse the multitude of unique papers they had in stock, before they closed.

After Danielle moved in with her grandparents, she had joined her grandmother in a springtime ritual Danielle now looked forward to every year. Her grandmother loved to make flowers out of colored paper and tie them to the shrubs and bushes that lined the lane leading to her house. From a distance, it looked like she was the world's greatest gardener, producing gorgeous flowers that bloomed from early spring till late fall. It was only when people walked right up to them and touched them did they realize they were not real.

When Danielle was living with her grandmother, all that was available was tissue paper. After Danielle left at age seventeen, she'd found and brought home brightly colored waterproof paper, which her grandmother had never seen before. Her grandmother was thrilled by it.

It became an exciting ritual after that. Always on the hunt for more spectacular waterproof papers, Danielle looked very much forward to presenting her finds to her grandmother every Easter. The new art supply store in which she was currently standing had the best selection she'd ever seen anywhere.

She found several papers that were gorgeous, but Danielle couldn't tell if they were waterproof or not. She didn't want anything that would have the color run out of them during a rain. She looked around for a sales associate, but didn't see one. She started walking toward the sales counter when she noticed Lilly's friend, Nathalie, examining the journals and notebooks, with two already in hand.

Danielle touched Nathalie's shoulder. "Hello."

Nathalie startled, jumping back.

"I'm sorry, I didn't mean to startle you," Danielle said.

"Oh. Sorry. I was just in my own world—I tend to live there a lot." Nathalie smiled the briefest of smiles before settling back into a somber look. "And what are you doing here?"

"I'm trying to pick out some paper for my grandmother. She loves making flowers."

"Origami?"

"Um, I think so. Daisies, carnations, origamis…"

Nathalie smiled as she explained, "No, I meant origami, the Japanese art of paper folding." She quickly pointed in another direction. "They have specialty paper for that over there."

"Oh." Normally Danielle would have been embarrassed by her faux pas, but she found Nathalie's manner so warm and genuine, she wasn't. "Is it waterproof? I was looking for someone to tell me if the papers I was looking at were, when I saw you." Danielle noticed Nathalie's dimples for the first time. When she smiled they were prominently displayed.

"You know, you might be better off choosing plastic instead of paper. I'll show you what I'm talking about."

Nathalie led Danielle to a small selection of brightly colored sheets of very thin plastic. Danielle looked them over, but hadn't yet decided which colors to buy when an announcement came over the speaker that the store would be closing in five minutes.

Danielle quickly picked one of each color, then both she and Nathalie headed to the cash register with their purchases.

Nathalie insisted Danielle go first, so Danielle was finished before she was. Danielle stood at the door waiting. She hadn't told Nathalie she'd wait for her, she just found herself doing so. When Nathalie approached the door, Danielle opened it and followed her outside.

"Would you like to grab a tea, Nathalie? I know it's getting late, but a chai latte would really hit the spot for me right now."

Nathalie hesitated, then said, "I should probably get back."

"Oh, come on. You can spare fifteen minutes, can't you?" Danielle placed her purchase on the top of her head, raised one leg and extended her arms out. "If I'm not a good conversationalist, I could entertain you with tricks."

Nathalie's stoic stance was shattered by a giggling grin. Danielle repeated the improvised balancing act for good measure. Nathalie's dimples deepened as she tried to suppress laughter, releasing such a smile it looked like her cheeks might explode.

Danielle smiled back in kind, while she tried to capture Nathalie's eyes with her own, but they evaded her.

Nathalie turned in the direction of the nearest coffee shop. "I suppose I could spare a few minutes."

Danielle paid for a chamomile tea and chai latte, then chose a private table in the corner for them to sit at.

After exchanging a few general comments about the shop and their tea, Danielle said, "Lilly tells me you met at a dance class?"

"Yes, hip hop. It's not really my kind of music, but I love to dance, and I wanted a fun exercise class. She and I hit it off because we were the only two who were of legal drinking age." Nathalie smiled, but ever so briefly.

Danielle noticed Nathalie kept looking at her tea, not at her. "Are you and Lilly dating?"

Nathalie glanced at Danielle. "You get right to the point, don't you?" She then turned her head and looked out the window.

Danielle noticed the other night, Nathalie didn't hold eye contact. "Guess that's the police officer in me," Danielle told her as she continued to observe Nathalie.

"Are you Halifax City, or RCMP?"

"RCMP."

"So, you're a Mountie. Do you work twelve hour shifts?" Nathalie was staring at her tea again and scraping at the side of her cup with her fingernail.

"No, I don't. I'm an investigator. Regular business hours, Monday to Friday, eight to four."

"And what do you investigate? Your friends' dating practices?"

That was unexpected, but Danielle supposed she deserved that. "I know Lilly is quite taken with you."

Nathalie didn't respond, just took a sip of her tea.

"Are you interested in her too?" Danielle asked.

"Excuse me?" Nathalie shifted, and though she leaned back and crossed her arms, she exhibited a forward expression in her face. "I don't mean to be rude, but I don't think who I may or may not be interested in, is any of your concern. I can appreciate you wanting to look out for your friend, but Lilly is a grown woman. I don't think she would appreciate your interference either."

"I'm not interfering. I was just curious if you felt the same way, is all."

"I thought I was coming to a coffee shop, not an inquisition," Nathalie snapped. Nathalie gripped her paper cup so hard that the tea inside raised almost to the rim.

Danielle didn't know what to make of this swift transformation in Nathalie. She changed from feeble to forceful so quickly, it took Danielle by surprise. "I just wouldn't want to see my friend hurt."

"Is that a threat?"

"It's not anything. I'm just telling you, I wouldn't want to see my friend hurt."

"Well, I'm just telling you. How I feel about Lilly—or anything else for that matter—is *none* of your business." Nathalie got up and tossed her entire cup, tea and all, into the garbage before storming out of the coffee shop.

Nathalie was at the end of the block before Danielle caught up with her.

"Nathalie!"

Nathalie ignored Danielle's arrival and kept walking forward, turning the corner.

"Nathalie, please…" Danielle touched Nathalie's arm.

Nathalie stopped and turned to face her. It was dark, but her face was illuminated by a street light. She had tears in her eyes and looked so very sad. "Message received, Danielle."

"No, you don't understand. I…" Danielle realized she didn't know what she was thinking or feeling herself, so how could she explain it to Nathalie? She just knew she couldn't leave it like this. "Listen, if Lilly likes you, you must be a good person. She's got good instincts, I know that much about her. I just—she's my friend. I was just looking out for her."

"I can appreciate that, Danielle, but you can't protect your friends from life. And that's exactly what life is, mostly hurt. Maybe a few joyous moments here and there, but for the most part, life hurts like hell."

Danielle sensed such deep, saturated pain behind Nathalie's words she didn't know how to respond. When Nathalie started walking away again, Danielle just stood there, watching…as Nathalie faded off into the distance.

❦ 11 ❧

When Danielle left Halifax on Friday morning she had planned on using the long drive to think about her relationship with Rachel. She had clearly reached an impasse this week and needed to think seriously about whether or not she should stay in the relationship. But as she drove the two hours from Halifax to the New Brunswick border, then another five through nearly that entire province, one of the last things that entered her mind, was Rachel. Instead, Danielle's head was filled with random thoughts of Lilly, Nathalie…and the dead woman whose face had a letter "S" carved into it.

Although she had told herself she wouldn't, Danielle couldn't stop herself from thinking about the case, about the evidence she had reviewed, and what it might mean.

She thought a lot about what had been done to the woman's face. Clearly, the carving was a message. But what sort of message, and to whom? What did the letter "S" stand for?

Danielle pressed the record button on her digital voice recorder and let words roll off her tongue: "Slut, snake, snitch." She had to think harder to come up with any others, and it took more and more time between each word. "Scumbag. Skank. Skag. Stoner."

Danielle turned the recorder off. God knows what the letter "S" really meant. Maybe it was a message, or maybe the guy was just so messed up himself, he didn't even know what he was doing, and it wasn't a message at all. Maybe he was just hallucinating some creature on her face and followed the trail with a knife.

Danielle quickly dismissed that thought, though. It took precision to carve the "S" as well as it had been. Whoever did it was sober. Whoever did it had the clarity, the coordination, and the presence of mind to carry out their plan. And it had been a plan. Danielle was sure of that.

Ketamine isn't like a knife or the base of a lamp that just happens to be nearby and gets grabbed during a heated argument. It's a drug that isn't so common, and has particular properties that must have served the killer's specific purposes.

So what properties does ketamine have that other drugs don't? Danielle tried to recall notes she'd taken while talking to Sergeant Carvery and mentally went over them.

It doesn't knock a person unconscious. They remain conscious and aware, even though that awareness would be intermingled with hallucinations.

Danielle felt the most important factor she needed to consider about the killer's use of ketamine is that it's a paralytic.

They chose a drug that would keep her conscious, but physically incapacitated and unable to defend herself. Perhaps they wanted to torture her first?

But she hadn't been. The medical examiner reported no signs of physical restraint or trauma of any kind—other than her face.

It didn't make any sense to Danielle. It seemed so contradictory. And so did the use of ketamine, when she thought more about it.

Why use a drug that puts the body to sleep, but keeps the mind awake? And if they wanted her mind to remain awake, why then put enough of it into her to kill her several times over?

Now that Danielle knew more about ketamine, she knew the amount was absolute overkill. It was no accident. When someone Kristina Buchanan must have known walked into her house that night, they had arrived with the intent to kill.

One thing was clear, the killing was not sexually motivated. There was no semen—though he could have used a condom. But there was no physical evidence she'd been sexually assaulted in any way. She was found fully clothed, and she had no pre-mortem bruising, scratches, or defensive wounds.

So if you exclude sexual gratification as a motivator, Danielle asked herself, *what other motives remain?*

Interested in working homicide for the last few years, Danielle had done a lot of reading and agreed with the experts that premeditated murder was usually motivated by sexual gratification, financial gain, business or political power or gain, an extreme fear of losing something or someone, mental illness, or…revenge.

Buchanan didn't have much financially. She had an okay-paying job, but typical of many single, working women who owned their own home, she didn't have a whole lot left over after each pay. Certainly not enough to kill for. Her mother had been the beneficiary of her life insurance, most of which was used to cover debts left behind and funeral expenses.

She was just a nurse, so any political or business power struggle could not have been a motive either. *Unless…she was trying to get into the drug trade?* Danielle talked into her recorder again. "Thoroughly investigate Buchanan's drug use and possible drug trade involvement."

As far as mental illness, it was all too well organized. Any cases Danielle read where the perpetrator was mentally ill, they always left a mess. This one was too clean, too meticulous. They certainly would not have placed the victim's wallet into her pocket, wanting her to be identified quickly.

That left just two possibilities in Danielle's mind. She must have been killed by someone who was afraid to lose something or someone, or for revenge.

Danielle spoke into her recorder for the last time on her trip home. "Interview all of Buchanan's friends and associates again, no matter how unlikely it may be they were involved in her murder."

Danielle had never been seasick, but the ferry from Dalhousie to the Gaspé peninsula was as close as she'd ever gotten. It was mid-April and the bay's currents were unusually strong and choppy. She was glad to be back on land again. This was the last leg of her trip, and she was eager to get home.

She drove along winding, twisting roads that curved around mountains with magnificent views. The Gaspé area of Québec was blessed—and cursed—with the Appalachian Mountains. As beautiful as they were, they could also be treacherous—especially in winter.

Danielle's pulse began to race when she finally reached Chemin LaCroix. She drove just half a minute before turning onto a long, dirt lane. The old farmhouse was now painted lavender and Danielle felt like a teenager again when she opened the door and entered.

"Allo, Grandmère!"

Danielle's grandmother stood up from her rocking chair with a large, toothy smile that spanned ear to ear.

The evening went as Danielle expected it would. Her uncle, who was single and lived with his mother (Danielle's grandmother), was waiting for Danielle to arrive so he could get a break from caring for his mother for a few days and spend time at his girlfriend's house.

Her grandmother behaved as excitedly as a child at Christmas. She told Danielle all the gossip—the majority of which she'd already told Danielle on the telephone earlier in the week—but it was very heartwarming for Danielle to listen to her grandmother's voice no matter if she'd heard it all before. Grandmère forced her to eat, even though Danielle wasn't hungry—she'd eaten in Dalhousie before getting on the ferry.

"Your friend didn't come with you?" Grandmère asked.

"No, she…couldn't come." Danielle had actually forgotten all about Rachel. Rachel hadn't even entered her mind until Grandmère mentioned her. And now that she did think of her, Danielle figured she should call.

She used her cell to call home, but there was no answer, so Danielle tried Rachel's cell.

"Hi, it's me. Just wanted to let you know I made it home safely."

Danielle had no idea what to expect, but Rachel was sweet as pie. "Thanks, honey. How was the drive?"

"Long."

"One of the reasons I didn't want to go," Rachel said.

Danielle was uncomfortable and didn't want to be engaged in conversation with Rachel even if it was civil. She truly wanted—*needed*—a break from her. "Grandmère's calling me, I have to let you go. I'll call again whenever I get a chance."

"You'll have to call my cell. I flew to Toronto this morning to take advantage of some Easter sales."

Danielle's body went rigid. "You never told me you were going to Toronto. When did you decide this?"

"Did you think I was going stay in Halifax all by myself on a long weekend?"

Danielle sensed an argument coming, and was so not in the mood for it. "Okay, Rachel. Have a good time."

Danielle was tired. She hadn't felt so when she arrived, but it hit her all at once. Maybe it was hearing Rachel's voice. She definitely needed to relax. So relax, she did.

For the rest of the evening Danielle and her grandmother made flowers and chatted in French about nothing that mattered, just knowing that hearing each other's voice and being in each other's company was a comfort to them both.

It was 10:20 p.m. when Danielle rested her head on the pillow in the bedroom she'd slept in as a teenager. She thought about Lilly, and wondered if she was still on her date—and if the date would continue till morning. She tried to shove it out of her mind, but she couldn't. She wasn't sure why either. Lilly had been a close friend for nearly three years. Yes, she was very attractive, but was Danielle attracted to her? She only started having strange feelings and strange dreams this past week. Maybe it was just all of the recent stress, the new assignment, the fighting with Rachel.

At 11:00 p.m.—midnight Halifax time—Danielle still wasn't asleep, and kept thinking about Lilly being at Nathalie's.

Chances are she's still at Nathalie's house. It wouldn't hurt to call Lilly's just to get confirmation, Danielle told herself. It would satisfy her intense curiosity and she'd be able to put her mind at rest. She'd just leave a casual message, no harm in that.

Danielle didn't expect it when Lilly answered on the first ring. "Oh! Hi! I was expecting to get your voicemail. Just thought I'd leave you a quick message telling you I made it home okay."

"How was the drive?" Lilly asked.

Danielle noticed the lack of enthusiasm in Lilly's usually upbeat voice. "You sound sort of down. Everything okay?"

"I'm not sure." Lilly paused for a few seconds. "Nathalie left me a message today canceling our plans this evening. She also told me she couldn't come to the powwow either, that it conflicted with something she couldn't get out of. I don't believe her. I know she's lying, I just don't know why."

Danielle was speechless.

Lilly didn't appear to notice and continued talking. "Everything was perfectly fine last night. I talked to her around seven, and she told me a few of the ingredients she had picked up for the meal she was planning on cooking for us tonight, and how much she was looking forward to the powwow. So I don't get it. Today out of the blue she calls to cancel not only dinner but the powwow too. It doesn't make any sense."

Danielle felt like a dirt sandwich. It didn't sound like Lilly was aware of her "chat" with Nathalie last night, but Danielle needed reassurances, so as much as she was afraid to ask, she did. "She hasn't told you why, has she?"

"No. She won't answer my calls. I even unblocked my number so she could see it was me phoning, but she didn't pick up or call me back even though I left two messages asking her to."

"Maybe something came up and she's just busy or something."

"No. By ten o'clock tonight I was—well, I guess I just needed to know what was going on. I drove to a gas station and called her apartment from a payphone there. She answered."

"What did she say?"

"I didn't talk to her. I just hung up. I was upset, knowing for sure she was screening my calls after all. I just don't understand, Danielle. Why, all of a sudden, out of the blue?"

Danielle sighed the deepest of sighs. "Lilly, I'm so sorry."

"Nothing for you to be sorry about. It's not your fault."

Danielle closed her eyes and pressed hard on her temples. "I should let you go, Lilly. I just wanted to tell you I was home safe. If you need to talk over the weekend, you can reach me on my cell."

"You sound really tired. Make sure you get a good night's sleep. Oh, Danielle!"

"Yes?"

"Thanks for being such a good friend."

Danielle felt like getting out of bed, kneeling on the hardwood floor with bare knees and saying fifty Hail Marys and fifty Our Fathers for her penance.

When she was growing up—and believed in what she'd been taught by the nuns at the convent school she attended—Danielle judged the severity of her sins based on the penance given to her by the priest after hearing her weekly confession. She was always given three Hail Marys. That was for the typical: fought with her brother, or perhaps stepped on a bug by mistake, crushing its life in the process.

But one day, when she was in grade six, the priest asked her if she had committed "le péché de la chair" (the sin of the flesh). She had no idea what that was, but figured if the priest was asking, God must have seen her do it and told the priest about it. After all, God saw and knew everything. If He had told the priest about it, she *must* have done it. And if that was the case, she would do the right thing and admit it.

"Yes," she answered.

But when she did, the priest responded by giving her the harshest penance she'd ever heard of, let alone received. She left the confessional shocked, scared, hurt, and confused.

When she returned to her pew to get on her knees and recite the many extra prayers, she leaned over to some of the other girls and in whispers asked if the priest had asked them the same question. He had. Some of them had responded yes, some had responded no, but none of them knew what it was either.

The following week, a nurse—who was a married woman, not a nun—showed up at the convent and gave them their very first sex education class.

But as tempted as she was to atone for her sins by giving herself penance tonight, Danielle did not pray anymore. She stopped praying twenty-one years ago. The day she lost faith in God, the very same day her suitcases had been packed up…and dropped off at her grandmother's house.

Danielle's sleep was disturbed. She was over-tired and dreamt choppy dreams she couldn't remember, but left her feeling unpleasant. Visions of Lilly and Nathalie, the ocean, mermaids, whales, flowers, her mother, father, brother, and flying hockey sticks, inundated her. Her mind was on over drive even though her body was exhausted.

She first heard some sort of banging coming from downstairs, but was so tired it didn't rouse her completely from sleep. That was quickly followed by her grandmother yelling repeated French versions of, "Danielle, are you awake?"

When Danielle came out of fractured sleep long enough to realize her grandmother was calling for her, she ran downstairs to the sitting room that had been converted to a bedroom.

"What's the matter, Grandmère?"

Danielle's grandmother was sitting on the side of her single bed, banging her foot on the hardwood floor.

Her restless legs must be bothering her, Danielle thought. Danielle's grandmother often suffered from a condition she described as "tickles" in her legs. "Would it help if I rubbed your legs?" Danielle asked.

Grandmère's blue eyes sparkled as she smiled at Danielle then reclined and moved over so Danielle could sit by her and rub her legs.

As tired as she was, Danielle knew this was important. It was her grandmother's way of asking for affection. Grandmère, although a kind woman, had always been stoic. She didn't know how to openly express the giving or receiving of affection, thus relied on very subtle methods for getting those needs fulfilled. Which is why Danielle spent the next half hour rubbing her feet and legs.

Danielle was back in bed and about to drift into a deep sleep when the banging started again. Danielle groaned. She looked at the clock. It was almost 1:30 a.m.—2:30 a.m. her time. She loved her grandmother, but Danielle was so exhausted. Nonetheless, she went back downstairs and entered the sitting room again.

"Grandmère, are your legs still bothering you?"

Her grandmother was driving the heel of her left foot on the hardwood floor. "Boyz, I wish I had a marrawanna cigarette."

Did Danielle hear that correctly? "What?"

"I said, I wish I had a marrawanna cigarette."

Danielle knew she was exhausted, but she was pretty sure she was awake. "What do you mean, marijuana cigarette?"

Her grandmother's only response was to grin.

"Grandmère, do you smoke that stuff?" Danielle was still trying to figure out if this conversation was real or not.

Her grandmother giggled demurely, then spoke like a child too excited to be able to stop from telling on herself. "Remember when I fell and I ended up in the hospital for four days?"

"Yes…" Danielle became apprehensive as she waited for her grandmother to elaborate.

"Well, I bought ten cigarettes that afternoon."

"What kind of cigarettes?" Unfortunately, Danielle's grandmother had always smoked. Not a lot, but perhaps a few each day. *Please say DuMaurier…*

"Marrawanna cigarettes."

Danielle was *wide* awake now. "*What?* From *who?*"

"Teegar."

Tee was short for *Petit*—which means little—and Gar was short for *Garcon*, which means boy. Teegar was the French equivalent of *Little Boy*. Which was fine when he was five years old, but Teegar was now a grown man. His real name was Claude, but nobody called him that.

He and his girlfriend rented the house across the road. They were in their late twenties, did whatever they could to eke out a living, and didn't have a phone. They often walked across the road and down the lane to use Danielle's grandmother's phone.

"You're telling me you bought ten marijuana cigarettes from Teegar two months ago, and that's why you ended up in the hospital?"

"Yes," she said with an impish grin.

"How many of them did you smoke?"

"Well, at first I was feeling pretty good after I smoked a couple of them. But after I smoked the rest—"

"You smoked all ten?" Danielle's voice shot up several increments in volume and alarm.

"Lots of people smoke a whole pack, one cigarette after another, and it doesn't bother them."

"Grandmère! It's not the same thing!"

"I was okay until I got really hungry. My God I was hungry. I could have eaten the bowels out of a bear, that's how hungry I got. I went to make myself something to eat, but when I got to the kitchen, the floor started to move."

Danielle couldn't force any comments past her lips. She was so shocked—and angry—all she could do was listen as the story unfolded, as it was being confessed to her by her grandmother in the middle of the night.

"I fell, and I couldn't get myself back up. The floor and the walls were moving. I had to yell for André to come downstairs and help me. He called the ambulance even though I told him not to."

"That's why you were in the hospital for four days?"

"Yes," Grandmère sheepishly admitted. "I figured it was the marrawanna cigarettes but I was scared to tell them the truth."

As much as Danielle wanted to scold her grandmother, to tell her how she had terrified the entire family, how Danielle had been called to attend her hospital bedside not knowing if she was going to live or die…

Danielle wanted to, but their roles were reversed now. Danielle looked at her grandmother the way a mother would look at an innocent child who just didn't know any better. What she wanted to tell her, was different than what she did: that as long as she was okay, that's all that mattered.

Danielle was back in bed, thinking about her grandmother's hospital stay. No wonder they couldn't find anything wrong with her. Other than unexplained low blood pressure, they couldn't find anything at all. Of course it had never occurred to any of the hospital staff to check for illegal drugs in an eighty-four-year-old woman. Not even her own family considered that a possibility. But now her grandmother's illness and sudden recovery made *perfect* sense. She'd just been stoned for four days.

Despite the shocking late-night confessional, Danielle slept soundly after finally getting to sleep around three a.m. When she rose at nine, her grandmother was still sleeping. Danielle took the opportunity to phone her uncle in privacy, stepping out into the woodshed that also served as an entrance to the house.

The first question Danielle had for her uncle after filling him in on Grandmère's confession was, why hadn't he noticed she had been smoking marijuana—ten joints no less. The smell alone must have been unmistakable.

He had indeed noticed the smell, he said. He just assumed Teegar had been smoking-up in the house while using the phone. He didn't think too much about it, just went directly upstairs after checking on Maman because his shows were coming on and she always kept the TV in the sitting room on the country music channel. He heard her yelling for him later that evening.

Danielle wasn't impressed, but knowing how exhausting and demanding her grandmother could be, she didn't say much. He hadn't abused or neglected Grandmère. Danielle had to admit, prior to her knowing what she now knew, it would not have occurred to her either that Grandmère had been the one doing the smoking up.

Danielle then asked her uncle to come by and stay with Grandmère for about an hour while she ran an errand. He said he'd come by in the early afternoon.

When Danielle returned to the kitchen, her grandmother was awake and hunched down on the floor in front of a lower cupboard, looking for something.

"What are you looking for Grandmère? I'll get it."

Danielle heard her grandmother's fist smash down on a shelf with such force that the canned goods lifted and banged back down.

"A-ha!" she yelled, as she drove her fist into the sides of the cupboard with full force, back and forth, three or four times.

"What are you doing?" Danielle knew her grandmother was very strong and healthy, despite her complaints to the contrary, but using her fists to fix the plumbing or whatever it was she was trying to do, was way too much for her at her age.

"I finally got ya!" Danielle's grandmother wasn't talking to Danielle. She pulled her arm out of the cupboard, then stood up. When she turned around to face Danielle, her face lit up as she posed and proclaimed, "I told him next time I saw him in there he was gonna get it."

Like an athlete proudly displaying a gold medal, Grandmère's arm was up in the air, holding the tail of a mouse that was now either knocked out—or dead.

When her uncle arrived in the early afternoon, Danielle asked her grandmother if she needed anything at the store. Then, not wanting her to know where she was really going, Danielle drove out the lane and in the opposite direction of her intended destination. Only when she thought Grandmère would no longer be watching from the sitting room window did Danielle head for the house she had grown up in.

Danielle felt herself needing to take a few deep breaths before knocking on the door. The house she had lived in for the first thirteen years of her life was clearly decaying.

Teegar answered the door. He didn't appear to recognize her, so she introduced herself as Evangeline's granddaughter. He asked what he could do for her.

"I'm visiting my grandmother for Easter. I was hoping to connect with my guy before I left Halifax, but I had to leave before we hooked up. It's been a few days, so I was hoping you could help me out."

Teegar looked at Danielle suspiciously, but he didn't ask her what she was hoping he could help her out with. To Danielle's relief he just invited her to come in and have a seat.

First, Danielle made small talk to put him at ease. It seemed to work. When she thought the time was right, she asked, "So can you hook me up? I haven't had any grass since Thursday. I just need a few joints to tide me over till I get back to Halifax." Danielle placed fifty dollars on the table in front of him. "I'm willing to pay you more than double."

Teegar stared at the money.

Danielle watched and waited. *Come on…take the bait…do it.*

Teegar grabbed the fifty dollars and said, "I'll be right back. I have to go outside for it."

Knowing every view from every room in that house, Danielle walked over to the bathroom and watched from a small window so she could keep an eye on Teegar. He walked around the house toward a woodpile stacked near the back shed. Danielle saw him remove something from between blocks of chopped wood just as a car came into the driveway. It was his girlfriend, Lisette, who was a few years younger than Danielle. They had never been friends, but their older brothers had been best friends, so they definitely knew each other.

Lisette hightailed it to the woodpile as soon as she spotted Teegar near it. They appeared to talk anxiously. Danielle noticed Lisette looking in the direction of the bathroom window where she was standing, so she went and sat back down at the kitchen table. She'd wait for them to come in and take it from there.

Lisette was first to enter, with Teegar behind her. He placed a frozen, skinned rabbit wrapped in plastic wrap, on the table.

"All I sell is rabbit. They're five dollars, but I don't have any change." He gave Danielle back two twenty dollar bills and stuffed the ten into his pocket.

Danielle raised from her chair, and with her boots stood the same height as Teegar. She stared him down as she said, "You were selling more than rabbit when you took a hundred dollars from my grandmother for ten joints."

"I did no such thing."

"She almost died, Teegar! How would you like to have an attempted murder charge hanging over your head?"

"What are you talking about?"

"You know exactly what I'm talking about. You saw the ambulance take her to the hospital that night."

"So she went to the hospital, big deal. She's an old lady. She must have had the flu or something."

"She was hallucinating that the floors and walls were moving!"

"Hey, I never laced it with no K. It wasn't even bud."

"No? She seems to think it was, and according to my uncle, that's exactly what it smelled like too."

"Look, every time I went over there and André wasn't around she threw hints that she wanted to buy some marijuana. She said she had the worst disease in the world and the new doctor wouldn't give her any decent nerve pills for it. I tried to ignore her at first, but in February we ran out of oil and didn't have any money to buy more. So the next time she asked, I told her I might have a few."

"Ten is more than a few, Teegar."

"Hey, she's lucky I only gave her ten. She wanted a hundred dollars worth!"

"And you just had to take the hundred from her?"

"Look, she takes this key from around her neck, hauls a cash box out from under the bed, unlocks it, pulls a hundred dollar bill out of it, and hands it to me. I never asked her for it."

Oh great. Now he knows about the box.

"Look, if Teegar wanted to rob your grandmother," Lisette said, "He could have done it long ago. Your grandmother's idea of a lock is a butter knife stuck in the frame of the door."

Danielle knew this to be true. "I'm going to ask you one last time, Teegar. What did you sell my grandmother?"

"It was just shake. Leaves and stems, hardly anything in it."

"There was enough to send her to the hospital for four days. Was there anything else in it?"

"No, absolutely not. I wouldn't waste any K on an old lady, it's too hard to come by. All I gave her was shake, I swear. She wouldn't-a-gotten much of a buzz off one of those."

"One? You gave her ten!"

"How was I to know she was gonna toke them all at once? Man, she's friggin' lucky it was *me* who sold it to her. If she'd-a-bought a hundred dollars worth of bud from anybody else and smoked it all, she'd-a-been in a coma for a month!"

"Are you aware, Teegar, that you get the same stretch for trafficking no matter what part of the marijuana plant you illegally sell?"

Teegar smirked, "Look, if your grandmother wasn't already flyin' high from poppin' nerve pills, that shake wouldn't-a-bothered her no matter how many she toked."

Fury erupted from Danielle as she pulled out her badge and shoved it in Teegar's face. "Anybody ever tell you what I do for a living, Teegar?"

Teegar backed away from the badge as though it were a crucifix and he a vampire.

"I'm RCMP, Teegar. That means I have the authority to make arrests in any province, whether I'm on or off duty at the time." Of course Danielle didn't add that the arrest would be dicey, with defense lawyers no doubt screaming entrapment—*if* it ever even made it to court. But terrifying Teegar was more important than that right now.

Lisette jumped to Teegar's defense once again. "Hey! Listen! You have no proof that Teegar sold your grandmother anything. All you have is her word against his, and if you want to go to court and accuse him of selling something your grandmother thought was marijuana, then you'd better be prepared to go to court for the same charge yourself."

Danielle's face didn't go red this time—it went white.

"Yeah, I know all about the little side business you and Armand had going. My brother Michel told me all about it."

Danielle lowered her badge.

"Look, Danielle. We don't want any trouble. Teegar never meant to hurt your grandmother, and he learned his lesson. He'll never do it again. Just like you never did it again. Look at you now, a cop no less. Bet your customers back then had no idea you'd end up becoming a Mountie."

Danielle put her badge back in her jacket pocket but walked up to Teegar and put her face in his. "If you *ever* step foot in my grandmother's house again, I'll have the RCMP ripping this place *and* your woodpile apart."

⤖ 13 ⤘

Danielle's grandmother was in her rocking chair when Danielle returned from Teegar's.

"Did you go visit your parents and brother?" she asked.

"No, I just went for a drive."

"You should go soon, it'll be too dark to visit them after supper. I'll be okay here by myself for an hour. Go ahead, go see them."

Danielle hesitated, not wanting to leave her grandmother by herself. "Why don't you come with me? You probably haven't visited them in a while either." Danielle knew her grandmother would say no, but she asked anyway.

Danielle was surprised when her grandmother got her coat and boots. She knew how much her grandmother hated graveyards.

Danielle was crouched at the foot of the only triple grave in the cemetery. The headstone, shaped like three hearts intertwined, contained the names of her father, mother, and brother.

They'd been returning from a hockey game when a pulp truck slammed into their small car. "They're angels in heaven now," is all she remembered people saying. The rest of it is still just a blur. All she really remembers is her grandmother's house suddenly becoming her home, and her uncle André becoming a sweeter version of what he had been before she had been orphaned.

"What would you like for supper, Grandmère?" Danielle asked when they returned from the cemetery.

"How about some moose?"

"Mmmm, moose. Yummy." Danielle loved animals and absolutely abhorred hunting, but she couldn't deny she loved moose meat. She thought it was better than the most expensive steak she'd eaten anywhere.

After they finished a delicious supper Danielle so clearly enjoyed, her grandmother told her to pick out a few moose steaks to take with her when she left. Danielle picked out six of them, then thought she'd better check to see how much room there was in the refrigerator freezer at home.

Rachel didn't cook, but would rarely eat what Danielle made in any case, as Rachel was vegetarian. Except for bacon, pepperoni, chicken breast in clubhouse sandwiches, and, oh yes—donairs (a mixture of lamb and spices)—but other than that, she was strictly vegetarian. Plus, even though Danielle had spent countless hours either researching or preparing vegetarian recipes, Rachel had never been interested in eating her home-cooked meals.

"Hi!"

"Uh, hi." Danielle didn't expect Rachel's cheery hello. "Do we have much room in the freezer?" *There should be, there's never any food kept in it.*

"Yes, why?"

"Grandmère gave me some moose steaks to take home. There's some deer and partridge too. I was just wondering how much room we had before I chose anything else."

"Oh, you are *so* not putting dead flesh into my freezer."

Danielle's patience went from sixty to zero in a fraction of a second. "First of all, it is not *your* freezer, it is *ours*. And so is the sofa by the way. I paid half for all of the new furniture and appliances that went into the condo."

"You French people disgust me! You're just like the savages you hang out with, making pies out of animal flesh. You're animals yourselves. Before you met me, you dressed like one too. God, you can dress her up, but once a savage, always a savage."

Danielle did something her grandmother hadn't heard her do since she was thirteen, the day she found out she'd never see her parents or brother ever again: she screamed every word that came out of her mouth. "You would not be here today if your ancestors hadn't eaten meat! There wasn't any herbed tofu or soy protein shakes when your parents were feeding you either, so get off your high fiber horse! You're the one who refuses to wear anything *but* animal hide on her feet! You have no problem wearing a cow on your back, or using a snake to carry your sunglasses in—" Danielle stopped only because she realized she was hearing a dial tone.

Danielle punched her phone off, then screamed as it went flying across the kitchen and into the sitting room where it miraculously landed safely in a padded chair.

Her grandmother, meanwhile, was clutching the arms of her rocking chair…her knuckles deathly white.

Danielle went for a run after the phone incident so she could calm down. When she returned, her grandmother was still in her rocking chair, knitting. Neither of them said anything for a while, then Danielle's grandmother asked a question she was convinced she already knew the answer to.

"Are you on your nerves, Danielle?"

"No, Grandmère, I'm not on my nerves. I just lost my temper. I'm sorry."

"Well, you know that the nerves runs in our family. You should get yourself some nerve pills. Your friend there, maybe she could give you some good ones."

Danielle did not want her grandmother getting the idea she could get medication or anything else from Rachel, so she told what she considered just a little white lie. "No, Grandmère. She's not that type of doctor. She doesn't prescribe pills."

"She doesn't give pills?" Grandmère asked in disbelief. "What kind of doctor is that?"

"No, Grandmère, she doesn't give out pills," Danielle reiterated, preferring to ignore her grandmother's last question.

"Well, there should be a doctor in Halifax who can give you some nerve pills. The nerves, there, it's a horrible disease."

"Grandmère, what you call the nerves, is just stress. People go through it all the time, and they don't need pills for it."

The blue in Danielle's grandmother's eyes turned a dark, icy grey, like the sea in the middle of winter. Danielle knew rage was setting in, and she pictured a dark, smoky monster forming inside of her grandmother. Danielle knew when she'd speak, it would sound like a hiss.

"Stress! It's not stress, it's a disease! Sixty years ago, the doctor didn't tell me I had stress, he told me I had the nerves!"

Danielle knew the story all too well. After giving birth to Danielle's mother, a severe depression had set in, and Danielle's grandmother had ended up in "the mental" over it. The doctors there prescribed her Valium, and when the prescriptions ran out her grandmother suffered a relapse. Danielle knew the initial "attack of the nerves" had most likely been postpartum depression, and that the subsequent relapse had no doubt been a result of withdrawal symptoms from the Valium, but Danielle could not convince her grandmother of this, no matter how hard she tried.

Danielle had often wondered if perhaps her grandmother held on to this because she could not bear the thought of having suffered electric shock therapy for a normal, hormonal shift that would not be treated so inhumanely today. Regardless of what it truly was, or had been, she had been given the terrible diagnosis of—and according to her grandmother, what was one of the worst diseases in the world— "the nerves".

Danielle had been trying to win this battle for over twenty years, and she knew she never would, so she gave up—sort of.

"Okay, Grandmère, you have the nerves. But at least it's not going to kill you."

"It killed Papa."

Danielle was exasperated. Papa was Grandmère's father who had lived a very, very, long life. "Grandmère, Papa was a hundred and four years old when he died."

Danielle's grandmother raised her finger at a snail's pace while she declared, "It's a *slooooooow* killer."

Lilly and Nathalie were sitting on a very unique looking leather sofa.

"Thank you for coming over," Lilly said.

"I'm sorry I canceled dinner on such short notice, Lilly."

"Why did you cancel both? I can understand if something came up and you had to cancel dinner, but you canceled the powwow too."

"I'm sorry, Lilly. It wasn't you. Honestly."

"What was it then?"

Nathalie crossed her feet and looked at them. After a pause she said, "I ran into someone Thursday night, and…it just threw me into a tail spin."

"Was it an ex?"

Nathalie looked at Lilly. "What makes you think that?"

"Seems the most logical. Everything was fine Thursday night. You had bought ingredients for dinner, and said you were looking forward to the powwow, so I figured it had to have been someone who made you change your mind about our date. Only person I can think of that would be is an ex."

Nathalie stared at a sculpture of a whale that rested on Lilly's coffee table.

"So was it an ex?" Lilly asked.

Nathalie asked a question rather than answer the one posed to her. "Do you have an ex who…haunts you?"

"Haunts me?"

"Is there anyone from your past that…" Nathalie pressed on each knuckle of her hand. "Keeps showing up in your dreams?"

Lilly saw a considerable sorrow overtake Nathalie. She was tempted to reach for her, but Nathalie had always pulled away from any type of physical affection. She was definitely not the strong, silent type, but Nathalie often reminded Lilly of a frightened animal who shunned contact for fear of being harmed.

"One or two I might think about once in a while, but not usually." Lilly hoped she wasn't pushing Nathalie too far by asking, "Is the reason you can't stop thinking about her, because you're still in love with her?"

Nathalie hesitated, then quietly said, "I try my best never to think about her." She pressed the back of her hand against her mouth as though suppressing something. "But it's not easy."

"How long since you broke up?"

Nathalie ran her fingers nervously through her hair. "We've had no contact whatsoever in well over a year—going on two."

"Did she cheat on you?" Lilly was aware that cheating—or a perception of it—was the most common reason for most domestic-related offenses and breakups.

Nathalie's eyes didn't leave the sculpture of the whale as she pressed and rubbed the fleshy part of her left palm. "I arrived at her place once, and her ex-boyfriend had crashed there the night before—she was one of those who discovered her sexuality later, by the way. She claimed he slept in the living room, but the bed she'd made for him was still made up. She was acting all nervous and went on about how he had fallen asleep on top of the blankets. I could tell she was making the story up. She then ran upstairs to her own bed and ripped off the sheets, saying she forgot to change them." Nathalie bit down on her lip for a few seconds then released it. "Did she really think I was that stupid?"

"I'm sorry," Lilly said in response.

Nathalie stood up. "I should go."

Lilly stood up also and touched Nathalie's arm. "Please don't go."

Nathalie looked up at Lilly. She was so very attractive. Lilly had the most perfect skin Nathalie had ever seen. It was so smooth and flawless, with a tantalizing brown tone that made her glossy, dark hair and eyes remind Nathalie of the phrase, "a vision of loveliness".

She had a beautiful body—tall, with long legs that were so tempting to wrap oneself around. Nathalie wished so badly she could allow herself to feel again, to trust again. Perhaps even to love again…

When Lilly put her arms around her, Nathalie hoped she could respond. She wanted to. So she tried, instead of pulling away like she really felt like doing. She stepped into Lilly's tall body and rested her head against Lilly's breast. She could feel Lilly's powerful heartbeats under her cheek, and Lilly's fingertips making their way up her back, under her hair, to the back of her neck.

Nathalie was trying. She was trying so hard not to give in to her desire to flee. She was hoping she could feel a building of excitement and pleasure from Lilly's touch, but—

Nathalie felt herself shutting down. She wished so badly she could enjoy this, but she could feel her body oozing an invisible barrier between her and Lilly's touch. She also felt herself floating away, going off into another realm where the sensation of another body against hers could not be felt...

Nathalie's arms began to fall away, and she began to step away from Lilly. But perhaps with Lilly's head clouded by intense physical desire, she interpreted the move as preparing for a kiss. She pulled Nathalie's face forward and opened her mouth, lowering it onto Nathalie's.

When Lilly's tongue touched her lip, Nathalie shot back as if she'd been burned. She set off for the bathroom so quickly, Lilly was left holding nothing but air.

Nathalie was in the bathroom a full five minutes before Lilly knocked on the door.

"Nathalie? I'm sorry. Come out, please. I won't try anything, I promise." Lilly went back to the sofa and waited.

Nathalie came out and sat in a single chair. "I'm sorry, Lilly."

"No, I'm the one who should apologize. I shouldn't have pushed."

"You didn't push, Lilly. If anything, you've been very patient. I just—I'm just not capable. I'm not capable of feeling anything anymore."

Lilly wished she knew the source of Nathalie's reluctance. She just knew Nathalie always pulled away and never allowed herself to feel or respond to anything even remotely loving or romantic. Which confused Lilly, because Nathalie's songs were the most heartfelt, passionate songs she'd ever heard.

Nathalie looked toward the floor, and the sides of her mouth—which when smiling, curved up in the direction of deep dimples—now curved downward and began to tremble.

"You're more than capable, Nathalie. Your songs are proof of that. You just have to open yourself up to—"

"I can't!"

And with that, Nathalie, who normally joked, chuckled, or laughed at least ten times an hour, began to weep...and ran out the door.

After Danielle's grandmother retired for the night, Danielle called Lilly's house.

"Hi, Lilly. You busy?"

"No."

Lilly didn't sound her usual self again. "Everything okay?"

"I just have a migraine."

"Oh." Danielle got the occasional headache, but had never suffered a migraine. She felt pity for anyone who did. "Do you want me to let you go?"

"No, I'd like to talk. I could use the distraction."

"Distraction from what?"

Though Lilly didn't usually sigh, she did. "Nathalie was over."

Danielle's stomach tensed so much she couldn't respond.

"I sent her an email today, asking her to please tell me what was wrong."

As much as Danielle wanted to know what Nathalie's reply was, she couldn't bring herself to ask. She was relieved when Lilly kept talking.

"She didn't answer my email, but she phoned, and I convinced her to come over so we could talk."

"And?" One word was all Danielle could force herself to get out.

"She told me she didn't think she could feel anything anymore, that she didn't think she was capable."

Danielle was on pins and needles. "Did she say why she canceled dinner and the powwow?"

"Apparently, she ran into her ex Thursday night."

"Her ex? Did she tell you that? Is that exactly what she said?"

"No, not exactly word for word, but it must be what happened."

"What makes you think that?" Danielle regretted asking the question as soon as it came out of her mouth. It was in her best interest to let Lilly think that.

"Because right after I asked her if it was her ex she ran into, she asked me if I had an ex who haunted me. That's probably who she ran into on Thursday. I mean, if it upset her so much that she canceled our date and the powwow, it seems pretty obvious, don't you think?"

Danielle swallowed. "I suppose."

Perhaps Danielle's mannerisms were rubbing off on Lilly, because she sighed again. "I screwed it up."

"What do you mean?"

"We actually got close. Physically. I put my arms around her, and she hugged me back, sort of. Until I tried to kiss her."

Danielle's stomach was hurting.

"Then she took off," Lilly said.

"She what?"

"She took off. First to the bathroom, and then when I finally convinced her to come out of there, I couldn't leave it alone, I had to push. All I ended up doing was pushing her out the door."

"What happened?"

"She ran out the door. Literally. I couldn't be content with just holding her, *no*. I had to try to shove my tongue down her throat."

Danielle kept picturing Nathalie running away from Lilly's kiss— and tongue. It somehow made her feel better.

"Well, Lilly. You've known her for how long now, seven or eight months? You're not fifteen anymore. Nobody our age waits that long to sleep together, let alone just kiss. If after all this time she can't even kiss you back, she's obviously got major issues and you're better off without her."

"I suppose," Lilly said, though not very convincingly.

"Cheer up. There's plenty of fish in the sea."

"There might be plenty of fish, but there aren't very many mermaids."

Lilly's remark brought memories of Danielle's recent dream to the forefront. Danielle considered telling Lilly about it, but for some reason she didn't understand, Danielle wasn't comfortable telling her.

"I didn't think you were looking for a mermaid, Lilly. I thought you were quite happily single, playing the field."

"Maybe Nathalie's making me rethink that."

Danielle's gut felt like it was on fire. She didn't know if she wanted to hear the answer to the question she was about to ask, but she asked it because her gut was forcing her to. "Are you in love with Nathalie?"

"I don't know. How do you know when you're really in love anyway?"

"If you have to ask, Lilly, then you're not. When you're truly in love, there's no questioning it. You absolutely know it."

"Have you ever been in love?"

"Yes," Danielle admitted, but she did not want to talk about it. "But not with Rachel," is all she said.

"Who, then?"

"I'd really rather get off this subject, Lilly. It's about as depressing as most lesbian movies," Danielle said with a forced, weak laugh.

"Oh no, you don't. You can't tell me something like that then just change the subject. I want details. Spill, or I'll turn all CP on you."

"CP? Do you mean Crown prosecutor, or crazy person?"

Lilly laughed.

"Speaking of crazy persons, you never told me how trial went last week."

"Nice try, Danielle, but you are not changing the subject. Who were you in love with? Or is it *are*?"

"Lilly, my grandmother is calling for me. I seriously have to go."

"I didn't hear her call your—" Lilly pulled the phone away from her ear and stared at it in disbelief. Danielle had hung up on her.

ജഇ

The water was so choppy and cold, Danielle dove under it to escape its turbulence. Somehow, she knew it would be calmer underneath, where she felt the mermaid's presence.

Danielle instinctively knew where the mermaid was and swam in her direction, but when she approached, she saw a whale circling. The whale was not menacing, but Danielle feared crossing its path to get to the mermaid.

✎ 15 ✎

Although Danielle worried her grandmother would be annoyed with her for not understanding the "disease of the nerves" the night before, she wasn't at all. She was gentler with Danielle this morning. Perhaps she understood Danielle was having a rough go of it relationship-wise. Although she wasn't the type to put her arms around Danielle and console her, or even offer her any motherly advice, she expressed her love, concern, and affection, the best way she knew how.

Early afternoon her grandmother made a sueslette pie—a strange but very tasty combination of flour, raisins, butter, brown sugar, molasses, and bacon—Danielle's favorite. It was a recipe so old, carried down for so many generations, Danielle had not been able to find it in any cookbooks anywhere. When she asked her grandmother how to make it, her grandmother cupped her hands and told her to use "two of these" of flour, then marked the third line that appeared on the knuckle of her thumb for an amount of butter.

As they drank hot tea and ate a slice of warm, fresh sueslette, Danielle's grandmother said to her, "Remember Antoine's girl, the one that used to come here with you all the time?"

Danielle swallowed hard even though there was no food in her mouth at the time. "What about her?"

"I saw her at the doctor's office a couple weeks ago with one of her boys. She asked how you were, and said to say hello. You should give her a call or go visit her. She lives just around the turn from Isabelle's."

"I know where she lives, Grandmère."

"Why don't you go visit her then?"

"I don't think we have anything in common anymore." Danielle could feel her throat narrowing, making it more difficult for her to breathe. The last person she ever wanted to see again was Véronique.

Danielle heard a car come down the lane. She looked out the window and saw it was her aunt, Isabelle.

All three sat at the kitchen table as Danielle and her aunt got caught up on each other's news. Danielle and her aunt spoke on the phone perhaps once a month, not as frequently as Danielle and her grandmother did, so they had more to catch up on.

"I was telling Danielle, I saw Antoine's daughter at the doctor's office the other day." Danielle's grandmother interrupted their conversation as if Danielle and Isabelle hadn't been talking. "She was there with her oldest boy. I remember when she was just a teenager herself, and now she has a son that age."

Isabelle glanced at Danielle. "Yes, time sure does fly." Then smiled warmly at her. "How's Rachel?"

Danielle rubbed her neck. "She's…okay."

"They had a big fight on the phone yesterday," Danielle's grandmother announced.

Danielle was taken aback by her grandmother's indiscretion, but didn't react to it. Danielle was getting used to expecting the unexpected from her grandmother as she got older.

Danielle's aunt responded in her usual kind, understanding way. "Everybody has arguments. They'll be okay by the time Danielle goes back home."

Danielle surprised herself by responding at all, let alone at what came out of her mouth. "I don't think we will be."

"Are you going to leave her?" This was the first time Danielle's grandmother had even come close to acknowledging Danielle's relationship with Rachel.

"I don't know, Grandmère. It's useless to stay if—"

"Yeah, she's useless all right."

"Why do you say that?" Danielle had never confided in her grandmother how Rachel did very little housework, or anything else requiring any effort, so was amazed Grandmère would have picked up on that.

"Any doctor who doesn't give out pills is useless."

After Isabelle left, Danielle's grandmother suggested Danielle keep her company in the sitting room. As always, the television was on the country music station.

Danielle sat quietly and stared mindlessly at the country music videos. She did this for almost an hour until she bolted upright when she saw the title "I'll Be Over You When I'm Six Feet Under" appear on screen. She asked her grandmother to raise the volume.

"I'll Be Over You" was a much better song than Danielle expected it to be. It was a haunting and mournful melody, yet ironically soothing. Danielle couldn't help but feel very moved by it. The song very well expressed the haunting remnants of a painful relationship, which Danielle knew all too well.

Danielle's thoughts drifted to Véronique. She had spent seventeen years trying to forget Véronique ever existed. But with one sentence, Danielle's grandmother had brought back a flood of memories from the most painful—and most wonderful—period of Danielle's life. A period Danielle had not been able to stop thinking about all day.

After supper, Grandmère expressed an interest in playing cards. Danielle didn't generally care for cards, but she enjoyed it because her grandmother did.

As she placed her bid on the table, Grandmère said to Danielle, "I'm sorry I smoked that marrawanna. I didn't mean to scare the family. It was stupid."

Danielle could see her grandmother's remorse was very heartfelt and genuine. "It's okay, Grandmère. I've done some stupid things too."

"Like what?"

"Uh...well, I'm just saying."

"What stupid thing did you do?"

Danielle might have brought up Rachel, but she and Grandmère never talked about Danielle's sexuality. Grandmère wasn't against it per se—at least not in front of Danielle—it was just something they never talked about. So Danielle decided to confess something she'd kept secret for many years.

"The summer I turned thirteen, the last summer Armand was alive...well, we sort of had a summer job."

"A summer job? I don't remember that."

"We didn't exactly tell you—or Maman and Papa."

"Why not? What was the job?"

"Okay, well this is what happened." Danielle was already trying to come up with excuses for herself, even though she knew none would hold water in her grandmother's eyes. "Armand was out playing near Henri's farm when he ended up inside Jean-Marc's shack. Remember him? The guy who was out of it all the time?"

"Uh-huh."

Danielle didn't think she'd ever heard her grandmother say "Uh-huh" before. She cautiously continued her story. "Armand came to me, scared to death. He said Jean-Marc offered him ten dollars to get him three joints—of marijuana."

"Where was Armand going to get that?"

"Exactly. But Armand took the money anyway. Spent it all in half an hour, then panic set in. He realized Jean-Marc would skin him alive for taking the ten dollars and not getting him the marijuana."

"What did he do?"

"He came to me."

"To buy marijuana?"

"Of course not! I didn't know where to find marijuana."

"How did you help him, then?"

Danielle winced.

"What did you do, Danielle?"

"Well, you see. Um…well…"

"Okay, Danielle, get on with it. I'm already eighty-four, I don't have too many years left to spare."

Danielle started talking faster. "Okay, well, what I did was, I mixed together some stuff. I took some dried parsley from the pantry, ripped open a tea bag, crushed up an aspirin, and mixed in a tiny amount of mayonnaise."

Danielle's grandmother grimaced in disgust. "Mayonnaise?"

"It was dry! And I figured maybe the mayonnaise—you know, with the oil—hey, give me a break. I was thirteen. I hadn't seen real marijuana in my life."

"Where'd you get the papers to roll the joints?"

Danielle was taken aback for a moment, then remembered her eighty-four-year-old grandmother probably had more direct experience with marijuana than she did.

"Armand stole them from Grandpère."

Danielle's grandfather had smoked loose tobacco in hand-rolled cigarettes most of his life before succumbing to lung cancer when Danielle was fifteen.

Danielle glanced over at the lone rocking chair in the corner. There used to be two there. An empty one sat next to Grandmère's for a full year until one day Danielle came home from school and it was simply gone. Danielle never asked where it went. She just found it one day when she was bored and had climbed up the rafters in the old barn.

"I didn't know how to roll cigarettes, but Armand did. He rolled three and brought them to Jean-Marc."

Danielle's grandmother made another bid, then looked up at Danielle for the rest of her story.

"I thought Armand would just hand him the three fake joints and that would be it. But you'll never believe what happened. Jean-Marc lit one of them, took a few puffs, then said it was the best stuff he'd ever smoked!"

Danielle's grandmother's face lit up like a Christmas tree. "Really?"

"Yes! Then when Armand arrived with twenty dollars—ten for me, ten for him."

"And how long did this—summer job—actually last?"

"Just the summer. When school started, I got scared. I told Armand to tell Jean-Marc the supply had dried up. Which in truth it had, because there was no parsley left."

Danielle's grandmother was silent for a very long time.

Danielle was afraid to ask, but summoned the courage to do so. "Do you have anything to say about what I just told you?"

Without looking up from her cards, her grandmother said, "Yeah...make sure you write me out that recipe before you go back to Halifax."

❧ 16 ❧

Grandmère had gone to bed early, so Danielle sat in the kitchen by herself. She couldn't get Véronique out of her mind. After staring at the phone book for half an hour, Danielle finally opened it and scanned the pages until she found the number she was looking for. She nervously picked up her cell and dialed. It rang only once, and Danielle's heart felt like it might pound right out of her chest.

What the hell am I doing? She hung up before anyone answered.

Danielle was rocking in her grandmother's chair reading a magazine when she heard a car driving very slowly down the lane. A black Pontiac appeared, but the person did not get out. Then as the car door opened in slow motion, Danielle's stomach lurched to her throat. The woman stepping out looked almost identical to what she did seventeen years ago.

Véronique had long, dark, wavy hair, olive skin, and dark brown eyes, with perfect teeth so white, her very full lips reflected off them. Véronique's body was even more alluring now than it had been in her teens. Although still trim, her breasts were more than twice the size they had been.

When Danielle turned the door knob to let Véronique in, her hand was trembling.

"It *is* you!" Véronique wrapped her arms around Danielle as if nearly two decades hadn't passed. "Somebody called my house, but it stopped ringing before I could answer. I looked up the number and it said it was a cell phone from Nova Scotia, so I thought, maybe a long shot, but maybe you were home for a visit. And you are!"

Véronique made her way to the kitchen table and sat down as if she'd just been visiting yesterday. Danielle had no idea what to say. She hadn't seen her secret high school sweetheart since she was seventeen.

"How are you?" Véronique asked, smiling brightly.

It took all of Danielle's training to keep her composure as she replied, "I've been...good. You?"

"I've been okay. Where's Grandmère?" Véronique had always called Danielle's grandmother that, as though she and Danielle were married and Danielle's grandmother were part of her family, too.

"She went to bed early." Danielle pointed as she added, "Her bedroom's in the sitting room now."

Danielle remembered the last time she and Véronique had been in that room together. They had spent the entire evening kissing and making out, touching and pressing into each other.

"Danielle, I'd like to talk to you. I've been wanting to talk to you for a long time."

Danielle walked over to the stairs and sat on them—they were the furthest away from Grandmère's room without being in the bathroom or upstairs. Danielle motioned for Véronique to join her.

She did.

Danielle said nothing. She couldn't.

"Danielle, you have no idea how much I've thought of you over the years." Véronique appeared entranced as she stared at Danielle. "You have no idea how many times I dreamt about you, these eyes..." Véronique traced Danielle's high cheekbone structure.

Danielle turned her face away.

Véronique clasped her hands between her legs and looked at them. "I did love you, Danielle. I just wasn't—"

"I know, don't worry about it." Danielle had already figured out Véronique was straight. After all, she was married now, with two teenage sons.

"I heard that..." Véronique wiggled her feet and looked at them. "You're a lesbian now."

Danielle sighed. "I was a lesbian then, Véronique. I just didn't have a label for it at the time."

Véronique glanced in the direction of the sitting room then said, "Remember the night we kissed all night till morning? Our lips were all red and chapped the next day. We told everyone we used the same lip gloss and had a reaction to it." Véronique was smiling at Danielle again.

"Of course I remember," Danielle admitted, even though she had spent all these years trying to forget.

"Danielle, I've never felt anything like that ever since, not even with David. I never stopped thinking about you." Véronique reached out and touched Danielle's hand. "Have you thought about me?"

Danielle pulled her hand away and was suddenly reminded of Nathalie. "Véronique, do you have any idea what I went through that summer? I wanted to *die*. The only reason I didn't is because after

Maman and Papa and Armand, and then Grandpère… I couldn't do that to Grandmère. But I didn't want to live, not after what you did to me." Despite Danielle's best efforts, tears escaped from her eyes. She hadn't felt this pain in a long time, and she did not welcome it back again.

Danielle and Véronique had met at the beginning of grade ten when they were both fifteen and quickly became best friends. Then, Danielle's world took another major turn—but up instead of down this time—as she fell completely, head over heels in love…with a girl.

For two years, they spent almost every waking moment together, slept in each other's arms, and made out like the hormonal teenagers that they were every chance they got. Danielle was so happy again for the first time since losing her family, for in Véronique she felt all the love, emotional fulfillment, and sense of family that had been so lacking after her parents and brother were killed. Véronique had simply meant the world to Danielle, was her life, her only reason for being—back then.

They had planned on attending CEGEP together—Québec's version of college, which normally preceded further studies at university. They had both applied and been accepted to CEGEP in Québec City. They were going to attend McGill University after CEGEP, with Danielle planning on going into engineering and Véronique medicine. They had even discussed having children, for they planned on living happily ever after—*together*—for the rest of their lives.

But one month before they were to go to Québec City to find an apartment, to move into their first home, to start what was to be their wonderful, blissful, life *together*…Véronique ran off—and got married.

"I wanted to die, Véronique. I was hurting so severely, I didn't know how to get through each day. I stayed in bed for two whole months that summer wishing I would just die so I could escape the pain."

"I'm sorry." Véronique whispered.

Danielle thought about Rachel, knowing now why she let herself get—and stay—involved with her. She knew she had never been in love with Rachel, but she didn't think she'd ever fall in love again, so she simply settled. If she hadn't fully realized it then, she certainly realized it now.

"I wanted to write to you, Danielle, but I had no idea where you went. I'd heard you joined the army, but—"

"What else was I supposed to do, Véronique? Go to CEGEP on my own? Without you, after all the plans we had together?"

"I'm sorry. I just, I knew. I did love you, Danielle. I still do. I just wasn't—" Véronique shook her head.

Neither of them spoke, though they looked at each other intently now. Danielle couldn't move, but felt her eyes drink Véronique in.

Véronique placed her hand on top of Danielle's. Danielle didn't move her hand at all, but her thumb, the only part of her that didn't seem frozen at the moment, instinctively raised and met Véronique's palm, grazing it, so lightly yet deliberately, in an attempt to confess her interest still, after all these years.

Véronique caressed Danielle's hand with her own, lingering in some spots, roaming along in others.

Danielle breathed in very deeply as her thumb followed the natural crevice in Véronique's palm, past the two fleshy upward curves to its center. She swirled her thumb around that center, as intuitively as she followed the crevice back past the palm, to the underside of Véronique's wrist.

Danielle's entire hand then turned upward, meeting Véronique's full on. The rush and intensity of sensations that hit her full force with this full hand-to-hand contact was too much for Danielle though, so she lifted her palm off Véronique's, leaving just their fingertips connected.

Danielle hadn't been able to take her eyes off their hand holding, but she now looked at Véronique, and her right hand, which hadn't moved from its resting position between them, reached across Véronique's lower back and pulled her closer.

Danielle stared into the deep, dark irises of her first love. She could almost see hints of blue, the reflection of her own eyes in Véronique's.

Danielle heard the swallowing of excess saliva. She didn't know if this had come from Véronique or herself. She lowered her gaze, then stopped when Véronique's full lips came into view. Danielle's mouth opened slightly, then, like metal to magnet, felt an energy pull her face toward Véronique's, her lips targeting the full lips she'd not been able to stop thinking about since she fell in love with them—and Véronique—so many years ago.

Danielle's left hand touched Véronique's cheek, while her right one pulled her even closer. Danielle's bottom lip first touched the underside of Véronique's top one, then her top one closed in, capturing it. It was only when Danielle heard Véronique gasp did she realize her tongue had instinctively started caressing Véronique's lip.

Véronique suddenly pounced. Her right leg swung over Danielle's lean frame, and she pressed her body against Danielle's while her mouth opened wide and her tongue acquainted itself with every part of Danielle's inner mouth. She devoured Danielle's mouth with her own, as if she'd been starving for years and Danielle was her buffet.

Véronique straddled Danielle's thigh and pressed herself hard into it, driving Danielle's back into the stairs. Danielle's ribs were so sore she thought she might pass out. Or was that because Véronique, the woman she'd loved for nineteen years, had her tongue in her mouth and was driving herself into her?

Danielle managed to release herself from the lock Véronique had on her open mouth long enough to whisper, "Let's go upstairs."

Véronique was up the stairs, into Danielle's old bedroom, and onto the bed before Danielle even reached the bedroom door. When Danielle arrived behind her, she saw her sitting there, with a fervor and demi-smile that made Danielle feel as though she were about to enter a lion's den. It suddenly dawned on Danielle that she, the experienced lesbian, was the hesitant one.

❧ 17 ❧

Danielle sat on the side of the bed and put her arms around Véronique. She just wanted to hold her for a moment, to take in the fact that this was real. Not a fantasy, not a dream, not wishful thinking. This was *real*. Seventeen years after the love of her life ripped her heart out, Danielle was holding her in her arms again. Danielle wanted to lie with her, to hold her and be held by her, to bring comfort to so many years of pain…and longing.

Danielle lowered herself onto the bed, but rather than following Danielle's move to lie down, Véronique jumped on top of her, straddling Danielle's hips with her thighs and pinning her arms up over her head. Véronique clamped on to Danielle's mouth, and though Danielle tried to oblige, it was a little too frenzied for her liking. She pulled her face away and started gently kissing Véronique's cheek and neck in an attempt to slow things down. Véronique started licking and sucking Danielle's neck.

"Don't leave any marks," Danielle warned her.

Véronique lifted her face and looked at Danielle. "Sorry." Her breathing was so heavy she could barely get her words out. "I just…want this…so much." And with that, Véronique attacked Danielle's breasts over her shirt, squeezing and rubbing them.

In turn, Danielle touched Véronique's breasts, though much gentler. They were remarkably larger than Danielle remembered—her nipples especially. Danielle couldn't stop her inquisitive mind from wondering if pregnancy had contributed to this dramatic increase, and then thoughts of Véronique's children…her husband…and what Véronique had done to her, that almost killed her off, brought her back to reality.

"Véronique, we should stop. You're married and—"

"Please, Danielle. You have no idea how much I want this. More than anything." Véronique rubbed all parts of herself against Danielle, then pressed herself very hard into her. "Please don't take me this far and…" Véronique began to grind her pelvis against Danielle's thigh.

Danielle didn't respond. Not verbally, nor physically. She felt in limbo, unable to decide.

Véronique turned on her side, rested her head on Danielle's shoulder, then placed her hand on Danielle's stomach. Véronique began to move her hand south as she breathlessly husked in Danielle's ear, "I want this so much."

When Véronique's hand reached between Danielle's legs, Danielle felt like she'd been pushed off a diving board. Gasping for air, knowing she couldn't hold back no matter how hard she tried, she opened her legs and lifted her hips, wanting, needing, Véronique's touch so badly, that her clitoris was pulsating against the seam of her jeans.

But when she pressed Véronique's hand into her, Véronique panicked. "I don't know what to do!"

Without a word, Danielle unzipped and kicked off her jeans, stripped off her shirt and bra, then unzipped and peeled off Véronique's jeans while Véronique discarded her own top and bra.

They just looked at each other for a moment, each of them naked except for their panties, which were both very distinctively moist at their center. Danielle seized the sides of Véronique's panties and pulled them down. Véronique raised herself so they could be released from her body. When Véronique's eyes returned from witnessing their landing on the corner of the bed, Danielle was completely naked.

Véronique's eyes moved from Danielle's breasts and very erect nipples, to her long waist and washboard abdomen, which ended at a patch of blond hair. Danielle, in turn, was staring at Véronique's breasts. Véronique fell back and spread her arms out, inviting Danielle to partake.

Danielle's mouth opened wide and took in as much of Véronique's right breast as she could. She swirled her tongue all around the outside, then up and over, across Véronique's nipple. Danielle brought her hand over to Véronique's left breast and began to gently touch and caress.

As Danielle's arousal grew, so did her moves. Though Véronique kept pushing her, Danielle was very patient and teased Véronique before slowly building up to all-out sucking. She couldn't believe how enormously erect Véronique's nipples were. They were a mouthful indeed.

"Stop teasing me!" Véronique put her hand on the back of Danielle's head, pulling it into her as she lifted her hips. Danielle had been touching her very delicately everywhere but there as she licked and sucked those incredible nipples.

For the next ten minutes, Danielle explored Véronique's inner thighs and the surface of what was situated between them. Her finger followed strands of course, kinky hair, the upper portions damp, leading to a complete soak as she reached lower. Véronique kept opening herself up, but Danielle wasn't giving in, even as Véronique's juices dripped from her, and her clitoris throbbed so much Danielle could feel it when she pressed into the thick outer surface of skin and hair that cushioned it.

When Danielle finally opened Véronique up, she laid a wide swath of her tongue from bottom to top. She took a few more licks with the broad, top side of her tongue, from midway up and above, savoring the taste and feel of Véronique's engorged clitoris. Danielle brought her tongue down, reached in as far as she could inside Véronique, then gently pulled out while also sucking the enormous amount of wetness oozing out of her.

Danielle had always enjoyed the taste of a woman, but enjoyed it even more at this moment, knowing it was *her* who was making this woman so wet. *This* woman. *Véronique.* The woman she'd loved and longed for ever since she was a teenager. This woman who Danielle now had her face buried in, tasting, licking and sucking…into an absolute frenzy.

Véronique was moaning so loudly, Danielle worried she'd be heard by her grandmother just a few floorboards below. With some quick thinking, Danielle replaced her tongue with fingers, then brought her face up to kiss—and muffle—Véronique.

The scent of Véronique's juices was all over Danielle's face and tongue. Danielle loved tasting herself off another woman's lips and tongue and got very excited at the thought of Véronique licking her own juices off her now.

She approached Véronique, but Véronique turned her face away. Danielle was so taken aback, she almost stopped. But she didn't want to spoil this now, so she shoved it out of her mind and lowered herself back.

"Stay there!" Véronique's hand pressed into the back of Danielle's head.

Okay, Danielle thought, *You want it, you got it.*

Danielle eased two fingers inside Véronique as she started licking under the hood of Véronique's clitoris at a faster pace. Danielle could feel the warm, wet, slippery, flesh surrounding her fingers as Véronique's vaginal muscles repeatedly clenched around them. Danielle reached up and forward till she found the familiar row of ridges. *Ah, you think you're wet now?*

Danielle's tongue was now moving at a clip, pointed and darting, sometimes a direct hit against the clitoris, sometimes a dash and swirl. As she did this, she stroked Véronique's G-spot with the tips of her fingers and maneuvered her thumb near the entrance, simulating slow, gentle penetration.

If Véronique's eyes hadn't been closed, Danielle might have seen them rolling to the back of her head. If Danielle's face hadn't been buried between Véronique's legs that is.

Véronique was panting so much, her mouth should have been dry with all the air being forced across her open mouth and curled tongue, but she was so extremely turned on, every part of her capable of producing fluid was doing so.

She was drenched and dripping between her legs, her bangs were soaked from perspiration on her forehead, and the feel of a woman's tongue lapping away at her was making her mouth water so much, it was keeping her hydrated.

Véronique was in such a sexual frenzy, she almost didn't recognize her own body. She couldn't stop herself from squeezing and pulling at her own breasts and nipples while she gyrated her clitoris against Danielle's tongue, and also impaled herself as much as she could onto Danielle's fingers. Then, just when Véronique thought she was feeling the most sexual pleasure she'd ever experienced in her life, Danielle topped it.

Danielle reached up with her left hand and pinched Véronique's nipple. It created a sensation that traveled all the way to Véronique's belly button, and even further down to the nucleus of her clitoris where Danielle's tongue danced all over it while she stroked her internally.

Véronique had no idea what body part Danielle could be stroking to produce such an intense sexual pleasure, but whatever it was, it was so beyond incredible, Véronique had no words for it. Good thing, because she would not have been able to speak right now if her life depended on it.

Another nipple pinch caused a chain reaction so intense, Véronique's entire body erupted into an orgasm unlike any she'd ever experienced before. First, her eyes careened even further back into her head. They went back so far, so fast, it actually hurt. But what she experienced next took her mind off it very quickly.

Véronique's nipples spasmed, her stomach muscles sucked her belly button in, then expelled it back out, and continued to do so as her body kept convulsing. Her clitoris shot out of its hood, quivering from over-exposure despite being covered by the moist heat of Danielle's tongue. Her vagina kept sucking Danielle's fingers in and out as she continued to ride this very long-lasting orgasm.

Danielle had eased off, but was still slowly stroking and lightly sucking, milking every last drop of orgasm out of Véronique. It was only when Danielle felt Véronique's toes uncurl from underneath her leg that she stopped. Yet she stayed there, fingers still inside Véronique, and her cheek now resting on Véronique's pubis for a few minutes, before sitting up and very gently easing her fingers out.

Danielle wanted so badly to kiss Véronique right now, but the memory of Véronique turning her face away was still fresh in Danielle's mind.

If Véronique couldn't handle a smidgen of her own vaginal juices on my lips, she's definitely not going to be able to handle a quarter cup of her own ejaculate all over my face, Danielle thought, so she propped herself up onto her elbow and traced the contours of Véronique's face with her fingers instead.

Véronique's eyes opened, met Danielle's, then looked away.

Was she embarrassed? Danielle wondered. "You okay?"

"Oh. My. God."

"Nique?"

Véronique breathed in very deeply then exhaled. "*Wow.*"

Danielle smiled. "I take it you enjoyed that?"

"My God, Danielle. That was…" Véronique took a deep breath then swallowed. "Mind-blowing."

Danielle's eyes grew as wide as her grin. "Mind-blowing?" she repeated, to confirm what she'd just heard. Danielle reacted excitedly by pressing her lips against Véronique's very quickly. Danielle's mouth opened and her tongue emerged, but Véronique kept her lips tightly closed and moved her face away.

Danielle responded by pulling her own face back. "What's the matter?"

"Nothing. I just don't like the smell."

"You don't like the smell?" Danielle felt like someone just told her the Loch Ness monster did exist, and he was also the tooth fairy. Her wide stare at Véronique became very narrowed as the realization set in. "What are you saying, that I don't get my turn?"

Véronique sat up and shifted further away from Danielle. "I don't—I wouldn't know what to do."

Danielle's mood grew dark. Despite the fact she'd gotten so close to coming herself when Véronique did, she still hadn't, and she needed to release so badly, it physically hurt between her legs. "You knew what to do when you were shoving my face between your legs."

"Don't be gross, Danielle."

"Oh, now that you've gotten off, it's gross? You wanted me so badly for the past two hours but now I'm just gross to you?"

"That's not what I meant and you know it."

"Well, what if at the height of your excitement I'd have just left you hanging?"

Véronique's expression softened. She reached over and put a hand on Danielle's hip. "Tell me what you want me to do."

"What I want you to do is whatever comes naturally to you."

Véronique turned her face away, and stayed like that for a full minute.

Was she thinking?

Véronique let out what seemed like an uncomfortable sigh, then said, "Okay." She lowered her mouth onto Danielle's nipple and started sucking. *Hard.*

Danielle didn't know if it was the extended, unreleased hyper-arousal, or the anger she'd just experienced, but it took everything in her mind power to tweak any pleasure out of the pain she felt with each suck.

She tried to gain pleasure from the thought that this was Véronique, the woman she'd loved and longed for, for so many years, who was now sucking hard on her left nipple, but it felt nothing like she'd desired and fantasized about for so long. The reality she was experiencing right now was just very uncomfortable and downright painful.

She guided Véronique's face away from her breast and asked for what she really wanted. Danielle raised and angled her legs to give Véronique full access. "Put your tongue on me...down there."

Véronique looked like someone had asked her to jump out of an airplane without a parachute. She hesitated at first, then started to dry kiss Danielle's stomach, creating a reluctant trail that lead to that line, where a triangular patch of blond hair began.

Véronique's quick and mechanical kisses reminded Danielle of her grandfather. When his cheek would draw near she'd smell the rancid odor of cigarettes, so she'd kiss him so quickly, half the time she wasn't sure if her lips had touched his cheek at all. It was therefore no surprise to Danielle when Véronique sat up and instead put her hand where Danielle was aching for her tongue to be.

Véronique then shoved—quite literally—two fingers into Danielle. Danielle emitted a painful groan that Véronique mistook for pleasure. Véronique immediately started pumping forcefully, slamming the joints of her thumb and two fingers, which were boney and jutting out, into Danielle's external genitalia.

Danielle started to pant, but it was purely out of frustration and agony. Véronique started digging inside of Danielle, at each interval in which she slammed her hand into her.

Danielle audibly and physically winced, then squeezed her legs tightly, cutting off Véronique's movements. Keeping her legs gripped around Véronique's hand so it could not move and cause her further pain, Danielle exhaled very pronounced breaths of relief.

"You came awfully fast," Véronique said to Danielle.

Danielle felt shock—and relief—that Véronique thought it had been pleasurable for her. It was really Danielle's deceitful response that came quickly. "Yes, I did."

Danielle waited a few moments, then feeling secure her lie made it safe for her to re-open her legs, she did so, encouraging Véronique to pull her hand out.

"I need to go to the bathroom to wash my hand." Véronique held it extended from her body as if it were covered in cooties.

Danielle reached for a nightshirt resting on top of a dresser. "Here, put this on." The only bathroom in the house was downstairs, near the kitchen.

The second Danielle heard Véronique on the first stair on her way to the bathroom downstairs, she started touching herself. *Gently.* She needed to come so badly, but her arousal had been tempered with such pain and discomfort, she wasn't aroused anymore—she was physically frustrated.

She was close to coming, but not there yet, when Véronique reached the top stair on her return. When Véronique re-entered the bedroom Danielle was just lying there, left arm behind her head, right arm keeping the sheets and blankets in place over her.

"I need to go," Véronique said as she rummaged through scattered clothing looking for just her own. "I'll get dressed in the bathroom."

The old Danielle of just an hour ago would have confronted Véronique, made remarks about how her tongue had just been inside her, how she'd been undressed and lying naked in front of her for two hours, that having to go to the bathroom to get dressed in private was now ridiculous…

But Danielle realized that she too just wanted Véronique gone. "Just leave my shirt in the bathroom. I'll wear my pajamas."

Danielle waited till she heard Véronique's car exit the driveway before finishing herself off, then going downstairs and slipping a butter knife into the facing of the door.

When in Rome, she thought. *When in Rome.*

Danielle couldn't wait to get back to Halifax. She had enjoyed her time with her grandmother, but she felt like she'd been run over by a truck. From her grandmother's marijuana confession, to the confrontation with Teegar and Lisette, to Véronique…

She had carried a painful torch for Véronique for almost two decades. Like tinnitus, a constant, low-grade siren your brain thinks it has gotten used to and no longer notices, until one day it finally stops, and only then do you realize how peaceful the silence is—and how disturbing that sound had been to your life all along.

For the first time in nearly twenty years, Danielle saw Véronique for who she really was—not for who Danielle wanted her to be—and realized…not only was she no longer in love with Véronique anymore…she didn't even like her.

Nonetheless, this realization caused Danielle to picture herself sitting back with a pack of cigarettes and a bottle of whiskey…and she thought of Nathalie.

Danielle normally listened to CBC radio when she drove, but she decided to scan for a country western music station. It wasn't long before Nathalie's song, "I'll Be Over You When I'm Six Feet Under" came on the radio. When Danielle first heard the song yesterday, she felt it perfectly expressed how she had felt about Véronique all these years. But twenty four hours later, Danielle no longer felt anything for Véronique. And Danielle felt so at peace about that. *Finally.*

Danielle dragged her suitcase and cooler filled with frozen wild game behind her as she walked from the elevator to her front door. When she tried her key, however, it didn't work. It wouldn't even go in.

She knocked on the door but there was no answer. She called the condo, and thought she could hear Rachel inside, but she didn't pick up. Danielle then called Rachel's cell. No response there either.

After waiting ten minutes, exhausted and wondering what to do, Danielle left her luggage at the door and took the elevator down to the security office. Her fears were confirmed when the building manager's master key did not fit either. Sometime during Easter weekend while she was in Toronto, Rachel had gotten a locksmith to change the locks.

Danielle was sitting quietly at Lilly's kitchen table, barely able to keep her head up and eyes open, listening to Lilly's reaction to the news.

"I can't believe that bitch. She changed the locks? And she's not answering the phone? If it weren't for my job, I'd be over there wringing her neck."

Lilly was livid. Danielle was too tired to be.

"She can't do that, you know. Even if she owns the condo solely, you've got a rental agreement. You can prove you've been paying her rent. She can't change the locks on you, and she can't terminate your rental agreement without providing you notice. What are you going to do, Danielle?"

"I don't know, Lilly. Can I decide after I've had some sleep?"

Having Lilly as a friend and ally was the best thing that could have happened for Danielle in this situation. When Danielle woke from her much needed nap, Lilly had already prepared and filed an Originating Notice—a legal document notifying a party they were being sued—and how she did it on Easter Monday in a matter of three hours, Danielle had no idea. But Lilly had gotten it approved, stamped, and filed with the courts while Danielle slept.

When Danielle arrived at the condo with notice of legal action already filed with the courts, her legal counsel (Lilly), and two Halifax Regional Police officers at her side, Rachel had no choice but to let Danielle in.

All Danielle wanted were her clothes and a few personal items for now. She didn't trust Rachel one bit though, so as she packed her belongings, Lilly took photographs of every inch of the condo, documenting what furniture, personal items, and other possessions it contained.

Rachel stood in the middle of the bedroom, seething, while she watched Danielle pack. "Going to shack up with your savage, are you? If there's any mail for you, should I just follow the smoke to your teepee? I wish her luck in the sack, Dannie. You haven't been interested in pussy in a long time."

"You know what, Rachel?" Danielle turned to face her only because she wanted Rachel to hear very clearly what she had to say. "I'm more than interested in pussy. But *you*, you're nothing but a cunt."

Rachel responded with something, but Danielle had already pressed the mute button in her brain and didn't hear another word Rachel spewed. She picked up the last suitcase and placed it on the living room floor next to Lilly.

Rachel stood in the doorway of the bedroom, watching them as they went over a list and agreed they'd gotten everything on it. Rachel cast her eyes in Lilly's direction and said, "Just so you know, she's really lousy in bed—when she's not frigid."

Lilly handed the list to Danielle and gave Rachel her full attention. "Rachel, lying next to an iceberg night after night would turn anybody frigid. And by the way, the smoke you'll see coming from Fall River tonight won't be from any teepee. It'll be a smoking hot Danielle and I burning up the eight-hundred-count, Charmeuse silk sheets. But don't worry, I'll have her so wet, she won't catch fire."

Rachel slammed the bedroom door so hard, her favorite photograph—of herself—fell off the wall.

Danielle and Lilly were driving back to Lilly's house when Danielle asked, "Where did that come from?" Danielle had seen Lilly speak extremely well in a courtroom, but had no idea she was so quick-witted.

"Actually, that came from Nathalie."

"Nathalie?"

"I hope you're not upset with me for this, but I sort of told Nathalie I couldn't stand Rachel, that she was cold and hateful, and I didn't understand why you were with her."

Danielle couldn't fault Lilly for not understanding. She herself did not understand. At least she hadn't, until she saw Véronique again and realized why she'd just settled.

Danielle wondered how much of her personal life Lilly had shared with Nathalie, and why Nathalie found it necessary to comment on something that was none of *her* business.

"So Nathalie suggested you tell Rachel that you and I were burning up the sheets?"

"No, I came up with that after I overheard her say what she did about a teepee. But Nathalie sort of gave me the idea. She said maybe

Rachel's frostiness had slowly numbed you to the point where you didn't realize how frozen you'd become."

Danielle thought about that, then admitted, "Good analogy."

"Yes, I thought so. Nathalie has lots of good analogies. Probably why she's such a successful songwriter."

"And how much about my personal life did you reveal to Nathalie?"

"Oh. Sorry. It's not like I was talking about you, or revealing personal details. I just told her I wished I knew what to do for you—as a friend. She said I should find you a woman to get you all hot and bothered, that it would thaw you out—including your brain—and you'd finally be able to see Rachel for what she was and leave her."

"I see." Danielle found herself somewhat irritated by Nathalie's advice. *Who was doing the interfering now?*

When they got to Lilly's house, Danielle unpacked just a couple of suits and a few essentials before calling it an early night. She'd had an extremely stressful day to say the least. She did find the bed in the guest room somewhat uncomfortable, but she was so tired she didn't notice it much.

She awoke at six and went for a run, returning at seven-thirty with a chai latte and a newspaper. After circling nine places, she called and made appointments to view the apartments as soon as possible.

By late afternoon though, Danielle was frustrated. She had seen seven places and none of them suited her needs. They were either dives, had too many students in the building, or they were in a location too far from downtown. She told herself she'd take the next place no matter what, but when she saw it, and the last one too, she didn't.

"Any luck?" Lilly was in the kitchen making biscuits when Danielle returned at five.

"No. I didn't realize how hard it would be finding a decent place near downtown Halifax. Everything I saw was either too big, too small, or filled with students."

"God, you don't want that."

"I sure don't."

"Um, Danielle?"

"Yes?"

"Well, with everything going on I didn't get a chance to tell you that Nathalie is coming over for dinner this—"

"Oh, sorry. I'll make myself scarce, don't worry."

"No, you don't need to do that. Actually, it works out even better because Nathalie has a friend—"

"I'm less than twenty-four hours single and you're trying to hook me up with Nathalie's friend?" Danielle was not impressed.

"I didn't mean to upset you. I just thought—"

"You don't have to shove anyone my way, Lilly. I started to unthaw all on my own last week. I had already decided on leaving. Rachel locking me out yesterday just sped things up."

"It's not a date. It's just a friend of Nathalie's coming over. Nathalie and her friend, having dinner with me and my friend. Four friends getting together for a meal, that's all." Lilly looked at Danielle as though she needed a huge favor. "Truth is, I need this, Danielle. I think it would help put me and Nathalie back on track if there were other people around to cushion things." Lilly's eyes pleaded. "Please?"

Danielle smiled then said, "Okay, just tell me what I can contribute to the meal."

Lilly leapt to Danielle's side, kissed her on the cheek and cheerily said, "Thank you!"

Danielle wiped her cheek. "You're welcome. Now what should I bring to this dinner?"

"Well, since you're so sweet, how about dessert?"

❧ 19 ❧

A hot shower had done wonders for Danielle's mood. She looked at herself in the mirror and had the surprising urge to put on makeup. She wouldn't even have makeup if Lilly hadn't packed it for her. It hadn't exactly been on her priority list.

Danielle, who rarely took more than ten minutes to get dressed, was still trying on different outfits half an hour later. She finally settled on a pair of dark blue flared trousers and a very stylish, light blue blouse with a wing-tipped collar and matching wing-tipped sleeves. She looked at the two open buttons at her neck in the mirror, then undid a third before joining Lilly in the kitchen.

"Wow!"

Danielle smiled at Lilly's reaction. "I'm just practicing looking sexy for when I'm ready to get back out there."

"You're making me rethink my outfit." Lilly was wearing blue jeans and a green, tight fitting, crewneck sweater.

"You look great, Lilly. You always do. Do you have any water?"

"There's a pitcher in the fridge. Aren't you going to have any wine?"

"I will, but I'd like some water first."

The doorbell rang as Danielle was opening the fridge. She poured herself a glass of water and was taking a drink when Lilly returned to the kitchen with her two guests.

Danielle almost choked when she recognized the woman standing behind Nathalie. The woman looked equally unimpressed and literally rolled her eyes in disgust, without even trying to camouflage her reaction.

"Danielle, this is Nathalie's friend, Melissa. Melissa, this is Danielle."

"We've met." Melissa Lambert, the DNA technician from the crime lab, did not sound very enthusiastic.

"You have?" Lilly and Nathalie asked in unison.

"We met last week at the crime lab," Danielle replied. She reminded herself that this was for Lilly, so she extended an olive branch to Melissa. "I might have been a bit snappy the other day. I hope you won't hold it against me." Danielle held out her hand to shake Melissa's.

To Danielle's extreme relief, Melissa obliged and replied, "Nice to meet you—again." Then Melissa leaned into Nathalie's ear and whispered, "And if she believes that, I've got some swamp land to sell her," not seeming to care that Danielle could hear her.

After a glass of wine and a chat about the latest movies each had seen and recommended or not, Lilly served dinner.

Melissa brought something Danielle had never had before, a fiddlehead salad. Lilly put out the biscuits she'd made earlier, and Nathalie warmed up what she'd brought, a homemade seafood chowder.

"Wow, this is the best chowder I've ever had," Danielle remarked.

"Nathalie's a great cook. I never ate so well as when we were dating," Melissa said matter of factly.

Both Lilly and Danielle stopped eating mid-stream. Lilly was first to react.

"You two?" Lilly pointed to Nathalie and Melissa with open scissored fingers. "You used to go out?" Lilly's surprise was more evident than Danielle's.

"Just for a couple of months. Seems so long ago now, I hardly remember it," Nathalie said somewhat defensively.

"Oh, thanks. Glad to know I was so memorable." Melissa rolled her eyes and shook her head.

"You know what I mean, Melissa. We were always more friends than—and I mean, it was ten years ago. To me it's like it never happened."

"When were you together? Were you friends first, or just friends later?" Danielle was now curious as to how lovers became friends, and vice versa.

Nathalie replied before Melissa could. "We met playing softball. We sort of dated briefly, but we were more friends than anything else. It just naturally took the course it was meant to."

Melissa's eyebrows clenched closer together. "It was seven years ago, not ten. It would be exactly seven years next month, on your birthday. Remember?" Melissa angled her head while looking directly at Nathalie. "Or did you forget that too?"

Danielle had guessed Nathalie's age to be early to mid-twenties— at most—which was at least ten years younger than Lilly. She was curious as to Nathalie's exact age now, to know how much of an age difference there was, but she had heard her mother say to her brother once, "You never ask a woman any question in which the answer is a number."

Tension permeated the room as Melissa continued to stare at Nathalie.

Lilly was first to break the silence. "Nathalie, don't suppose you have any vacancies in your building? Danielle's been having a really hard time finding a place near downtown, and your building would be the perfect location."

Danielle saw fear flash across Nathalie's face. *What's up with that?* she wondered.

"No, sorry. Have you considered downtown Dartmouth, Danielle?" Nathalie directed the question at Danielle of course, but had her eyes locked on Melissa's.

"Only briefly. I know I could just hop the ferry and be across the harbor in fifteen minutes, but I like living on the Halifax side."

Everyone went quiet again until Lilly asked about Danielle's annual Easter ritual. "Danielle, how did your grandmother like the flowers you made for her this year?"

"Oh, she loved them. We didn't put them out though. She waits till the long weekend in May to do that." Danielle smiled in amusement. "It would tip off the neighbors that they aren't real if she put them out too early. She gets my uncle to go out after dark and put them out so they miraculously appear the next morning in full bloom."

Nathalie grinned. "She sounds like a character." Nathalie glanced at Danielle for a second, but averted her eyes just as quickly again. Danielle noticed Nathalie had no problem looking Melissa in the eye when she spoke to her. Or Lilly, for that matter.

"She is, believe me. You don't know the half of it. Oh! I saw your video, by the way. Well, not yours, but your song's."

"The one Sammi Tyler sings?" Nathalie was playing with her spoon.

"Yes. It's a really nice song. It really is."

"Thanks." Nathalie seemed uncomfortable with the compliment. "Melissa, I love the dressing you made for the fiddlehead salad. It goes perfectly with the chowder. You'll have to give me the recipe."

"Prime Minister's Choice, Blue Cheese & Garlic."

Everyone except Danielle laughed when Melissa disclosed the name of the generic grocery store brand of salad dressing. Danielle chose to ignore it and move the dinner along. "Guess it's time for my contribution." Danielle got up and opened the freezer as Lilly cleared everyone's dinner plates and bowls.

Danielle placed a small bowl of French Vanilla ice cream in front of everyone.

Melissa wasn't touching hers.

"Is there something wrong with your ice cream?" Danielle thought she couldn't go wrong with vanilla.

"I don't eat ice cream unless there's sauce over it," Melissa replied.

Danielle stared at her. *You've got to be kidding me. How old are you?* Danielle stood up. "I suppose I could run to the store and get some."

"Don't do that." Nathalie motioned for Danielle to sit back down.

"No, don't bother running to the store, Danielle." Melissa said. "You already went out of your way once by going to the store to buy the ice cream."

Nathalie shot Melissa an unimpressed look, then stood up and pulled on Danielle's arm. "Danielle will have her homemade sauce ready in five minutes."

When Lilly saw Nathalie grab a sauce pan from her pot rack, Lilly started picking up bowls. "Guess that means I should put these back in the freezer so the ice cream doesn't melt."

"Danielle, get some butter," Nathalie instructed. She then picked up two bananas from a fruit bowl, and a knife from a wooden block next to them. Nathalie passed the knife and bananas to Danielle.

As Danielle sliced the bananas, Nathalie asked Lilly if she had any hard liquor in the house. Lilly led her to a small bar that contained an assortment of rum, scotch, gin, and vodka. Nathalie chose a spiced rum.

When Nathalie returned to the kitchen she said to Danielle, "Okay, now put some butter in."

"How much?"

"About a cup."

Danielle retrieved and unwrapped a rectangle of butter and sliced off a measured cup before tossing it into the sauce pan.

"Okay, stir that around till it's melted." Nathalie reached around Danielle and lowered the heat.

"Anything else?" Danielle asked.

Nathalie kept her eyes on the pan as she answered, "A half cup of brown sugar."

Danielle opened some cupboards until she found brown sugar while Nathalie came back from the fridge with some milk.

"Put the sugar and bananas in, and keep stirring. Let me know when you start to see bubbles. Lilly, do you have a lighter or matches?"

Lilly walked over to her fireplace mantel and retrieved a box of long, wooden matchsticks. After handing them over to Nathalie, Lilly returned to the table and her conversation with Melissa.

"We've got bubbles!" Danielle announced.

Nathalie grasped the spoon Danielle was stirring with. "I'll keep stirring while you measure out a quarter cup of rum." Nathalie's hand brushed Danielle's when she took over the stirring, and a look of alarm came over Danielle. "It's okay. Trust me," Nathalie said in response.

Danielle's alarm had nothing to do with the cooking, however. It was something she noticed when Nathalie reached for the pan.

"Okay, now pour the rum slowly into the pan." Nathalie continued to stir as Danielle poured. "Next is to light one of the matches."

"Don't set my house on fire!" Lilly cautioned the cooks.

"Don't worry, Lilly. I'm very good at stroking a fire. I mean, stoking." Nathalie grinned and winked at Lilly.

"She's really cute, isn't she?" Lilly said to Melissa, in reference to Nathalie.

"Yeah, she's kinda cute. But she's not beautiful like you are..." Melissa's eyes roamed over Lilly's frame, pausing temporarily at her breasts, then parked themselves in front of Lilly's face. "You have a thing for Nathalie?" she asked Lilly.

Lilly shrugged a little. "She does have a type of playfulness and charm that is quite seductive."

"Playfulness and charm, eh? Hey, if that's your thing, I could borrow my niece's sandbox and her charm bracelet..." Melissa grinned as she leaned in and winked.

Lilly's full lips parted, revealing perfect bright white teeth, as a smile developed.

Nathalie was holding the pan over the heat. "Okay, lower the match, but stand back." The pan exploded in a burst of flames, then Nathalie raised it, rocking it back and forth as the alcohol burned off. "Okay, last thing now is to pour in some milk." Nathalie handed Danielle the carton of milk.

"How much?"

"Just pour in slowly and keep stirring. I'll tell you when it looks right."

Danielle smiled. She thought of a warm, wonderful memory of her and her mother making fudge together one cold, winter's night.

Nathalie poured the hot sauce into a bowl, inserted a ladle, then said to Danielle, "You may serve us your homemade rum and butter sauce, Mademoiselle." Nathalie then whispered something in Danielle's ear.

As Nathalie, Lilly, and Melissa sat at the table with their ice cream in front of them, Danielle poured a generous amount of what she'd just made into each bowl. When she got to Melissa, Danielle scooped out as many bananas as she could find, then poured the remaining sauce all over them.

Danielle looked at Nathalie who was smiling in such amusement she looked like she was about to break into a giggle. Danielle couldn't stop from smiling gleefully either as she sat down to enjoy her very own culinary delight that to her, looked and smelled to die for.

While everyone else ate their sauce and ice cream all up, Danielle keenly observed Melissa Lambert foraging through hers and eating very slowly. Danielle looked at Nathalie and winked, still thinking about what Nathalie had whispered in her ear: "Melissa hates bananas."

❧ 20 ❧

"That wasn't very funny." Melissa was standing outside having a cigarette, and even though Nathalie hated cigarettes and smoking, she had joined Melissa so she could explain.

"Melissa, you weren't very nice to Danielle. I felt bad for her."

"*You* felt bad for her? I'm the one who had to eat around the bananas."

"Oh, you don't hate them that much. You've eaten my banana bread."

"Well, you know I hate raw bananas."

"They weren't raw, they were cooked in rum and butter." Nathalie giggled.

"Don't be flippant, Nathalie."

"What is your problem with her, anyway? It's like you hated her from the first second you laid eyes on her."

"Not the first second, just the first scene."

"What does that mean?"

"She comes into my lab like she's in a Clint Eastwood movie or something, acting like Dirty Harry, and treating me like I was an idiot who didn't know how to do my job. When she wasn't acting like a four-year-old that is, asking why and why not every two seconds. Christ, I had a similar conversation with my four-year-old niece the other day. She wanted to know why cows couldn't shit cheese if they could pee milk."

Nathalie ignored the subject of Melissa's conversation with her niece. "Funny, I don't see any squinting or hairy chest when I look at her."

"No, I'm sure you don't. But you sure do see something you like."

Nathalie rolled her eyes. "Melissa, are we going to go through this again?"

"I'm not jealous."

"I know you're not jealous, but how many times do I have to tell you, I don't sleep with my friends?"

"Hey, haven't you heard about friends with benefits?"

"Melissa, we've already talked about this."

"Yeah, yeah, yeah. I'm not allowed to go there. If I cross that line, you'll stop being my friend again. Blah, blah, blah."

"Melissa, you know you're not romantically interested in me. Just because we had sex once upon a time and you enjoyed it, doesn't mean we should base a relationship on that."

"I'm not looking for a relationship, Nathalie. A relationship is the last thing I want, you know that."

"You know I'm not the type who can—"

"But why not? Why can't you just allow yourself to have some fun? It would be perfect for both of us. Neither of us wants a relationship. No strings attached. Why not just have fun with each other?"

Nathalie glanced at the house, specifically the windows, to see if any were open, then lowered her voice to almost a whisper. "Melissa, I've enjoyed your friendship again this past year, but—"

"Year and a half."

"Okay, year and a half. Twatever."

Melissa chuckled. "Twatever. I like that. Why did you, by the way?"

"Why did I what?"

"Why, after years of keeping your distance from me, did you contact me again? I mean, you were polite and everything if I saw you somewhere, but you never did contact me when I gave you my phone number or email. Why did you all of a sudden decide to be friends with me again?"

"I don't know. I suppose I figured enough time had gone by, that we could be friends without you wanting sex." Nathalie hoped her half lie had come out naturally enough to be believed. It was true she hoped Melissa would no longer be interested in a sexual relationship, but rekindling their friendship hadn't been Nathalie's reason for contacting Melissa again. It was because of what Melissa did for a living.

"Okay, I won't ever ask you for sex again. But if you ever change your mind…" Melissa grinned. "Hey, how come you lied to Lilly earlier?"

"What are you talking about?"

Melissa scrutinized Nathalie's face for a moment, then said, "Yeah, okay. If that's how you want to play it, I'll play along."

Nathalie slapped Melissa in the back of the head. "I'm going back into the house. You can stay out here and smoke yourself to death if you want."

"Wait for me, I'm done." Melissa dropped her cigarette butt on the ground and walked toward the door.

Nathalie walked over to the butt, extinguished it by stomping on it, then said to Melissa, "Come pick this up. Nobody wants your cancerous leavings left on their doorstep."

Melissa was holding her crushed cigarette butt in her fingers when she went back into the house. "Where can I put this?"

Lilly got up and showed Melissa where the garbage was. Meanwhile, Nathalie sat down next to Danielle on the small sofa, leaving two empty chairs across from them for Melissa and Lilly to sit down in. This surprised Danielle—until she figured out Nathalie was more comfortable looking across at Lilly and Melissa than at her.

"Are you a Clint Eastwood fan, Danielle?" Melissa asked.

Danielle had no idea what Melissa's motive could be for asking that, but knew there must be one. And felt it probably was on the more sinister side, since Melissa's face was just too spiteful looking as she asked it. "Not particularly. Why do you ask that?"

"Oh, I just—"

"I'm not a fan either," Nathalie interrupted to say. "I don't like any of those old geezers. They're sixty or seventy years old with twenty or thirty-year-old love interests. Give me a break. We're supposed to believe that every young woman's fantasy is to have sex with her grandfather?"

Danielle and Lilly emitted creeped out sounds.

"And what's your ultimate sexual fantasy, Nathalie?" Melissa's spiteful look turned mischievous.

"None of your business!"

"Oh, come on. We're all girls. Girls who like girls," Melissa prodded.

Nathalie didn't budge.

"Okay," Melissa said. "What about you Lilly? Do you have the guts to answer, Madam Prosecutor?"

Lilly scanned the faces of all three women, but Danielle's in particular. Danielle got the impression she was trying to decide whether to answer or not.

Lilly took a sip of wine then said, "I love dominance. I love it a little rough."

Danielle's face didn't show any reaction, but she was surprised, to say the least. She never expected Lilly to be into that. "How rough?" Danielle asked her.

"Not beating or anything. But I love role play. It's very exciting when someone tells you what to do, and when you can come."

Danielle felt her stomach churn. She was so turned off by BDSMXYZ, or whatever it is they called it. She couldn't get over the fact that this is what turned Lilly on.

"What about you, Danielle?" Lilly leaned forward, appearing eager for her reply.

"Um…well, I guess, nothing really."

"Oh, come on, you're not getting away with that. Quid pro quo, remember? I told you guys, now you each have to tell yours." Lilly leaned back in her chair and crossed her long legs.

"I'm sure you'd find mine quite boring compared to yours."

Lilly's eyes appeared glazed as she stared into Danielle's and said, "Try me."

Danielle was so uncomfortable. Having been raised Catholic she was not comfortable discussing sex so openly—especially in a group setting. "I don't know. I've never really thought about it."

"Oh, that's a cop out, if I've ever heard one," Melissa blurted. "Pardon the pun. Have you never pulled over some gorgeous woman, then went home and fantasized about what you'd have done to her with your baton while she was handcuffed?"

Danielle rolled her eyes and angled her body away from Melissa.

"So Nathalie, are you going to be a party pooper too?" Melissa wasn't drinking any wine as she was driving, but didn't seem to need any to say whatever she wanted, whenever she wanted.

Nathalie hesitated, but not for very long. "My ultimate sexual experience would be to make love on the beach on a hot summer's night, just the two of us spending hours making love to each other's entire bodies, from hair to toes while the waves lapped at our feet."

Lilly stared at Nathalie in disbelief. "Okay, truth now."

"That is the truth," Nathalie stated.

"You're serious?" Lilly didn't not appear to share in that fantasy.

"Yes, I'm serious. I don't need any toys or role playing." Nathalie's face reddened as she seemed to remember Lilly's fantasy, then added, "I mean, not to say that hey, if that's your thing…" Nathalie fidgeted nervously with a ring on her right hand. "All I'm saying is, for me, bodies and tongues and love are all I need." Nathalie took her first sip of wine. Though it was more like a gulp.

Lilly turned sideways, facing Melissa, and draped her legs over the arm of her chair. "Have you been saving the best for last, Melissa?"

"My ultimate sexual fantasy? Yeah, I know what makes my animal side grow wild. I can definitely relate to the dom-sub thing, and putting somebody in their place. I think it would be extremely hot to tease a woman and not allow her to come until I decide to let her."

Lilly leaned way back and put her arms behind her head as she continued to focus on Melissa, her erect nipples visibly protruding from her tight-fitting sweater.

"You're the only one left, Danielle," Melissa pointed out. "You sure you're a cop? You look more like a chicken to me."

Danielle ignored Melissa, and inched even further away from her—till she felt Nathalie's thigh against hers.

Nathalie jumped to her feet. "I need to get home, Melissa."

"What? It's still early."

"I need to go, Melissa."

"I can't stand that Danielle," Melissa told Nathalie as she drove away from Lilly's house.

Nathalie said nothing.

"She thinks she's hot shit, investigating a homicide."

Nathalie still hadn't said a word by the time they were crossing one of the large suspension bridges that spanned Halifax harbor. She was barely listening to Melissa and just looked at the beautiful skyline of downtown Halifax while trying to think of anything that was mindless.

"She's not as smart as she thinks she is. She's definitely not thorough. She didn't even know her star victim's face had been carved up. All she wanted to know was if we could get DNA from somebody's breath. Idiot. A team of homicide investigators couldn't figure out who killed her, but she thinks she can by getting DNA of the last person who took a breath in her direction while she was alive."

Nathalie whipped her head around toward Melissa. "What?"

"I said, she thinks she's going to solve a homicide by getting DNA from somebody's breath."

Nathalie leaned forward with a sudden alertness. "Can they do that?"

"Of course not. The biggest clue in that case is the carving on her face, and all *Clit* Eastwood wants to do is try get DNA from whoever panted on her last."

"What case are you talking about?"

"Buchanan. You must remember that hitting the papers a year and a half ago." Melissa turned down Creighton Street, as she headed toward the lower end of Maynard, where Nathalie lived.

Nathalie felt her stomach convulse. She tried to hold it back, but it didn't help that Melissa kept talking.

"Yeah, there was a big letter 'S' carved in her face. Oh, that's confidential by the way. It was never released, so don't mention it to anybody. Friggin' stupid bitch thinks she's going to figure out what an entire squad couldn't. Thinks all she has to do is bat her pretty blue eyes and—"

Nathalie opened the car door even though Melissa was still driving. Melissa hit the breaks and careened into an opening on the side of the street. When the car stopped, Nathalie simultaneously undid her seatbelt buckle and jumped out, half a second before throwing up on the sidewalk.

"What the—" Melissa put on her emergency flashers and got out of the car. "My God, what's wrong?"

Nathalie straightened herself up. "Nothing. I just get car sick sometimes." That was true, but not the reason she had thrown up. "I'm going to walk home. The air will do me good."

"You're not walking from here, it's still four blocks away."

"I'll be fine. I really need some air."

"Nathalie, get in. It's dark, and I'm really uneasy letting you walk by yourself. I'll drive really slow. At least you'll be safe."

"Melissa, I'll be sick again if I get in the car, no matter how slow you drive. I'll be okay."

"Nathalie, please get in."

"I need some air." Nathalie placed her hand on her stomach and started walking.

"Okay, here's the deal. I'm going to drive beside you, even if it's just one kilometer an hour."

Nathalie acknowledged with a nod and kept walking. Melissa got back in the car and drove beside her till she got to her building.

When Nathalie entered her apartment she went straight to the front window and looked down below. She saw Melissa still parked, looking up at her. Nathalie waved, and in response, Melissa produced a thumbs up, then drove away.

Nathalie sat down in the middle of her sofa. She looked in the direction of her bedroom. She didn't want to go to sleep. She was too afraid to.

She looked toward the back yard window where she saw a maple tree. She hated looking at that tree. She almost didn't buy her building because of it. Had it been visible from the bedroom, she would not have bought it for sure.

Nathalie got up and harshly pulled the curtains shut. She then clutched the fabric, twisting it around her hand, as tears began to flow. She sobbed uncontrollably now, as she pounded the wall with the curtain wrapped around her fist like a boxing glove. She punched and punched—and punched—until she fell into a heap on the floor, bringing the curtain down with her as she collapsed.

She stayed there for a while, till the last tears fell and dried from her cheeks. Then, as if a switch had been flicked, she swiftly picked herself up. She wasn't crying anymore. She wasn't angry. She wasn't sad. Her face had less expression than a mannequin's.

She robotically walked into the bedroom and sat down on the edge of her bed. She opened the bottom drawer of her bedside table and reached far back, underneath everything else in there, and grasped a frame she hadn't touched in a while.

She pulled it out, not knowing what she would feel—or if she would feel anything at all. When the hidden photograph was extracted and flipped over, Nathalie ran her fingertips over it, in an "S" formation...over Kristina Buchanan's face.

❧ 21 ❧

Danielle tossed and turned in bed for hours. Despite two glasses of wine, sleep did not come easily. She realized she was stressed. That's the simplest word she could come up with to define what she was feeling, experiencing. In one week she went from routine to chaos, and not just in one area of her life, but in almost all of them. A new job, uprooted from her home, the end of a long-term relationship. All of it ricocheted around in her head until she surrendered.

❧❧❧

Danielle was swimming again, but this time, in a heart-shaped pond. Flames of blue, orange, and yellow lined the pond, illuminating its dark surface like a cinematic screen, upon which split-second frames of various images from the past week's events flashed across.

Danielle felt a sense of foreboding. She did not want to leave, but danger lurked. She could feel it.

She swam toward the bottom of the heart and hit an icy cold spot. She turned to go back, but an iceberg thrust itself out of the water, blocking her way.

Danielle was scared.

A whale swam by and Danielle grabbed its fin, holding on as the whale submerged and navigated the cold, murky waters to safety. When Danielle felt warmth, she let go and let herself rise.

She rose into a hot, buttery, sweet sauce that surrounded her. The cozy warmth swaddled and comforted her. She closed her eyes and breathed in very deeply, feeling tension release from her as she exhaled.

Danielle did this twice, then opened her eyes—to see a mermaid smiling at her, from a face covered and blurred by the thick, rich sauce. The mermaid's only distinguishable feature was her long dark hair, which was also drenched and dripping in sauce.

Danielle began to lick the hot, sticky, sweetness from the mermaid's face, with an intent to unveil her layer by layer. But the mermaid wrapped herself around Danielle and Danielle was so lost in loving, contented bliss...that she succumbed to a wonderfully deep, restful sleep.

Danielle felt refreshed when she got back to her desk on Wednesday morning. She had gone for an early run, and felt alert and eager to get back to the investigation. She reviewed her notes and organized what she would do today: speak with the medical examiner, then interview Gillian Stevens and Maurice Coultier.

"Thanks for taking time out to talk to me again," Danielle told Dr. Peterson.

"No problem. You were saying on the phone you had some questions about Buchanan's cause of death?"

"Yes. Your report states cause of death as being polydrug intoxication. I was wondering if you could explain exactly what that means."

"Polydrug intoxication simply refers to a combination of drugs, which if taken in safe dosages, would not result in death on their own, but when combined with certain other drugs, particularly alcohol—"

"Why alcohol?"

"Alcohol depresses the nervous system, slows down breathing and heart rate. When you combine alcohol with other drugs that also depress the nervous system, you're playing Russian roulette. Too many times I've heard from a family how their loved one had always had one or two drinks, then taken a sleeping or anti-anxiety pill, and it had never hurt them. Then one night the same thing they got away with for months, maybe even years, kills them."

"Any drugs in particular?"

"We're seeing a lot of accidental polydrug intoxication involving prescribed medications, painkillers, antidepressants and anti-anxiety drugs especially. Those combined with alcohol can be lethal. But not just alcohol. Even over the counter cough medications, if combined with particular drugs, can cause lethal polydrug intoxication."

"Even cough medicine? That's scary."

"If you take all medications as prescribed, they are safe. But any drug that alters your mood or makes you feel drowsy, especially, don't ever combine it with alcohol or any other type of drug no matter how tempted you are, or how safe you think it might be." Dr. Peterson spoke as though it were a personal warning.

Danielle rarely got colds, and when she did she never took cough medicine. She had also never taken an antidepressant or anti-anxiety pill in her life, and ibuprophen was the strongest pain reliever she'd ever ingested, so she did not take it personally. She suspected Dr. Peterson just took every opportunity to warn individuals of this very serious risk.

"How does one actually die when it's polydrug intoxication?" Danielle asked.

"Usually it causes respiratory failure. If you take a sleeping pill for instance, you get drowsy, everything slows down, and you fall asleep. Add alcohol or other drugs that also depress the nervous system, and you risk slowing everything down to the point where it just stops altogether. But that's not what happened to Buchanan."

"But you said her cause of death was polydrug intoxication."

"She did die of polydrug intoxication, but not respiratory failure—more like respiratory eruption."

Danielle was confused. "Okay, talk to me like I'm a five-year-old. Or give me the, 'How Buchanan Died For Dummies' version."

Dr. Peterson smiled, then proceeded to explain. "Early in the evening, Buchanan had perhaps four to six beers and smoked a fair amount of marijuana. The deposits in her liver tell me she was a chronic user."

"How chronic?"

"Definitely daily. And when I say daily, I'm talking probably had it for breakfast most mornings."

"You can tell that from her liver?"

"Like most drugs, the body develops tolerance over time, and heavy users need to take more and more to experience the same high. In the case of marijuana, the liver begins to store the THC—that's the active ingredient in marijuana that makes people high—and the liver will hold on to it for months, even years. That's why chronic users have such a hard time kicking the habit. Even if they don't smoke or ingest any marijuana for months, the liver will start releasing the THC that it stored, triggering very severe cravings. If chronic users tried to quit cold turkey their hands would shake, they'd get headaches, have sleep disturbances, and like I said, extremely severe cravings."

"Did any other drugs show up in her liver, or any other organs?"

"Other than ketamine hydrochloride, just alcohol. There was mild cirrhosis, so I'd say she drank alcohol to excess on a regular basis, but not daily—not like the cannabis."

"You're sure she smoked a lot of it every day?"

"The liver is an incredible organ, Constable. It reveals secrets one might never have admitted to anyone. That's what I love about my job. Some people have lots of secrets, and though they might go to their grave without confessing them, their remains will tell on them. What her liver tells me is that she was a chronic user. It was loaded with THC, and you don't get those types of deposits by smoking it once in a while."

"But she was a nurse."

"Constable, you'd be surprised at who is addicted to what. I'm not surprised anymore. Haven't been in years. Doctors, nurses, little old ladies. Addiction has no borders or boundaries. You start using, you risk addiction, plain and simple. And once you're addicted, no matter what your profession is, no matter how much you tell yourself you should quit, that you can quit, it's one hell of a battle. So the key is, don't ever start."

Danielle was a little uncomfortable with Dr. Peterson's mini lecture even though she thoroughly understood where he was coming from. "Don't worry, I don't plan on it."

Dr. Peterson raised his thumb.

"Could you tell if she was a regular user of ketamine, or if that might have been the first time she'd taken it?"

"I can't say she had never done ketamine or any other illegal drugs before, whether once in a while or on a regular basis. Drugs like cocaine for instance, don't stay in the liver, but do damage it. She could very well have done other drugs, but if she did, they were either of the type or not frequent enough to leave any tell-tale signs."

"Did she have any needle marks anywhere?"

"No. I looked very closely and there were none at all."

"Okay. Getting back to the evening of her death, she drank alcohol, smoked marijuana. And then?"

"And then she snorted maybe two lines of ketamine, and after that, ingested another higher dose before an enormous amount was blown into her lungs."

"You're sure she snorted the first dose?"

"She definitely snorted it. I swabbed from her nasal openings down to her lungs. About two lines worth of ketamine were drawn in all the way through the entire respiratory system. That first dose was snorted willingly, not blown in by force.

"You said last week that she was in a drug-induced stupor when the ketamine was blown into her. My research into ketamine is that it would take a large amount to put a human to sleep, and that they'd probably start to vomit quite violently long before that happened."

"We found no vomit in her mouth, on her body, or in her home, which is where she was killed."

Danielle wanted to know how he knew she was killed at home, but didn't want to jump around, so she just made a quick note to get back to that.

"Was there food in her stomach?"

"Looks like she'd eaten supper around five o'clock, then had some potato chips and popcorn in the evening, but no, she never threw it up. Which tells us something very important."

"What's that?"

"It means that she ingested a fairly high dose of ketamine very soon after snorting the two lines. The amount of marijuana she smoked would have quelled the urge to vomit after ingesting the two lines, but she would have still been nauseous."

"Would the two lines she snorted have paralyzed her enough to allow whoever killed her to blow the twenty grams into her?"

"No. After the two lines she'd still be able to move, although not very well. She'd be somewhat in a stupor, but still have enough motor control to at least try resisting. She had no defensive wounds whatsoever, though, so she had to have taken that second dose willingly. Whether she was aware it was ketamine or not I couldn't tell you, but I can tell you that the second dose was ingested."

"The second dose is what knocked her out then?"

"No, not knocked out, but definitely incapacitated. She wouldn't have been able to defend herself even if she was aware enough to try. She would have been paralyzed and hallucinating, but still conscious."

Knowing now that liquid ketamine was very potent and could easily be dropped into a drink, Danielle asked Dr. Peterson, "Do you know if any of her drinking glasses or beer bottles were tested for the presence of ketamine?"

"You'd have to check with the crime lab for that. I just deal with the body and cause of death."

Danielle jotted down a note to check with the lab for ketamine residue in anything Buchanan might have drank from, then she thought of Melissa Lambert and rolled her eyes. Luckily for Danielle, Dr. Peterson was flipping through the reports in front of him and didn't notice.

"How do you know she died at home?" Danielle asked.

"The feces found in her panties and pants was matched to the feces found on her sofa. The crime lab can confirm that for you."

"How does that prove she died at home?"

"When you die, your sphincter muscles—like everything else—stop functioning. If anything is in the rectum at the time of death, the sphincter muscles cease to function and out it comes. That's how we know she was lying on her back on her sofa when she died." Dr. Peterson paused for a moment, then added, "We also know she died with her eyes wide open, but that's not unusual considering she would have been experiencing extreme hallucinations prior to death."

"How do you know she died with her eyes open?"

"Because of the *tache noire*."

Danielle recognized the French phrase as meaning "black stain" but did not understand what it meant medically. "What's *tache noire*?"

"It's when the conjunctiva—that's a colorless membrane that covers the eye—dehydrates, and that happens when a person dies with their eyes open. It causes the membrane to turn black."

Danielle recalled the eerie darkness of Buchanan's eyes in the photographic evidence. She had one last question for Dr. Peterson.

"Can you explain to me exactly how she died? If her heart didn't slow down and stop, then what happened?"

"She already had alcohol and marijuana, both of which slow down respiration, in her system. Ketamine is unusual in that it actually raises respiration, so the initial dose she snorted would have raised her heart rate despite the alcohol and marijuana. When the twenty grams was blown into her…let me tell you, Constable, you've either got an ingenious killer on your hands, or an incredibly stupid and lucky one."

"How so?"

"If the person who killed Kristina Buchanan chose ketamine hydrochloride specifically, knowing exactly what would happen, how it would kill her…then you've got someone who not only wanted her eyes to turn black…but for her heart to literally rip apart."

Although Danielle had planned to pay Gillian Stevens a visit after leaving the medical examiner's office, she chose to go back to the crime lab instead.

Melissa Lambert was hunched over a microscope when Danielle was escorted into the lab. Melissa looked up but didn't speak.

"Hi." Danielle expected a similar greeting in return but Melissa didn't respond. "I was hoping you would have a few minutes to help me make sense of some of the lab reports. You're the expert, and I thought maybe you could simplify things for me." Danielle hoped this little flattery would go a long way.

Melissa hesitated, then asked, "Which reports?"

"One in particular is regarding the carving of the letter 'S' in Buchanan's face, and I also have a question regarding the duct tape found at the scene. The medical examiner says she was already dead when her face was cut, but I was wondering if the duct tape was used on her."

Melissa walked over to a computer and started typing. "There was duct tape residue found deep inside her facial tissue, which means her face was carved after the duct tape was placed on her. The duct tape itself was not cut though, so it was removed before he took a knife to her face."

"How do you know it was a knife? I thought Sharp Trauma couldn't definitively identify the object used to cut her face. You don't have any training in ST, have you?" It was more of a statement than a question.

"No, I don't," Melissa answered dryly. "I was just using the term 'knife' as a generalization."

"I need concrete facts, not generalizations," Danielle retorted. "So let's just stick to what you do know for a fact. Was there any DNA on the tape?"

A blue vein deepened on Melissa's temple so quickly, Danielle thought she could see it pulsing. She expected Melissa to lose her temper—or for her cooperation to come to an abrupt end—but Melissa remained remarkably composed and provided the information asked of her. "Just the decedent's skin cells and a few of her own hairs, nothing foreign."

"I know the tape was found near the edge of the pond. Were your tests able to show exactly where the duct tape was placed on her body?"

Melissa typed again. "There were two strips covering her ears, one on each. One strip was across her nose and squeezed tight around the nostrils, then a fourth piece was used across her mouth."

"No tape over her eyes?" Danielle thought this unusual.

"No, that was it. Not around her wrists or ankles either, just nose, mouth, and ears. Different, isn't it?"

"Hmmm. Different indeed." For the first time ever, Danielle agreed with Melissa on something. "I was also wondering if any of her drinking glasses or the empty beer bottles or cans were tested for any other substances in them—ketamine hydrochloride in particular."

After a few moments of searching, Melissa reported, "We tested the empty beer cans found in her home. They contained her DNA, Maurice Coultier's DNA, and Gillian Stevens' DNA. No other DNA found, and no other substances found in any of the drinking glasses or cans, so it doesn't look like anything was slipped into her drink."

Danielle had to admit Melissa was very sharp. She then felt a pang of unexpected remorse. "Um, Melissa. I'd like to apologize for my attitude last time I was here."

Melissa's eyes widened in surprise.

"It's just this job sometimes, you know? I didn't mean to take it out on you. I hope you'll accept my apology."

Both Melissa's physical stance and voice relaxed. "Okay...sure. Apology accepted."

"Why don't you let me make it up to you? What's your favorite food? My treat."

"Whoa. Well, I didn't expect that," Melissa admitted.

"Do you like Morrie's Feast?"

"Love it."

"Are you free tonight?"

Melissa hesitated, then said, "I...am, actually."

"Meet you there at seven, then?"

"Ooh-kay." It was a very hesitant okay, but it was one nonetheless.

"Great." Danielle then turned and walked away, but just before she got to the door she turned back to look at Melissa and smiled.

It was a smile that caused Melissa's nipples to harden.

When Danielle got to her vehicle she made a quick call to the medical examiner. He confirmed Kristina Buchanan was already dead when her nostrils and mouth were taped over.

"There was no petechial hemorrhaging," he explained. "If she had been alive, the duct tape would have suffocated her and the eyes would have displayed petechiae under the conjunctiva, but there were none."

Danielle thanked Dr. Peterson and wrote this down in her notes.

When Danielle went to see Gillian Stevens, her first questions were related to what was already in the files.

Gillian reiterated how she and Kristina had worked together and often hung out on their days off, that Maurice Coultier and Kristina had lived together as a couple for a few years until Kristina left him for a woman several years prior to her death, and that they started hanging out again after Kristina and the woman she'd left him for, split up.

Gillian also went over the timeline of events as she knew them on the last evening of Kristina's life. Kristina had picked up Maurice, then Gillian, then drove them to her place around seven in the evening. Gillian and Maurice had visited till nine-thirty, then left when Maurice's brother, Joseph, picked them up and drove them back to Gillian's apartment.

"Were you and Maurice dating?" Danielle asked.

"No, he had a girlfriend. Well, they weren't committed to each other. At least he wasn't committed to her. He was still in love with Kristina and hoped they'd get back together."

"How do you know that?"

"Everybody knew that."

"Even Kristina?"

"Especially Kristina."

"How did she feel about that?"

"It didn't bother her if that's what you're asking."

"Was she interested in getting back together with him?"

Gillian raised both eyebrows. "Hardly."

"What does that mean?"

"I mean, no, she didn't want to get back together with him. She was dating other people."

"Did he know about that?"

"She didn't keep it a secret from him. If anything, she always made sure he knew whenever she was with somebody else."

"Why?"

"When it came to Maurice...I don't know. It's like she enjoyed taunting him or something. I don't know why she did it. It was cruel sometimes, but she didn't seem to care. Sometimes she really seemed to—I don't know—take pleasure in it."

"How would he react to that?"

"He didn't like it of course, but what could he do? They weren't together anymore. Just because he followed her around like a puppy dog and did whatever she wanted, didn't mean she owed him anything. Maurice was...well, he didn't have much of a backbone. Kristina had him wrapped around her finger, and she knew it."

"Was she sleeping with him?"

"You'd have to ask him about that. It was none of my business if they were or weren't."

"Tell me about that night. What did you do after you got there?"

"We just hung out."

Danielle scanned the small kitchen and larger living room. There were several lighters in various locations throughout the apartment, and on an end table next to the sofa was a small tin box, a lighter, and a small pair of surgical scissors that appeared to have a gum-like substance on them. Danielle didn't have any direct drug investigation experience, but she knew enough to recognize the paraphernalia of a chronic pot user. "Did your hanging out with Kristina always involve doing drugs?"

The question appeared to get Gillian's back up. "I don't know what the hell you're trying to get at, but I don't appreciate it. Why are you trying to make her out to be a criminal? So you can justify not finding her killer?"

"I'm not trying to vilify her, Gillian, I'm just trying to solve her murder. We know she smoked pot regularly, and I just have a few questions about that since it might shed some light on who might have killed her."

"Her smoking up once in a while didn't have anything to do with her murder. Some psycho killed her, not a drug dealer."

"What makes you think I was thinking a drug dealer killed her?"

"Kristina wasn't involved in drugs the way you make it out to be."

"I didn't make it out to be anything. I just said we know she smoked pot regularly. It was every single day, actually. That's not just once in a while."

"She wasn't dealing drugs," Gillian snapped.

Danielle snapped back. "Then why were there two mature marijuana plants with all their buds stripped off them in her spare bedroom, and a half pound of bud soaking in a pot of alcohol on her kitchen stove?"

Gillian stared at an empty glass that sat on the table in front of her and started chewing the nails of her right hand.

"She was trying to make hash oil, Gillian."

"I have no idea what you're talking about."

And that's where the interview—and information from Gillian— ended in the files. But Danielle was determined to get more than that, because she knew Gillian had more to tell, and Danielle was more determined than ever to be the one to get that information.

"I know nursing is a stressful job, Gillian. Lots of people use pot to relax. That's not what this is about. It really isn't. It's about whose path Kristina crossed, who had the audacity, the menace, and evil within them, to end her life. Maybe somebody made a delivery to her that night, or maybe she found somebody to sell the oil to and when it didn't turn out, they killed her. We've got lots of missing pieces, Gillian, and you—*you*—are the one holding back on some of those pieces."

There was a long stretch of silence before Gillian responded quite apathetically to Danielle's dramatically emotional appeal. "I told you, I don't know anything."

Danielle walked over to the end table in the living room area. As she did so, she removed a secondary clip-on RCMP badge she normally kept in an inside pocket, and attached it to the front of her belt where it would beacon attention when she turned to face Gillian again. She then tucked the right side of her jacket behind her nine-millimeter gun so it was fully exposed, turned in Gillian's direction, and pointed to the tin box with her left hand while she held onto her holster with her right.

"That's in plain sight, Gillian. Might not be much in there, just enough for a small personal possession charge, but enough to give you a drug record and get the hospital's attention."

Gillian glanced at the tin box then stared forward again.

"Gillian, you're very lucky to be working in a hospital that doesn't require its nurses to submit to mandatory, random drug tests. Right now it takes very serious allegation or proof of misconduct for the Halifax Health Authority to force its nurses to submit to a drug test, but if I walk in there, flashing my badge, announcing you've been charged with possession and start asking questions, how long do you think it'll take for them to haul you in for a test? And we both know, Gillian, what the results would be."

Gillian reached for a pair of glasses resting on the table. Her right hand trembled slightly as she placed them on her face.

"It really is up to you, Gillian. You can divert my attention away from this by answering my questions now, or I can charge you with possession, then go to the hospital and start asking questions there."

Gillian crossed her arms in defeat. "What do you want to know?"

❧ 23 ❧

Danielle was quite clear on what information she wanted from Gillian Stevens.

"I want to know *everything* concerning Kristina's drug use. What she used, how much she used, what she bought, what she sold—and don't leave anything out."

After going on about how hard nursing was, after feeling she had justified why nurses had so much more of a need to "relax" and "wind down" than anyone else, Gillian began to talk about Kristina's drug use.

"Yeah, Kristina smoked up most days, but she wasn't the only one."

"Did she ever smoke up while she was at work?"

A few seconds passed before Gillian answered. "Not *at* work."

Danielle was well trained in how to recognize honest, yet deceitful answers. "Did she ever smoke up during a work shift?"

Gillian looked at Danielle apprehensively, and Danielle surmised Gillian's reason for it.

"If you reveal to me your participation in a work-violation that happened in your past, Gillian, it'll stay in your past—as long as you know never to repeat such serious mistakes ever again."

"Well it's not like it happened all the time."

Danielle looked at Gillian sternly.

Gillian hesitated for a moment, then said, "It was just once or twice, I swear, and it's never happened since."

"What hasn't happened since?"

"A couple of times we went out for a burger instead of eating at the hospital. After we finished eating we shared part of a joint. Just a few tokes. Nothing extreme."

"Other than pot, what other drugs did Kristina do?"

"If it was in front of her she'd do coke or acid, ecstasy a few times, but she didn't usually go looking for it. It was mostly pot she smoked regularly."

"Do you know how much she smoked?"

"Maybe half, or a full bud, maybe more each day. If she was partying, could be a lot more."

"A bud is what, about a gram? How much does that cost in Halifax these days?"

"Usually, fifteen. BC bud or medicinal, twenty or twenty-five."

"Do you know who her dealer was?"

"She didn't have a dealer. She was really paranoid about buying it from dealers. Always got somebody else to buy it for her—always."

"Who bought it for her?"

Gillian started chewing her nails again. "Mostly me. And Maurice."

"How often would she buy it, and how much at a time?"

"Two, maybe three times a week she'd buy two or three grams."

"That must have taken quite a chunk out of her pay each week."

If Gillian had any opinion on the matter, she didn't share it with Danielle.

"Was she selling any to support her own habit?"

"No."

"You sure about that?"

"Yes, I'm sure. She was too paranoid to even buy it, let alone sell it."

"Then why was she growing it at home, and trying to make hash oil?"

"The plants she had at home were for her own use. Maurice got her some seeds and helped her put a small setup together in her spare room—only two plants survived. When they were ready, she stripped the buds off and put them out to dry. We tried some for the first time that night, but we smoked six joints altogether and we barely got a buzz off it."

"Is that why she decided to make hash oil out of it?"

"No, that was Maurice's brilliant idea. She was really pissed at him for how bad the bud turned out. I think we'd have gotten more of a buzz off banana leaves."

"According to the drug unit, it was a very bad attempt at making hash oil."

"Yeah, it was more like soup than oil. Kristina flipped right out when she looked at it and realized he didn't have a clue what he was doing. At least with the dried bud she could have smoked it. Might have taken her ten joints to get stoned, but it was completely useless after what Maurice did to it."

"You say she flipped right out. What exactly did she do?"

"She told him he owed her a couple thousand dollars, to get out, called him every name in the book and told him she never wanted to see his face again."

"What names did she call him?"

"Stupid, shithead, simpleton. Those were some of the nicer things that came out of her mouth."

"How did he take to that?"

"Well, he didn't like it. Who would? But he was his usual, just tried to do whatever it took to please her. Maurice was the type—well, he could be wish-washy—especially when it came to Kristina."

"Did he leave when she told him to?"

"No. That's when it all kinda went crazy. When she told him to get out, that he wasn't spending the night, he went berserk."

"Describe berserk."

"He started slamming different parts of the house, yelling and screaming that he built this, fixed that. Said he didn't build the swing in her maple tree for her to sit in it with somebody else."

"He didn't get angry when she called him terrible names, but he went berserk when she told him he couldn't spend the night?"

"Yeah. He said he wasn't leaving, though. He said she promised he could spend the night, and he hadn't done everything he did for her to just use him, or something like that. He sat in the chair and said he wasn't budging."

"And then what?"

"And then Kristina grabs his cell and calls Joe. And believe me, if you think he was mad after she told him he couldn't spend the night, you should have seen him after she called Joe."

"Do you mean Maurice's brother, Joseph?"

Gillian nodded a yes. "We didn't know it was Joe she was calling, but after she dialed she said, 'Come get your brother or he'll be sleeping in the ditch tonight.' Maurice tried to grab the phone from her, but she'd already hung up. He was so mad, he was shaking."

"What did he do?"

"Nothing. He was mad as hell, but he didn't scream or yell, or bang his fist like he had done before. He just bore holes into Kristina with his eyes."

"What did Kristina do?"

"She just turned on the TV and started watching it like we weren't even there."

"Were you supposed to have been spending the night too?"

"No. My sister was going to pick me up at 11:00 but I decided to get a lift with Joe instead. After we got in the truck I borrowed Maurice's cell to call her and tell her I was getting a ride home."

"Why did Maurice go to your place instead of going home?"

"He was so mad, all he wanted to do was get wasted. He said he'd pay for the beer if I had anything to toke at my place. Joe stopped at the liquor store and Maurice picked up a two-four. We went back to my place and drank and toked till about two in the morning."

"When Joe arrived to pick Maurice up, did he go into Kristina's house?"

"No. Soon as I saw lights in the driveway I hauled Maurice out of there."

"How did Maurice explain Kristina's call to him?"

"He didn't."

"Joe didn't ask?"

"No."

"Kristina calls Joe to come get his brother or he'll be sleeping in the ditch, and he doesn't ask Maurice about it?"

"No."

"What did they talk about?"

"Nothing really. It was pretty quiet in the truck. Maurice was still so mad, I could feel his leg shaking against mine."

"Was he still mad when you got back to your place?"

"He was upset. He smoked one joint after another, and drank a lot more beer than usual. All twenty-four bottles were empty the next morning."

"When did you hear about Kristina's death?"

"The next day. Her mother phoned me after the police notified her, in the early afternoon. The cops showed up at my apartment soon after that."

"Was Maurice still with you?"

"No, he left early, about eight o'clock in the morning."

"How did he get home?"

"Called a cab."

"Did you call him when you found out about Kristina?"

"Yeah, but I couldn't get a hold of him. I kept calling his cell and his house, but there was no answer. I even tried his work a week later, but he never called me back."

Danielle brought her head forward. "Never?"

"Ever."

Danielle's eyes widened. "Are you telling me you haven't spoken to him since?"

"Not a word."

"What about at the funeral?"

"He wasn't at the funeral."

Danielle looked back as if someone was standing behind her, then at Gillian again. "Don't you think that's odd? If he was with Kristina for a few years, and was still in love with her—"

"We all just figured it was too hard for him. He did show up at the funeral home for a couple minutes just before it closed the last night of the wake. I had already left, but I guess he asked Kristina's mother if he could spend a couple minutes alone with her coffin. She knew he loved her, so she let him. It surprised her though—it surprised us all—that he didn't come to the funeral."

"The medical examiner thinks she was killed between midnight and four a.m. Any chance he could have slipped out while you were asleep?"

"No, he was passed out when I went to bed. He wouldn't have hurt her anyhow, he was too crazy about her."

"Can you think of anyone or any reason someone might have wanted to hurt Kristina, not just want her dead, but hurt her too?"

"Kristina had lots of...exes. Maybe one of them snapped or something, I don't know."

"Can you give me the names of the people she dated, and any other information you might know about them?" Danielle already had a fairly long list, but thought she'd ask just in case anyone had been left out—intentionally or unintentionally. "I know it's a lot of work, but it might help us find the person who killed Kristina. Anything you can recall about them too, like where they lived, or worked, or what kind of vehicle they drove."

Gillian nodded. "Okay, but give me a few days."

"Sure. Just call me when you've finished." Danielle handed Gillian her card.

"Oh, you know who might know, too? Caroline."

"Who's Caroline?"

"Kristina's ex-girlfriend. I don't know her phone number, but I think she's listed. Caroline Corkum—lives in Tantallon. Or maybe you could get her number from the hospital. She's a nurse too. Same hospital as me and Kristina, just a different floor."

A man answered when Danielle called Caroline Corkum's home phone number.

"Honey, phone's for you."

When Caroline said hello, Danielle introduced herself, explained she was working on the Buchanan case, and would like to meet with her to ask a few questions. Caroline sounded nervous, and responded now wouldn't be a good time, but she was working the next day till three p.m. and could meet with Danielle after work at the station. Danielle said that would be fine and gave Caroline the address before hanging up.

Danielle looked at her watch—it was almost three o'clock. She had an appointment to view an apartment at six, but she figured she still had time to talk to Maurice Coultier. She had noted from the files he worked at the rail station from seven a.m. till three p.m., so he should be getting home just about the same time she would arrive if she left now. She thought it best to catch him off guard, so she didn't call ahead to warn him.

Danielle arrived at the change of address Registry of Motor Vehicles had for him at about three thirty. It was a very pretty and well-to-do street in Bedford, and the house itself was equally impressive. There was a BMW in the driveway.

Danielle was admiring the house and its pristine landscaping when she heard the door open. She turned to see Lucy Miller standing there with her baby in her arms.

Danielle remained outwardly calm, but to say that some quick thinking was required on her part, was an understatement. Danielle's neurons never fired so fast.

"Hello, Ms. Miller. I just wanted to let you know we've officially closed the case on the break-in at your clinic."

"You came out here to tell me that?" Lucy Miller looked at Danielle suspiciously.

And rightly so. But Danielle did not want Lucy Miller to be suspicious. She did not want her to be tipped off that she'd just become a murder suspect.

Danielle had to do some very quick thinking to come up with something—anything—to throw Lucy Miller off any such trail.

"Okay, you caught me. Truth is, I was wondering if you were single. I don't know if you're gay or not, but if you are—"

The come-on set Lucy Miller's eyes on fire. "I do *not* swing both ways, Officer!" Lucy said before slamming the door shut.

Danielle walked so fast to her vehicle her steps were in time with her racing heartbeats. As she drove out to the street and on to the Bedford highway, she was trying to decide if she'd just done something incredibly smart—or incredibly *stupid.*

Danielle's first instinct, when she saw Lucy Miller opening the door of Maurice Coultier's home, was to haul them both down to the police station and interview them separately, but she had learned some valuable lessons already. She heeded Sergeant Carvery's advice, and decided to think things through before she made any moves.

She pulled into a gas station parking lot and called Vital Statistics. In less than five minutes she learned Maurice Coultier and Lucy Miller had married last year on Valentine's day, and that they'd had a son six months later, in August. Danielle mulled this all over, then decided to call it a day in terms of the case. She'd be better off making decisions about what she'd just learned after a good night's sleep.

She looked at her agenda and glanced at the address of an apartment she'd made an appointment to view. Normally Danielle would have declined viewing a sublet, since those were normally student accommodations, but as soon as she noted the location of this particular apartment, Danielle was extremely eager to take a look at it. She really didn't care what the apartment looked like. She was more curious to find out if the landlord was aware it was being sublet—or if Nathalie had lied when she said there were no vacancies in her building.

The young man who advertised a flat for rent on Maynard Street introduced himself as Rob, was very friendly, and showed Danielle around the empty second floor unit of a large, three-level, shingled house.

"It's a large one-bedroom, and as you can see a fair-sized living room with open concept dining and kitchen. There's a front view of the street, and a back view of the yard. It has a beautiful maple tree and lots of shrubs and flowers—the owner loves flowers. She's out of town a lot, but a really good landlady—you'll like her."

"I've never sublet a place before," Danielle said truthfully. "How does it work? Does the landlady know you're subletting?"

"It would be pretty hard to keep it from her—she lives upstairs," Rob said with a smile as he pointed to the ceiling. "I have a lease till the end of July. That means you take over the end of my lease from now till then, then it's up to you if you want to renew or not. I have a sublet agreement here, if you think you want it. I only advertised this place yesterday. It'll probably be gone by tonight."

Danielle looked around the apartment with genuine interest. It really was a very nice apartment, and it was in a terrific location. She heard herself saying, "Absolutely. When's it available?"

"As you can see, it's empty and ready to be moved into right away."

"It certainly works for me. It's practically downtown, and it's bright with a nice yard. Do I give the cheques to you?"

"You don't pay me, pay Nathalie—the landlady."

"Do you know if she's home right now? I'm very interested in the apartment, and would like to give her my rent cheques right away if I could."

"I think she is. Oh, if you ever call or knock but get no answer, even when you know she's home, she's not ignoring you. When she's composing she wears earphones so her music won't bother anybody. She's very considerate like that."

Danielle followed Rob upstairs to the top-level apartment as he told her, "Two guys live on the first floor, and Nathalie's above you. But like I said, she's gone a lot. She's always got someone you can call if you have any problems though. Although I've never had a problem—this is a great place."

Rob knocked on the door.

"Just a minute!"

Rob turned to Danielle and said, "She loves animals too, so if you have a cat or a dog that'd be no problem."

Danielle knew she was very interested in seeing Nathalie's reaction, but her heart raced faster than expected when the door opened.

Barely a hint of recognition crossed Nathalie's face as she stood almost directly in front of Danielle. Danielle felt a mixture of disappointment and bewilderment as Nathalie focused her eyes on Rob only.

"Hi, Nathalie, this is Danielle Renaud. She's interested in subletting the apartment."

Nathalie looked through Danielle, instead of at her, even as she welcomed them in.

Rob didn't enter. "Actually, I need to get back. Can I just give the keys and sublet agreement to Miss Renaud, and you can work out the details?" Rob handed the keys and agreement to Danielle, and was halfway down the stairs before Nathalie could say anything.

Nathalie shut the door behind Danielle, then yanked the sublet agreement from her hand. "You don't have to take over Rob's lease. I'll rent it to you month-to-month." She fed it through a shredder under a small desk, then pointed to a black leather sofa and said, "Have a seat."

"I don't mind taking over Rob's lease," Danielle said.

"Nope, I'll not take no for an answer. I'm happy to rent it to you for as long as you want, but who knows where you'll want to live after the dust has settled." Nathalie looked nervously at her feet. "By the way, I just found out this morning that Rob decided to sublet." Nathalie glanced ever so briefly at Danielle, then very quickly away again, her eyes drifting to various areas of the room while she spoke. "He'd been posted for just a two-month course, so he was going to keep the apartment thinking he'd be back, but they decided to post him for two years instead. That's the military for you. Never know when you're going to be moved from one place to another. It took them no more than two hours to pack up his stuff and get it out of here this morning."

Danielle considered herself a very good judge of character, and could always rely on her instincts as to whether someone was lying or not, but as she watched Nathalie's body language and listened to her speak, she really couldn't tell if Nathalie was lying or telling the truth. Danielle wished Rob hadn't left. She would have definitely dropped in for a casual conversation and at least found out if the military did clear all of his things out just this morning.

But did it really matter? Even if Nathalie was lying, maybe it was only because she didn't want someone she'd just recently met on a personal basis, living below her. It's not like wanting your privacy was a crime. So why was Danielle so curious as to whether or not Nathalie had lied? Why was she so curious about Nathalie at all?

But she was. *Very.*

"I really don't mind taking over the lease, Nathalie. It's a great apartment, and the location couldn't be more perfect."

"You don't have to do that, Danielle. With the hospital just a ten-minute walk away, and the downtown core and universities so close by, a month's notice would be lots to rent it again. The only reason I rent it by yearly lease is because I prefer to have long term tenants who will treat the apartment like a home, not just a temporary stopping place. But for you I'll make an exception," Nathalie said as she smiled briefly at Danielle and tucked her hair behind her ears.

"Okay. Well, thank you." Danielle smiled back at Nathalie and looked at her closely, noticing small details in her face she hadn't noticed before. Nathalie had very round eyes, a small, cute nose, adorable dimples, and naturally cherry red lips. The light danced in her earrings—a beautiful purple crystal cut with so many angles, one could easily get lost in them. Without thinking, Danielle spoke her thoughts out loud. "You have perfectly shaped ears."

Nathalie laughed shyly, and Danielle was suddenly embarrassed, realizing how utterly dim-witted that sounded.

"Well you know, they do go into the plastic surgeon's office asking for ears just like mine," Nathalie said.

"They do?"

Nathalie broke into another laugh. "Of course not. I was just kidding."

Danielle's caramel skin reddened to a more coppery hue, the layers as deep as her embarrassment. "Sorry, I'm not usually this gullible. It's just been a very long day."

Nathalie turned serious. "I bet most of your days are very long in your line of work."

"Some days are better than others. How long have you owned this building?"

"Almost two years. Sold my old place, then bought this building and a cottage down the Valley—it's on the beach near Blomidon."

"Oh, I love that beach. It's my favorite one in Nova Scotia."

"Really? I love it too. That's why I bought it, so I could have a view of the beach and the cliffs while I composed."

Danielle looked around the room and saw a keyboard and three guitars resting in stands. "Do you write your songs on the piano or guitar?"

"Sometimes piano, sometimes guitar. I have a baby grand at the cottage, but I use an electric piano when I'm here."

"What was your inspiration for 'I'll Be Over You When I'm Six Feet Under'?"

Nathalie got up and walked to the window that faced the back yard. "Oh, that was just my attempt at country music, and the title 'My Wife Left Me, My Dog Died, and I'm Outta Whiskey' was taken." Nathalie attempted a chuckle, but there was clearly no humor in her voice. "What types of cases do you investigate?" Nathalie asked, as she peered out the window as if looking for something.

"I'm working on a cold homicide at the moment."

"What's a cold homicide?"

Did Nathalie really not know, or was she just playing dumb? Danielle really couldn't tell, so she answered the question sincerely. "It's an unsolved homicide investigation that has exhausted all its leads and is more than a year old."

"How do you go about investigating something like that?"

"You start from scratch, look at everything all over again. See if anything was missed, or look at what you have from a different perspective."

"Which murder are you investigating? Or can you tell me?" Nathalie was still looking out the window.

"It's not an undercover operation, so yes, I can tell you. It's the Kristina Buchanan case."

Nathalie did not comment. She opened a door to the left of the window that led to a balcony.

"There you are! It's about time." A longhaired, grey and tan cat meandered in. Nathalie picked it up and pointed the cat in Danielle's direction. "Chai, I want you to meet our new tenant. Her name is Danielle. Danielle, this is Chai."

Danielle walked over to the cat and petted its head. "Nice to meet you, Chai. And where did you get a name like that?"

"I named her after chai tea, because it's what the color of her fur reminded me of."

"Her fur is so soft. It doesn't even feel like fur, it's more like very soft hair."

"That's why I chose her. Even people who are allergic to cats can be around her and they won't react."

"A non-allergenic cat?"

"Yepper."

"I didn't think there were any non-allergenic breeds—unless they were hairless."

"Oh, she wasn't bred to be non-allergenic. Her breed's been around for centuries. They're just naturally non-allergenic."

"You know a lot about cats?"

Nathalie put the cat down and walked toward the kitchen. "A little. Would you like some tea?"

"Sure," Danielle replied.

When Nathalie entered the kitchen she asked Danielle, "This case you're working on, how do you go about investigating it? Do you do a media thing asking the public for new information?"

"That was done last fall, on the first anniversary of her death. Nothing new came of it though. How long have you lived in Halifax?" Danielle could see only glimpses of Nathalie through the archway that led to the small kitchen, but could hear her very well.

"Since I was fifteen. Guess that makes it about seventeen years."

"You're thirty-two?"

"Will be, next month."

Danielle walked across the living room and stood near the kitchen where she could see Nathalie more clearly. "You look much younger than that."

"Flattery is not required. You've already got the apartment."

"It's the truth."

"Speaking of truth, do the police really use lie detectors like they do on TV?"

"Polygraph tests are used, yes."

"Can someone be forced to take it?"

"No. But even if someone does willingly take a polygraph, it's not admissible in court, so we can't really rely on them as far as court is concerned."

"If they're not admissible, why are they used then?"

"It's a useful interviewing tool. It's also often used on convicted pedophiles who are up for parole to see if there's a risk of re-offending. It's also part of the entrance exam for becoming a police officer."

"You had to take a polygraph when you joined the RCMP?"

"I did."

"How was that?"

"Somewhat nerve-wracking. Even if you're an honest person who's never done anything wrong, it's intimidating to be strapped to an instrument and have your responses measured as you answer questions."

"I can see that. Do you take milk or sugar? I don't have any sugar actually, but I do have honey."

"Just milk, please."

Nathalie set Danielle's tea down in front of her, then sat with a black tea for herself. She looked at her tea as she spoke. "Do you have any suspects?"

"If I did, I wouldn't be able to tell you."

Nathalie's questions stopped and Danielle thought she looked quite pensive. Danielle wondered if it was the conversation they were having or if something else altogether was on Nathalie's mind.

"Did you know Kristina Buchanan?" Danielle asked.

Nathalie grabbed the handle of her mug and stared at her tea as she spoke. "No, I don't think so. What did she do for a living?" Nathalie brought the cup to her lips, tipped it, and appeared to take a drink, but didn't swallow.

"She was a nurse—worked at the hospital just over here." Danielle pointed in the direction of Summer Street. "She was a lesbian. Or at least she had been for the past few years of her life."

"Oh, one of those." Nathalie rolled her eyes.

Danielle found Nathalie's remark—and how she expressed it—amusing. "How long have you been out?"

"Officially? Since my early twenties, but I always knew. Not when I was a kid or anything, but by the time I was a teenager, I knew I had stronger feelings for girls than boys. What about you?"

Danielle thought about Véronique for the first time since arriving back in Halifax. Danielle wanted to tell Nathalie all about Véronique. She felt like pouring her heart out all of a sudden—something Danielle rarely did—but of course she didn't. "Pretty much the same for me."

There was an awkward silence after that. Danielle would have normally taken it as a cue to leave, but she didn't want to. "Dinner was fun last night," she said, to prolong the conversation.

"Yes, it was."

Danielle smiled at the memory. "Don't think I've ever enjoyed bananas so much."

Nathalie let out a soft giggle, and Danielle at that moment could picture her as a giddy four-year-old child.

"Melissa does have a chip on her shoulder, but I'm not scared to knock it off her once in a while." Nathalie smiled demurely as she said this, then her smile faded as she looked at a clock on the wall. "I can't believe it's after seven already."

Danielle whipped her head around to look at the clock, then checked her watch. "Oh my God." Danielle leapt to her feet. "I was supposed to meet Melissa ten minutes ago."

"Melissa? Lambert?"

"Yes, I saw her at the lab today and we made dinner plans. God, I don't even have time to shower or change." Danielle looked at Nathalie apologetically. "Sorry, I have to go."

As Danielle ran down the stairs, Nathalie walked to her front window. She watched Danielle exit onto the street and run to a grey Toyota Matrix. As the Toyota drove away, Nathalie closed her eyes and continued to watch Danielle from her mind…until Kristina Buchanan's face appeared. Then, with her eyes still closed and Kristina's face all she could see in her mind, Nathalie traced a large letter "S" over the glass with her fingertips.

❧ 25 ❧

Melissa looked pleased as punch—*not*—when Danielle plunked herself down across the small table at seven-twenty-five.

"I was starting to think you'd set me up," Melissa said seriously when Danielle arrived.

"I'm really sorry." Danielle considered telling Melissa where she was, but then thought better of it. "This job sometimes…"

"I didn't know if you were going to show up or not, and I was getting hungry, so I already ordered something for myself," Melissa informed Danielle. A waiter approached and Danielle ordered what she thought would be the fastest.

"How was your day?" Danielle crossed her arms and leaned forward, as though she were genuinely interested—even though she wasn't—and noticed Melissa was wearing makeup. Even her heavy, dark burgundy glasses did not mask her extra long, extra dark, lashes and eye shadow.

Her straight hair was perfectly bobbed just under her chin and each strand was exactly the same length. Though most of the strands were black, some were dark burgundy. Her lips were also deep burgundy, with a heavy, glossy lipstick. All in all, Danielle thought it was a youthful, funky look—and an attractive one—a contrast to Melissa's plain look at work.

Danielle wondered if she too looked plain during the day—and right now—since she had not had time to dress up or put on any makeup. All she had time to do was remove her ponytail and let her hair loose. Not that she would have put much of an effort into her appearance this evening. After all, it was only Melissa Lambert. Danielle had only asked her out to dinner to mend fences since she was a colleague of sorts.

"It was good. I like my job—it's always interesting. How about yours?"

"Hectic," Danielle replied. "It flew by."

"Are you making any progress on your case?"

"A little."

"Oh, yeah? Like what?"

"I can't talk about that."

"Hey, I'm on your team, remember?"

Danielle knew that despite confidentiality agreements, other members sometimes confided to spouses or close friends, but Danielle had never done this. Perhaps because she never felt close enough to anyone to trust them, or perhaps she was just used to keeping things to herself. Lilly was the closest confidante Danielle had, but Danielle still did not tell her many things. Perhaps she should start. Lilly was a Crown attorney, on her side of the law, and a good, trusted, personal friend.

"Sorry." Danielle pressed her lips together, zipped across them with her thumb and index finger, then pretended to throw away the key.

"Well, you're no fun."

"I'll have you know I am tons of fun."

"Oh, really. And *how* are you so much fun?"

"Oh, I can't tell you that sitting in a public place." Danielle said, then winked.

Is she flirting with me? Melissa felt her nipples harden for the second time today. She was definitely physically attracted to Danielle—who wouldn't be? She was gorgeous. But maybe too gorgeous. Melissa didn't trust overly attractive women.

"Nathalie told me you're just recently single?"

"Three days," Danielle confirmed.

"What? Only three days?" Melissa was concerned at first, but then realized this might actually be perfect. Not ready for a relationship, but in need of some "comforting", i.e., *sex*.

Melissa leaned in so close that her face was mere inches away from Danielle's. She stared at Danielle's lips as she said, "Getting back to that fun. I don't mind we're in a public place. Might be *fun* for us to go into the washroom together."

Did she just proposition me for sex in a bathroom? Danielle leaned back in her chair, as far back as she could, away from Melissa. "You and Nathalie are pretty good friends?"

Appearing to get the message loud and clear, Melissa leaned back in her chair as well. "We hang out. Go to Parrot's a lot, listen to the up-and-comers."

"What's Parrot's?" Danielle rarely went to bars even though she loved listening to live music.

"The Parrot's Prose on Gottingen. It's a great bar not far from Nathalie's place here in the city."

"Is it a gay bar?"

"No, it's a live music venue. But it's owned by a lesbian, and she often books acts of interest to lesbians, so a lot of us do go there."

Despite having ordered at separate times, their pizzas arrived at the same time. As Melissa took her first bite, Danielle asked her, "How well do you know Nathalie?"

Melissa furrowed her brow and asked, "Why do you ask?"

"Just making conversation. She seems stand-offish, but you seem to have a good rapport with her."

Melissa shrugged. "I guess. She's different, but I like her a lot. There's definitely a lot more to her than meets the eye."

"Like what?"

Melissa smiled. "Let's just say that your friend Lilly might be in for a treat."

Danielle dropped her slice of pizza. "What kind of treat?"

Melissa leaned forward again, and did a vocal impression of Kathleen Turner. "The kind that would make a mute scream her head off." Melissa quickly leaned back, then added in her regular voice, "Do I have to paint you a picture?"

Danielle's stomach knotted. She didn't know if she could speak, but there was something she wanted to know, so she forced herself to. "Do you think Nathalie and Lilly would make a good match?"

"Who cares if they would or not? As long as the sex is great— and with Nathalie, it definitely would be. All that passion she puts into her music? When she directs it as sexual energy..." Melissa then made sounds Danielle never wanted to hear coming out of *her*.

Several seconds passed before Danielle commented. "Sex isn't everything, Melissa. And just because sex is great with one person, it may not be with somebody else. Plus, a good relationship requires a lot more than sex. It requires deep love and strong support."

Melissa was on her last slice, but Danielle hadn't picked hers back up. Melissa bit down on the heel of her pizza slice and gave Danielle an "Are you for real?" type of look.

Danielle chose to ignore the look and asked, "Do you think Nathalie has feelings for Lilly?"

Melissa took her time chewing then swallowing her last bite of pizza before replying. "I have no idea if Nathalie has feelings for Lilly or not. She tends to keep her feelings to herself."

"But you know her quite well, and you're very smart. Just because she's never verbalized it, you must have some idea."

Melissa looked intently at Danielle, as if trying to figure out her motives, or trying to decide whether to respond or not. After some hesitation, she said, "Actually, I can't figure Nathalie out sometimes. She's got opportunities to hook up, but she turns them down all the time. Believe me, I've tried."

"What do you mean, you've tried?" Danielle was sitting on her hands now, and leaning forward.

"Even when we've left the bar really tipsy and I've crashed at her house, Nathalie would never give in. I asked her once how could she not be the slightest bit tempted and she said that sex without love made her feel too empty. I don't really get it, to be honest."

"Do you think she's romantically interested in Lilly?" Danielle asked the question again because Melissa hadn't answered it the first time.

Melissa tossed her napkin on the table, and glared at Danielle. "Why did you ask me out to dinner? All you've done since you've sat down is grill me about Nathalie and Lilly. The second I put the picture of them having sex together in your head, you stopped eating, and you haven't been able to swallow a bite since."

Danielle glanced at her half eaten pizza, then back at Melissa as Melissa continued to berate her.

"I don't know which one it is you've got the hots for, but do me a favor. Next time you want some inside information on whoever it is you're looking to lay, don't use me to get it."

Melissa stood up and picked up her jacket. She took two steps forward then turned back around to face Danielle. "And by the way, if I'd have known, I'd have ordered the lobster pizza and the eighty dollar bottle of wine. Cheque, please!" Melissa yelled at the waiter and pointed at Danielle's head before strutting out.

Danielle had told Lilly she would be late this evening because she had invited Melissa out to dinner to mend fences with her. She knew if she arrived back too early, Lilly would start asking questions as to why dinner had not only ended so early, but abruptly. Danielle wanted to avoid all that. She wanted to avoid having to explain why she was asking Melissa so many questions about Nathalie—and Lilly. Danielle therefore decided to spend an hour or two working on her case, and hopefully Lilly would be in bed by the time she arrived.

As Danielle began to drive away from the restaurant, something felt and sounded very wrong. She pulled over, got out, and checked her tires. One of the tires on the passenger-side was completely flat.

After changing the tire, Danielle drove up Gottingen Street until she saw the gay flag flying over a glassed door entrance. She parked, then entered the building. She was immediately met with a steep flight of stairs and quickly ran up them. She looked around, seeing all sorts of small rooms with chairs and sofas in them. She walked through a dark hallway that led to a dance floor and a bar. There were perhaps a dozen people milling about, and six people sitting at the bar.

Danielle sat on one of the bar stools and ordered a beer. When the bartender served her, she asked him how long he'd been working there.

"Four years," he said.

She pulled out a photo of Kristina Buchanan and asked if he had seen her there before. He turned on a lamp behind him and looked at it very closely.

"Can't say that I have. She might have come in once or twice, but she's definitely not a regular."

Danielle's cell phone rang. She said hello without checking to see who it was.

"Allo, Danielle?"

Danielle recognized Véronique's voice at the first syllable. She grabbed her beer and walked out of the bar area where she found an empty side room with chairs facing a fireplace. She shut the door and asked Véronique to repeat what she'd said.

"I wanted to tell you I had a great time Sunday night."

Danielle didn't comment.

"You wouldn't believe how hot it's been between me and David ever since. I told him every detail about what we did, and he got so turned on, we had the best sex ever. We were thinking of going to Halifax. Maybe the three of us—"

Danielle pressed the "end" button on her phone, then pushed a few more buttons. She put the phone back up to her ear and heard the tail end of a confirmation message. "Eight, seven, three…has been blocked."

Danielle left the room, walked across the bar area, and into another room where two men and a woman were playing pool. She sat down in a chair and watched them. As soon as their game was over, one of the men asked Danielle if she'd like to join them. Danielle hadn't played pool in a long time, but she joined in.

They introduced each other, made small talk, and Danielle nursed her beer, taking such small sips, hardly any passed her lips. They played two games and an hour passed before Danielle decided to sit out the next game. The other woman—Wendy she said her name was—decided to sit out as well and sat next to Danielle. While Danielle still nursed her first drink, Wendy was already on her third.

Wendy was an attractive woman. Not stunning, but attractive in her own right. Her cleavage was showing considerably more than it ought to, and Danielle could not help but notice—especially when the woman bent over the table attempting a shot. Which may be why the woman now inched closer to Danielle and touched her several times as they chatted.

"Are you a lesbian?" she asked Danielle.

"This is a gay bar, isn't it?"

"Lots of straight people go to gay bars with their friends sometimes."

"Are you straight?" Danielle asked her.

She looked at Danielle with obvious lust. "I'm *extremely* curious. I would love to experiment. Especially with a hot, sexy, lesbian." Wendy ran her finger along Danielle's chin, down her neck, toward her breast.

Danielle grabbed Wendy's hand, stopping it in its tracks. "I'm a lesbian—not a laboratory." Danielle stood up, dropped her beer off at the bar, and left.

❧ 26 ❧

Beulah Hunt sat across from her unscheduled eight a.m. appointment. Normally sessions were booked no earlier than nine, but sometimes a client was in acute need, usually because of some unexpected traumatic event or other triggers which resulted in a need for an unplanned but necessary session.

"You say your nightmares are back with a vengeance. What's happened to trigger that?" she asked her client.

"I don't know."

As frustrating as it could be, Beulah was accustomed to this all too frequent answer, but as a psychologist, it was her job to ease out what her clients did know—just weren't ready, willing, or able, to yet face. "Is it the same recurring nightmare?"

"Yes and no. There's an added element to them this time, but I still keep seeing her face."

"Whose face?"

When Beulah's client first came to her for grief counseling, Beulah thought it would be typical bereavement therapy. But after more than a year of biweekly sessions, it had turned into one of the most puzzling cases Beulah had ever had. Someone had died, but her client would not say who. Her client felt tormented by this death, but would not say why. So it was no surprise to Beulah that her client did not answer the question. She therefore decided to ask again in a different manner.

"We've been having sessions for well over a year now. Are you ready to tell me who died?"

Beulah's client was silent for a very long time. Sometimes half the sessions were just silence. At first Beulah would ask questions, trying to get her client to open up, but she now knew that allowing the silence was often necessary. Beulah knew if she pushed, that her client would shut down, maybe leave, and perhaps never come back again. So Beulah now allowed the silence, hoping that one sliver at a time, she could draw her client closer to the epicenter of her turmoil. It was agonizingly slow, but it was progress nonetheless.

Beulah's client stared eerily into space. "For over a week now, every time I close my eyes, I see her face again."

Beulah cautiously raised the question once more. "Can you tell me whose face it is?"

Once again Beulah's client didn't answer. She didn't answer anything else either, as she spoke not a single word for the remainder of the session.

In the early afternoon Danielle and Lilly were having lunch on Barrington Street, not far from Lilly's office.

"This seems like the longest week of my life."

"It's no wonder, Danielle. Look at everything you've gone through in just a week. Have you gotten in touch with Rachel yet?"

"No, I haven't had a chance. I wish I didn't have to contact her at all, but I'll have to. I'd like to get the rest of my things as soon as possible."

"So a sublet came up in Nathalie's building. How fluky is that?"

"Isn't it? What's up with you two by the way?"

"Nothing much is up. We haven't spoken since dinner the other night. I think she's pulling back."

"Are you still interested in her?"

"In one way, very much so, yes. But God, landing somebody shouldn't be this much work."

"You know what they say, Lilly. If it's meant to be, then it'll happen all by itself—no assembly required."

Lilly smiled in response, then complained, "You know, I think I've seen you less since you've been staying with me than when you lived with Rachel."

"I know. It's been crazy. How about next weekend you come over to my new apartment and I'll cook us dinner?"

"You? Cook? *Can* you cook?"

"Of course I can. Remember that delicious rum and butter sauce? I'm not just a crack investigator with a pretty face, you know."

"Might I remind you, you had help with that?" Lilly picked up her buzzing cell phone, looked at the display, then set it back down on the table. "Speaking of crack investigators, how's your case coming along?"

"Actually, I've been meaning to talk to you about something pertaining to that. I need some work-related advice."

"What about?"

Danielle related her encounters with Lucy Miller, then said, "I wanted to haul her and her husband down to the station and keep them there till one of them broke down and told me what they were up to, but I didn't want to jump the gun. I need to figure out a good plan before I start playing Maverick."

"Tell me everything you know so far." Lilly took a drink from her water glass.

"I looked at every supply order from the vet clinic she works at, and she's good. I mean, really, really, good. I looked it over three times before I caught it. For four months prior to Buchanan's murder Lucy Miller ordered an extra two, ten milliliter vials of ketamine each week. Problem is, those extra vials were never used.

"When you look at the inventory and the invoices everything adds up. Except—and here's where I caught it—when you calculate all of the surgeries, and how many injections, and the dosages logged during those surgeries, we're talking a discrepancy of twenty milliliters a week for sixteen weeks. And you know what else?"

Lilly licked her lips and swallowed. She took another drink of water. "What?"

"After Buchanan is killed, the discrepancies stop. No more extra ketamine orders."

"Maybe it's just a coincidence."

"I don't think it is. Regardless, what was she doing with the ketamine? Twenty mils of high concentration ketamine every week for sixteen weeks? If she turned that into powder, that's thirty-two grams, Lilly. *Grams!* She had to have been selling it, Lilly. In those four months she would have made at least fifteen thousand dollars. It's not a fortune, but it's a nice chunk of extra change for an inventory clerk."

Lilly leaned back and crossed her arms. "Don't take this the wrong way, Danielle, but what does this have to do with your murder investigation?"

"Are you seriously asking me that? Come on, Lilly. She's stealing ketamine, and ketamine just happens to be the drug that killed Buchanan, and she just happens to be married to the guy who was with Buchanan on the last night of her life."

"Coultier's got a solid alibi, right? If you know he didn't kill Buchanan why are you wasting your time on an avenue of investigation that's not viable?"

"Well, maybe *he* didn't do it, but maybe *she* did. Maybe she was selling it, or maybe she was stashing it away till she got enough to do Buchanan in. Either way, she was up to no good. It can't be just a coincidence, Lilly."

Lilly gripped her empty water glass. "Does *she* have an alibi?"

"I don't know. I haven't checked yet," Danielle sheepishly admitted.

"Danielle," Lilly released her hand from the glass and placed it on top of Danielle's. "Maybe this isn't the best time for you to be investigating something like this. You're going through a lot right now, and maybe you're seeing things you want to see instead of what's really there. Why don't you give me the paperwork you've got and let me take a look at it? It sounds like you could use an extra set of eyes and an objective opinion."

Danielle's eyes were fixed on Lilly's hand.

"Danielle?"

Danielle removed her hand from underneath Lilly's and took a sip of water. When she set her glass back down, she tucked her hands under her legs. "Yes, maybe you're right. I suppose it wouldn't hurt to show you the information and see what you think."

"I don't have court this afternoon. I could go with you now to pick it up, and I'll look it over first chance I get."

When Lilly returned to her office with all of the paperwork Danielle had received from the Victoria Veterinary Clinic, she looked it over then picked up the phone. When the person on the other end answered, Lilly said, "We have a problem—a serious one. Do you think you could make it to my office without being seen?"

"Why don't I just come to your house after it gets dark?"

"No. All we need now is to have Danielle seeing you at my house. She's staying with me right now."

"What?"

"I'll fill you in on that later—it's not important. What's important is we've got a major problem."

"What's the problem? Or should I be asking, how bad is it?"

"I'll explain it when I see you, but we're going to have to put our thinking caps on. Meet me in my office as soon as you can. I'll be here all afternoon."

"You're absolutely sure you want to risk my being seen talking to you?"

"Just wear a hat and sunglasses and keep your head down. All the security cameras are above eye level, so whatever you do, don't look up while you're anywhere inside the building."

Danielle was able to speak with Rachel by asking the receptionist if Rachel was free to talk with her, otherwise she would leave a detailed message. Danielle knew Rachel would not risk having staff gossiping about her personal life, and it worked.

When they spoke, they agreed Danielle would collect the remainder of her things on Saturday morning. She also negotiated with Rachel—if you could call it that—that Rachel would keep all of the furniture, and Danielle would take only her own personal possessions. Danielle was fine with that since she just wanted a clean break. But it meant buying new furniture, and she hated shopping.

Later in the afternoon Danielle was putting pieces of the Buchanan case together in her mind. Early evening on October fourth, Buchanan picked up her friend and ex-boyfriend, then brought them to her house. They all drank beer and smoked marijuana, and her guests left at nine-thirty in the evening. Then...someone she must have known, arrived later—and killed her.

It couldn't have been after she was in bed, as she was found wearing the same clothing she had on when her friends were there. According to the alarm company, she turned her alarm on at 9:37 p.m., then back off again at 10:33 p.m. and it remained off after that. So chances are, that's when whoever killed her arrived.

She willingly snorted a few lines of ketamine. *Did she know it was ketamine?* Then she ingested a larger dose of ketamine, but it was not slipped into anything she drank out of. *Unless...whatever she drank from was taken away by the killer?* The only fingerprints and DNA found belonged to people who had admitted to being there, and been checked out and cleared.

Where do I start, where do I start?

Danielle was at a loss. She felt stuck—and overwhelmed. Maybe she would fail after all. She had been so eager and excited at first, but now she was starting to feel like a rat trapped in a maze leading nowhere.

Danielle thought perhaps she just needed a break and some fresh air, so she went outside and walked around the parking lot for a few minutes. She thought as she walked, then got the idea to go back to square one: the scene of the crime. Although Kristina Buchanan had been killed at home, Danielle felt the location chosen to dump Buchanan's body was significant. She got in her vehicle and headed for the park.

❧ 27 ❧

If Danielle hadn't used her GPS, she doubted she would have found the entrance to Hemlock Ravine Park. It was not marked, and she doubted the accuracy of the GPS as she drove up Kent Avenue until it ended at a very steep, downhill driveway that led to the park's entrance.

The sign at the beginning of the footpath welcomed her to the entrance of Julie's Pond and gave a brief history of it. Danielle walked less than a minute before arriving at the now infamous heart-shaped pond where Prince Edward once declared his love for his French mistress, Julie St. Laurent, where love-struck couples got engaged, and where Kristina Ann Buchanan was found lifeless—with her face desecrated.

The area surrounding the pond was surprisingly vacant. The few benches that surrounded it were empty, and there wasn't anyone on the trails.

Maybe it's still too early in the season, Danielle thought. It was mid-April, and though the hot sun was warming up the soil, the cool wind that prevailed still had a wintry bite to it.

The entrance led to the top right side of the heart, where Buchanan's body was found. The left top was inaccessible—unless you were a duck or other small animal. The bottom of the heart pointed to the rest of the park, which from the map seemed to go on for quite a distance before reaching residential streets and the highway.

The pond did not appear to be very deep. She recalled it had been measured at two feet in some places, three to four feet in others. She walked toward the pebbled concrete that lined the pond. Obviously, the concrete was more modern, and probably put in place shortly after the city took possession of the park.

Danielle walked around the left side of the heart-shaped pond, and peered up at a vertical rock face that shot so far up it reminded Danielle of a mountain. Very few people knew it, but Danielle was afraid of heights. She hadn't been, but after her family was killed she started having nightmares of them, and cars, and hockey sticks—and her—flying off a tall, steep mountain…to death. Since then she avoided mountain top views or sitting at the window seat of an airplane.

Danielle's thoughts shifted to her mother, father, and brother. She felt compelled to touch the rock, to press her cheek against it and feel their beating hearts. Did their souls now live within that rock—and the sea and sky? Or were they actually in "heaven"? Or…did they simply no longer exist, except in her memories?

Danielle had to maneuver around a large mound of debris to get to the exposed rock that was drawing her. It wasn't easy to walk through, but she eventually made her way, and pressed her cheek and hands against the rock. It was cold. So very cold. Danielle shivered. She hoped her parents and brother were not any part of that rock at all. Danielle turned her back to it and closed her eyes.

A minute later Danielle opened her eyes and started moving some debris with her foot. She did this mindlessly as thoughts—perhaps not even thoughts, just feelings surrounding the loss of her family—swept through her.

Then, Danielle's brain went into investigative mode again, when she noticed the debris she'd been kicking at was not a random collection after all, but that the twigs and branches were woven together. Danielle lowered herself to the ground and took a closer look. She got back up and looked at the top of the debris. She could see through some of it, and viewed what appeared to be black plastic hanging from the inside.

She lowered herself back down, then crawled in. Once inside, she was amazed at what she saw. It was a very roomy den. Danielle pulled out a small penlight. She took a quick look around, then quickly exited the den. She ran to her vehicle and pulled out her evidence kit. She retrieved a larger flashlight, a pair of latex gloves, large tweezers, a professional digital camera, a permanent marker, and some clear evidence bags.

When Danielle returned to the den first thing she did was take photographs. After photographs were taken, she picked up a rusted, closed, tin box and tried to open it. She struggled with it at first, as it was almost rusted shut, but she did manage to get it open. Inside were a large number of cigarette butts and a half spent package of matches. She closed back the tin, and put it in an evidence bag.

She also collected a very thin, very moldy, ragged blanket, and removed all of the black plastic and any duct tape she could find. An empty rum bottle was the last item she placed in an evidence bag.

Danielle didn't go directly to the crime lab when she left the park, but to her office instead. There was something she needed to check first as she did not want to be wasting her or the crime lab's time.

She logged on to the computer and searched for photos taken at the pond the morning Buchanan's body was discovered. Most were close ups, which were useless, but she soon found what she was looking for. In the background, the engineered den of debris was indeed there the day Kristina Buchanan's body was discovered.

Danielle picked up the phone and called the crime lab. She was relieved when she learned that the Latent Prints section was on the second floor, not the first, where Melissa Lambert worked. Then she realized she would also have to submit a request to the DNA lab if she wanted the blanket tested for any blood or bodily fluids.

I don't have to see Melissa to submit a request though, Danielle reminded herself.

Danielle then went to the crime lab and submitted two requests: one to Melissa's section to check the blanket for any DNA, and the other to Latent Prints to see if they could lift any prints from the black plastic, duct tape, or items in the tin box. She considered asking for DNA to be taken from the cigarette butts, but knew how expensive that would be. And since the butts were more than likely scavenged from the park, it would probably be of no use anyway. She thought she'd await the results of the blanket before deciding if that would be necessary.

Melissa Lambert was walking around the parking lot smoking a cigarette during her afternoon break when she recognized the vehicle she had flattened a tire of the night before.

Melissa wished she had her keys on her. She would have liked to have taken a walk alongside Danielle's vehicle and scraped the side of it. But then again, that would be too obvious—and too risky. She worked for the RCMP now. No doubt there were cameras covering the parking lot. Plus, Melissa would never allow her emotions to cause such impulse. After all, she hadn't gotten away with what she had so far by being careless. As much as she would have enjoyed taking her keys to the side of Danielle's car, that would only be an appetizer. Melissa was quite willing to bide her time and wait for the main course. Danielle would get what was coming to her, just as that snitch had.

She threw her cigarette down, then walked around the building so she could enter from the back entrance. Danielle was walking out the front door when Melissa poked her head out toward reception. When Danielle was completely out of the building, Melissa walked over to the clerk who was in charge of evidence logging.

"What did Clit Eastwood want?"

"Pardon?"

"Constable Renaud. What did she want?"

"One for you, and several for Eric."

"Which one's for me?"

"Looks like some sort of blanket—or what used to be a blanket."

"Might as well take it while I'm here. You finished logging it?"

"Yep."

Melissa took the paperwork and evidence bag containing the blanket then returned to the lab. Went she got there, she unlocked the door of a rarely used cabinet, tossed the paperwork inside, and relocked it again. Even her eyebrows were smiling when she then tossed the blanket into an incinerator.

๑ 28 ๏

Lillian Marsh greeted her guest at the elevator so they would not have to introduce themselves at reception. It was clear they were together, as Lilly walked past reception and into her office. Lilly sat down at her desk, not attempting to mask her worried look.

"Danielle's figured it out," Lilly informed her guest.

"But you have everything, right? She gave you all the paperwork?"

"Yes, it's right here." Lilly picked up several sheets of paper off her desk and dropped them back down.

"Couldn't you just lose it?"

"She'd only go back and get copies. I knew she was a dedicated officer and could be tenacious, but I never expected her to get this far. Honestly."

"Any chance you can get her off the case?"

"Doubt it. I'm the one who called in favors to have her recommended in the first place, remember? I thought it would be safer for us, that I could keep an eye on the investigation in case it headed your way. But she got there so fast, I didn't even get a chance to steer her in another direction."

"What do we do now?"

"We need to stop her is what we need to do. But that's easier said than done."

"If we can't lose the paperwork, can the paperwork lose her?"

"Even I can't follow that, Lu."

"What if you give her back the paperwork, but it doesn't show what she thought it did?"

Lilly's pupils expanded and a smile ensued. "You're brilliant, Lu."

"Indeed I am. Except I can't be burning the midnight oil doctoring paperwork. I have an infant child needing midnight feedings, as you know."

"Don't worry, I'll have it finished before midnight tonight."

Danielle barely made it back in time to meet Caroline Corkum. The woman—tall, thin, with sun-damaged skin already in April—seemed ill at ease.

"My fiancé doesn't know, and I don't want him to," Caroline said even before sitting down in the interview room.

"Your fiancé doesn't know what?"

"About me and Kristina."

It was apparent to Danielle that Caroline was uncomfortable discussing her prior sexual relationship with Kristina Buchanan, but after reading the statements of Kristina's friends, family and coworkers, Danielle knew it was not unknown to them, it was simply never openly discussed. Danielle wondered if Caroline knew their relationship had been an open secret.

"I understand, Caroline. I will respect your privacy, but I need some information from you."

"What do you want to know?"

"I need to know about Kristina's drug use."

"Kristina didn't do drugs around me."

"But you knew she was doing them."

"I knew, yes. She'd go out on the balcony for a cigarette—she used to smoke then—I could tell she'd been smoking grass instead of cigarettes when she came back in."

"Did she keep it hidden from you during your entire relationship?"

"She tried her best to. Then after we split up, she didn't care anymore. If she felt like smoking a joint in front of me, she did. But I always left when she did."

"Why is that?"

"I didn't like her personality when she was high."

"What was it like??"

"Nasty."

"Could you tell me exactly what you mean by nasty?"

Caroline brushed the bangs from her face. "Kristina had some really wonderful points, but when she'd get high, she'd get this mean streak in her. She would get defiant and really cocky. You could tell she was picking for a fight, you could see it in her eyes. It's like she had to hurt somebody on purpose. When she was like that, I didn't want to be around her."

"Do you know if she was buying or selling drugs of any kind?"

"Honestly, I don't know anything else other than what I've already told you. What drugs she did and how often I couldn't tell you. She knew I didn't approve, so she kept that part of her life hidden from me."

"But you said after she moved out, she didn't seem to care, that she did it in front of you."

"There were just some days, if I was at her house, and if she was angry with me. She just did it because she knew it disgusted me. I really don't know how to explain this, but if Kristina knew there was something you hated, or you were afraid of…when she'd get into that mean streak, it's the first thing she'd do to you."

Danielle felt Caroline Corkum had nothing new to provide as far as Buchanan's drug use was concerned, so she moved on to another line of questioning.

"Can you think of anyone who might have wanted to hurt Kristina? Not just want her dead, but hurt her?"

"I can't think of anybody who would have wanted her dead. Nobody that I know of, at least. But hurt her, maybe. A few people didn't think very highly of her."

"And who would that be?"

"One woman in particular springs to mind. Kristina called her Dee. I don't know her last name, and I'm assuming Dee was just a nickname. Apparently they were…involved. And Kristina being who she was, I think she ended up hurting Dee a lot."

"What makes you think that?"

"Kristina and I had gone to a movie a few months before she died. We went to the washroom after the movie finished, and when I came out of the stall, Kristina was standing next to this woman. I didn't know it at the time, but it was this Dee. I don't know what Kristina said to her, but I heard her say to Kristina, 'Get out of my sight.' And she said it in the most…I don't know if I can even describe it. She didn't yell it or say it loud even, but she said it really slow like…she was seething."

"How did Kristina react?"

"She spun around and left the washroom in a hurry. And believe me, you didn't see Kristina react like that very often. I was washing my hands when I heard Dee's friend ask her what that was all about. I'll never forget what Dee answered. She said, 'That was just a beast that tries to pass itself off as a human being.'"

Danielle wrote the harsh statement down in her notebook then asked, "What did Kristina say about it?"

"She didn't want to talk about it. She did tell me it was Dee when I asked her who it was, but that's all."

"What did Dee look like?"

"About the same height as Kristina, so maybe five-one or five-two. Short, curly brown hair."

"Dark, medium or light?"

"Dark I think. No—medium. Or maybe it was dark brown with lighter highlights in it, I don't remember exactly."

"What about her eyes?"

"Sorry, I didn't really notice them much either, but I'm thinking brown too." As Danielle wrote this down, Caroline revised her answer. "Actually, Kristina mentioned once how Dee's eyes looked brown from a distance but that they were actually green. It was one of those times when she wanted to let something slip on purpose. She said she only noticed after they were lying in bed together." Caroline turned her face away, opened her purse and pulled out a tissue, which she dabbed at her eyes with.

"Is there anyone else you can think of who might have wanted to hurt Kristina or get back at her for something?"

"I know there was no love lost between her and Maurice's brother, but he wouldn't have killed Kristina."

"Are you talking about Joe Coultier?"

"Yes."

"Why do you say there was no love lost between them?"

"Just things Kristina would say. I think she felt the reason Maurice would never marry her is because his brother didn't like her."

"Kristina wanted to marry Maurice and he wouldn't?" Danielle was quite surprised by this piece of information, considering everyone else said Maurice was in love with Kristina and wanting to get back together with her.

"She did at the time, when they were together. She had wanted to get married, but he wouldn't. Maybe deep down he knew she would never be faithful." Caroline pressed the tissue she was holding back up to her eye. "She and I were together when same-sex marriage became legal. I wasn't surprised when she asked me to marry her too. I remember wondering who'd be the next person she'd ask." Caroline licked her dry lips. "If she hadn't died, I'm sure she would have found someone to say yes…eventually."

Danielle was aware Maurice and Kristina had broken up because Kristina and Caroline had started having an affair. According to friends and coworkers, Kristina claimed to have left Maurice before she and Caroline became involved, but no one believed it. For over a year, while Kristina lived with Maurice, she and Caroline spent most of their free time together, and shortly after Kristina moved out of the apartment she shared with Maurice, she moved in with Caroline.

It was also clear to Danielle that Caroline now considered this period of her life as a phase she was now embarrassed about. It seems Caroline had only been with men prior to her relationship with Kristina, and had only been with men ever since.

"Was Kristina bisexual?" Danielle asked.

"After she left Maurice she called herself a lesbian, but…I think she was capable of sleeping with either." Caroline ran her finger along her eyebrow. "Whenever it suited."

"Whenever she wanted something from someone?" Danielle did not think this was an inappropriate question based on what she had learned about Kristina Buchanan so far, but nonetheless Danielle was relieved when Caroline Corkum was not offended.

"Pretty much," Caroline admitted.

"Do you know why Maurice's brother didn't like Kristina?"

"He probably felt Kristina was just using him."

Danielle would have asked why, but after speaking with Gillian and reading many other statements, Danielle already knew why anyone would come to that conclusion. Danielle dropped her pen and leaned forward.

"Caroline, I think whoever killed Kristina did it for very personal reasons. And by that I mean, I think she did something to somebody that angered them so much that they not only wanted to get rid of her but to also send a message. Either to her…" Danielle thought about the fact that the letter "S" was carved after Kristina was dead, so the message had to be for someone else. "Or to someone both of them knew. I really think whoever killed her was driven to do what they did to her by something she did to them, or to someone they loved. Is there anyone else you can think of that Kristina might have hurt or done something to?"

"If she did anything to anybody who was involved in drugs or anything like that, I wouldn't know who they are. Like I told you, I never approved, so it's not something she shared with me. I know she hurt some people she dated, but I doubt very much—"

"No matter how unlikely you think they may have killed Kristina, just anybody who might have had a bad experience with her."

Caroline thought for a moment, then said, "Kristina used to boast about this woman who had fallen in love with her and moved to Vancouver because it hurt her too much to stay around here." Caroline then added, "But they reconnected after Kristina and I—

after she moved into her own place. I guess Kristina got in touch with her, and they renewed their friendship."

"Do you know her name?"

"Erin Walker. Kristina was planning to visit her before she died. There should be an address for her in Kristina's address book, if the police still have it. Her mother told me they took a lot of her things and never returned them."

Danielle felt she had to defend that, so she said to Caroline, "Yes, I'm sorry about that. It's never easy when we have an investigation that…is more complicated. Not knowing what will end up as evidence, we have to keep everything until we know what we'll need, and what we can release back to the family."

Danielle wrote herself a note to check Erin Walker's whereabouts the night Kristina died, and to investigate a possible drug connection, since British Columbia was a source for some of the most potent marijuana in the world.

"Is there anything else? I really need to get home."

"Just one last thing. I was wondering if you could take some time—when you get home is fine, and you can take a couple of days if you need to—but I need you to write down the names of all the people Kristina dated and any information you might know about them."

Caroline's neck craned forward. "*All* the people she dated?"

Danielle got the impression it was an insurmountable task for Caroline. "How about just the past two years of her life, then? Would that be easier?"

Caroline nodded.

After Caroline left, Danielle spent some time reviewing the notes she'd taken during their interview. In addition to checking out Erin Walker's alibi, and any possible drug connection between her and Kristina, Danielle now had one other strong lead to pursue: locating Dee.

❧ 29 ❧

Rather than going to Lilly's straight after work, Danielle went to her new apartment to measure the windows. She had her tape stretched across one of the front windows facing the street when she heard a knock on the door. When she opened it, Nathalie was standing there.

"Hi. Saw you through the front window when I was coming in. How are you doing? You need anything?"

"You mean, other than curtains, a sofa, bed, blankets, dishes…"

Nathalie laughed. "Yes, it does look mighty empty at the moment."

"I'll be getting my things from the condo on Saturday, but I don't have any furniture. I still have to buy it." Danielle groaned. "I hate shopping. I was hoping Lilly could join me but she's working late tonight."

"I'll go with you if you want."

"Really?" Danielle's look of surprise was then cast off by a smile and twinkling, blue eyes. "That would be great!"

Instead of smiling back, Nathalie diverted her eyes from Danielle's face, and focused on the measuring tape. "I already know all the measurements, so you can put the tape away. I just need a minute to check on Chai and give her fresh water."

Before Danielle could thank her, Nathalie was sprinting up the stairs.

Danielle had finished a round of speed shopping in which she had purchased a bed, bedside tables, and bedroom lamps. She discovered Nathalie had simple tastes just as she did—except Nathalie's was much more colorful and vibrant—and that Nathalie was great company. She found humor in everything, was very pragmatic and financially conscious, and surprisingly had a head full of information regarding consumer reports on almost every item imaginable. Danielle was very impressed, and was pleased Nathalie had joined her.

Danielle suggested they have dinner before she tackled buying the remainder of her furniture.

"I like how you shop," Nathalie said as they shared a seafood pizza.

"I like how you know your consumer goods. I had no idea you were so well informed."

"After six years of—" Nathalie abruptly stopped in mid-sentence as though she just remembered something, then said something else. "I just hate shopping so much, I prefer to know exactly what I'm going for so I don't have to spend much time in the stores."

"Same here. I don't like shopping either."

"My motto for shopping is, 'when in doubt, do without.'"

Danielle was again impressed by Nathalie's humor and laughed heartily in response.

"So…the furniture you bought tonight will be delivered Saturday afternoon, and you said you were getting the rest of your things from your old place Saturday morning?"

"Yes. Guess that means I'll no longer be homeless by Saturday." Danielle smiled and raised her glass.

Nathalie smiled briefly before turning serious. "Danielle, Melissa phoned me today. She mentioned you might be interested in Lilly. I just want to say that I'm not—if you have romantic feelings for Lilly—"

"I don't have feelings for Lilly," Danielle cut Nathalie off to say. "Not those types of feelings. Melissa may have misinterpreted my…" Danielle didn't want to say, "…questions about you and Lilly", so she fudged. "…positive comments about Lilly, for interest. But Lilly is just a close friend, nothing more." Danielle pointed to a scar on Nathalie's hand. "How'd you get that?"

Nathalie ran a finger along the scar. She looked a million miles away. "Um…I really don't remember. Playing Batman and Robin maybe?" She attempted a smile but it didn't mask the sadness behind it.

Danielle thought she'd struck a painful nerve. She smiled warmly at Nathalie, attempting to lighten the mood. "You mean, you're not the singing siren by day and Wonder Woman by night, dodging bullets with your gold bracelets?"

"Singing siren? I don't sing, I just write and compose. Believe me, if I was a mermaid trying to lure love with a song, I'd be living a very lonely life. I'm a terrible singer."

"I find that hard to believe. It would be like a boat builder saying they didn't know how to sail."

"I keep forgetting you're a cop," Nathalie said. Her hand was under her chin now as she stared sideways at the wall.

"Are you from Halifax?" Danielle asked.

Nathalie put both hands under her chin and looked down at her plate. "Not originally."

Danielle expected Nathalie to tell her where she grew up, but she didn't. So Danielle asked her. "Where are you from?"

Nathalie slowly finished chewing her food, then took a drink of water. Just when Danielle thought she wasn't going to answer, Nathalie said, "I grew up in Cape Breton, but I moved here when I was a teenager, so it's home to me."

"You know, I've never been to Cape Breton. I hear it's beautiful."

"Yes, it is..." Nathalie looked at the wall again.

"You didn't like it there?"

"I have very mixed feelings about it."

"I can understand that. I'm from a rural area myself. It's got its good and bad points. Did your parents move here for work?"

"No."

"Do you have any family in Halifax?" Danielle asked.

"No, I don't." Nathalie did not elaborate, and Danielle got the impression she had ventured into sensitive territory. Nathalie turned her face away again, and stared at a painting on the wall as she slowly resumed eating.

Danielle suddenly feared what others had often assumed about her, that her family was alive and well, when in fact they were deceased. Danielle was about to ask Nathalie about her family, but instead surprised even herself by blurting out, "My family was killed when I was thirteen."

Nathalie stopped chewing in mid-bite.

Danielle was shocked at herself, that she revealed what she just did.

"What happened?" Nathalie looked directly into Danielle's eyes with a deep empathic look in hers. Danielle felt such an intensity from them—until Nathalie abruptly looked away.

"They were coming home from a hockey game, my parents and my brother. A pulp truck came around the turn on the wrong side...

"The impact sent my parents' car over the guard rail, down the mountain. They found empty beer bottles inside the pulp truck. He survived of course, and he was charged with drinking and driving, but...that was no consolation."

Nathalie bit her bottom lip and her face was overcome with sorrow. Both of them were silent for a few moments, then Nathalie quietly asked, "Do you have any other siblings?"

"No, I just had Armand—my brother. He was fourteen." Danielle noticed tears forming in Nathalie's eyes.

"I have to go to the washroom," Nathalie told Danielle as she stood up, then walked briskly away from the table while keeping her head down.

Several minutes later, Nathalie sat down with red eyes, but was acting chipper. "Ready for shopping spree number two?"

Danielle felt she probably shouldn't say what she was about to, but since she really meant it, she felt compelled to. She had only intended to speak, but as she did, she saw her own hand cross the table and place itself on top of Nathalie's. "I didn't mean to upset you."

Danielle fully expected Nathalie to pull her hand away or to make a joke, but she didn't. She surprised her by turning her hand over, taking hold of Danielle's, and squeezing hard.

When Danielle and Nathalie returned to Danielle's apartment, it was dark and the light switch didn't work.

"Did you remember to call the power company to get your power hooked up?" Nathalie left the door open so the stairwell light could cast some light inside the apartment.

"Yes, they're supposed to do it tomorrow. Phone too. They said they didn't need anyone to be home." After Danielle set down some of the smaller things she had purchased and was able to carry, she turned to Nathalie and gave her a hug. "Thanks for all your help, Nathalie."

Nathalie didn't react, but she didn't move away either, so Danielle didn't break her hug. Then…Nathalie raised her arms up and surrounded Danielle's back with them as she pressed her face against Danielle's shoulder. Danielle loosened her grip just so she could lower herself to meet Nathalie's lesser height, and hugged Nathalie so that each other's chins now rested on each other's shoulders. No one said a word, and no one moved for a long time. They just stood there wrapped around each other, and no one spoke for fear of acknowledging that they were not just hugging…but holding each other.

30

"She what?" Lilly was evidently surprised.

"She propositioned me for sex in the bathroom," Danielle reiterated. "I can't believe I forgot to tell you."

Lilly grinned wide and poked Danielle. "Why didn't you go for it?"

"You're kidding me, right?"

"No, I'm deadly serious. She's pretty good looking, and it's spontaneous. The sex might have been sizzling."

"No, thank you."

"What—spontaneity isn't your style?" Lilly poured Danielle a small glass of wine.

"There's a difference between spontaneity and lewdness, Lilly. It was a restaurant, not a cabin on a lake. Not to mention, it was Melissa Lambert."

"What's wrong with Melissa Lambert? She's attractive, and smart—"

"And psycho, if you ask me."

"*Psycho?* Where does that come from? She's a friend of Nathalie's, and she works for the RCMP."

"I don't care who she works for or who she's friends with. There's something not right about that woman. My spidey senses tingle every time she's near."

"That's called sexual arousal, Danielle." Lilly laughed, then teased Danielle. "I know it's been a while for you, but…"

"Ha, ha. Good one. But I'm not dead in that department, I'll have you know."

"Oh, really? So if it isn't Melissa Lambert who's making you tingle, who is it?"

Danielle could still feel Nathalie's arms around her, could still feel her breasts pressed against hers, and how while they held each other, Danielle's hands did not physically move, but in her mind, had slipped under Nathalie's shirt and touched her bare skin…

Danielle wanted to tell Lilly this but she couldn't.

"Did you get a chance to read over the material I gave you?" Danielle very much wanted to change the subject, and did.

"Yes, I did." Lilly got up and retrieved some papers from her briefcase. "I hate to break it to you, but you must have mixed up some calculations—or just been too tired to see the numbers properly. Everything's accounted for. The surgery logs match the inventory exactly."

"What?" Danielle grabbed the paperwork and looked it over. She was floored. "I can't believe this."

"You're tired, Danielle. You're sleeping in a strange bed, and you're dealing with a stressful breakup. It's not surprising you're seeing things that aren't really there."

Danielle kept staring at the sheets of paper she was holding.

"Danielle, I've looked them over very carefully. There's no mistake. In the morning, you can go over every single calculation again for yourself."

"But I could have sworn…"

"I know. But that's why it's important to have another set of eyes sometimes. Especially when you're tired. And speaking of which, we both need sleep."

८०C3

Danielle was swimming in a chalice of chai tea. The tea was not warm and soothing, but cold and stale. She looked for the mermaid but could not find her.

"Fifty laps around the chalice," the voice commanded.

Danielle cried tears of remorse as she did her penance.

First thing Danielle did Friday morning after she got to work was go over the figures from the paperwork Lilly returned to her. Lilly was right. It *did* add up. Danielle felt somewhat deflated by this, but she refused to let it get her down. She picked up the phone and called Gillian Stevens. When she answered, Danielle made arrangements to meet with her again in the afternoon.

Danielle then went to the train station where Maurice Coultier worked. He was nothing like she expected. He was short, balding, and Gillian's description of wishy-washy was kind. All he had going for him were nice eyes. The rest of him was…well, quite effeminate. He wore a mechanic's jumpsuit covered in grease, but the man looked barely strong enough to wield a hammer, let alone a sledge.

In the eye of the beholder, Danielle thought to herself.

At Maurice's request, they sat in a small, private office with the door closed.

"Are trains a lot more complicated than cars to maintain?" Danielle tried some casual conversation to put Maurice at ease, as he seemed jittery.

"A lot easier in some ways. Just takes a lot more crawling underneath."

"Ah," Danielle said as she nodded. Maurice wasn't aware Danielle was nodding in response to how his smaller size would be an asset in that case. "I don't want to keep you from your work very long, Mr. Coultier, I just have a few quick questions."

"I don't have anything more to tell you than I told the police already."

"There are a couple of things I need to ask you that the previous investigators didn't."

"Like what?"

"My first question is regarding your brother."

"My brother?" Maurice rubbed his moustache.

"It seems your brother didn't like Kristina very much."

"He liked her."

"That's not what I've been told."

"Joe's always been protective of me. I'm his younger brother. It's not that he didn't like her, he just didn't think anybody was good enough for me."

"How does he feel about your wife?"

"He likes her."

"Why does he like her then, when he didn't like Kristina?"

"I don't know what you're getting at."

"Kristina didn't treat you very well, did she?"

"I didn't kill her."

"Why did you only marry Lucy after Kristina was killed?"

Maurice shoved his hands in his pockets. "I married Lucy because I love her."

"But you were *in love* with Kristina, and you were hoping you and she would get back together."

Maurice flashed some unexpected anger. "Well, we couldn't after she was dead, eh?"

"Do you know where Lucy was the night Kristina was killed?"

"Don't be so foolish!"

Maurice's reaction had Danielle convinced he didn't believe for a second Lucy killed Kristina. But Danielle wasn't about to put her faith in a man who had a history of being blinded by women.

Maurice may not have taken the question seriously, but Danielle most certainly did. "Do you, or do you not, know where Lucy was that night?"

"Look, I've got nothing more to say than I told the cops already." Maurice stood up.

"Sit down, Mr. Coultier." Danielle always had a more authoritative attitude when she carried her badge and gun, but she was even more authoritative as she stood up and towered above the man before her. "We can finish this conversation here in a matter of minutes, or I can take you to the station and keep you there for twenty-four hours."

Maurice sat down and shoved his tongue in his cheek.

Danielle was okay with dropping the subject of Lucy, since she'd already concluded Lucy was a definite suspect without an alibi—unless of course, she could provide one for herself—but she had more questions for Maurice at the moment. "According to Kristina's phone records, you called her from your cell phone about ten minutes after you arrived at Gillian's apartment. What did you talk about?"

Maurice's eyes froze in place.

"Do you remember talking to her that night?"

Maurice paused, then replied, "Yeah. I guess I just wanted to let her know we made it there okay."

"You guess? Do you *remember* talking to her?" Danielle repeated, and emphasized.

"Yeah. Like I said, I just wanted to let her know we got to Gillian's okay, so I gave her a quick call."

"How was she?"

"What do you mean, how was she?"

"Was she still angry with you or was she calmed down?"

Maurice started pulling on his moustache again. "Look, I really need to get back to work. I have to get the train serviced before it leaves for Montreal."

"The faster you answer my questions, the faster you can get back to work, Mr. Coultier."

"She was fine. I just said we were there, and then I hung up."

"Okay, Mr. Coultier. I'll be in touch if I have any more questions. In the meantime, if you remember anything else, please give me a call." Danielle handed Maurice Coultier her business card—which he promptly tore up and tossed in the garbage.

When Danielle got back to the office, she put in a request for electronic surveillance. Her gut told her Maurice Coultier and Lucy Miller were hiding something, and she was determined to find out what it was. She had the authority to do the visual surveillance on her own—watching from a distance and taking pictures, video, and notes—but what she really wanted was wiretaps, and that required authorization.

"I'm glad you didn't cancel our regular appointment," Beulah Hunt told her client as she placed a glass of water and tissues next to her. "How have you been?"

"Tired. The nightmares are every night again."

Beulah was sure the nightmares stemmed from some unresolved issues regarding the person who died. "Are you ready to tell me who died?"

Instead of answering, Beulah's client stood up from her chair and walked over to the window. The blinds were closed, but she looked at them, as though looking at the view. She had always requested the blinds be closed when they had a session, and Beulah had always obliged this request.

Until today.

Normally Beulah would never confront a client with such a tactic, but this had gone on for far too long. Without warning, Beulah opened the slats and light streamed in. To Beulah's surprise, her client did not budge. So Beulah did the unthinkable, and raised the blind completely open, leaving a huge square hole that invited the world—and whatever else was out that window—to stare her client in the face.

"What can't you face out this window?" Beulah asked.

Her client's focus traveled to her feet.

"I can't help you if you don't tell me what you see when you look out that window," Beulah urged.

Beulah's client wouldn't look out the window, but she said, "Seeing a maple tree close to a window like that, brings it all back."

"Brings what back?"

"The image…that's burnt into the back of my eyes and brain."

Beulah stood quietly, waiting for her client to reveal what that image was. After a full minute of silence, Beulah gently prodded, "What image do you see?"

Her client closed her eyes and said, "A dead face with black eyes."

After a quick lunch, Danielle met with Gillian Stevens again.

"I don't have that list finished yet," Gillian told Danielle.

"That's okay, that's not why I'm here. I'm here to ask you about a woman named Dee."

"Dee? What do you want to know?"

"Anything and everything."

"I don't know much. Just that she's somebody Kristina dated."

"Do you know her full name?"

"I think it was Dee-Ann. I can't remember her last name, though I think it was French."

"Do you know how it's spelled?"

"Not sure. D-e-e-a-n-n, maybe?"

"Do you know how old she was, where she lived, or where she worked?"

"I know she was a vet."

"A veterinarian?" Danielle shifted her weight to one leg, then eagerly asked, "Do you know where she worked?"

"No idea. Seems to me she lived in Halifax somewhere, but she could have worked anywhere in HRM."

The Halifax Regional Municipality was made up of several cities and towns. The number of veterinary clinics within HRM probably numbered three or four dozen.

"Did you ever meet her?" Danielle asked.

"No. Kristina kept things like that separate."

"How do you mean?"

"If she spent time with one person, if it was somebody she was maybe sleeping with or interested in, she spent time alone with them. She didn't mix them together."

"Are you trying to say she juggled different people so they didn't know she was sleeping with anybody else?"

Gillian shrugged. "Depends on who it was. Some people she didn't care if they found out or not, some she made a point of telling them."

"Like Maurice?"

"She told Maurice, yes. But other people I think she preferred to keep it from them."

"Like Dee?"

Gillian looked away, as though embarrassed.

"Did Kristina ever mention where Dee was from?"

"Halifax, I think. She said once how Dee had attended some really expensive private school on Spring Garden Road. Guess she must have come from money."

Danielle considered the attraction someone like Kristina might have had to someone with money. "Did Dee give Kristina any gifts?"

"Kristina never asked for them."

"What gifts did she receive from her?"

"Kristina never asked for anything," Gillian said again, defensively. "Dee was just a really generous person. Kristina told me Dee insisted."

"Were any of those gifts drugs?"

"No. One thing I do know for sure, is Kristina said Dee didn't smoke up, or do drugs of any kind."

"Was Dee aware of Kristina's drug use?"

"Might be why they stopped dating, but I'm not really sure. Kristina was the type to move on and never look back. She just did her usual for a while."

"What was her usual?"

Gillian fingered her earring. "Put the person down. She did say some pretty awful things about Dee after they split."

"What kinds of things did Kristina say about her?"

"That she was a loony tune, and unstable."

"Unstable? And you didn't think to mention this before?" Danielle chided Gillian.

"I didn't take her seriously. Kristina was a fun person to hang out and party with, but if you crossed her, or got her mad or embarrassed her, she could turn on you on a dime."

Danielle wasn't surprised by this. She already had enough information to form a fairly accurate picture of who Kristina Buchanan was as a person. It was enough for Danielle to deduce that Kristina's behavior might have driven someone to a crime of passion. A deduction that told Danielle she very much needed to locate Dee.

"Do you know what type of vehicle Dee drove?"

"I don't know what kind it was, but it was silver. Kristina had borrowed it once when hers was in the shop."

"Was it a car, an SUV, a truck?"

"An SUV."

"Do you know the model?"

"Sorry, I don't know much about cars. All I can tell you is that it was silver."

"Do you remember if there was a spare tire attached to the back door of it?" This information would at least narrow down the model types.

"Yes, there was, actually."

Danielle finished writing this down before moving along to her next series of questions. "You said you thought Dee's last name was French. Do you remember what letter it started with?"

"I really don't remember. I just have a vague memory that it might have been French."

"Okay. There's something else I'd like to ask you. When you and Maurice got back to your apartment that night, did Maurice call Kristina?"

"Not that I know of. It wasn't in front of me if he did."

"Do you recall if you were in the same room with him for the first half hour let's say, or did he go to the bathroom or outside and take his cell with him?"

"Not that I noticed. I do know when he called for a cab the next morning he used my phone, but that's not unusual."

Danielle looked at her notes. "You called your sister from Joe's truck using Maurice's cell, didn't you?"

"Yes."

"Thanks for talking to me again. This has been helpful. If you think of anything else in regards to Dee, please give me a call."

"I will," replied Gillian.

31

"What's this regarding?" Mrs. Joyce Coultier asked before replying as to whether or not her husband was home.

"I'm investigating the death of Kristina Buchanan. I'd just like to go over a few things with him."

Joyce Coultier welcomed Danielle in. "Joe's at work right now, but he'll be home soon. Would you like some coffee or a cup of tea?"

"No, thank you."

Joyce poured herself a cup of coffee, then joined Danielle at the kitchen table. "What goes around, comes around," she said.

"Pardon me?"

"Kristina. How her life ended. You reap what you sow."

Danielle sat forward in her chair. "You weren't surprised she ended up murdered?"

"Not in the least."

"Why not?"

"She was a wicked woman, and it might sound terrible, but she probably got what she deserved."

"Why is that?"

"She was a drug addict for one thing. Did you know that about her? A nurse on drugs, and she still kept her job. Can you believe it?"

"What kinds of drugs did she do?"

"Probably everything she could get her hands on."

"Had you ever seen her do drugs yourself?"

"She never did them right in front of me, no, but it wasn't hard to tell. When she was with Maurice, she'd always make excuses to leave the room, and she'd come back with eyes so red, she looked like a snake. Probably the only time she showed her true colors, was when she looked like the snake she was."

"I take it you didn't like her very much."

"She was an evil snake who slithered into Maurice's life and even after they broke up she kept tempting him, even after she made a fool of him by leaving him for a woman. He kept saying she was the apple of his eye. She was an apple all right. The same apple that was in the Garden of Eden. She might have been scrumptious looking on the outside, but she was poisonous and pure evil on the inside."

"That's a pretty harsh description, Mrs. Coultier. What did she do to warrant a portrayal like that?"

"All she did was jerk Maurice around and use him for what she could. She only called him when she wanted something. But it wasn't just that, she was really evil. You could see it in her eyes. They might have looked green on the outside, but on the inside, those eyes were as black as her heart."

"Did your husband share this view?"

"Anybody who saw how she treated Maurice shared this view."

"How did she treat him?"

"Kristina was the type of person to kick somebody in the face, then make fun of them when their teeth fell out."

Danielle was more interested in actual incidents than descriptive expressions. "Are there any specific incidents you can tell me about?"

"We were at a Christmas party at their house once, and she was mad at Maurice over something. Probably something she wanted and didn't get, or maybe she wanted to step out and he forced her to stay at the party, I forget what it was. She's standing on the stairs, and he's coming down the stairs, and the mental case sticks her foot out."

"On purpose?"

"Yes, on purpose. And she didn't care that she almost killed him."

"Did he fall down the stairs?"

"Fall? He tumbled down like a bowling ball and almost broke his neck."

"What did she do after he fell?"

"She laughed."

"She didn't run to his aid, or express any concern?"

"No. She just stood there, with a mental grin on her face."

"Did she say why she did it?"

"No, she didn't say anything at all. Like I told you, she just stood there like some mental case, grinning from ear to ear."

"What did Maurice do?"

"The usual. Tried to cover up for her, said he tripped coming down the stairs. But I saw what she did. Saw it with my own two eyes."

"Was she doing drugs that night?"

"Oh, for sure. She tried to hide it, but it didn't take much of a genius to figure it out. She'd go outside supposedly for some air, or upstairs to the bathroom, and come back with bloodshot eyes and right out of it."

"Do you know what drugs she took?"

"No, but I think she'd have done anything. This guy arrived at one of their parties once and asked her if it was okay if he did cocaine in her house. She told him only if he shared it with her. They went into the kitchen and did it."

"Did Maurice join them?"

"No. Maurice was none too pleased, but that's the way it always was. She did what she wanted, and if he didn't like it, too bad for him. She didn't give a flying leap." Joyce Coultier ran her finger around the rim of her coffee cup. "I tell you, his life has been a hell of a lot better since she died."

"How so?"

"He wouldn't settle down with anybody else while she was alive. All he did was pine over her, hoping they'd get back together. He finally moved on after she died, settled down and got married. But when she was alive, everything he did was for her. He didn't even go fishing once that last summer she was alive. Spent all his days off working himself to death on that shack she bought."

"Did she pay him for any of the work he did on her house?" Knowing now what kind of person Kristina was, Danielle would have put her own money down on the fact that Kristina hadn't.

"Not a penny. She led him on, making him think they'd get back together again, but she was just using him. He rebuilt most of that house. It was falling apart and all rotted. It was an old cottage, really. After Maurice was done with it, it looked like a real house. I suppose he thought he'd end up living there one day."

"My sources tell me she made it clear to Maurice that she was dating others. Maybe she was telling him they'd never get back together and he just wouldn't believe it?"

"It wasn't like that at all. One time, Maurice came over to borrow some of Joe's welding equipment so he could build her a pot rack, and she was with him. My niece was here with her baby and Maurice was holding her. Kristina leaned her chin on Maurice's shoulder and said, 'Maybe you and I will have one of these one day.' Then a half hour later she blurts out that they need to get going because she has a date. That woman had a black heart. She didn't care how much she was hurting Maurice, she just loved showing off that other people wanted her. Man or woman, she didn't care, she just loved attention."

"How did Maurice handle her death?"

"He took it hard at first, but it was the best thing that ever happened to him. He's very happy now. After she died, he started living again. Instead of wasting all his time working on her shack for nothing, he started his own business. He makes lots of money now and provides for a wife who truly loves him. They have a beautiful baby boy now too, and Maurice is so happy. Happier than he's ever been. Might not sound like a very nice thing to say, but it's true. The best thing that ever happened to Maurice was Kristina dying."

"Maurice started his own business?" This was new information for Danielle. "What kind of business is it?"

"Body shop. He adds fancy stuff to cars. That's why he makes so much money. Lots of people with lots of money to make their cars look fancier than they already are."

"How does he find the time to run a business when he's working full-time at the rail station?"

"He's a very hard working man, and he's smart. He's got a few men working for him to look after things while he's at the train station, and Lucy helps too."

Danielle made a few notes then switched up her line of questioning. "Were you here when Kristina called Joe to go get Maurice the night she was killed?"

"Yes. Joe was so mad. Maurice had just brought Kristina wood for her fireplace the day before. Cut it, chopped it, and delivered it to her. All for free of course. She had told Maurice he could spend the night if he went there the next night, but I guess she told him to get out after he was there. He didn't have his truck with him, so what was he going to do? It would have cost him a fortune to get a cab back to his place from Hubley."

"What time did Joe get home?"

"Probably…from here to Hubley, then to town and back here, it's—"

"Were you not home when your husband got back?"

"Yes, I was home, but I was asleep."

"So you don't know the exact time your husband came home, then?"

"We didn't know anything was going to happen, that we were going to have to record the exact time."

Danielle nodded. "Understandable. So tell me, how did Joe feel about Kristina?"

"The same as the rest of us felt. Joe tried to tell Maurice what she was, but Maurice wouldn't hear it."

"Did Joe and Maurice ever fight over it?"

"No, not fight. Joe called Maurice a sissy sometimes, but he said it to his face. With Kristina he was the biggest sissy there was.

Anything she wanted, she got. She told him jump, he asked which direction."

Danielle heard a vehicle come in the driveway. Joyce Coultier opened a curtain and said, "Here's Joe now."

After Joseph Coultier dropped his lunch box and joined his wife at the table, Danielle asked him a few routine questions. He confirmed getting the call from Kristina, picking Maurice and Gillian up at her house, stopping at the liquor store, then dropping them both off at Gillian's apartment afterward.

"Did Maurice tell you why Kristina threw him out?

"No."

"Did you ask him?"

"No."

"Why not? Seems to me you'd be curious as to why she was throwing Maurice out."

"I stopped trying to make sense of Kristina long before that night. I figured she was in one of her fits, so I just picked him up. I didn't want to embarrass him. Gillian was with him, so I didn't want to say anything in front of her."

"But Gillian was there, she knew what happened. It's not like you'd be bringing up something she knew nothing about."

"Like I told you, I didn't want to embarrass my brother. Kristina was always making a fool of him, and I didn't want to rub it in his face. I just picked him up and got him out of there soon as I could."

"Did you see any other vehicles or anyone hanging about her place when you arrived?"

"I wasn't paying any attention, so I have no idea if there was or wasn't. There was only her car in the driveway, but there could have been somebody parked alongside the road waiting, I suppose."

"Did you come straight home after you dropped them off at Gillian's house?"

"Yes."

"And what time was that?"

"About ten-thirty."

"Was your wife awake or asleep when you came in?"

"Was she awake or asleep? What kind of question is that? She's sitting right here, why don't you ask her yourself?"

"She says she was asleep."

"Well, if she says she was asleep, then she was asleep." Joe rolled his eyes.

"Does your brother do drugs, Mr. Coultier?"

"What?"

"Does he smoke pot, do cocaine, or any other drugs?"

"Look, just because she was a druggie doesn't mean my brother was. If he ever did any of that stuff, she's the one who dragged him into it. My brother didn't do that garbage before he met her and he doesn't do it now. He's a good, decent, hardworking man."

Joyce Coultier was just as defensive. "Why are you asking about Maurice? He didn't kill Kristina. You should be asking the hospital why they let drug addicts work as nurses. They should do drug tests on nurses, you know."

Joyce Coultier had a very good point. Danielle had wondered why a nurse would risk her career by doing any illegal drugs at all. Surely she would have gotten caught at some point during the random drug testing.

As an RCMP officer, Danielle was subjected to random drug tests periodically, but when she looked into the Halifax Health Authority's drug testing policy, it turns out they rarely test their employees, and that includes doctors and nurses. Only if they have extremely strong reasons to suspect a nurse of misconduct or of compromising patient care due to substance abuse will they test, and even then, the decision to do so is not taken lightly.

Although to a certain degree Danielle understood how privacy laws, the *Charter of Rights and Freedoms*, and the *Human Rights Act*, restricted the Health Authority from implementing mandatory random drug testing for all employees on a regular basis, she did not feel that what they currently had in place to identify addicts in the workplace was adequate. Danielle had learned that the hospital relied on self-compliance of the *Registered Nurses' Code of Ethics*, and put great effort into producing awareness campaigns aimed at educating nurses and physicians about the seriousness of substance abuse among their own, but for the most part, this meant that the hospital relied only on a whistle-blowing format to identify which of their staff were substance abusers.

After reading countless statements and interviewing many of Buchanan's colleagues, it became apparent to Danielle that nurses were reluctant to report any of their own, and that most turned a blind eye as to what their colleagues might be engaging in while they were off the clock—even if that behavior had long-lasting effects that might pose a risk to their patients while on duty.

While Danielle understood the hospital's stance from a legal point of view, this knowledge troubled her deeply as a regular citizen.

Knowing what she knew now, Danielle would certainly not trust a loved one's care to a nurse like Kristina Buchanan. This thought prompted Danielle to write herself a note to check if any of Buchanan's patients had ever died while she was on duty.

"Do you know who might have killed Kristina, Mr. Coultier? Or why?"

"If you ask me, she got mixed up with some drug dealers or something. That's usually what it is. Knowing Kristina, she probably screwed over some drug dealer and he killed her for it."

"According to the information we've gathered, Kristina never associated with drug dealers. She never bought it herself." Danielle observed Joe Coultier carefully as she revealed her next piece of information. "Your brother's the one who supplied her with most of it."

"Oh yeah, oh yeah!" Joe Coultier jumped up out of his chair and started flailing his arms. "Blame it on Maurice, now. She was the druggie pulling the strings, but blame it on him because he was her puppet!"

His wife was also severely antagonized by Danielle's remark. "You know what? I feel sorry for her mother, but other than that, I'm glad that slut is dead. As far as I'm concerned, whoever did it, did everybody a favor. God knows how many deaths she might have caused had she lived, going to work stoned all the time."

It was not up to Danielle to evaluate whether or not Kristina's death might have spared others their lives—her job was simply to find her killer—so she ignored Joyce Coultier's commentary.

"Mr. Coultier, why do you think a drug dealer might have killed Kristina?"

"Makes the most sense to me. It's normally drug dealers or gangs that kills somebody and leaves a type of message."

"What message are you talking about?" Since the carving of the letter "S" on Buchanan's face had never been made public, this remark piqued Danielle's interest.

"It was all over the papers that she was dumped in a heart-shaped pond. That's some kind of message right there."

"What do you think the message was?" It sounded as though Danielle were seeking Joe Coultier's advice, but of course she wasn't. She was scrutinizing his every move and studying his body language as he replied.

"It probably meant, 'you're not gonna screw me over and get away with it.'"

"Mr. Coultier, if I asked you to give me one word to describe Kristina Buchanan, what would it be?"

Joseph Coultier didn't take very long to answer, "Slut."

"And you Mrs. Coultier?"

"Snake."

And on those fine notes, Danielle thanked Mr. and Mrs. Coultier for their time and left.

❧ 32 ❧

Danielle spent the rest of the day hitting the bars—for information. She went to as many as she could, starting with the gay and alternative bars, showing Buchanan's photo and asking if she was a regular or looked familiar. But every one of them was a dead end. It appeared she was not a barfly at least, and certainly not part of the club-drug scene.

At four o'clock, just as she was about to end her work week, Danielle's cell phone rang. It was a delivery truck informing her they were at her apartment, but that no one was there.

"It was supposed to be delivered tomorrow, not today," Danielle informed them.

"Do you want us to take it back?"

"No, don't take it back. I'll be there in fifteen minutes."

By six-thirty, Danielle was sitting in her very own apartment filled with furniture, and even had power and telephone service. Her first phone call from her new apartment was to Lilly.

"Have you eaten yet? I'd invite you over for that home cooked meal I promised you, but I forgot to buy pots. We could have takeout though."

"No, I haven't eaten, but I think I'd feel safer eating something delivered anyway," Lilly joked.

"How does Greek sound? It'll arrive around the same time you do if I call now."

"Sounds great to me."

When Danielle hung up she thought she heard clumsy footsteps on the stairs, so she opened the apartment door and looked out. She saw Nathalie on her way up the stairs with several grocery bags in her arms, and one of them was falling. Danielle rushed to catch the bag, surprising Nathalie.

Nathalie first punched Danielle, then kicked her hard in the ribs before recognizing the blond hair and female form as groceries dropped everywhere.

"Oh my God! I'm so sorry! I didn't know it was you." Nathalie rushed to Danielle's aid.

Danielle was sore, but did not want to show she was. "It's okay."

"I'm really sorry. I didn't even think, I just reacted." Nathalie extended her hand in an effort to lift Danielle up.

"It's okay. I know you couldn't see it was me. It didn't help that I just grabbed. I'm actually proud of you."

"Sure you are. Proud of me for assaulting my tenant—an RCMP officer at that."

"I won't tell if you won't. Our little secret," Danielle said as she reached out and touched Nathalie's lips with her fingers. Nathalie turned away awkwardly and started placing groceries back into bags.

"Here, let me help." Danielle picked up some groceries, carefully placing them back in the bag, and insisted she carry at least one up to help Nathalie.

When Danielle dropped the bag on the dining room table, Nathalie said to her, "I thought your furniture was only arriving tomorrow."

"They mixed up the date and delivered it a day early. I'm glad though, since I might need some extra time to get my things out of the condo tomorrow."

"How do you think that'll go?"

"She'll be spiteful. But I'm experienced at ignoring her."

Nathalie let out a small laugh.

Danielle then said to Nathalie, "You know, I ran out of here so fast the other night I forgot to give you my rent cheques. I was about to write them out just a few minutes ago when it dawned on me I don't even know your last name."

Nathalie's eyes remained focused on the grocery items she was removing from bags and placing on the counter one by one. She only answered Danielle after her back was turned, while she put the items in a cupboard.

"It's Boudreaux. With an x at the end." Nathalie spelled it out for her.

Danielle sat at the dining room table and filled in Nathalie's last name on several cheques.

Nathalie walked over to the table and pulled something from a bag. "Here, I have something for you. I was going to give it to you tomorrow, but since you've moved in tonight..." Nathalie handed Danielle a gorgeous plant, a mass of fuchsia ruffled flowers.

They were so gorgeous, they didn't seem real, but they were. Danielle touched them, just to be sure.

"It's your housewarming present." Nathalie smiled as she presented Danielle with the colorful plant.

"Oh, it's so beautiful, Nathalie." Danielle put the plant down and hugged Nathalie. "Thank you." Danielle was aware the hug was lasting too long, but she didn't want to let go. She was disappointed when Nathalie did. Nathalie returned to the kitchen where she put away the remainder of her groceries.

"Does the evening sun glare through your back window? Seems to me it shouldn't set that far back," Danielle observed.

"No, it doesn't. Why do you ask that?"

"I've noticed you keep one side of your curtain closed."

"Oh. That's... It's just the way it reflects sometimes." Nathalie began to fidget unnecessarily with the position of canned goods.

"Hello!"

Danielle and Nathalie could hear a voice calling from the stairwell. Nathalie walked to her door, opened it, and yelled, "Up here!"

When Lilly arrived, she said, "I know you're used to living in a fancy condo Danielle, but there's no security guard at the entrance of this building—no offense Nathalie. Do you realize you left your apartment door wide open?"

"Oh, geez." Danielle headed for the door.

"I shut it for you," Lilly said. Danielle turned back and stood by the plant she'd just received from Nathalie.

"Hi, Lilly." Nathalie waved.

"Hi, Nathalie. So this is what your place looks like." Lilly looked around the organized, functional space with admiration. There was color everywhere. Reds, oranges, and deep yellows. "I fully expected your place to be really wild and creative, and it is, except—"

"Except what?" Nathalie asked.

"Except I didn't expect it to be so orderly."

"Why not?"

"Well you know, the creative personality and all that."

"Creating order out of chaos is what creativity is all about," Nathalie said with ardor.

"Not according to some paintings I've seen. Looks more like paint just thrown all over the place," Lilly responded.

"Music is different. The notes have to correlate and flow. Sometimes like a trickling stream, sometimes like the roar of a raging, swollen river, but no matter how much force you put behind it, it has to be controlled and manipulated to take whatever course you want it to."

Danielle was awed by Nathalie's creative response. She easily pictured a stream, a river, and a waterfall.

"Sometimes you answer the simplest questions in the most profound manner, Nathalie," Lilly said. "You're definitely a philosopher."

"Oh, no I'm not. I stopped trying to make sense of this world years ago," Nathalie said with a seriousness that seemed tinged with bitterness.

Danielle told herself she should go down to her apartment and let Lilly and Nathalie talk privately, but the thought of them being alone made her stomach churn. She realized she didn't want Lilly and Nathalie to be alone, or to share anything privately, not even a conversation. Danielle never used to be jealous, or selfish or self-serving, but she could not help herself. Instead of going downstairs she stayed put.

"Nathalie, I was just about to order some Greek food. Would you like to join me and Lilly in my new apartment?"

"Oh, no. I don't want to interrupt, plus—"

There was a quick knock on the door then Melissa Lambert entered. "What's this? A surprise party for me?"

"I was just about to tell them you were on your way over. Danielle's moved into the apartment below."

Danielle expected Melissa's reaction to be uncensored, maybe even dramatic, but it was quite subdued. "I see," is all she said. Though she said it with a bit of disgust in her voice. She walked into the kitchen as if it were hers, opened up a six-pack carton of blueberry beer she brought, and put them in the fridge. "Nathalie, they're already cold. Do you want one now? I'll pour it for you." Melissa shut the fridge door and looked at Lilly as she said, "Don't know if you know this or not, but Nathalie can't stand drinking out of beer bottles."

"Just bring the beer downstairs, Melissa," Nathalie told her. "We're going to join Danielle and Lilly in celebrating Danielle's moving in."

"*Great.* I'll get the cauldron," Melissa muttered under her breath.

Two wine glasses and two beer glasses accompanied a myriad of Greek dishes on Danielle's dining room table. Lilly was pouring Melissa a second glass of wine when she accidentally spilled a few drops on Melissa's hand and wrist.

"Oh, I'm sorry," Lilly told Melissa.

Melissa wiped the few drops from her hand with her napkin as she said, "Gee, Lilly, all you had to do was lift your sweater and flash me if you wanted to get me wet."

Lilly responded with a grin.

Danielle ignored what she interpreted as Melissa's crassness. Melissa, quite frankly, turned Danielle off in a big way. But for Nathalie's sake, Danielle had welcomed—no, tolerated—Melissa at her table.

"Well, this is a very nice way to christen my new dining room table," Danielle said as she raised her beer glass in a toast.

Melissa didn't skip a beat when she responded with, "I found a better way to christen mine—though my back was awfully sore the next day."

Lilly roared laughing. Nathalie just shook her head. Danielle rolled her eyes in disgust, and that made Nathalie giggle.

Afterward, Nathalie looked around the room and said to Danielle, "I can't believe you got all your furniture unpacked and curtains up, in just a couple of hours."

"I am woman, hear me roar. My cordless drill at least," Danielle said.

Nathalie giggled again.

"It's the blueberry beer," Melissa said as she pointed with her wine glass. "Puts her in a good mood." Melissa had abandoned her beer for the wine Lilly brought. "And what puts you in a good mood?" Melissa asked Lilly seductively as she leaned toward her and smiled.

To Danielle's surprise, Lilly grinned flirtatiously, then leaned over and whispered something in Melissa's ear.

Danielle and Nathalie glanced at each other, then Nathalie got up from the table. "I have to go check on Chai." Nathalie walked toward the door.

"I'll come get that frying pan I want to borrow for the morning while I'm at it," Danielle said to Nathalie.

Danielle and Nathalie burst out laughing the second they entered Nathalie's apartment.

"Oh...my...God!" Nathalie managed to say despite hysterics.

Danielle was laughing so much, she could hardly talk. "Do you think...I'm going to have to...burn the table tomorrow?" Danielle collapsed onto the sofa, and Nathalie followed suit.

After their laughter finally subsided, Danielle was very aware they were leaning on each other, but pretended not to notice. Except Danielle wanted so badly to touch Nathalie, to feel her skin, and…to kiss her.

Danielle's hand moved ever so slowly down Nathalie's forearm until it reached Nathalie's hand. Danielle worried this might be too much for Nathalie, but since Nathalie didn't move her hand away, Danielle continued touching Nathalie, and moved her thumb lightly across Nathalie's hand. Nathalie moved her head closer. So close, Danielle could feel Nathalie's breath on her neck.

Danielle could not conceal her own breaths, which were now coming harder and louder. Danielle took Nathalie's hand in hers, and Nathalie squeezed tightly as she pressed her face deeper into Danielle's neck.

Danielle gulped when she felt Nathalie's lips purse against her neck. She did not expect it of course, but the excitement that Nathalie's kiss upon her neck stirred within her made her no longer able to restrain from giving in to her intense desire to kiss Nathalie back—on the lips.

Danielle simultaneously turned her head and guided Nathalie's chin away from her neck so she could lower her lips onto Nathalie's. When their lips made contact, Nathalie's mouth opened and Danielle's tongue entered it.

Nathalie's tongue explored Danielle's. It was not frenzied like Véronique's, and it was not stale and mechanical like Rachel's. It was the type of kiss that made Danielle see stars. (Then she remembered to breathe.)

Nathalie's tongue slowly touched, tasted, and felt its way up and down and all around Danielle's, then did the same to her lips. Danielle was inspired to do the same, so her own tongue traversed the surface of Nathalie's lips until it met Nathalie's. When their tongues intersected, they entwined and suckled each other before continuing their erotic journey along—

A bang on the door caused both Nathalie and Danielle to shoot up like two fired bullets. They were in flight, then standing apart, before the door flung open and Melissa Lambert announced, "We need more wine downstairs."

Nathalie straightened her hair and clothing as she asked Melissa, "Are you taking a cab home tonight?"

"Can't I crash here?"

"Actually, Melissa, I'm feeling tired tonight, and I have to be up really early—"

"Knock, knock!" It was Lilly this time.

Melissa was opening and closing cupboard doors as if she owned the place. "Hey, Lilly. Looks like Nathalie's out of wine too—and energy it seems."

Danielle walked toward the door. "I'm beat too, and I have to get up early and face Rachel." Danielle then tried to make eye contact with Nathalie, but Nathalie was avoiding her gaze.

"Why don't we take the party to my place, then?" Lilly suggested to Melissa.

"I'll call a cab," Nathalie said quickly. Without waiting for a response, she picked up the phone and dialed.

"I'm going to go downstairs and clean up," Danielle said. She really wanted to stay with Nathalie, and tried to send her a subliminal message telling her she'd like to rejoin her after Lilly and Melissa left, but Nathalie seemed to be somewhere else in her mind now.

Danielle had just finished cleaning up when she saw a cab pull up and heard Melissa and Lilly come down the stairs. She wanted to go straight up to Nathalie's, but she waited to see if Nathalie would come down. Fifteen long, agonizing minutes went by.

Danielle knew she shouldn't, but she was drawn. She walked up the stairs and knocked quietly on Nathalie's door. There was no response, so she knocked harder. Danielle listened, but she couldn't hear anything. She knocked one last time, praying the door would open.

It didn't.

It didn't, because Nathalie was in her bedroom…listening to Kristina Buchanan's voice for the very last time.

8003

Danielle was swimming in her new bed, and she felt so alone in it. The mermaid, the whale, and all the other creatures that normally swam about, were eerily missing. Danielle submerged, swimming down to the ocean floor. She saw a dim light in the distance and swam toward it. It was coming from a small opening in a large den made of forest debris that had turned into a type of coral.

Danielle noticed that the opening was completely sealed with a black plastic that glowed like embers as the bright light from the other side penetrated it. She couldn't see what was happening, but she knew that those inside were having a party. She didn't want to join them, however—even though she felt so terribly alone—because she somehow knew that the mermaid was not in there.

Danielle swam away from the den and surfaced. A hockey stick drifted by and the sight of it made her cry. When her tears hit the dark water, Danielle noticed they were almost identical in color to the water.

Danielle now knew why there was no one else in this water. This was not an ocean after all, but a bay of tears. She also knew now that only the interior of the den was filled with seawater, sealed safely shut against the tears with black plastic and duct tape, and that the reason she was alone is that she was the only one who instinctively knew how to traverse the unusual currents in this bay of tears.

But whose tears were these?

Danielle looked at the small puddle her own tears had created on the surface. They were thinner, not as dense and concentrated as those that surrounded her. She tasted them, and they were sour. She was curious as to how the bay's tears compared to hers, so she tasted them too. They were equally vile, they were just different. They were harsh and bitter.

Danielle heard water now. Water that trickled, then grew louder, more forceful. She swam toward the sound, but the roar got so loud she had to turn around and swim to the edge of the bay, which was lined with some sort of ledge. Danielle held on to this ledge and turned to see a waterfall. Her eyes drew up, trying to view the source of this waterfall. She let go of the concrete edge, but when she did, she floated up instead of down.

"Order must be created out of chaos," the voice bellowed over the loud waterfall.

Danielle then felt her body float up to the top of the waterfall, and began to glide like a bird, upstream toward the source of the river.

When Danielle arrived at its origin, where it all began…the mermaid sat as tears flowed from her sunburst eyes, down her face, over her porcelain white breasts, further down her body, then onto the earth, and created a stream, which turned into a river, which roared over a waterfall, and upon its landing below…carved out a heart-shaped bay that was lined with pebbled concrete.

Danielle ran the perimeter of the Commons—a large park in the heart of the city just a couple of blocks from her new apartment—and let her mind go where it may. It helped to clear Danielle's mind when she ran, but this afternoon it seemed to do the opposite. Danielle's head was filled and getting fuller with each stride.

That morning she had retrieved items from her former home without incident—thanks to two police officers and the threat of legal action still looming—which was a good thing, since Lilly was not around to legally intimidate Rachel.

Lilly had gone home with someone. Melissa, of all people. Danielle knew she wasn't jealous, but there was something about Melissa. Danielle just didn't trust her, and it bothered Danielle that Lilly might be getting mixed up with her.

Nathalie...

Danielle had spent a good part of the night staring at the ceiling, knowing Nathalie was just above, and couldn't stop thinking about her. *Why?* What was it about Nathalie that drew Danielle to her?

Danielle completed her run then spent the rest of the day shopping for items she still needed, or had forgotten to get—like pots and pans. She would have liked to have had Nathalie by her side as she did so, but Danielle sensed Nathalie needed some space. And she was right about that.

Nathalie had gotten up early and driven to the Annapolis Valley. With each kilometer she drove further away from Halifax, the better she felt. Nathalie couldn't wait to get to her cottage, to get away from her building on Maynard—and Danielle.

It was a mistake renting the apartment to Danielle. Nathalie thought she could handle it, but it was already obvious, less than twenty-four hours after Danielle's moving in, that she couldn't.

Nathalie felt fear. Terrible fear. Because deep down she knew...that if what she felt was happening again really was...that Danielle's days were numbered.

Nathalie had left Halifax feeling anxious and apprehensive, but as she turned onto Pereau Road she felt calmer, knowing that her refuge was just around the corner. She'd bought the cottage the summer before Kristina died. She had needed a place to hide, a place where she could deal with the fear.

After settling in, Nathalie went over to the piano and started playing. As so often happened when she played, Nathalie's emotions poured out of her. At first she played softly, expressing her sadness. Then as her emotions heated up and simmered, they then turned into a thunderous rumble, which boiled over as she played turbulently, while streams flowed from her eyes.

Then…she stopped.

Nathalie got up from the piano and picked up a pencil and notepad. She sat in a rocking chair in front of the fireplace and wrote.

I don't live in fear of you anymore, Kristina.

Nathalie closed her eyes and threw her head back. She sat like that for a few moments, then opened her eyes and scribed one more sentence on her notepad.

But I'm starting to feel fear again.

Nathalie brought her pencil lower onto the page, and slowly drew a letter "S". She traced this letter over and over, back and forth without lifting the pencil, until it almost tore through the paper. On the last tracing, Nathalie kept going onto a new path without lifting the pencil, and drew a giant letter 'D'. She stared, keeping the pencil in place for a moment, then watched as her hand slowly added the letters a-n-i-e-l-l-e.

Just then the phone rang. But instead of answering, Nathalie ripped the sheet from its notepad, threw it in the fireplace, and watched it slowly burn.

Nathalie had showered before leaving Halifax, but she had to shower again before going to the shelter. She needed to wash away the tears—and everything else—before she started with surgeries.

By five o'clock she had performed three spays, two neuters, and repaired a broken leg.

"Think I'll skip dinner today, Vivian," Nathalie informed her assistant. Normally they ended surgical days with a meal at one of the many scrumptious eateries known for their locally grown, organic produce, but Nathalie wanted to get back to her cottage and be alone. She had some thinking to do.

"It's not healthy to skip meals," Vivian reminded the veterinarian she'd worked with for almost two years.

"I'm just going to pick up a few things at the market and take them back to the cottage," Nathalie replied.

"Dianne—before you go," Vivian said to her, "the drug company you order our Ketaset from wants you to be consistent with your name. They said you're registered under Dianne Boudreau, but that the last time you ordered, you signed Nathalie Boudreaux with an 'x' at the end of your last name, and they either want proof of a legal change of name, or for you to update your records with a certified copy of your birth certificate and diploma if they've got the name wrong. They said they won't send us any more Ketaset until you clear the matter up with them."

Nathalie responded tersely. "They should already know that my given names are Dianne Nathalie, but that's fine, I'll straighten it out with them." Nathalie didn't address the minor spelling change of her surname.

"We could avoid the whole thing if I placed the orders. I know you like to order the drugs and maintain inventory yourself, but you're only here twice a month."

It was a hint that was not lost on Nathalie. Nevertheless, she ignored it. "I'm the surgeon who uses the drugs, I'm the one responsible for them. Thanks for offering, but I don't mind doing it myself. It shouldn't matter to the drug company which of my given names I use, at any rate."

Vivian looked at Nathalie crossly. "I guess they figure most people stick with just one."

Nathalie ignored Vivian's comment. It was, quite frankly, none of Vivian's business if, or why, or when, she had started using her middle name. Nathalie had enough to worry about. She hoped she didn't have to start worrying about Vivian too.

Danielle waited until six o'clock in the evening to phone Lilly.

"How did your evening go after you left here last night?" Danielle asked.

"It was all right."

"Did you and Melissa sleep together?"

"Maybe we did, maybe we didn't."

"What's the big secret? She went home with you, you're both single."

"And I'm interested in Nathalie."

Danielle wished Lilly hadn't said that. "Well, that wouldn't stop Melissa from trying. If anything, she would probably enjoy it more if she knew you were interested in somebody else. Does she know you're interested in Nathalie?"

"I didn't think it was anything she needed to know," Lilly said.

"So did you, or didn't you?"

"Why are you so curious? I thought you weren't interested in Melissa."

"I am *so* not."

"Well, you seem awfully interested."

Danielle realized she'd better change the subject before Lilly caught on—if she hadn't already. Danielle was hoping Lilly would find someone other than Nathalie to be interested in, but on the other hand, Danielle did not want it to be Melissa. "I just don't trust Melissa. I know you're a grown woman and you've got good instincts, but…" Danielle decided not to complete her sentence.

"Danielle, I appreciate your concern, but I really think you're just overly stressed and overly sensitive these days."

"I'm not overly sensitive."

"Look, it's understandable. You've just had a relationship end and you've had to find a place to live quickly—not to mention the stress of working on a case that's so important to your career. Believe me, you're doing exceptionally well considering the circumstances, but don't push yourself or you'll crash."

Danielle had to admit she was feeling stressed, and perhaps Lilly was right. Perhaps the stress was making her overly sensitive and she just wasn't aware of it. Danielle sighed loud enough for Lilly to hear it through the phone. "Yes, you've got a point."

"Do you know if Nathalie's home?" Lilly asked.

"I'm not sure." Danielle didn't want to admit she knew for a fact Nathalie wasn't, because she'd been checking for her every five minutes for the past four hours.

"Is her car parked out front? It's a silver Toyota Prius."

Danielle looked onto the street again. Most of the houses on Maynard were built right next to each other, and almost none of them had parking, so residents had to park on one side of the street.

"I don't see it," Danielle said without revealing her continued disappointment.

"Maybe she went to her cottage. I've called there too though, and there's no answer. Oh, well. I've left her messages at both places, guess she'll get back to me when she can."

"Have you ever been to her cottage?" Danielle wanted to know.

"No, I haven't. You were in her apartment before I was, even."

"Really?"

"Yes, really. The night I was supposed to have dinner at her house was the first time she'd ever invited me to her place, and then she canceled. Boy, you must really be stressed, because you normally don't forget anything."

Danielle didn't feel it was stress affecting her memory, but her preoccupation with Nathalie—a preoccupation Danielle couldn't quite understand.

"You said you called both places—did you try her cell phone?" Danielle hoped Lilly would interpret her question merely as a helpful suggestion.

"Yes, but I didn't even get voicemail. It just rang and rang. Nathalie's a little odd when it comes to being accessible. You'd think she'd be publicizing herself all over the place, and have her cell phone on twenty-four hours a day, but she seems quite reclusive. I find that strange for someone in the entertainment industry."

"Maybe she doesn't want to be famous."

"Oh, I think all musicians want to be famous," Lilly said.

"I don't think Nathalie wants to be famous at all. I think that's why she writes stuff for other people to record."

"Oh, and you know this based on knowing her for a whole two weeks?"

Lilly's sarcasm stung like a blow dart, but Danielle refused to let it show. "Who's the sensitive one now?"

"What are your plans tonight, Danielle?"

Danielle was well aware that Lilly's skill of steering a conversation extended beyond the courtroom, so she wasn't surprised by the abrupt change of subject. But Danielle didn't want to tell Lilly she was hoping she'd see Nathalie and invite her down to her apartment for a movie. "I'm just going to hang out here, put more things away and get used to being in my own space. Might watch a movie, or see what's in the last few boxes I haven't opened yet. You know how you keep saying if you're looking for something and can't find it, start looking for something else and it'll show up right in front of you? I'm going to start looking for my garlic press— might find myself, instead," Danielle chuckled.

Lilly chuckled too, and it appeared to diffuse some of the tension between them. "Okay, well you have a good evening."

"You too, Lilly. I'll call you later if I don't crash early."

After she hung up, Danielle looked out the window again. Evening was setting in now, and the empty spot on the street where

Nathalie normally parked felt like a gaping hole to Danielle, a hole that made her feel hollow.

She turned on the television and inserted the suspense movie she'd rented. She opened the fridge and grabbed a beer she had purchased for the evening. Danielle almost never bought beer. When she popped the cap, the scent of blueberries was stronger than she expected.

As Danielle stared at the television and drank a blueberry beer, she wondered why, after being with Rachel for over three years, that she did not miss her at all, but after knowing Nathalie mere weeks, missed her terribly.

Nathalie listened to Lilly's message when she got back to the cottage, but did not return her call. Nathalie did not want to speak to anyone who reminded her of Danielle, who reminded her of Kristina, who reminded her of the worst hell on earth she'd ever experienced. And while Nathalie had felt just so much relief after Kristina was dead, that relief was now being replaced by a building tension and fear. She had hoped and prayed she would never feel this way again. Nathalie truly did not want anyone else to die. But if she could not find a way to stop these growing feelings, Nathalie knew...that a *third* woman would have to die.

There were so many previews and commercials at the beginning of the movie, the movie itself had barely started when Danielle heard footsteps above her head. Danielle leapt up excitedly and rushed to the window. Nathalie's car wasn't there, but perhaps she had parked elsewhere.

Danielle listened intently. They were definitely footsteps, and they were definitely coming from Nathalie's apartment.

Danielle ran up the stairs and listened first before knocking on the door. She could definitely hear someone inside. Yet when she knocked, Nathalie did not come to the door. Danielle listened again. All she heard was silence.

"Nathalie, it's me, Danielle."

Silence.

Danielle took her cell phone out of her pocket and dialed Nathalie's number, then pressed her ear against the door. She could hear Nathalie's phone ringing, followed by soft steps walking past the door and fading into the direction of the kitchen counter, where

Danielle knew Nathalie's phone was located. When Nathalie's voicemail picked up, Danielle hung up without leaving a message.

Disappointed, Danielle walked slowly back to her apartment. When she went in, she picked up her landline and dialed Nathalie's number again. Again she heard footsteps go toward the location of the phone, but Nathalie did not pick up.

She's obviously hearing the phone ring, and walking to the caller ID to check who it is, Danielle construed. *So she must be deliberately avoiding me.*

Danielle responded to her conclusion by pouring her blueberry beer down the drain and going to bed.

Nathalie was not aware of this. She was not aware Danielle had picked up blueberry beer because she knew Nathalie liked it so much. She was also not aware that Danielle had gone to the video store to pick up a suspense movie with a theme she thought Nathalie would enjoy, with the intent of inviting Nathalie to watch it with her. Nor was Nathalie aware Danielle surmised she was avoiding her. Nathalie was not aware of any of this at all. Just as she was also not aware that Melissa Lambert had broken into her apartment and was rifling through her personal belongings at this very moment.

Lilly expected it to be Danielle again when her phone rang late Saturday evening, but it wasn't. It was Melissa Lambert.

"Hi, how was your day?" Melissa asked.

"Busy. Worked some of it. Finished my dress though, and plan on relaxing the rest of the evening."

"I bet I could help you relax," Melissa flirted.

"Oh, really. And how would you accomplish that?"

"Do you have any ice cubes in your freezer?"

"What does—"

"I bet an ice cube would feel great against your..." Melissa chose to breathe hard into her phone instead of saying the word, preferring Lilly to use her imagination. She then used a very sultry tone of voice to complete her seduction. "And if it got too cold, my hot tongue could warm it right up—"

"Get over here!"

❧ 34 ❧

On Sunday Danielle repeated her periodic checks looking and listening for Nathalie all day, but Danielle did not see or hear her. She also called Lilly three times, but did not let Lilly know she was calling to see if she'd heard from Nathalie. Through their casual conversation, Danielle learned Lilly had not heard from her either.

What Danielle had not learned, that Lilly kept to herself, was that Lilly and Melissa had spent another night having sex—and very good sex indeed. With cold ice cubes and hot candle wax, they had brought each other's arousal up to great heights, then forced that arousal to remain sustained without reaching climax until one decided it was time for the other to be finally sated. The result was that both of them intensely released from a powerful lust they felt very comfortable sharing with each other.

By early Sunday evening Danielle had every last thing unpacked and organized. She was grateful to have this to do, as it distracted her from just watching the clock, and the street, on the lookout for Nathalie.

Danielle made one last check along the street looking for Nathalie's car before going to bed. It still wasn't there.

An hour after going to bed Danielle was staring up at the ceiling, and realized she felt just as she had after her parents died, feeling such longing for her family's return. Except tonight, the person Danielle wanted so badly to just come home…was Nathalie.

Nathalie had purposefully waited till very late before driving back to Halifax. She didn't like driving in the dark, but she had her reasons. Well, one reason. And that one reason being that she did not want Danielle to see her arrive. She had things to do—and put into place—before she encountered Danielle again.

Early Monday morning Danielle was making notes on how she would organize her day when Staff Sergeant Kline appeared in front of her, looking annoyed.

"What's this?" Kline dropped Danielle's request for electronic surveillance on her desk.

"It's a wiretap request," Danielle replied.

"I know that much. But why Coultier? He's got an alibi."

"Did you know he's now married to someone he was dating, but wouldn't marry, until his ex, Kristina Buchanan, died? Someone who worked at a vet clinic and was responsible for ordering all their ketamine?" Danielle was about to add, "Who was ordering extra ketamine for herself," but now knew that wasn't the case after all.

"No, I didn't. Does his wife have an alibi for the night Buchanan was killed?"

Danielle hadn't checked yet because she wanted to get more information before she tipped Lucy off that she was a suspect. "Not yet."

"Not yet?" Kline clenched his teeth as if he were trying to stop himself from saying something he might regret. Then he slowly said, "The woman could have an airtight alibi, and before you know if she has one or not, you're asking for electronic surveillance?" Kline's speech came faster as he scolded Danielle. "Do you realize how difficult it is to get the Crown's approval for that? It's like a search warrant, Renaud. We can't do it without reasonable and probable grounds."

Danielle should have been embarrassed, but she wasn't. Something told her she was right about this, and she was sticking to her guns on this one. She took the request and shoved it in a desk drawer. "Okay, I'll hold on to it until I get it—reasonable and probable grounds, that is."

The way Kline was looking at Danielle, she was sure he was going to rake her over the coals. But he didn't. He stared at her intently for what felt like an hour but was really just a minute, then to Danielle's great relief, he just walked away.

Danielle wasn't sure how she was going to ask Lucy Miller where she was the night Kristina Buchanan was killed without tipping her off, but she was going to have to find a way. Then again, perhaps tipping her off is exactly what would shake things up. Tipping her off, then watching where she scurries is exactly what would be best, Danielle ultimately decided. But Kline was right, wiretaps required the Crown's approval. Danielle wasn't worried though—she knew she had friends and allies there.

When Danielle submitted her warrant for approval to the provincial Crown, she was told that the federal Public Prosecution Service would have to grant the warrant. That was unusual, but Danielle didn't see it being a problem since Lilly worked for the Feds.

"Sorry, Danielle." Lilly raised her hands in defeat. "I tried, but there's just not enough evidence."

"All I'm asking for, Lilly, is forty-eight hours. Tap their phones and place GPS devices on their vehicles so we can see where they go or who they talk to after I ask for her alibi."

"First of all, Danielle, wiretaps don't happen overnight. It can take weeks or even months to put them into place. And second of all, you're requesting electronic surveillance on somebody who, for all we know, could have an ironclad alibi."

"But what if she doesn't have an alibi? What if, the minute I leave her house after asking her where she was that night, she picks up the phone to talk to somebody, or does something that could tell us exactly who killed Buchanan?"

"Sorry, Danielle. The Crown can't approve this. You just don't meet the substantive requirements for granting the application."

This was one area of her work Danielle hated. She didn't see it as justice, she saw it as a game. A game that people in robes and suits played. Even if someone was found drenched in their victim's blood, still holding the knife and confessing, as soon as lawyers got involved, it became a trial in which the games began. Which lawyer can get what evidence thrown out or admitted? It wasn't about justice, it was about who played the better game. There were times Danielle hated Lilly's profession, and Lilly knew it.

Danielle grabbed the edge of Lilly's desk and propelled herself forward with great force. "Who did you talk to?"

Lilly thrust her shoulders back. "What?"

"I want to know who you talked to. I want to talk to them myself. I don't understand why a warrant that would normally be granted by the provincial Crown suddenly needs federal approval."

Lilly sat upright and crossed her arms. "Danielle, this is your first major crime. I know you're keen, and I know how frustrating it must be, but you have to understand, we can't intercept private communications without—"

"No, I don't understand, Lilly! I don't understand why we work our tails off to investigate something, we find the person who did it, and you guys screw us over by telling us this evidence or that evidence isn't admissible because some judges got together over cocktails one afternoon to interpret some legal mumbo jumbo!" Danielle's face was so flushed, and her breathing so vigorous, she looked like she'd been running a marathon. Except she was wearing patent leather shoes instead of sneakers, and a suit instead of a t-shirt and shorts.

"Danielle, calm down."

"Who do I talk to? I want them to tell me *to my face* why I can't get evidence that's just waiting for me!"

"Danielle, she hadn't been swiping ketamine, remember? The logs matched the inventory perfectly. You bring that to a judge as reasonable and probable grounds, and you'll be laughed at."

"Okay, well maybe she wasn't selling ketamine, but something is wrong there Lilly, I *know it*. And I know I could find out what it is, if only I could get some support around here."

"I'm sorry, Danielle. What you have just isn't enough. You can't come to the Crown with just a hunch."

"But I'd have more if—"

Lilly slammed her hand on the desk so hard, her coffee spilled. Danielle had never before seen this in Lilly, and it silenced her. "Listen, Danielle! I'm telling you, let—it—go!"

✖ 35 ✖

Melissa Lambert retrieved the brand new blanket she had purchased over the weekend and ran tests for bodily fluids and DNA on it, knowing full well none would be found. When the tests were completed, she printed the report and threw the new blanket into the same incinerator she had tossed the blanket Danielle had brought in. Normally items brought in for testing would be placed in storage after tests were completed, but sometimes mistakes happened and items got tossed out by mistake—especially with evidence that contained no evidence at all.

Melissa then filed the results of her report under the identification log number assigned to the original blanket Danielle had brought in.

"You processed that pretty fast," the clerk who logged the results said to Melissa.

"I aim to please our city's finest," Melissa replied.

"Especially when they just happen to be drop dead gorgeous and gay?" she teased Melissa.

Melissa rolled her eyes. "Oh, please. Constable Renaud? I'd rather have my nails pulled out one at a time."

"Turned you down, did she?"

"I'll have you know, I got fabulously laid both nights this weekend, and Constable Renaud was the last thing on my mind." That wasn't entirely true, but close enough.

Danielle had hit a roadblock with Lucy Miller, but was confident she could plow through it. She just needed to figure out how. In the meantime she decided to follow up on her other leads.

Contacting Erin Walker proved to be easy as she still had the same phone number that was in Buchanan's address book. Danielle would have preferred to interview Erin Walker in person, but a plane ticket and accommodations across the country wasn't exactly in the budget.

Erin told Danielle how Kristina had contacted her about a year before she died. She had learned of Kristina's death a week after it happened, when a friend who still lived in Halifax had heard the news and emailed her.

When Danielle asked Erin where she was when Kristina was killed, Erin disclosed her battle with breast cancer—she'd been in the hospital getting a mastectomy. Danielle would confirm this with the hospital, but believed she was telling the truth.

Danielle also asked Erin if she did drugs. She didn't expect Erin to answer truthfully if she did, but Danielle would be able to tell if Erin was lying about it. She did not appear to be, however. She told Danielle Kristina had hinted she'd love to get some high quality BC bud, but Erin told her she couldn't help her, that she didn't do illegal drugs of any kind, and had no connections whatsoever. Danielle only had one more line of questioning left for Erin.

"Did Kristina ever mention a woman named Dee?"

"Yes, she went on and on about this super expensive bracelet Dee had gotten custom-made and given to Kristina for her thirty-sixth birthday. She said it had thirty-six emeralds in it—emerald was Kristina's birthstone and green was her favorite color."

"Did she mention which jeweler made the bracelet?"

"No, but she did say it was eighteen karat white gold."

"Did she mention where Dee was born, or where she went to school?"

"Let me think…" After a brief pause Erin said, "She said she was really smart, that she had put herself through university with scholarships, but I don't remember if she mentioned which one. I suppose it would have been a veterinary college, because she did mention she was a vet."

Since Danielle was already aware of this, it was not useful information. "Did Kristina ever mention Dee's birthday, or her astrological sign, even?"

"Same sign as Kristina—Taurus. As a matter of fact, her birthday was just a few days after Kristina's. I don't know the exact date, but Kristina said she was relieved that she didn't have to buy Dee a birthday gift. I guess when Kristina asked Dee what she wanted for her birthday, she said she wanted Kristina to spend the weekend with her at some expensive resort. That was typical. Instead of buying somebody else a birthday present, Kristina got the birthday girl to give *her* an all-expenses-paid weekend in the Cape Breton highlands."

"Is there anything else Kristina said about Dee?"

"Not that I remember. At that point, to be honest, it just turned my stomach. Kristina was doing the same old, just with a different person."

Danielle didn't want to offend, but she was curious. "I hope you're not offended by this, but what was it about Kristina? I mean, if you knew she was the type to just use people…"

"You just had to know Kristina. She would never come right out and ask for anything, or make you feel like she was making you do something, she just had a really good way of making you want to do it for her. I guess you could say she was the perfect con artist."

Feeling there was nothing new Erin could provide, Danielle ended the interview and thanked her for her time.

Danielle hadn't learned much more than she already knew, except for something that didn't jive. Gillian said she thought Dee had come from money and had attended an expensive private school, while Erin said Dee had put herself through university with scholarships. Danielle didn't know if there was anything to this inconsistency, but she still made a note of it.

Danielle then faxed a request to the Canadian Veterinary Medical Association asking for a list of all female veterinarians practicing in the Halifax Regional Municipality two years ago, and to include their dates of birth.

She quickly received a phone call informing her that their registration information did not include dates of birth, just registration year. They also could not be specific as to if, or where, a particular veterinarian had been working two years ago, only where they were currently working, as they didn't track a veterinarian's work history, only kept track of their current workplace for contact purposes.

Fearing Dee may have left the Halifax area and be practicing elsewhere, Danielle modified her request. She knew of course that the name Dianne was pronounced "Dee-Ann" in French, and since Gillian Stevens thought Dee's last name was French, she wanted to search for any names that were even vaguely possible matches. In computer terms, this was called a soundex.

"In that case, what I want then is a list of all female veterinarians working in Canada, but filter the results for any given names with a soundex containing Dianne or Deeann."

"You know your computers, Constable," the database administrator complimented Danielle.

Danielle had tremendously enjoyed the computer courses she'd taken as part of her training. So much so, she had considered going into computer forensics. But when she thought of sitting at a desk for eight hours a day, investigative work won out. Danielle enjoyed the variety and fieldwork of being an investigator.

After hanging up with the Canadian Veterinary Medical Association, Danielle contacted the hospital Kristina worked at, and learned that no patients had ever died while under her care. That extinguished that lead.

Danielle used the rest of the afternoon to compile a list of custom jewelry shops in the city. There were a lot more than she expected, and she'd only gotten a chance to call a few before quitting time.

Danielle looked for Nathalie's vehicle as she drove up Maynard Street, but it still wasn't there. She had supper, then went for a long run.

It was dark when Danielle returned, and she noticed some lights on in Nathalie's apartment. Danielle was tempted to walk up to her door and knock, or call, but she had already left Nathalie a message. She would just wait for Nathalie to return her call.

But Nathalie didn't.

❧ 36 ☙

Tuesday morning Danielle started her day with an early morning swim. Citadel pool was just across the street from her new office, and the swim refreshed Danielle before she went to work.

She was pleased when the information she'd requested from the Canadian Veterinary Medical Association arrived sooner than expected. The list contained about forty names, all categorized by province. Danielle started with Nova Scotia, which had five names listed under it: Diane Redden, Dian Tidwell, Deanna Ward, Dianne Boudreau, and Deeyana Paris.

Danielle had to call one of the women at home for when she called her work number, Danielle was told it was her day off. Another, Danielle learned, was actually retired, but still worked one day every two weeks, and had just been in on the weekend. Danielle figured if she was retired that she would be too old to be Dee, so rather than hunt the woman down, Danielle simply left a message with the shelter asking for Dr. Boudreau to return her call.

Beulah Hunt chose not to start off today's session by asking her client about the dead face with black eyes, but to build some trust by asking about her client's early years.

"Were you and your siblings close growing up?"

Beulah's client tensed. "I only had one. A sister."

"Were you close in age?"

Her client lowered her eyelids before replying. "One year apart." She then crossed her arms and looked at the floor.

Beulah sensed she should pull back, so she veered the conversation toward a more carefree time in siblings' lives. "What was your favorite game to play together?" Beulah hoped a warm memory would relax her client.

But it didn't. Her client started bouncing her leg off the ball of her foot and bit down on her lip instead of answering.

Beulah recognized a road block when she saw one. Time to take a detour. "Are you and your sister on speaking terms?"

"No," came an unusually swift reply. Followed by a very sad one. "Well, I talk to her. Guess I should say I write to her. Though not as often as I used to."

"Does she answer you?"

"No," the client whispered.

"Never?"

Beulah's client fingered her chin. She didn't address the question, but she at least continued to speak, and that was progress. "My sister was very angry with me the last time we spoke."

"What was she angry with you about?"

Beulah's client stood up and walked to the window, but closed her eyes and kept them closed. She didn't speak, which was a message Beulah got loud and clear. Another roadblock requiring another detour.

"Do you look more like your mother or your father?" Beulah asked.

Beulah's client walked back to her chair and sat down. "Have no idea. We never had a father growing up, and our mother never mentioned one. Though I always suspected my sister and I had different fathers, because we didn't look alike and we were so different from each other."

"How were you different?"

"We were just different. Though we both enjoyed playing with dolls when we were young, but..." Beulah's client pressed her legs tightly together and cradled her knees with her arms before finishing her sentence. "...she would often do terrible things to them."

"Like what?"

"Once, she dug the eyes out with a pen. What she couldn't dig out, she scribbled up with a black marker. She'd break the arms off and stick them...in places. She cut a slit into one of them once, then broke an arm off and shoved the hand into the slit."

"Where was the slit?"

Beulah's client took a very long time to reply. When she finally did, her answer was almost a whisper. "Between the doll's legs."

"Were you and your sister sexually abused?" Beulah asked very softly.

Nathalie Boudreau's body turned in her chair and pulled tighter. She was almost in a fetal position when she whispered, "Yes."

Danielle was going over the work the original team had done, comparing their results with hers so far, and making sure she didn't just re-trace dead-ends.

In terms of locating Dee, they hadn't broadened their search beyond Halifax because their sources told them she worked in Halifax. Why they didn't expand their search or why they stopped looking, there was no reason indicated in the files. Danielle considered asking why but thought that might ruffle some feathers, so she decided to concentrate on being as thorough as she could be rather than question the investigative skills of the original officers.

Danielle reviewed her own notes, which brought her back to Lucy Miller. Danielle pulled out the electronic surveillance request she had tried to submit.

Wracking her brain trying to figure out how to find "reasonable and probable grounds", Danielle began at the very beginning and replayed all of the events she knew in regards to Lucy Miller. When she did, what stood out was recalling how Lucy Miller had arrived at the clinic and offered to be interviewed there. She claimed knowing Danielle was there because a coworker named Shelly had called to tell her.

Why? Why would her coworker feel compelled to call and tell her?

Danielle decided to take another look at the information she got from the clinic Lucy worked at. There might not be a discrepancy in ketamine orders after all, but maybe there was something else that might explain why the coworker called Lucy.

The original paperwork was at her apartment. Once Lilly pointed out there was no discrepancy after all, Danielle hadn't bothered filing it at work but had made a photocopy of the original paperwork before handing it over to Lilly, and Danielle did have that copy at the office. It's not that she didn't trust Lilly, it was just a habit of Danielle's to photocopy documents and keep backups in case something happened to the originals.

Danielle pulled the photocopy she'd made and took another look. It didn't take very long for her to be very confused. The information she was looking at now was identical to what she'd seen when she first noticed the discrepancies. She wasn't losing her mind, it was right there in black and white.

"Nathalie, it's not uncommon for children to exhibit the different traits you and your sister had. Some children will react to abuse with anger and hostile behavior—like your sister. And some will quietly retreat keeping everything inside, just like you did. Your sister wasn't angry at you, Nathalie, she was angry at her abuser."

"No, she was angry with me. She was definitely extremely angry with me personally, and she had every right to be."

"Why? What did you do?"

Nathalie clenched her fists but didn't reply.

Sensing a greater risk that Nathalie might flee if she was forced to go where it was still too painful for her to bear, Beulah asked a different question to keep the conversation flowing. "Where's your sister now?"

Nathalie relaxed her fists but grasped the flesh of her upper thighs and squeezed hard. "In Cape Breton."

"Do you visit her often?"

Nathalie let go of the flesh she had clenched in her grasp and started rubbing. "Rarely."

"What about your mother?"

"My mother's dead," Nathalie said quickly. She closed her eyes then rubbed her forehead. "Actually, that's not true. She's not dead." Nathalie lowered her hands and opened her eyes but didn't look at Beulah. "It's just easier for me to think she is."

"Why is that?"

"Because…" A single tear came down Nathalie's face, and her lip began to quiver. "It's easier for me to think she couldn't be there for me rather than the fact that she just didn't want to be."

Beulah would have liked to have asked who had died if it wasn't her mother. She was hoping she'd finally learn the identity of the person who was the source of Nathalie's torment, but she also knew she couldn't push or Nathalie would undoubtedly shut down again, so Beulah veered the conversation away from the decedent in her life.

"Where's your mother now?"

"She's in Cape Breton—I think. At least she was, last time I spoke to her."

"When was that?"

Nathalie's single tear was soon followed by several more. She bit down on her bottom lip then released it just long enough to say, "At my sister's funeral."

Danielle knew what she was seeing, but just to make sure, she walked upstairs to Sergeant Carvery's office.

"Hey, how's it goin'?" Sergeant Carvery smiled at Danielle.

Danielle spied a brand new pacifier on the corner of Carvery's desk and pointed to it. "Gum's not taking the cigarette cravings away anymore?"

Sergeant Carvery laughed. "That's for my infant granddaughter. My wife and I are babysitting while her mother recovers from some minor surgery. What can I do for you?"

"I've got something here you might find interesting. Care to look at it?"

"Sure. What is it?"

Danielle explained where she got the information and how she discovered the discrepancies proving Lucy Miller was ordering more ketamine than the clinic was using.

Sergeant Carvery stared at the information in front of him. His hand rose to his forehead then swept its way down, stretching his face in the process. "Kinda looks that way," he said. He paused, still staring at the information, then asked, "Do you mind if I hold on to this? I'd like to cross-reference it with some of our undercover operations."

"Sure, just let me make a copy of it first."

"I'll do it. I need the exercise," Carvery said as he patted his stomach. "I'll bring this back down to you in a few minutes."

Danielle wasn't comfortable with that, but before she had time to object, Sergeant Carvery was out of sight.

An hour later, Sergeant Carvery still hadn't brought Danielle's paperwork back, so she ran up to his office, only to find him out of the office. Danielle decided then to take a quick run to her apartment for the original she had given Lilly, which she knew was sitting in a box of papers she hadn't yet gotten around to shredding.

When she drove up Maynard Street, she noticed Nathalie's car parked on the street. After retrieving the paperwork she wanted, she called Nathalie again, but to no surprise, Nathalie didn't pick up.

Instead of going back to the office, Danielle walked up to Nathalie's apartment and knocked on the door. She heard footsteps approach on the other side, and an eye appear through the peephole. Danielle expected the door to open, but it didn't. She waited another half minute, and when the door still didn't open, she knocked again and waited.

Danielle leaned against the door and said, "Nathalie, I know you're in there. I know you can hear me."

Danielle turned her back to the door and leaned against it. She waited another moment, then took out her pen and notepad. She scribbled something down then slipped the note under the door. She then loudly hurried down one flight of stairs, removed her shoes, then tiptoed back up. She waited a good ten minutes—during which time Danielle had very quietly put her shoes back on—before Nathalie's door finally opened.

When it did, Danielle launched her foot inside, and shoved her badge in the opening. "RCMP—step away from the door!"

To her relief, Nathalie did.

When Danielle stepped in, she could hardly see anything. All the curtains were closed, and it was dark inside.

"I take it this means there's really no package for me that was accidentally delivered to your apartment, which you left in front of my door for me to retrieve?"

Danielle replied with a hint of Catholic guilt. "Sorry, but you've been avoiding me, and—do you mind if I turn on a light? Or open the curtains? I can barely see you."

Nathalie walked over to the windows facing the street and opened the curtains, then raised the heavy blind behind them. Light flooded that side of the apartment.

"Is this official business?" Nathalie asked, with her arms folded and her body language making it clear she wasn't happy she'd been tricked.

"Why have you been avoiding me?" Danielle's voice was soft and sad sounding.

Nathalie, whose face was expressionless, repeated her question brusquely. "Is this official business?"

Danielle wanted to say, "Yes, it is. I'm arresting you for breaking and entering. You've entered my heart, and now you're breaking it." But didn't. Instead, she sighed. Sighed very deeply, and sat herself down in a chair near the sunlit window. "I'm sorry if what I did—"

"You didn't do anything, Danielle. I've just been busy." Nathalie walked away from the window and closer to the darkness at the opposite end of the apartment. She stared at the shut curtains over the back window, keeping her back to Danielle. She placed her hands across her temples and forehead and rubbed.

"Nathalie?" Danielle spoke very softly. "Do you have a migraine?"

Nathalie heard the blind behind her close, and the light simultaneously disappear. "I'm sorry, I didn't realize."

Danielle walked toward Nathalie, but Nathalie walked away and sat down.

"Can I get you something? A wet face cloth?" Danielle asked.

Nathalie leaned her head back against the sofa and closed her eyes. "Thanks, but it won't help."

Danielle wanted to tell her to lie down, to rub her temples, and to relieve her headache for her, but she knew better.

Nathalie kept her eyes closed as she bent forward, placed her hands behind her neck, and pulled as far down toward her knees as she could.

Danielle sat down next to Nathalie. She knew she shouldn't, but she couldn't stop herself from gently placing a hand on Nathalie's upper back.

Nathalie stiffened at first, but then relaxed and her breathing slowed.

Danielle moved her hand up under Nathalie's hair, to the back of her neck, and said, "Sometimes applying pressure here helps." Danielle pressed her thumb across the base of Nathalie's skull. She pressed deeply but gently, as if squeezing out the last bit of toothpaste from its shell.

Danielle did this repeatedly until she could not hold back any longer. With her right hand pressing along Nathalie's neck and skull, Danielle brought her left hand up to Nathalie's cheek…and lovingly touched it.

Nathalie stood up and quickly made her way to the bathroom. She was there longer than she needed to be, so Danielle knew she had crossed a line again.

When Nathalie returned, she opened the curtains and blinds of both windows. "My headache's gone away, thanks."

Danielle wasn't quite sure she believed Nathalie, but she was glad to have light in the room. She saw Nathalie clearly for the first time since entering her apartment and noticed she looked terrible. Her eyes were red, her skin was sallow, her thin lips looked even thinner, her hair was frizzy—and all over the place. And yet…Danielle longed to kiss her.

"I haven't been feeling well, and I had to meet a deadline, so I sort of holed up for a few days. I know I should have taken just a minute to call you, but I just forget sometimes that the world is going on out there when I'm composing." Nathalie sat on the love seat, as far away as possible from Danielle while still remaining in the living room and looked at the floor.

"Do you regret what happened last Friday? Between you and me?" Danielle tensed as she waited for Nathalie's reply.

Nathalie rubbed her forehead. "It's complicated, Danielle."

"I know, Nathalie. But sometimes things happen that you don't expect—they just happen naturally because they're right. And sometimes you think something should be a certain way, so you try, but you just can't, because it's not right." Danielle didn't come right out and say it, but she hoped Nathalie knew when she said that last part, that she was referring to herself and Rachel—and Nathalie and Lilly.

"Danielle, you don't want to get involved with me."

"Why not? You're smart, and talented, and funny—."

"I just can't, Danielle. And it's for your own good, I assure you."

Danielle walked over to Nathalie who was now standing by the door. She placed her right hand on Nathalie's waist. "I know you feel it too, Nathalie. I know you do."

Nathalie opened the door. "Please leave, Danielle."

Danielle was back at her desk looking at a totally different set of numbers again, but this time she knew she wasn't just seeing things. As much as she didn't understand it, it was clear that the paperwork Lilly returned to Danielle wasn't the same paperwork Danielle had given her. What Lilly returned to Danielle…had been altered.

Danielle rushed out of her office and went to Lilly's. She didn't wait for reception to announce her arrival. She stormed past reception and opened Lilly's door, not caring who was inside or what she might be interrupting.

Danielle's already existing anger and confusion rose even higher when she saw Sergeant Carvery sitting there holding her paperwork in his hand.

"What the hell is going on here?" Danielle snarled like a woman who just discovered her lover in bed with another.

"Lillian, should I call security?" The receptionist who chased after Danielle and was now standing behind her asked.

"No, everything's fine, Frances, thank you. The three of us are going to be in a meeting though, so please hold all of my calls."

"I want some answers right now," Danielle demanded as soon as the door was closed.

"Have a seat, Danielle. I'll let Lu fill you in."

"Lu, is it? I suppose being on a first-name basis is why you took my paperwork to Lilly instead of a photocopier? So she could alter that too?" Danielle lunged toward Lilly and shouted, "I thought you were my friend! What are you trying to do to me?"

Sergeant Luis Carvery guided Danielle into a chair. "Let me explain, Renaud."

Danielle sat, but glared at Lilly.

Sergeant Carvery detailed the year-long drug investigation of Maurice Coultier. "He gets the goods from several sources in Halifax. Heroin and cocaine from ships coming into port, and all sorts of pills from labs crooked chemists are cooking up on the side. He then secures the drugs underneath the rail cars of the train heading for Montreal. Some of it is retrieved when it makes a stop in Moncton, and the rest continues its journey to Montreal."

Danielle recalled how climbing underneath rail cars was part of Maurice Coultier's job. "That's all very interesting, *Lu*." Danielle emphasized Sergeant Carvery's nickname quite sarcastically. "But that's no reason for Lilly to sabotage my case."

Lilly seemed undaunted by the glare that was directed squarely at her. "You don't *have* a case, Danielle," she rebuked. "Maurice Coultier has an airtight alibi, and your meddling is only going to cost us a large drug bust if you keep this up."

"His wife doesn't have an alibi, and she's my suspect," Danielle reminded Lilly.

"You don't know if she has an alibi or not. You haven't checked, have you?"

Danielle was too enraged to be embarrassed. "The only reason I haven't is I wanted surveillance on her and her husband when I did ask."

"You're not going to get your wiretaps or any other electronic surveillance, Danielle. The drug unit's already got theirs in place, and we can't put theirs at risk for just a hunch you might have. I've presented this to the provincial Crown and they agree."

Even though Danielle was offended by Lilly's use of the word "hunch", she offered a compromise. "Okay, so if the Feds already have wiretaps in place, just give me a report on who she calls and what she says after I ask for her alibi."

"Can't," Lilly proclaimed.

"And why not?" Danielle asked with renewed anger—and disgust.

"Because nothing obtained from a federal investigation would be admissible in a provincial one."

"What are you saying? That even if Lucy Miller confessed to Buchanan's murder in a telephone conversation recorded by the drug unit, the Crown wouldn't let me use that confession to arrest her?"

"That's right."

Danielle's voice was vile as she glared at Lilly once again and said, "I don't believe you."

"No? Look up the McWade decision—*Larson versus Canada.*" Lilly picked up the paperwork Sergeant Carvery handed to her after Danielle sat down and put it through a shredder sitting on the floor next to her desk. "I've already documented my concerns in regards to your hunch, Danielle. I can't stop you from going back to the clinic to get the information again, but you'll never be able to use it to get approval for electronic surveillance—I'll make sure of that."

Danielle was wounded by what she perceived as her friend's betrayal. "Lilly, I thought you were my friend."

"I can't sink a case over a friendship, Danielle."

Danielle's anger melted into hurt. "What you really mean is, you've got no problem sinking a friendship over a case."

Sergeant Carvery's eyebrows constricted so much his eyes were barely visible, even though he was giving Lillian Marsh a long, lingering look. "The McWade decision?"

"Caught that, did you?"

"I'm impressed with your improvisational skills Lilly, but what's going to happen when she finds out that no decision exists and that you flat out and out lied to her about any information obtained from our wiretaps not being admissible in provincial cases?"

"Lu, I know Danielle is eager to prove herself, but her career isn't on the line—*mine* is. I can't let Danielle or anyone else interfere with this case. I can't afford to take that chance, and you know it."

"Even for a friend? A very *good* friend?"

Sergeant Carvery leaned forward as Lilly's composure crumpled before him in response.

Melissa's findings in Nathalie's apartment on Saturday disturbed her. Which is why she took the day off so she could drive to Nathalie's cottage, knowing Nathalie would be in the city.

She didn't have a copy of Nathalie's key to the cottage, but she suspected there was a copy stuffed into one of the planters near the door, just as Nathalie had one in a planter in her back yard in the city.

They had come home from listening to some live music one night when Nathalie couldn't find her key, so she went to the back yard and stuck her hand into one of her planters, retrieving a key that was protected by the dirt and rain by a zip-lock bag.

Even though Nathalie was frequently away, she never asked Melissa to watch Chai. She would always put her up in a motel for pets—which Melissa thought was absolutely ridiculous. And when Melissa said so, Nathalie told her she felt better knowing Chai had twenty-four-hour care instead of just a few minutes each day. That's when Melissa decided, if there was any such thing as reincarnation, she wanted to come back as Nathalie's cat.

So despite Nathalie never giving Melissa a key, Melissa had copies anyway. She'd snuck in the back yard one day when she knew

Nathalie was at her cottage, retrieved the key, had two copies made, then returned the key to its planter. Nathalie was none the wiser.

She hoped Nathalie had done the same at the cottage, and to Melissa's glee, she had. She pulled a zip-lock bag out of the third planter she dug through and removed the key.

When she got to the door though, she saw something that caused her to exclaim, "Oh my God!"

Shelly Boutilier's eyes darted in Danielle's direction the second she walked in the door at the Victoria Veterinary Clinic. Danielle noticed this and walked up to her, telling her she wanted to speak with her privately. The nervous vet tech scrambled to find an empty room with a door that could be closed. When they were inside, she shut the door, and fear was evident on her face. Danielle knew vulnerability when she saw it, so she went for the jugular right off the bat.

"Do you know what the sentence for aiding and abetting is, Shelly?"

Shelly fell into a chair.

"You tipped Lucy off that I was here asking questions about the break-in, and that's because you knew she had ordered extra Ketaset to sell on the side," Danielle confidently summarized. "If you tell me everything now, I'll consider not charging you. As long as you tell me everything you do know. Otherwise, you're in one heck of a mess."

It took mere seconds for Shelly Boutilier to start blurting out everything she knew. She related a series of events that started just a month prior to Buchanan's death, when she temporarily performed Lucy's duties while Lucy was on vacation.

Shelly confessed how the morning after the clinic had been broken into she checked the inventory very carefully, and based on what was ordered and what was in inventory, she thought some of those vials had been stolen during the break-in, so she reported it. When Lucy returned and was told about the theft, Shelly thought she acted strangely about it. Though the matter was cleared up—by Lucy—and their manager called the police back to tell them that no Ketaset was missing after all, Shelly became suspicious, and confronted Lucy privately about it.

According to Shelly, Lucy admitted to ordering extra ketamine for herself but begged her not to tell. Shelly agreed, but only on the condition that it stop. Lucy said she would right after Christmas, that she just needed a bit more money, and then she would stop for good.

"But she stopped in September," Danielle told Shelly.

Shelly didn't display any type of surprise. "Yes, because I confided in my sister-in-law, and after that, all of a sudden it stopped. I guess Joe flipped a lid when she told him, and he put a stop to it."

"Who's your sister-in-law?" Danielle asked even though she knew the answer before it came across Shelly's lips.

"Joyce Coultier. She's married to Maurice Coultier's—"

"Brother," Danielle chimed in.

Armed with her new information, Danielle drove directly to Joe Coultier's home. She knew he'd be at work, and Danielle wanted to talk to his wife alone.

Danielle told Joyce Coultier what she learned from Shelly, then asked her, "Why do you and your husband think Lucy Miller was so much better for Maurice if she was dealing drugs?"

"She wasn't dealing drugs. She just ordered a couple extra bottles of cat sedative for the shelter she volunteered at so they could get it at cost. It was to do surgeries on animals people couldn't afford."

"Do you seriously believe that, Mrs. Coultier?"

"Of course. I do, because it's the truth."

"Is that what Joe believed?"

"Why wouldn't he?"

"Then why did he, to use Shelly's exact words, 'flip a lid' when he found out what Lucy was up to?"

"He was mad at first, but when he went and spoke to Maurice about it, Maurice explained everything. Lucy was just helping out at a shelter. They couldn't afford the huge prices the pharmacies charge, and Lucy was able to order it from the drug company directly. After Joe found that out, everything was okay."

Danielle wondered if Mrs. Coultier was really so gullible. She doubted her husband was.

It was almost quitting time for Joe Coultier when Danielle arrived at the dockyard where he worked as a welder. He didn't seem very pleased to see she was the reason for his being summoned to the office.

"Mr. Coultier, sorry to bother you at work, but I have something very important I need to ask you."

Joe Coultier didn't respond or even sit down.

"I want to know why you never told me you knew Lucy Miller was selling ketamine hydrochloride."

"What are you talking about?"

"I'm talking about the information your wife relayed to you, information that Lucy Miller was ordering extra vials of ketamine from work, and selling it for her own personal profit."

"Where'd you hear something crazy like that?"

"From your wife."

Joe Coultier's eyes looked like they'd just been shot out of a cannon. "When were you talking to my wife?"

"An hour ago."

"You went to my house when I wasn't there?"

"Yes, Mr. Coultier. It's your wife I wanted to talk to, so I went to *her* home. Do you have a problem with that?" Danielle had a very strong feeling Mr. Coultier needed putting in his place. "If you do, I have no problem taking her to the police station instead."

Joe Coultier's pale blue eyes darkened as the pupils opened up, like a double-barreled shot gun readying for its target. "Why are you here?"

"As I said, I'm here because I want to know why you never told me Lucy had been stealing ketamine hydrochloride from her workplace."

"She wasn't stealing it, she was paying for it. She just ordered some extra and paid for it herself, so cats in the shelter could get fixed."

"Joe, I know you're not stupid. Sure, you're just a welder, but I know you've got a brain in there."

Danielle was amazed at Joe Coultier's self-control. His eyes seared into her, with his face exhibiting such loathing it looked ten years older in a matter of seconds, yet he didn't even flinch.

"Are you aware, Joe, that any vet or vet tech can purchase ketamine directly from the drug companies? No shelter would have needed Lucy to order it for them."

The veins in Joe Coultier's neck popped out as he continued to drill his eyes into Danielle. It didn't bother Danielle in the least.

"Are you the reason Lucy suddenly stopped—"

"Look, I have nothing to say. I know you can't force me to talk to you, so I'm done."

It frustrated Danielle that certain television shows made her job so much harder these days. The steel stairs at the end of the hallway echoed and vibrated with each step as Joe Coultier irately stomped down each and every one of them.

As a result of discovering Nathalie had a security system installed at her cottage, Melissa Lambert looked around the exterior of the cottage for the phone line. When she found it, she used a small pen knife to cut the wire. Of course, she was wearing gloves. She hadn't expected the alarm system, so she hadn't anticipated needing electrical tape to repair the wire after she was done, but like a good girl scout, Melissa was always prepared—she had some in the trunk of her car.

Melissa knew that telephone wires contained very little voltage, so that was safe to cut. She also knew that most alarms contained a built-in emergency signal that was sent to the alarm company if its main wire was cut, but by cutting the telephone wire instead, the alarm would continue to display and report normal functioning to the alarm company doing the monitoring, it just would not be able to send any emergency signals out to anyone.

But that would not stop the alarm from screaming bloody, blue murder if it did go off. And in these parts, on the shores of the Minas Basin in the Annapolis Valley, sound traveled at the speed of light, and neighbors did check on each other, so Melissa had to make sure that didn't happen either.

She knew how to bypass that, too, however. All she had to do, once she got in, was to turn off power to the alarm to stop it from blaring. She was aware of a battery backup that allows the computer on these types of alarms to continue functioning during power outages, but with the main breaker off, at least the alarm horn would not sound. And though the backup might attempt to notify the alarm company that the power was off, with the telephone wire cut, that report would never reach its destination.

When she got in, the alarm started beeping its warning. She had forty-five seconds to find the main power panel and cut off power to the alarm before it would screech at eighty-five decibels. She found it in forty.

Danielle knew she was defeated when it came to obtaining any electronic surveillance of Lucy Miller, so she decided she might as well go ask Lucy for her alibi.

When Lucy opened the door, Danielle displayed her badge and officially stated, "Ms. Miller, I'm here because I'm investigating the death of Kristina Buchanan. May I come in?"

"No, you may not." Lucy held the door open a few inches, but would not open it any further.

Danielle was not deterred. "I need to know where you were the night Kristina Buchanan—your husband's ex-girlfriend—was killed."

"Unless you have a warrant, Officer, you are to leave my property immediately. You are not welcome here, and if you ever approach me again without a warrant, I'll have you charged with sexual harassment."

Wonderful, Danielle said to herself. *Just freaking wonderful...*as the door slammed shut in her face.

Danielle sat in her apartment that evening feeling lonelier than she'd ever felt in her life. It was one thing not to hear from someone because they were no longer here on earth, but it was in some ways even more painful when you knew the person was alive and well, just *didn't want* to talk to you.

Danielle felt her world falling apart. In one single afternoon, she'd lost her best friend, maybe even her case, and any chances for career advancement, too. And to top it all off, she had fallen—*hard*—for someone who couldn't care less about her. Or just didn't know how to.

❧ 38 ❧

Wednesday morning Danielle went for both a run and a swim before work. She awoke at five, and unable to fall back asleep, decided to just start her day earlier than usual.

When she got to the office she continued working on trying to locate Dee. In addition to calling more jewelry shops and asking them to search their records for a custom-made bracelet containing thirty-six emeralds in a white gold setting, she also contacted resorts in Cape Breton, requesting guest records for the May sixteenth weekend—the weekend following Kristina's thirty-sixth birthday, which was May tenth. Erin Walker said Dee's birthday was just a few days after Kristina's, so Danielle figured it was most likely the weekend they would have gone to the resort.

Danielle had just hung up from making an inquiry at one of the resorts when her phone rang.

"Constable Renaud, this is Eric MacPherson from Latent Prints. You asked for us to give you a call when we processed the items you requested."

"Have you finished already?"

"A lot of what you brought in was too degraded, but I had better luck with one strip of duct tape and the interior of the tin box. The prints I lifted all belong to the same guy."

"You ran them through the system?"

"Sure did, and we got a hit. Name is Hill. Tucker Canada Hill."

"*Canada*? His middle name is *Canada*?" This was a new one for Danielle. "Who in their right mind names their kid Canada?"

"Maybe his mother was on drugs or something," Eric joked.

"Really," Danielle agreed. "So how long before you'll have those reports uploaded?" All reports pertaining to an investigation was entered into a database investigating officers could access.

"Give me ten minutes."

"Wonderful. Thanks so much, Eric."

"You're welcome."

Fifteen minutes later, Danielle had Tucker Canada Hill's name, date of birth, social insurance number, and Record of Arrest and Prosecution—more commonly known as a RAP sheet.

Tucker Hill had been arrested four times in the three months prior to Buchanan's death. Oddly, he had a squeaky clean record up until that point. In all four cases, he had been picked up in the Bayer's Lake shopping district—three times for shoplifting, once for drunkenness—and at the time of his arrests, had no fixed address.

Danielle ran his name through the Registry of Motor Vehicles and discovered he had not renewed his driver's license even though it had expired two years earlier. His last address was listed as Margaree. Danielle did not know exactly where in Nova Scotia that was, but a quick search revealed it was on Cape Breton Island—which was not technically an island anymore, since they had built a causeway linking the island to the mainland of Nova Scotia quite a few years back. But one thing Danielle did know, despite a mere four years in Halifax, was that to the people of Cape Breton—causeway or not—Cape Breton was and always would be an island.

Danielle could not locate a phone number for Tucker Hill, though. She would have extended her search to his family but both his parents were deceased and he had no siblings.

Danielle plugged his social insurance number into a national database that linked healthcare, social insurance number, employment insurance, Canada pension, and other federal services in one hub. If he was drawing Employment Insurance benefits, paying into or receiving Canada Pension, or if he had even visited a doctor anywhere in Canada recently, his current address and phone number would be on file.

While Hill was a common surname, his given names—Tucker Canada—certainly were not. It took only seconds for Danielle to get a hit. The only problem was, a hit was all she got. Because of the strict privacy laws, she would have to go through a frustrating rigmarole and submit an official request to obtain any information about him, and that included his current address and contact number. Red tape was such a pain.

Danielle submitted a written request right away, then called to see if she could get the request fast-tracked, or even better, the information over the phone.

"Four to six weeks," the federal government employee informed her.

"Four to six weeks? This is a homicide investigation. I'm RCMP."

"Sorry. Doesn't matter who you are, no information over the phone. Written requests only—no exceptions."

But under FOIPOP I'm entitled to information from Vital Statistics without—"

"That's provincial—we fall under the federal Privacy Act. Like I said, doesn't matter who you are, no exceptions."

"Can you at least tell me if the address I have is his current one? What I have is—"

"No can do. I told you, can't tell you a thing over the phone. Submit your request in writing on official RCMP letterhead, and you'll get a response back in writing. That's why it can take up to six weeks."

Arrrrggggghhh! That's what Danielle wanted to yell into the phone, but resigned to the fact that she was at the mercy of "the system" yet again, she just thanked the gentleman for his time and hung up.

Sergeant Carvery spit out his gum before he spoke. "You're taking quite the risk, coming here."

"Crown attorneys and police officers confer all the time, Lu." Lilly knew she was taking a risk, but she didn't care—she couldn't afford to right now.

"Not when the Crown attorney is risking her job by going against orders from the top. You know if the brass finds out you're involved in this and it goes sour, it'll sink your career—*for good* this time."

"I know that." Lilly was pacing in front of Sergeant Luis Carvery's desk. "Believe me, I know that all too well."

"Do you think she'll let it go?"

Lilly shook her head. "Of course not."

"So what's the worst case scenario? Renaud goes there, spooks them, and they shut down operations for a while?"

"We can't afford another delay, Lu. We've already been at this for a year, and we've got Moncton and Montreal just about ready to roll."

"What if we roll now? Don't we have enough?"

Lilly's mind wandered to Danielle's anger and frustration at the judicial system. Lilly agreed with it at this very moment. "I need this case to be solid before you roll on it, Luis. Do *not* give the order until you have everything in place. *Promise* me."

"I don't want to lose this operation either. Especially not after a year's worth of work. But if Renaud causes the guy to cease operations, even if only temporarily—"

"I lost a major drug case once, Lu. A loss that almost cost me my career and had me sent back to—" Lilly interrupted her own speech when an idea came to her. "I just thought of something." She grabbed her cell phone and dialed a number. After a pause, she said, "Hi, Melissa? It's Lilly. I need a *huge* favor from you."

Yesterday morning had been an incredible breakthrough. Beulah had gotten Nathalie to finally divulge who had died. The session had not progressed any further however, because Nathalie had broken down weeping, and continued to do so until their session ended.

Beulah eased into this morning's session by purposefully not bringing up her sister's death, but something else altogether.

"Do you paint, Nathalie?"

"Do you mean like brush and easel paint?"

"Yes, artistic painting. You describe colors sometimes in such a way, I've wondered." Beulah thought this type of conversation would relax Nathalie, but it seemed to agitate her.

"I don't paint anymore."

Despite Nathalie's uncomfortable reaction, Beulah pressed. "Why not?"

Nathalie placed her index finger on the arm of her chair and started tracing what appeared to be a letter "S", back and forth, back and forth.

"Why don't you paint anymore, Nathalie?"

Nathalie stopped tracing and clutched the arms of her chair. "I don't need to paint anymore. I see all the colors I want to see when I dream."

Beulah knew it was a sidestep, but she knew when to back off. And when to seize an opportunity to head in another direction. "Did you have any nightmares last night?"

Nathalie quoted Mahatma Gandhi. "Those with the greatest awareness have the greatest nightmares."

Beulah found Nathalie frustrating at times. She was clearly very intelligent—to the point of being sly, even. And she had an incredible knack for answering questions without really providing an answer. But Beulah was well versed in the psychological dance of therapy.

"What was your last nightmare about?"

"About..." Nathalie began to trace something with her finger again. "Death."

"Your sister's death?"

Nathalie didn't answer.

Beulah took a risk. "How did your sister die, Nathalie?"

There was a very long pause. "Can I ask you something?" Nathalie finally broke her silence to ask.

"Yes, of course."

"Can you be forced to reveal what is said in our counseling sessions, or is it truly confidential, that no matter what I tell you, it stays between us?"

"It depends. All sessions are confidential, yes. But there is one exception, and that is when a client expresses a real intent to cause harm to themselves or to others. In such cases, I am obligated by law to report it to the authorities so that any harm can be prevented." Beulah wondered why Nathalie was asking this. Perhaps she was just feeling vulnerable and needed assurances? Or perhaps...

"Are you planning on harming yourself or anyone else, Nathalie?"

Nathalie didn't answer right away and when she did, didn't really answer the question at all. "What about in circumstances where a crime's already been committed? If someone confesses to a serious crime, let's say."

"Psychologists follow the Psychological Association's Code of Ethics. We are only allowed to break confidentiality when we believe a true intent to cause harm exists. Any confessions to crimes already committed are considered part of therapy and, therefore, we are not obligated to report them." Beulah wasn't sure if this convinced her client or not, so she added, "As a psychologist, my duty is to treat my clients' mental and emotional health, not to prosecute their past actions."

Nathalie was typically silent again.

"Is there something you'd like to tell me?" Beulah asked.

Nathalie said nothing.

"How did your sister die, Nathalie?" Beulah expected Nathalie to remain silent, but she didn't.

"I killed her," she simply replied.

"You're going to Cape Breton?" Staff Sergeant Kline asked Danielle after learning she'd put in an out-of-office notification.

"I found a possible witness to the Buchanan dumping."

"Really? Tell me all about it." Kline sat on the corner of Danielle's desk instead of a chair.

She told Kline what she found in the den, and how even after a year and a half, the talented latent prints technician had lifted Tucker Hill's prints from a piece of duct tape and interior of the tin box.

"What makes you think he was there the night her body was dumped?"

Still burning from her inability to follow her strongest lead with Lucy Miller, Danielle riled, "It's a lead, Staff. And if you'd allow me to do my job and follow the leads I do get—"

"Whoa, settle down. Nobody's stopping you."

"No? You might want to ask the judicial system."

"Danielle, I know it can be extremely frustrating. Believe me, I've wanted to haul a few judges and attorneys out into the parking lot and kick the you-know-what out of them myself a few times, but we've got no choice. If anything, it makes us more determined and forces us to be thorough. I'll be honest with you. I didn't have much faith we'd get any further on this case by bringing you in, but I'm starting to think we just might."

Kline got up and walked out the door, then popped his head back in. "When you get to Margaree stop at a small greasy spoon called Flo's Flounder—best fish and chips in the world."

Kline's encouragement and belief in her lifted Danielle's spirits somewhat, even though she was still crushed over Lilly's betrayal. Danielle understood the importance of a high-profile case to an attorney's career, but Lilly could have supported her. There were other options. Instead, Lilly hung her out to dry, and Danielle could never forgive her for that.

By the end of the day, Danielle had cleared every Nova Scotian veterinarian on her list—except for one. Dianne Boudreau had still not returned Danielle's call despite several messages.

After spending the entire day on the phone following up on the bracelet, the resorts, and the list of veterinarians, Danielle's workday ended with a much needed swim.

Danielle was sitting in front of the television not seeing or hearing what was on it when her phone rang. She looked at the caller ID and saw it was Lilly. Danielle was still very angry and hurt, and there was nothing Lilly could say to change how she felt. Lilly had betrayed her and sabotaged her case, plain and simple.

Danielle didn't even want her leaving a message though, so she picked up the phone and hung it back up immediately. She then turned the phone back on and shoved it in a drawer so she wouldn't hear the open-line signal.

❧ 39 ❧

"How did you kill your sister, Nathalie?" Beulah Hunt cut right to the chase this morning, if only to see how Nathalie would react.

"Did you read the files?" Nathalie asked.

"If you're talking about your medical records, yes I did. I was able to gain access based on medical grounds."

Beulah monitored Nathalie's body language very closely. Based on what she saw, she felt she should move Nathalie back to a more comfortable distance from the event, to start further back and move gently toward it.

"You didn't have an easy childhood."

Nathalie sat silently, with little reaction.

"I know this is difficult, Nathalie, but you have to talk about it if you want the nightmares to stop."

Nathalie was crouched in her chair. "I don't know where to start, Beulah,"

"Tell me about the last time the three of you were together. You, your sister, and your mother." Beulah knew she was pushing Nathalie into a minefield, but felt it was imperative.

Tears pooled in Nathalie's eyes, and some time passed before she answered. "I was eleven and Chantal was ten." Nathalie swallowed, and said no more.

Beulah realized she would have to do some major pulling and pushing over trap doors Nathalie wasn't expecting. "Was it your mother who called the authorities?" Beulah held her breath while she waited for Nathalie's reaction to the question Beulah already knew the answer to.

"No. She was too busy drinking the bottle of whiskey she had sold me for."

Beulah released an internal sigh of relief. That door brought them to level two. Now on to level three. Beulah was extremely cautious now, and monitored Nathalie very closely as she directed her toward a very specific memory—one that Beulah now knew encased the extremely volatile nucleus of Nathalie's torment. "Who alerted the police?"

Nathalie brought her arms across her chest. More than a full minute passed before she attempted a reply. "After it was done…there was blood all over, and…" Nathalie leapt out of her chair and bolted from the office.

Staff Sergeant John Kline was waiting for Danielle when she walked into work.

"Let me see the paperwork you have proving Lucy Miller was lifting ketamine."

"How did you—"

"I've been a cop a long time, Renaud. I know how to keep my ear to the ground."

Danielle handed him a copy of the information she'd gotten a second time when she was at the clinic to see Shelly Boutilier.

Kline looked it over, then said, "Very good work." He placed the paperwork down on Danielle's desk and asked, "Does her alibi check out?"

"She wouldn't talk to me. Said I'd better have a warrant next time I tried to talk to her."

"Then you'd best go get yourself one."

"But I'm not sure if any judge—"

Kline slid the paperwork back toward Danielle. "Here's your reasonable grounds, Renaud. Might not be enough for wiretaps, but it's definitely enough for a warrant to get her in here for twenty-four hours. You prepare the warrant, and by the time you're done, I'll have a judge ready to sign it."

For the first time in thirty-six hours, Danielle smiled.

Nathalie was in the washroom for almost ten minutes before returning to Beulah's office with a freshly washed face.

"Are you okay, Nathalie? Would you like to end our session for today?"

"I really need these nightmares to stop, Beulah. I'd like to continue."

Beulah nodded. "Okay. I was asking who notified the authorities when you left for the washroom. You're sure you're okay to continue?"

Nathalie breathed in deeply. "No…but I will."

"Take whatever time you need," Beulah told her.

After a minute or so, Nathalie spoke with some renewed strength. "As soon as he left the bedroom Chantal came in to see if I was all right. It terrified her seeing me like that, with so much blood all over. I was in so much pain, I could barely move, and I was having such a hard time breathing. She thought I was dying, so she snuck out the window and ran to a neighbor's. They're the ones who called."

"Did you get to see Chantal all that time you were in the hospital?"

"No, she'd been taken into protective care. I didn't get to see her till I was released. She must have been so terrified by herself, without me to look after her. When I got out we were put in the same foster home at least."

"You didn't stay there very long, though. Your foster parents wanted to keep you, but they couldn't deal with Chantal's anger and hostile behavior."

Beulah was hoping for some verbal confirmation from Nathalie, but Nathalie didn't provide it.

"You always refused to be separated from her though, even if it cost you the stability of a safe and caring environment. Did Chantal not receive the same counseling you did?"

"Yes, but it didn't do her any good. I suppose when your own mother can't even force herself to love and protect you…" Nathalie subdued her trembling lip by biting down on it.

"It wasn't your fault, Nathalie. Your mother was—"

"We were her children!" Nathalie exhibited a sudden anger Beulah had never seen before. Her emotional transformation was so swift, her face didn't even look like her own. "Everywhere in this world, all you hear is how the mother's instinct is so strong. A lioness protecting her cubs. The strongest bond that exists is between mother and child." Nathalie created a fist and punched herself as she shouted. "Well, what was so *fucking* wrong with *us* that our *own mother* couldn't even force herself to love us? Me especially. I was so damned *worthless* to her as a human being, that she sold me for a goddamned forty ouncer of whiskey!" Nathalie sobbed so forcefully, she began to hyperventilate.

Beulah waited for Nathalie's boiled over reaction to simmer down before she said to her, "Nathalie, your worth had nothing to do with your mother's inability to parent. Your mother was an alcoholic—a severe one—and alcoholics and addicts often act in ways they shouldn't or don't want to. Often, all they can think about is getting their hands on the substance they're addicted to." Beulah watched Nathalie very carefully as she spoke, because Nathalie was now curled up in her chair, rocking herself.

When Danielle showed up in Staff Sergeant Kline's office with her typed, unsigned warrant, he had good and bad news for her.

"The good news is that Judge Harrington is going to sign it. The bad news is, he can't until Monday morning, and no other judge will either—don't ask why. Just be grateful you'll have Lucy Miller here at the station on Monday. In the meantime, go to Cape Breton and see what you can get out of your—hopefully—witness."

"I'm surprised you were able to get your sister's juvenile records," Beulah said to Nathalie.

Nathalie didn't disclose how she got them, but she did say, "I had no idea she'd done half the things that were in there."

"Your sister was very troubled, Nathalie. Her records are classic of someone who's been through what you and she—"

"But *she* didn't go through most of it, I did. I protected her from most of it." Nathalie had a hard time saying her next words as she had to breathe in between sobs. "I'm...the one...who...went willingly...as long as they...promised to...leave her alone." Nathalie cried openly now.

Beulah sat in silence until Nathalie's crying subsided. When it did, Beulah said to her, "Nathalie, perhaps your sister was only angry at herself. She might have known you were sacrificing yourself to protect her, and she might have felt guilty that you suffered through that because of her. I'm not saying you did suffer because of her, because it absolutely was not her fault. Just as it wasn't your fault. You were just a child trying to protect your little sister. Maybe a part of her was angry with herself for letting her sister go through all that in order to spare her."

"That's not why she was so angry with me."

"How do you know that?"

"I just do!" Nathalie shocked Beulah by slamming both fists against the arms of her chair, propelling herself upright. Nathalie's anger disappeared as quickly as it had appeared, however, and the tears returned. "She left me a very clear message as to what she was angry with me about," Nathalie said with incredible anguish.

"What was her message?"

Nathalie walked over to the window. She stared through it, and stood silently for a few minutes before speaking quietly. "By the time I finished grade nine, I knew my sister and I were headed down different paths. I knew I was going to lose any chance I had, if I couldn't stay in the same school and have a good environment. Plus, I was so sick of the instability, of being shuffled from one foster home to another."

"Is that why you went to live with foster parents in Halifax while your sister stayed behind in Cape Breton?"

"I didn't even ask them to take her. I didn't want them to, because I knew she'd ruin it again."

"Those last three years of high school, you were with the same foster parents. Prior to that, the longest you and your sister had ever stayed in one place was eight months—and most were only three or four."

"I used to beg her not to mess it up. I *begged* her. But every time we found a home, she'd behave so badly nobody could deal with her. When she was younger, she'd scream and have violent outbursts, but as we got older, she started stealing, smoking and drinking, doing drugs. She never went to school. When she hit twelve, she'd run off and be gone for days. I was worried sick about her all the time."

"You had a nurturing nature, Nathalie. All the reports from your foster homes indicated you were very loving and protective toward your sister, that you were very kind and gentle, and loved animals."

"Yes, animals were my salvation. If I didn't have becoming a veterinarian as my goal, I don't know what would have happened to me. But then again, if I hadn't had that selfish goal Chantal would still be alive today."

"What happened to Chantal, Nathalie?" Beulah now knew, but she needed Nathalie to face up to it.

As Danielle was going over her notes in preparation for her interview with Tucker Hill, something started to nag at her, and it was pertaining to the bracelet Erin said Dee had given Kristina as a birthday present. No bracelet matching that description was ever found in Buchanan's home, nor had she been wearing it when her body was discovered.

Danielle picked up the phone and called Gillian Stevens. "Sorry to bother you, Gillian. I just have one quick question for you."

"What is it?"

"Do you remember Kristina ever wearing a white gold and emerald bracelet?"

"Of course. She wore it often—it was beautiful."

"Was she wearing it the night she was killed?"

"Yes."

"Are you sure?"

"I'm positive. Maurice pointed to it when he was saying he was sick of being used. He said she was probably using the person who gave her that bracelet too."

"This is really important. Did she still have it on when you left?"

"Yes, she did."

"Are you absolutely sure of that?"

"Yes. When she shut the door behind us, I remember thinking how beautifully the light reflected off the emeralds."

Nathalie took some time to prepare herself before she answered Beulah's question as to what happened to Chantal.

"It was summertime. I was fifteen, going into grade ten in September. A social worker drove me to Halifax to meet my new foster parents, but I didn't tell Chantal.

"I'll never forget when I saw their house for the very first time. It was the most beautiful house I'd ever seen. And the bedroom they'd set up for me...it had a desk, and even a computer. A *computer*. I couldn't believe it. And there were bookshelves filled with encyclopedias.

"It was like walking into heaven, Beulah. It had everything I'd ever dreamed of. Things I knew I'd never get if I didn't go live with them, things that would help me get really good grades."

"Nathalie, you were given that opportunity because they recognized your potential. You earned that, and you deserved it."

"I knew the only way I'd get to go to university is if I went to live there. I needed more than good grades. I needed fantastic ones to get scholarships, and scholarships were the only way I was going to be able to afford to go. And without Chantal around to screw it up..." Nathalie's voice began to break. "It was so selfish of me."

"No, Nathalie, it wasn't."

"You should have seen the look on Chantal's face when I told her I was moving to Halifax by myself."

"Is that why she was angry with you?"

"Partly."

"How did you make out at your new foster home?"

"They were so good to me. They sent me to an excellent private school. That's where I learned to play piano and guitar—the school had a fabulous music program. When I first went to live with them, I was allowed to call Chantal every single night if wanted to. And I did—if I could find her. At Christmas, they even let her come visit with me and gave her Christmas presents too. It was the best Christmas we ever had. Until..." Nathalie pressed her lips together—hard—and left them like that.

"Until what, Nathalie?"

Nathalie chewed on her lip before releasing it so she could speak. "The visit was going so well. Until this one night they went out to a dinner party and she raided their liquor cabinet. She got drunk and stole some jewelry."

"Bet that didn't go over too well."

"It sure didn't. She was a lawyer, and he was a judge. Chantal spent a couple of months in the youth detention facility over it. When she got out, they wouldn't even let me talk to her, let alone visit. They thought she'd be a very bad influence on me and said they were worried she would become violent toward me. I told them she never would, that she loved me, that I was all she had."

"They didn't believe you?"

"He came home one day with copies of Chantal's juvenile records."

"Ah, that's how you got them."

"Yes, I stole them."

"Did they know you took them?"

"I think they suspected, but they never asked me about it. Maybe they thought my having them would serve as a reminder of how not to turn out."

"They're pretty bad."

"But *she* wasn't bad. She was just—"

"I know, Nathalie." Beulah cut Nathalie off because she found it unnecessary for Nathalie to have to struggle to come up with a sentence to describe the effects of a decade's worth of abuse on a child.

"I wasn't allowed to call her after that, but I wrote her all the time. I got myself a mailbox they didn't know about, but I hardly ever got any letters back. The last one she sent me, she called me names, saying I had gotten uppity, and thought I was better than her. If it hadn't been written in my sister's handwriting, I'd have thought it was my mother who wrote it when she was drunk."

"Wasn't she back living with your mother around that time?"

"Not officially. Neither of us were allowed to live with our mother after...after what happened to me. Not that it mattered. They never went looking for Chantal, even when she'd run away and they knew where she probably was. She would often end up where my mother was—wherever that was at the time. She was fourteen by this point, and thought it was cool to party with our mother."

"Your mother was an alcoholic, Nathalie. She was irresponsible and had poor judgment."

"At fourteen Chantal became my mother's drinking buddy. She started putting me down for wanting to get an education, saying I thought I was better than the people I came from."

"When was the last time you saw Chantal, or spoke to her?"

Nathalie clasped her hands together so hard, her knuckles turned white. "She called me on my sixteenth birthday, May thirteenth. I picked up the phone before my foster parents did. She was drunk. I asked her where she was phoning from, but she wouldn't tell me—there was no caller ID in those days. She said she wanted to come visit me, but I told her they wouldn't let her stay with me if she came to Halifax. That's when she told me she was already in Halifax. She said she was cold and hungry, that she needed a place to sleep, and she asked if she could sneak into my room."

Nathalie began to cry again. Beulah waited patiently for her to be ready to continue again.

"I was scared. I was so scared they'd make me leave if they found her in my room. Without everything they were providing for me, I was so afraid I wouldn't be able to finish high school even, let alone get the marks and recommendations I needed for scholarships to university. I was terrified of losing all that."

"What did you tell her?"

"I told her something I'll regret for the rest of my life," Nathalie said with concentrated sorrow.

"What was that?"

"I told her..." Nathalie's voice vibrated. "I told her that for the first time in my life that I loved waking up in the morning, that when I opened my curtains I saw the most beautiful maple tree that squirrels run up and down on, and blue jays build nests in." Nathalie swallowed twice, then took a deep breath. "I told her I was scared to sneak her into my room, because if they found her I'd get kicked out, and we'd both be out on the street."

"What happened next, Nathalie?"

Nathalie pointed to the clock. Their session was already ten minutes over and Beulah's next client would be in the waiting room.

40

Nathalie was already seated in the restaurant when Melissa sat down to have dinner with her.

"Geez, you look like shit, Nathalie."

"Thanks, Melissa. Good thing I'm not trying to impress you."

"You okay?"

"I haven't slept well all week. It's just catching up with me, is all. How was your weekend?"

"*Fab-u-lous.*" Melissa's smile couldn't have held more satisfaction.

"I take it that means you got lucky?"

"I sure did. Lilly kept me up till the wee hours of the morning both Friday and Saturday nights." Melissa expected a shocked reaction from Nathalie, but to her surprise, Nathalie was quite blasé about it.

"Funny, she never mentioned a thing to me about it," is all she said.

"You don't mind, do you?"

"God, no. Not at all. Lilly is great, but—for me... Regardless, I'm just not ready."

"But if you *were* ready, would you be interested in Lilly?"

Nathalie placed a finger on top of the table and traced what looked like curves over and over. Only after a very long delay did she respond. "No, Melissa. That's the truth."

Lilly dialed and heard a busy signal for the umpteenth time, so she called Nathalie. At least her phone was ringing. But she wasn't home. Or not answering. She considered trying Nathalie's cell, but decided to just leave a message and hoped Nathalie would return her call when she got home. She did.

Danielle was finishing up the dishes when she heard a knock on her apartment door. She opened it to see Nathalie standing there.

"Hi," Danielle said. "This is a surprise."

"Lilly asked me to check on you. She says your home phone's been ringing busy since last night, and she keeps getting voicemail on your cell."

"Oh." Danielle had forgotten she'd put her kitchen phone with the line open in the drawer the night before.

Nathalie entered the apartment but stood by the door. "She also tells me you're furious with her. Anything you want to talk about?"

Danielle not only wanted to talk to Nathalie, but to wrap her arms around her too. But Danielle didn't want to risk Nathalie fleeing again if Danielle tried to, so she sat in one of her new leather chairs she'd purchased with Nathalie by her side. "I'd like that very much— to talk."

Nathalie sat down on the sofa next to Danielle's chair. "What happened?"

Danielle told Nathalie the whole story, and how she felt so betrayed by Lilly.

"Maybe her hands were tied," Nathalie said.

"Nathalie, she purposefully altered my evidence. I thought she was on *my* side. She's supposed to be my friend, not my enemy. I never in my wildest dreams thought she'd be plotting behind my back to sabotage me."

"I don't know much about the law or police procedures, Danielle, but what I do know about is the importance of friendship. Especially when you have very little family, and your friends become your only family." Nathalie touched Danielle's knee with her hand. "Please talk to her, give her a chance to explain herself."

Danielle didn't want Nathalie to remove her hand. She wanted Nathalie to touch her even more. But of course Nathalie didn't. She removed her hand as soon as her sentence was finished.

"I'll call her when I get back from Cape Breton," Danielle said.

Nathalie stiffened and her expression hardened. "You're going to Cape Breton?"

"Yes, for work."

"Which part of Cape Breton are you going to?"

"Margaree. Is that anywhere near where you're from?"

"When are you going?"

"In the morning."

Nathalie stood up. "I really need to go, Danielle."

"What's wrong?"

"Nothing's wrong. I haven't fed Chai yet, and she'll be chomping at the bit."

"Well, if you want to come back down after you feed her—"

"Call Lilly, Danielle. Don't wait till you get back from Cape Breton."

Danielle was very uncomfortable when Lilly answered her phone.

"It's me," Danielle said.

"I know." There was a slight pause before Lilly started to say, "Danielle, I'm really sorry, but—"

"I don't want to talk about it this evening, Lilly. I have to go to Cape Breton tomorrow, and I'll be back late tomorrow night. We'll talk on Saturday, okay?"

Lilly sighed audibly in the phone. "Okay, call me when you get back."

"Bye."

Lilly didn't bother saying goodbye, since Danielle had already hung up.

Danielle was brushing her teeth when there was another knock at her door. She smiled when she saw it was Nathalie again.

"You weren't already in bed, were you?" Nathalie asked.

"No, just brushing my teeth."

"I was planning on going to Cape Breton myself Saturday, but if you're going tomorrow…"

"Oh, it would be wonderful if you could join me, Nathalie, but it's work-related."

"That's okay," Nathalie said, even though she looked disappointed. "I understand. I wasn't sure if you were allowed to or not, just thought I'd ask since I was planning on going Saturday anyway."

"No, no." Danielle knew it was work, but her emotions swelled at the thought of having Nathalie's company for a ten hour round trip. "I'm not saying you can't come with me. I would love to have your company—the GPS tells me it's a five hour drive."

For the first time ever in her career, Danielle made a decision that would affect work, based strictly on personal desire. She was trying to convince Nathalie—and herself—that no harm would be done by taking Nathalie along when she said, "I would just have to make sure you aren't with me when I do my official business."

"Are you sure? I don't want to do anything that might interfere with your case."

"No, it won't. I just have to go talk to a potential witness and get a statement."

"What time are you planning on leaving?"

"Is five too early?"

Nathalie winced. "Actually, I do have an early meeting at seven-thirty. I can cut it short though, and be finished at eight o'clock. It's downtown on Barrington. You could pick me up there at eight."

Danielle was hoping to be in Cape Breton by ten a.m., but if they left at eight, she'd still be there in the early afternoon, leaving her enough time to interview Tucker Hill. "Sure, no problem."

"Great. See you in the morning."

Danielle very much wanted to hug Nathalie goodnight, but Nathalie had already made a hasty exit.

Lillian Marsh was on the phone with Sergeant Carvery even though it was very late on a Thursday night.

"The team needs to be ready four days earlier," she told him.

"Earlier? We don't know if we'll even be ready in time for the following Friday."

"We've got no choice—not if we want to do this right. Judge Harrington is going to sign Danielle's warrant Monday morning, and it'll be executed at ten a.m. Your team needs to roll at the exact same time. The distraction on Danielle's end while we're at the train station needs to be perfectly timed."

The following morning, Danielle decided to work at the office while she waited for Nathalie's meeting to finish. Although none of the jewelry shops left on her list would be open yet, Danielle left a message with a description of the bracelet for each of them and asked them to give her a call if they recognized it.

Had it been a request from any other client Beulah would not have rescheduled an eight a.m. appointment to an even earlier time—with less than twenty-four hours notice, no less. But Nathalie seemed more committed to her therapy than ever. Nathalie had not only booked and showed up for sessions every day this week, but had progressed so much further than Beulah had expected in such a short time—considering how agonizingly slow the pace had previously been. Moreover, their last session had ended in a cliffhanger. Beulah couldn't remember a time when she looked so forward to resuming a session.

"We ran out of time yesterday before you were able to tell me how your sister died," Beulah said, then prepared herself for the outburst of sorrow she expected from Nathalie.

Except that's not how Nathalie reacted at all. Nathalie eyeballed Beulah as she said, "You know how my sister died, Beulah." The layer of sadness that usually sat under Nathalie's skin was now gone, displaced by an eerie acidity in her voice.

Beulah pictured a dusty landscape with Nathalie stepping forward in wide steps, two pistols at her sides. Though Beulah responded only by shifting in her chair, she metaphorically stepped forward as well, with eyes fixed on Nathalie while delivering her firm response. "Yes, I do know Nathalie."

"How long have you known?"

"Does it matter?"

Nathalie shrugged. "Guess not."

Thinking Nathalie had already left the city, and having witnessed Danielle leaving for work, Melissa was relaxed as she made herself at home in Nathalie's apartment. Again, she took some time off work so she could go through Nathalie's things.

She was lounging on Nathalie's sofa, flipping through Nathalie's notebooks, when Melissa read one particular page and said out loud, "Hmmm…veddy eentarresting."

Melissa was looking at the original lyrics Nathalie had written for one of her songs. Although the song was published and recorded as, "I'll Be Over You When I'm Six Feet Under," the original lyrics in Nathalie's handwriting in her notebook were, "I'll Be Over You When *You* are Six Feet Under."

Melissa smiled and closed the notebook before picking up another. Melissa's smile, however, was wiped off her face when the second notebook naturally opened to the last page that had been written on. Every hair on Melissa's body bristled as she read a poem in Nathalie's handwriting, and next to the lines, *did not know you, do not know you, may never know you*…was a dated note documenting how Nathalie had been struck and mesmerized by Danielle…before they'd even met.

"Did you have any nightmares last night?" Beulah asked Nathalie.

"Yes," Nathalie said very quietly.

"About your sister, and how she died?"

"No." Nathalie moved her finger along the arm of her chair in what appeared to be an "S" formation, over and over. "About the slayer."

Melissa slapped Nathalie's notebook shut then went to her bedroom. She opened the bedside table and started rooting through it. It looked pretty much like the same stuff that had been there last Saturday, but Melissa pulled out the drawer and emptied its contents on the bed for a closer inspection. And when she did, that's when she noticed something taped to the back of the drawer.

"What—or who—is the slayer, Nathalie?" Beulah was keeping a close eye on Nathalie because she seemed so different.

"She's someone I used to live in fear of, until—" Nathalie got up and walked over to the window. "I had stopped living in fear of her, but..." Nathalie closed her eyes and rubbed her temples. "The fear is back again. And it's getting worse."

Melissa went to Nathalie's bathroom and retrieved a blow dryer. She put the setting on high and warmed the clear duct tape until its sticky residue softened and peeled away easily from both the envelope and the drawer. When she turned the padded envelope over, it was sealed.

"Geez, Nathalie. You're not making it easy for me, are you?"

Melissa brought the envelope to the kitchen. She filled the tea kettle with water, turned it on, and waited for it to boil. When it started to blast a full steam, Melissa placed the sealed flap of the envelope over it...and watched as it slowly blossomed open.

"What are you afraid of?" Beulah asked Nathalie.

"Of history repeating itself."

"Whose history? Yours or someone else's?"

"Have you ever been to an RCMP officer's funeral?" Nathalie asked instead of answering the question.

"Why are you asking me that, Nathalie?"

Nathalie shrugged. "Just wondering." Nathalie then traced a letter "S" on the window glass. "I bet there'd be lots of red."

"I hope you have a plan B," Sergeant Carvery told Lillian Marsh.

"I do, but I'm hoping I don't have to resort to it."

"Does plan B involve sending Renaud up the creek without a paddle?"

"More like down the river," Lilly admitted.

Melissa placed her gloved hand inside the envelope and pulled out the most beautiful bracelet she'd ever seen. It was eighteen karat white gold with thirty-six emeralds all around it. Melissa whistled, then said out loud, "This must have cost a fortune."

Nathalie was standing on the sidewalk waiting for Danielle when she pulled up.

"How was your meeting?" Danielle asked as soon as Nathalie got in.

"I got through it. Listen, I really hate to ask since I know I've already put you behind schedule, but could we just stop at the apartment for one sec? There's something I forgot, that I'd really like to take with me."

Danielle looked at her watch. It was 8:05 a.m. She was already more than three hours behind schedule, and taking a detour back to the apartment would put her even further behind. She opened her mouth to ask Nathalie if it really was that important, but the words that tumbled out were quite different than the ones she had intended. "Sure, no problem."

Nathalie's hurried footsteps sounded like a small herd of animals on the stairs.

"Shit!" Melissa ran like lightning to the living room, grabbed the notebooks she'd been rifling through, and placed them back on the shelf before running to the kitchen because she realized she hadn't unplugged the kettle.

"Fuck!" she said under her breath. She didn't have time to run to the bedroom and put the drawer back in—or anything else—because just then...Nathalie entered her apartment.

41

Melissa was crouched down on Nathalie's kitchen floor, behind the island, and stopped breathing.

Please don't come to the kitchen. Please don't go to the bedroom. Melissa repeated this mantra to herself over and over.

Leaving the door slightly ajar, Nathalie rushed to a bookshelf and grabbed a notebook Melissa had put back mere seconds earlier. Nathalie then rummaged through a pen and pencil holder. "It must be in the bedroom," she said out loud. She walked a few steps toward the bedroom but just then Chai escaped out the door. "Chai! Come back here!"

Nathalie chased Chai all the way down to the stairs. When she returned, Melissa heard her say, "Thanks to you I don't have time to look for my new pen. Now stay! I can't keep Danielle waiting forever."

Melissa was enormously relieved when she heard the door close, then Nathalie locking the door behind her.

Shortly after they started driving, Danielle said to Nathalie, "I hope it doesn't rain. Those dark skies look awfully menacing."

Nathalie didn't reply to that, or to much else, even though Danielle tried at first to make conversation. It didn't take long for Danielle to figure out though, that something was bothering Nathalie a lot, and that she clearly did not want to talk about it, so Danielle turned on the radio and they drove a long time in silence.

They were almost an hour away from Halifax before Nathalie finally spoke. "You traded in your Jeep for a Matrix?"

"This is my work vehicle," Danielle explained.

"You drive a different vehicle for work?"

"Yes. We can log a lot of hours driving to and from places, so we're assigned a work vehicle."

"Makes sense, I guess. I loved my SUV, but you can't beat the Prius for mileage. Most of the time I'm glad I traded it in."

"Was your father French?" Danielle was aware it was an abrupt change of subject, but it was something she'd been wondering.

"I don't know. Maybe. I never knew him."

"Your last name, Boudreaux—but with an 'x'."

"That's my mother's maiden name. She didn't speak French though."

After fifteen minutes of silence, Danielle asked Nathalie, "You okay? You're awfully quiet."

"I will be," Nathalie replied. Danielle thought she also heard Nathalie whisper, "I hope," when Nathalie turned her head away to look outside the passenger window.

"Rough meeting this morning?" Danielle asked.

"Kinda," Nathalie replied.

Melissa was still rifling through Nathalie's things when she came across an upside down photograph in the bottom drawer of the other bedside table. When she turned it over and saw Kristina Buchanan's face, Melissa said to it, "You got what you deserved you fucking snitch. I'd have defiled more than your face if I'd have gotten the chance."

"Do you mind if I ask how long you've been single?" Danielle asked Nathalie, trying to initiate conversation again.

Nathalie turned her face from the window and looked forward. "I haven't really dated anyone in a while."

"Are you and your ex still in touch?"

"No, she...hasn't been in my life in any way for a while."

"Do you miss her?" What Danielle really wanted to ask was, "Are you still in love with her?" But didn't.

"It was a painful relationship. I'm relieved it's over." Nathalie glanced at Danielle then back out the window again. "What about you?"

"What about me?"

Nathalie was still looking out the window as she spoke to Danielle. "I know you're the one who left Rachel, but I think no matter who does the leaving, the end of a relationship always hurts to some extent."

"The only hurting I did over ending my relationship with Rachel, was by overdoing the dance of joy."

It was shortly after 2:30 p.m. when Danielle pulled into an ocean-side bed and breakfast in Margaree. Danielle thought she still had time to interview Tucker Hill and drive back to Halifax before midnight, but Nathalie had convinced her they shouldn't drive back in the dark. It didn't take much convincing, since as soon as Danielle started ascending the majestic mountains she was reminded of how precarious twisting and turning roads around them could be. It was still light when they arrived, but soon it would be dark, with treacherous driving.

Eager to find Tucker Hill, Danielle left Nathalie back at the B&B and headed for his last known address. When she got there however, instead of finding Tucker Hill's house...all she found were charred remains.

Nathalie stood staring out the window from the double occupancy room she rented when they arrived. Danielle had planned on driving back to Halifax later that night, but since Nathalie had convinced her to stay, Nathalie had insisted she pay for Danielle's room as well as hers, since the only B&B yet open for the season was exceptionally overpriced, even though it had a gorgeous view of the ocean. Danielle was firm in paying for her own though, so it was only after some debate that Danielle agreed to let Nathalie pay—on the condition that they share a double occupancy room rather than having Nathalie pay for two rooms. Although Nathalie would have much preferred having her own room, she agreed. So Nathalie now stood in that room, staring at eruptions of sea spray that exploded like fireworks each time a dark grey wave crashed onshore.

How am I going to do this? Nathalie asked herself, as she stood with her left arm across her chest while rubbing her jaw with her right hand.

Nathalie had no more planned on coming to Cape Breton this weekend than she had planned on hiking through the Mexican desert. But she had invited herself along when Danielle told her she was coming to Cape Breton for something "work-related" because Nathalie knew that work-related meant Kristina-related.

Nathalie stared at the powerful and violent swirling of seawater. That's how her brain felt at the moment. Everything was swirling around in her head so fast and furious, she had a hard time staying in control. But she had to. She had an important reason for coming here with Danielle, and she needed to follow through.

It was just past five when Danielle returned to the bed and breakfast looking despondent. Over dinner she told Nathalie her frustrations.

"First, the guy's house is burnt to the ground, and it looks like it's been like that for a year or more. I figure someone around there must know who he is, so I knock on neighbors' doors. I went to the pub, to the legion, and even this little restaurant up the road, but not one person will admit to knowing him."

"Did you identify yourself as an RCMP officer?"

"The first two houses I did, but after that, I thought maybe that's why no one would tell me anything, so when I went to the other places, I didn't. Do you think they still figured me for a police officer?"

"In these parts? No, even worse."

"Worse?" Danielle asked.

"Yeah," Nathalie told her. "A bill collector."

Danielle smiled. She was too discouraged to laugh.

"Hey, cheer up," Nathalie told her. "I'll take you to somebody who'll talk to you so much your ears will hurt."

Following Nathalie's directions, Danielle ended up in the driveway of a funeral home.

"A funeral home?" Danielle asked.

"Hey, they're very lonely people. It's not like their clients talk to them much. And the best part is, they know everybody's secrets. All that family drama tends to unfold at wakes and funerals, you know."

Danielle learned that Nathalie was right. If she hadn't told the funeral director that she needed to go (four times), he would have talked to her till her ears fell off. It was already going on eight, and Danielle still had to drop Nathalie off, then go to where the funeral director said Tucker Hill now lived.

Nathalie asked Danielle for a favor as they left the funeral home. "Instead of driving me back to the B&B, do you think you could drop me off at the legion?"

"Dying for a drink are you?"

"No, I'd like to see if…my mother might be there."

Tucker Canada Hill was the suspicious type. Danielle had to show him her badge and tell him why she was there through a window before he would let her in.

"I never killed anybody," was the first thing he said.

"You're not suspected of killing anyone, Mr. Hill. But I'm thinking you might have seen someone who has."

"I haven't seen anything or anybody. I've been keeping to myself, getting back on my feet."

"That was a really good job you did building that den in the park. We found your prints, Tucker. Remember the duct tape? The black plastic garbage bags? Found an empty rum bottle and a tin box full of cigarette butts too, all with your prints on them."

"I never killed her, I swear."

"I believe you, Tucker. But I think you might have seen or heard something that night, so I need you to tell me what happened."

Tucker appeared to mull things over before deciding to reply. He poured himself a cup of tea that looked as dark and as thick as dirty motor oil before sitting down and telling his story.

"I was trying to sleep, but it was really damp that night, and foggy. I heard somebody wheeling something, and dump it in the pond. I couldn't tell you who did it, I never saw them. I waited for the sun to come up before I went to see what it was. The fog was still thick, so at first I just saw the dolly. I pulled on it, and there was a blanket stuck in the wheel. I pulled the dolly out first, then tugged on the blanket, and out rolls this dead body."

"Why didn't you report it?"

"Because I knew they'd blame me."

"We didn't recover a dolly or a blanket."

"That's cuz I took them."

"You took them?"

"Yeah. The blanket was a really nice one. I knew it would be really warm after it dried, and the dolly I could use to strap my stuff to. I put the blanket in one garbage bag, and all my things in another one, and used the dolly to carry them."

"Where are they now?"

Tucker pointed to a blanket draped across a small sofa in the living room. "Dolly's in the shed out back. That morning I hitchhiked back home with everything I owned strapped to it."

Despite Tucker Hill's fears he would somehow be implicated in a murder he did not commit, he reluctantly agreed to give Danielle the items he took from the pond—after she threatened him with an obstruction of justice charge, that is. Danielle made certain to photograph, bag, and log the evidence she acquired, then placed it in the hatchback of her vehicle.

Nathalie took a very deep breath before entering the legion. She walked up to the bartender, an older man who appeared to be in his late fifties.

"Hi. I'm looking for Rita...Rita Boudreau."

The bartender looked Nathalie over, but didn't speak.

"She's my mother," Nathalie explained. "I thought maybe she'd be here."

The bartender looked at her more closely, then put a shot glass in front of her. He poured Jack Daniels into it and said, "Better drink this."

Nathalie hated whiskey—Jack Daniels in particular—it was what her mother had sold her for. As disturbing as that memory was, Nathalie's sickening feeling was due to fear as to what the bartender might say next.

"Why?" she found the courage to ask.

The bartender looked at Nathalie apologetically. "Your mother died a few months ago. She was drinkin' her usual one night, and when she ran out of money she pulled out her nerve pills, sayin' they turn five drinks into ten. We always warned her not to do that, but she said she did it all the time. Guess she won't be doin' it no more, God bless her soul. Some people thought you were in Halifax, but we couldn't find you listed. If we'd-a-known how to get in touch with you, we'd-a-called." He moved the filled shot glass closer to Nathalie. "We buried her next to your sister, if that's any consolation."

Nathalie was standing in the legion parking lot shivering when Danielle pulled in.

"How did it go?" Nathalie asked as soon as she got in the car.

"He didn't see anyone, but I've got some evidence he took from the scene."

Nathalie turned quickly in Danielle's direction. "What sort of evidence?"

"A dolly and a blanket."

Nathalie hadn't put her seatbelt on yet, so she leaned across the console and looked in the back. Horror crossed her face.

"Are you okay? You look like you're going to throw up."

❧ 42 ❧

Danielle had intended to ask Nathalie if she'd seen her mother when she picked her up at the legion, but Nathalie had suddenly become ill. Danielle thought Nathalie might be distressed about something, but she wasn't talking. Danielle didn't want to pry, but she wanted to break the silence, and find out what was bothering Nathalie so much.

"Was your mother at the legion?" Danielle came right out and asked.

Nathalie replied in such a low voice, it was almost a whisper. "No."

"Did you try her at home?"

"I think I left my notebook in your vehicle, Danielle. I'm just going to run downstairs for it, okay?" Nathalie grabbed Danielle's car keys from the small table they were resting on without waiting for Danielle's approval.

Nathalie returned later—much later than it should have taken to just grab a notebook—and immediately prepared for bed. She got under the covers, but instead of going to sleep, sat up and started writing in the notebook she'd retrieved.

She wasn't writing anything important. She just needed to perform the act of putting pen to paper as it was a comfort to her—and she needed comforting after learning her mother had died. Even though she hadn't been a very good mother, Nathalie still felt a type of loss.

Nathalie had so often told others her mother was dead. And now she really was. For the first time since she started telling that lie, Nathalie wished she never had. Would her mother be alive now if she hadn't said so often that she wasn't? The thought made Nathalie's head feel like it was literally splitting in two.

Danielle was lying in her bed just a few feet away from Nathalie's, aching, longing for her. If Nathalie were any other woman, Danielle would have simply gotten up, slipped under the covers with her, and expressed her interest. But Nathalie wasn't any other woman. Danielle was very aware that Nathalie was unusually spooked when it came to intimacy.

Danielle was aching though, and not for sex. She just wanted to lie next to Nathalie, to be close to her. She wanted to hold Nathalie in her arms, just as the loving mermaid had been holding her in her dreams recently. Danielle wanted so badly to reach across that great divide between their beds and wrap her arms around Nathalie, but all she could do was lie there and listen to Nathalie's breathing. So close, and yet so far…

Danielle's longing finally faded into sleep, a sleep that was abruptly broken by a terrible cry. Danielle bolted up, not sure if the cry had been in her dreams or—

Danielle's head turned toward the pleas for help. It was Nathalie. She was having a terrible nightmare. Danielle quickly tossed her covers off and leapt out of bed. It didn't occur to Danielle to just call Nathalie's name and wake her. Instead, she towered over Nathalie and shook her shoulder.

Danielle felt the kick to her abdomen instantaneously as a scream of terror was discharged from the depths of Nathalie's gut. The kick was so powerful, it blasted Danielle half way across the room, slamming her back against the door. Nathalie then grabbed a bedside table lamp, and was approaching so fast, she was mere seconds away from bashing Danielle's head in…

"Nathalie!" Danielle was desperately trying to reach the light switch but her back had landed on the door knob and the kick had knocked the wind out of her. Danielle yelled her name again, screaming it this time. "Nathalie! It's me, Danielle! You were having a nightmare!"

Nathalie stopped approaching. There was so little light in the room, Danielle couldn't see if Nathalie was still asleep or awake. Though quite sore, she managed to pick herself up and flick the light switch on.

Nathalie looked confused for a few seconds, and looked around the room. Danielle got the sense that Nathalie had no clue where she was. Maybe even *who* she was?

"Nathalie?" Danielle's voice was gentler now. "Are you okay? You were having a nightmare."

Nathalie walked back over to the bed and placed the lamp back on the bedside table. She sat down on the edge of the bed, and looked around. She sat there for a full minute, looking around, before responding. "I'm sorry. I should have warned you if I have any bad dreams not to touch me, to just yell my name or something."

Nathalie grasped the cord that was still plugged in but had ripped away from the lamp when she grabbed it. She pulled it out of the socket, then wrapped it around the lamp, tucking the end that had ripped from its base when she went at Danielle with it. And then…she got under the covers and closed her eyes as though she were just going to go right back to sleep.

Danielle stared at her, not knowing what to make of this, as she rubbed the indentation in her back where the door knob left its imprint. With some slight difficulty, Danielle walked over to her bedside lamp and turned it on, then returned to shut off the main light. As Danielle walked painfully back to her bed, Nathalie opened her eyes.

"Are you okay?" she asked.

Danielle sat on the edge of her bed, rubbed her back with her right hand, and her abdomen with her left. "That's some mean kick you have."

"I kicked you? Oh my God, I'm so sorry." Nathalie rushed over to Danielle. "Let me see."

Danielle sat up off the bed just barely enough to pull her nightshirt up. She then turned so Nathalie could look at her back. "I hit the door knob here." Danielle touched the spot lightly.

"Oooh. It's already a deep red. What about your front?"

Danielle leaned back so Nathalie could look at her abdomen, and closed her eyes tight when the pain intensified as she leaned. She heard Nathalie take such a sharp breath, it sounded like a small gasp.

"What's wrong?" Danielle opened her eyes and looked at Nathalie, who was staring not at Danielle's abdomen, but lower. That's when Danielle realized she wasn't wearing any underwear.

"Oh my God, I forgot!" Danielle fumbled to cover herself.

Nathalie's face went red, but she didn't sound embarrassed or uncomfortable. "Don't worry about it. Not like I haven't seen a few of those before—and a lot more close up than this." Nathalie smiled shyly, displaying her dimples. "Your front doesn't look too bad, actually. Good thing you have abs of steel."

Danielle felt herself blush. "You've got quite the kangaroo's kick."

"Sorry," Nathalie said as though embarrassed. "It was dark, and I was asleep."

"It's okay, Nathalie. I understand. I know what it's like to have bad dreams." Danielle didn't know what Nathalie's dreams were about, but felt at this moment that the source didn't matter. Nathalie was clearly upset about something, and although the police officer in Danielle tugged at wanting to know what that was, the woman in her—and her overwhelming desire for Nathalie—was overriding that. All she wanted to do was wrap herself around Nathalie and bring comfort to her.

"Get on your stomach," Nathalie instructed.

"What?" Danielle was so wrapped up in her mind's creation of a loving scenario between her and Nathalie, that it took her a few seconds to be brought back to reality.

"That muscle in your back is going to be frozen by morning if you don't get it massaged."

Danielle lowered herself on top of the covers and pulled her nightshirt all the way down, covering herself fully from neck to mid-thigh.

Nathalie started massaging the area surrounding Danielle's sore spot over her shirt. Danielle lay there with eyes closed, listening to Nathalie's very quiet breathing, and feeling her palms magically alleviate away the tenderness and pain as Nathalie eased her way closer and closer to the injury.

When she arrived there, Nathalie pressed ever so lightly, then manipulated her movements so that each one delivered incredible relief. She did this very carefully for several more minutes, then...Nathalie just stopped.

Oh, please, please, don't stop. Danielle wanted more. So much more. "Could you do just a little more? If your hands aren't too tired."

Nathalie didn't respond to Danielle's request. Not verbally, nor by continuing the massage. She hadn't moved away, but she hadn't placed her hands back on Danielle either. Time stood still for Danielle as she waited for Nathalie's decision to continue massaging her or not.

Just as Danielle had come to the conclusion that the massage was over, Nathalie tapped Danielle on the side of her hip, directing her closer to the center of the bed. "It'd be easier if you moved over," she said.

When Danielle was in position, Nathalie clutched the seam of Danielle's nightshirt and gently pulled up. Danielle lifted her weight to allow the shirt to fully expose her injury. Nathalie then did something very unexpected by Danielle. She brought her leg over and sat on Danielle's behind, putting just half her weight on it as she leaned forward and slipped her fingertips under Danielle's nightshirt, touching bare skin.

Danielle's respiration shot up. She could feel Nathalie's fingers touch and press into her, and could feel her skin respond to that touch, follicles standing at attention as though begging, *touch me, touch me.*

Nathalie's hands marched up Danielle's back, along the muscles that banked her spine, and visited her neck and shoulders where they gently eased away tension and discomfort, before journeying back down again. Nathalie did this so many times, Danielle felt herself turn to gelatin, and her sighs grew so deep they now bordered on moaning. Then, as rapidly as a lightning strike, a multitude of powerful emotions was discharged through Danielle when she felt Nathalie's full weight and patch of pubic hair press into her—a patch that was unmistakably drenched.

Nathalie's hands moved to Danielle's sides, then delicately crept their way up under Danielle's shirt where they hesitated at her breasts.

Danielle moaned her approval.

Nathalie seized the nightshirt that was crumpled up around Danielle's upper back and peeled it away. Danielle released her arms from the shirt, then started to turn over so she could face Nathalie, but Nathalie held her back and whispered in her ear, "Stay on your stomach."

Danielle obliged, then saw Nathalie's nightshirt fall to the floor before Nathalie's hands fully covered her rear cheeks, caressing and tracing the line between them with her thumbs.

Nathalie continued her exploration up Danielle's back, across her arms, till she reached and wrapped her fingers around Danielle's hands. Nathalie's entire body was now resting on top of Danielle's, and Danielle felt so warmly blanketed by Nathalie, everything outside of that blanket ceased to exist. All Danielle felt—all Danielle wanted to feel—was Nathalie.

Nathalie traced her fingers back along Danielle's hands, down her arms, across her shoulders, to the center of her spine, slowly following the crevice back down again to where the center line between Danielle's cheeks began.

Nathalie then lowered herself further down, straddling Danielle's lower legs in the process. When Danielle felt Nathalie's tongue at the top of her cheek line, her clitoris tingled. Nathalie swirled her tongue in and out of the very beginning of the crevice, not going any further than just teasing the very top of it, as she stroked Danielle's rear cheeks first with her hands, then her lips. Nathalie then tasted her way up Danielle's spine, her nipples grazing Danielle's back as she moved her body up until she reached Danielle's neck again. Nathalie lifted Danielle's hair and started licking and kissing her nape, sending shivers down it, shivers that extended to Danielle's broad, hardened nipples.

Nathalie pressed herself into Danielle's rear again, and Danielle felt a drip land on her and slowly make its way down the curve of her left cheek, blending itself into her own wetness between her legs. Nathalie began to kiss and lick the side of Danielle's neck as she bore down harder into Danielle.

Danielle couldn't hold back her desire to kiss Nathalie anymore. She turned to face Nathalie so their tongues and lips could meet. Nathalie accommodated this time, lifting her weight so Danielle could turn onto her back.

Danielle looked deeply into Nathalie's eyes—and was startled. "Your eyes aren't brown," she said with great surprise.

Nathalie looked directly at Danielle without glancing away for the first time ever.

Danielle was mesmerized by what she saw. "They're actually green. Dark green with a brown *sunburst* around the pupil."

Nathalie lowered her head and rested it on Danielle's chest. "Not too many people notice that."

Danielle thought of her recurring dream. Of the mermaid, with sunbursts for eyes. She then picked up Nathalie's right hand and traced the L-shaped scar she noticed the night they made the sauce at Lilly's house. Danielle traced it just as she had the first night she dreamt of that scar, and of the mermaid—whom she now recognized as being Nathalie.

Danielle's reverie was broken by the sensation of droplets landing on her chest. She raised Nathalie's face up, and saw that it was stained with tears. "Please don't cry, Nathalie. You're the last person I ever want to cause any pain."

"You're not causing me pain, Danielle." A few more tears emerged as Nathalie said, "You're releasing it."

Danielle kissed Nathalie's forehead, the bridge of her nose, her cheeks, her chin, and lips. Nathalie returned Danielle's kisses, both of them engaged now ever so lightly, lip to lip, touching, grazing, gently capturing both and releasing, with a loving tenderness that shielded them from the outside world.

Danielle rolled Nathalie over and sat on top of her, focusing on the glassy sunbursts as she watched them expand. Nathalie brought her hands up along Danielle's stomach until they reached her breasts. Danielle closed her eyes and sighed deeply as she felt Nathalie's touch transmit every conceivable pleasure, pleasures that ensued wherever Nathalie's fingers made contact with her skin.

Danielle had never felt this type of arousal before. It wasn't just a physical, sexual response, it was as though the most loving, wonderful elixir were coursing through her, delivered into her skin by Nathalie's touch.

Nathalie brought her hands around Danielle's waist and gently pulled forward. She opened her mouth and elevated herself so she could meet Danielle's. Danielle's mouth opened wide expecting their tongues to make contact, but Nathalie just traced her tongue along Danielle's top lip, to the corner, down along the bottom one and to the corner again. Nathalie did this over and over until Danielle's clitoris started to quiver.

When it did, Danielle's tongue could not stop itself from sinking itself deep inside Nathalie's mouth. Nathalie engulfed it as though it were a popsicle, sucking it from narrow tip to wide base, then back up again. Each time Nathalie sucked on Danielle's tongue, Danielle felt yet another layer of pleasure coat and enlarge her clitoris.

Nathalie pulled her tongue out of Danielle's mouth and started kissing, tasting Danielle's chin, the side of her neck, occasionally nipping as she cautiously held back. "I won't leave any marks," Nathalie huskily assured, and a few seconds later released her mouth from Danielle's neck and began to lick and kiss her way to Danielle's breasts.

Nathalie moaned when her tongue reached Danielle's engorged nipple. Danielle felt immense pleasure as Nathalie devoured her nipple, licking, tasting, sucking, and swallowing. Danielle was so emotionally charged, wanting, having Nathalie feasting on her. She wanted to give herself completely to Nathalie, and she knew Nathalie wanted her too, there was no mistaking it.

Nathalie turned herself around, her head facing Danielle's feet. She began to kiss, lick, and caress her way down Danielle's body. She rubbed her facial cheek against Danielle's pubic hair then kissed it, but didn't stay there. She continued down Danielle's thigh, stopping at her knee.

Nathalie's tongue ran circles around Danielle's knee cap, then started sucking tenderly, as she touched and massaged every inch of Danielle's leg and foot.

She kissed her way to Danielle's ankle, stopping again, to swirl her tongue and taste Danielle as she made her way to her destination. She was squeezing and massaging Danielle's foot with her fingers when her tongue finally reached the base of Danielle's toes, and eased itself between them.

Nathalie licked up one side of Danielle's middle toe, then back down the other before going down on the entire toe with her mouth and slowly releasing it as she pulled her lips and tongue off it, only to bring her mouth back down on two of them together. Nathalie then captured Danielle's whole big toe with her mouth, while gently massaging the plump flesh of Danielle's smaller toes with her fingertips.

As Danielle felt the hot moisture of Nathalie's mouth surround her toe, it lit a virtual trail of gun powder that sizzled along her foot, up her leg, to her center where a miniature explosion occurred at her clitoris and shot up to her belly button and nipples.

As if sensing this, Nathalie followed this trail, licking, sucking, and nipping her way up the interior of Danielle's legs.

Danielle opened wide.

Nathalie's tongue entered Danielle immediately, and the sensation of Nathalie's tongue inside her took Danielle's breath away. Nathalie tasted and swallowed, from inside Danielle, then from the juices that rested on Danielle's inner lips, up and around her clitoris, before exploring the taste under Danielle's hood. She probed every part of Danielle's inner lips with her tongue, licking, tasting, and swallowing, as though sampling the differences.

Danielle felt high. As opposed to being frenzied, everything was carefully measured and perfectly placed. Every touch and every lick made Danielle want to give herself to Nathalie even more.

Danielle didn't want this to end, but when her pleasure reached its peak she could not hold on any longer. Nathalie's mouth now sucked hard and the floodgates burst open before Danielle could stop them from doing so.

Danielle's multiple orgasm started at her clitoris, then continued on, heaving its way up her stomach, to her breasts, neck, lips, and her glazed, blue eyes. As Danielle came, as she expelled and emptied all of her juices over Nathalie's face and tongue, intense emotions overwhelmed her, producing a trickling of tears from under her closed eyelids.

After her very lengthy, drawn out orgasm rippled away, Danielle felt like she was back in one of her dreams. Every part of her felt gelatinous, her muscles giving no resistance even to the air as her body basked in complete gratification and relaxation. She could have easily drifted off into the best sleep of her life, except she wanted to repay this incredibly loving pleasure.

Danielle reached down and stroked Nathalie's face, which was now resting on Danielle's lower stomach. In response, Nathalie came up and kissed her. Danielle's inner core swelled when Nathalie leaned in and Danielle could smell herself on Nathalie. As they kissed, Danielle breathed in deeply, taking in as much of her own scent and taste from Nathalie's face as she could. The mixture of Danielle's juices and Nathalie's perspiration was an elixir Danielle could not get enough of. But she wanted Nathalie to experience what she just had.

Danielle guided Nathalie onto her back and made her way between Nathalie's legs. Danielle slipped her tongue between Nathalie's lips and discovered a river. Danielle licked and swallowed as much as she could but the juices kept flowing.

Danielle raised herself up and kissed Nathalie. Both of them moaned as they tasted their juices off each other. Danielle started to head back down, but Nathalie held on to her. Nathalie instead guided Danielle's hand down.

Danielle rubbed her thumb over Nathalie's clitoris. It was so slippery, her thumb slid all over the place, whether it was intentional or not. They continued to kiss and taste each other as Danielle positioned herself so Nathalie could wrap her legs around Danielle's hips. Danielle then gently injected two fingers into Nathalie as they continued kissing.

Nathalie was so small inside, Danielle's fingers were tightly wrapped inside her flesh. Danielle applied more pressure with her thumb as she slowly increased her speed. She didn't want to thrust too far, afraid to hurt Nathalie, but Nathalie pulled at her arm, so Danielle went deeper.

Nathalie began to slowly pant.

Danielle transferred her kisses and licking to Nathalie's neck. When she did so, Nathalie made guttural sounds. She pulled on Danielle's arm even more and lowered her mouth onto Danielle's shoulder.

Danielle started circling Nathalie's interior muscles as she thrust her fingers inward and outward in rhythm to Nathalie's hand strokes along her upper arm. When Danielle started to stroke Nathalie's G-spot, she let out a yelp, then a high-pitched moan. Her vaginal canal, already clenched around Danielle's fingers, clamped around them even more, as Nathalie bit down on Danielle's shoulder, sucking and not releasing until she and her orgasm were completely spent.

Both of them just rested for a few minutes, with Danielle floating, drifting, feeling nothing but serenity. Danielle wrapped her arms and legs around Nathalie and breathed in their scent, intermingled and lingering heavily in the air, while Nathalie held on to Danielle and caressed her back. And if Danielle hadn't already fallen into a deep slumber, she might have noticed that those caresses…were all traces of the letter "S".

The parking lot of the bed and breakfast was at the back of the building. The first thing Danielle noticed when they rounded the corner after checking out, is that she couldn't see the dolly or blanket in the back of the Matrix. She turned to Nathalie, panicked.

"The evidence! It's not there! Did you take—did you put it somewhere?"

Nathalie put her hand over her mouth. "Oh my God. Maybe I didn't lock the car last night. I just, I had such a headache."

"You mean, you didn't put it somewhere? It really is missing?"

"I didn't touch it. Oh my God, Danielle. I'm so sorry. I figured if you were okay leaving it in the car, then it must be okay. I didn't think of it."

Danielle slapped her forehead. "I'm such an idiot! I knew I should have brought it in with me. I just assumed it would be safe if it was locked up." Danielle peered at the console inside. "The alarm didn't go off either. You must have forgotten to turn that on too."

"I'm so sorry, Danielle. I'm so, so, sorry."

Danielle slumped against the car, and slid to the ground. Nathalie crouched down beside her.

"It'll be okay, Danielle. We'll find it. We'll get it back."

"Why would anybody take it, Nathalie? I can see the dolly maybe, but the blanket too?"

"Maybe they thought there was something else in the bag. Maybe in the dark they just grabbed what they could really fast."

Danielle stood up and looked in the hatchback area. "The only thing missing is the evidence, Nathalie. Everything else is still there." Danielle opened the driver's door and opened the ashtray. It was filled with change. She slammed the ashtray back shut.

"Let's go."

Nathalie looked at her watch. "Do you think we'll make it back to Halifax by three o'clock?"

"I doubt it, Nathalie. Because we're going to the nearest RCMP detachment first."

Nathalie sat in the lunch room of the Port Hawkesbury detachment of the RCMP while Danielle had the exterior doors of her vehicle processed for prints. As an RCMP officer, Danielle's prints were already on file, but they needed Nathalie's prints so hers could be differentiated from any others they might find. It was no surprise to Danielle that the only prints found belonged to her and Nathalie.

Danielle wanted that evidence back so badly. "What about dusting the interior? Maybe they touched the rear seat?"

The officer in charge was not keen on that at all. "You say you worked GIS for a few years? How many vehicular break-ins did you investigate? Hundreds? Thousands?"

"What's your point?"

"My point is, in how many of those break-ins did you dust the vehicle for prints?"

Danielle didn't answer because she knew the only time a vehicle ever got dusted was if it was involved in a major crime.

"Renaud, we've already gone out on a limb here by dusting for prints on the exterior. We've done that as a courtesy because you're one of our own. But we don't have the money or the resources to hunt down some petty thieves who took advantage of an unlocked vehicle. You mentioned that the only two things missing were a dolly and a blanket. Unless there was something extremely special about them, I can't justify spending any money or time on them. As it is, I'll probably get my hide cooked if it gets out I authorized the dusting for prints on the exterior."

Danielle knew he was right.

"Why didn't you tell him it was important evidence that was missing?" Nathalie asked Danielle after they left the detachment.

"Because I did not want to be the laughing stock of the RCMP, that's why."

"You must hate me."

It would have been easy to blame Nathalie, but Danielle blamed herself. The evidence was her responsibility, and it was missing because she herself hadn't secured it properly.

"No, I don't hate you, Nathalie. It's my fault. I didn't like to carry large, bagged evidence into the bed and breakfast, but I should have. It was my responsibility to ensure my evidence was secure, and I didn't."

"I'm really, really, sorry," Nathalie repeated.

Danielle sighed. "I know you are."

Danielle and Nathalie had just arrived back in Halifax and were getting out of the car on Maynard Street when they heard the screeching of tires. They turned toward the sound and saw that an animal had been hit. Nathalie immediately ran to a cat lying on the pavement.

The driver of the car ran to the cat as well. "I didn't even see it! I just felt something hit the wheels. Oh, God. I hope it's okay."

Nathalie tried examining the cat, and though he was too injured to run away, he growled and hissed every time she touched him. "I'll be right back," she said to the driver.

Nathalie ran up to her apartment and came back with a tote bag, a towel, and a cat carrier. She opened the tote, prepared an injection, and gave it to the cat.

"This will calm him down and make him more comfortable."

Nathalie waited a few minutes for the medication to take effect before gently wrapping the towel around the cat, placing him in the carrier, and handing him to the woman who hit him.

"Bring him to the after hours emergency animal hospital on Burnside Drive, and when you get there, tell them I've already given him twenty-five milligrams of Ketaset—they'll know what that is. It'll calm him down and reduce his pain until you get him there. And don't worry about the carrier, you can leave it there and I'll pick it up sometime next week."

Danielle looked terror-stricken.

"The cat will be okay, Danielle."

It wasn't the cat's condition that terrified Danielle. "Why do you have Ketaset?" Danielle forced herself to ask.

Nathalie took a very pronounced breath before replying. "Because I'm a veterinarian, Danielle."

Danielle normally never went into work on a Saturday evening. She'd gone in the odd Saturday morning sometimes if the case was one that was more challenging, but never in the evening—Saturday evenings and Sundays were her down time. But Danielle needed to look at the list she'd received from the Canadian Veterinary Medical Association again.

When she got to her office she delayed pulling out the list only because she saw her phone flashing, indicating messages. There was only one, from Fire Wonders Custom Jewelry. The voice on the message let Danielle know that they had indeed created a custom designed bracelet in white gold containing thirty-six emeralds, and that the name on the order was Dianne Boudreau. She also stated that Ms. Boudreau had used cash to pay for the substantial amount.

Danielle closed her eyes momentarily before opening the list. Even though she knew what would be there before she even looked, her heart still sank when she saw a Dr. Dianne N. Boudreau—whose contact information was listed as a non-profit animal shelter in the Annapolis Valley—the same veterinarian for whom she'd left several messages but never got a return call from.

Danielle tried telling herself there was some logical, innocent reason. Perhaps it was just a coincidence. After all, both Dianne and Boudreau were fairly common names, and there was an 'x' on the end of Nathalie's last name, which wasn't on Dianne's. But deep down Danielle felt a terrible foreboding.

And rightly so.

When she ran Nathalie's real name through the computer, the result that came back hit Danielle like a shotgun blast.

Nathalie was lying on her sofa in the dark trying not to think, but it was all she could do. She knew she couldn't keep her real identity from Danielle forever. She knew Danielle would eventually put the pieces together. But Nathalie wasn't ready for that yet.

Nonetheless, ready or not, Danielle probably did know by now. And what would Nathalie do about it? What would—what *could*—she do about Danielle? That was a question Nathalie had asked herself all the way to and from Cape Breton, and she still didn't have an answer. Which is why Nathalie was now avoiding it all by lying in the dark with a cold, wet, facecloth on her face.

According to the Registry of Motor Vehicles, Dianne Nathalie Boudreau was born May thirteenth, and her address was listed as Pereau, which lies on the shores of the Minas Basin, near Blomidon Beach in the Annapolis Valley.

Danielle felt like there was hot, molten lava in her stomach. She felt like she did when she found out Véronique had run off and gotten married, and when she'd been told her family no longer existed. Nevertheless, she managed to remain focused and started putting the pieces of what she now knew, together.

The result was undeniable. Dianne Nathalie Boudreau— suspected of murdering Kristina Buchanan—and Nathalie Boudreaux, the woman Danielle had made love to the night before— were one and the same.

"You realize," said Constable Douglas Blanchard, "that we don't have to follow the Crown's advice. It's up to us when we roll, and if or when we lay any charges."

Sergeant Carvery looked at his best undercover officer and replied, "I'm quite aware of that Douglas, but this one's got some complications."

"Don't they all?" Blanchard retorted. "Getting some clarification might be useful here and there, but when have we ever let a Crown prosecutor tell us when we can or cannot roll?"

"The prosecutor isn't telling you—I am."

"I think you're getting too soft in your twilight years, old man," Blanchard, a cocky, super-fit, thirty-eight-year-old had no qualms saying to his boss.

"Monday, ten a.m. sharp," Sergeant Carvery ordered him. "Not one minute sooner, not one minute later."

"Suit yourself," said Blanchard. "But if this entire operation goes down the drain because you've allowed yourself to be led by the nose by a Crownie...I won't have your back."

Nathalie was still lying in the dark when the doorbell rang. She figured it was Danielle, and since Nathalie still didn't know what she was going to do in regards to her, she didn't answer it. She wasn't surprised when she heard footsteps approach her apartment door and knock. She was *extremely* surprised, however, when she heard a key being inserted into the lock...and her apartment door opened.

Lilly was on her fourth phone call regarding the same matter. "You have all your ducks in a row?" she asked the person on the other line.

"Exactly where you asked me to place them."

"Good," Lilly said.

"But are you sure about this, Lilly? I really don't know how you're going to get away with it."

Nathalie was sitting upright staring at the door when it opened and a female form slipped in. Whoever it was didn't turn on any lights, but used a penlight to make her way through the living room to Nathalie's bedroom. Nathalie would have called 911, but clearly whoever it was, was familiar with her apartment and knew exactly where they were headed.

Danielle ran Dianne Nathalie Boudreau's name through three more computer systems: Versadex, primarily used by Halifax Regional Police; PROS, the RCMP's computerized record of occurrence; and JEINS, the Nova Scotia Department of Justice's computer system.

It didn't surprise Danielle that Nathalie didn't even have a speeding ticket on record. All that meant, is she'd never been caught. She could very well have committed a serious crime such as murder, just had never been suspected or arrested. Yet. But Danielle planned on changing that. She headed back to Maynard Street.

"What the hell are you doing here?" Nathalie lowered the syringe when she recognized Melissa Lambert.

"Jesus, Nathalie. You scared the hell out of me."

"I scared you? What are you doing in my apartment?"

"I, uh, forgot my glasses last time I was here."

"In my bedroom? And where did you get the key?"

"Okay, you got me," Melissa said without any concern for the repercussions.

"You've got some serious explaining to do."

"Me? What about you, Nathalie? I knew there was more to it than just not wanting obsessive fans to know your real name. You almost shit bricks when I slipped and called you Dianne when we were outside at Lilly's."

"I don't have to explain myself to you. But you'd better explain to me why and how you've got a key to my apartment."

"How about you explain to me why you slept with that bitch?"

Nathalie was well aware Melissa despised Danielle. "How do you know? We just got back. I can't believe Danielle would—"

"Danielle? You and *Danielle* have slept together?"

Nathalie couldn't believe she'd just let that slip to Melissa by mistake. "That's none of your business, Melissa. And your attempt to change the subject isn't going to work. What are you doing with a key to my apartment?"

"You know, Nathalie, I used to think you were really smart. But Danielle? And Kristina?"

Nathalie let loose an inner fury when she heard Kristina's name. "You went through my things? My personal, *private* things?" Nathalie lunged for the phone. "I'm calling the police!"

"Go ahead, Nathalie. You can explain to them what the letter 'S' stands for."

Nathalie didn't dial, but kept the phone gripped in her hand.

Melissa began reciting part of a poem from one of Nathalie's notebooks. "'Beware the Slayer, Slaughterer of hearts. She'll slice it to pieces, then laugh as it falls apart.'" Melissa concentrated her attention on Nathalie's face as she commented on the poem. "Slayer. Big, capital 'S', Slayer. That was a real nice touch to the poem, capitalizing every letter 'S'. And a wonderful message you gave her on her face, too, if I do say so myself."

"What do you want, Melissa?" Nathalie gripped the phone so hard, the flesh in her hand appeared to have no blood in it.

Melissa plopped herself down in one of Nathalie's chairs. "Relax, Nathalie. Believe it or not, I'm on your side. That bitch got what she deserved. I know I certainly wanted to teach her a lesson when she snitched on me."

"You knew Kristina?" Nathalie pretended to be surprised by the news. She wasn't about to give Melissa any more ammunition than she already had.

"Yeah, I kinda figured you didn't know anything about it. Which surprises me somewhat, cuz that cunt was quite the bragger. Guess I really did scare her though when I told her I'd cut her tongue out if she ever yapped to anybody else."

"You're the lab tech who was selling information on organ donor matches based on routine blood analysis at the hospital?"

Melissa turned toward Nathalie. "So she did tell you."

Nathalie lied again. "She never told me your name."

"I got let go from the hospital because of that slithering snake. The only reason I got on with the RCMP is because I knew my boss at the hospital was having an affair with one of the techs. He gave me an excellent reference in exchange for keeping my mouth shut. If that bitch had succeeded in ending my career she'd have been dead sooner rather than later, I tell you that much."

Nathalie still wanted an answer. "Why have you broken into my apartment and read my notebooks and private journals?"

"Because I knew you were hiding something, Nathalie. At first, I was just curious. Especially about how much money you were making. It's a lot more than I ever thought, by the way. Don't know why you're living in an apartment with that bundle of money sitting in your bank account."

"How much money I have or don't have is none of your business, Melissa."

"Oh, your bank balance is just the tip of the iceberg of what I learned, Nathalie. At first I was just curious, but the more I learned, the more fascinating it got. I always wondered why you couldn't stand drinking out of beer bottles." Melissa's voice contained no empathy when she said, "It was just the head of a beer bottle, Nathalie. The guy could have used a lot worse to break you in."

"Give me my key, and get the hell out! If you ever set foot on my property again, I'll inform the RCMP that you disclosed extremely confidential information that could jeopardize a murder investigation. The carving on her face, remember? You told me when we were coming home from dinner at Lilly's."

Melissa stood up and sneered. "And I'll just tell them that you already knew about it because you're the one who did it to her. I've seen the painting, Nathalie. I know why you killed her."

Nathalie crossed her arms and stood defiantly in front of Melissa. "Really? Well, when you've figured out the how, you're welcome to go to the authorities. Now *get out*," Nathalie hissed.

Melissa smirked, then tossed Nathalie's key on the coffee table and left.

❧ 45 ❧

Danielle didn't expect Nathalie to answer her door, and she didn't. She checked the street for Nathalie's car, but to no surprise, it was gone. She went back inside and knocked on the door of the couple who lived below her.

"You didn't happen to see Nathalie?" she asked them.

"She was coming down the stairs with Chai in her carrier when we were coming in, so she's probably gone to her cottage. She seemed to be in an awful hurry, though."

Danielle thanked them, then went to her apartment to change. She would need better footwear—and her gun. It was seven forty-five p.m. She figured she could make it to Nathalie's cottage by nine.

Melissa hated losing. That's why she rarely did. She might have been mistakenly thought of as being down for the count, but she always found a way to bounce back up and clip her opponent at the knees. She called Lilly and invited herself over.

Danielle parked a fair distance from where her GPS told her Nathalie's cottage was located. Danielle wanted—no, *needed*—to catch Nathalie by surprise, so she made the final trek to the cottage by foot.

When she arrived at the cottage Danielle quietly crept her way around back. Through a small window with just a sheer curtain on it, Danielle could see Nathalie standing in front of a large painting resting on the floor and leaned against a wall. Danielle tried to make out what the painting was, but all she could see was that it had lots of red in it.

Danielle prepared herself by clipping her badge to the front of her belt and releasing the strap from her holster. She then placed her right hand on her gun and knocked on Nathalie's back door with her left. There was a short delay before the door opened.

"I really appreciate you doing me that favor," Lilly said to Melissa. Lilly was referring to her request that Melissa speed up processing of any items Danielle dropped off at the lab. Lilly hoped it would result in Danielle coming up with any suspects other than Lucy Miller. Lilly's very strong instinct was that Lucy Miller was not Kristina Buchanan's killer, and they already knew Maurice Coultier wasn't either. Lilly hoped the conflict that existed between her and Danielle would disappear with new results.

"No problem. It wasn't much help though."

"It must have been," Lilly said. "Because she went to Cape Breton."

"What did she go to Cape Breton for?" Melissa asked.

"Had something to do with the Buchanan case, that's all I know."

"That's quite interesting, because I spoke with Nathalie before coming here, and apparently, she and Danielle have slept together."

Lilly's eyes opened so wide, her eye shadow disappeared. "*What? When?*"

"Danielle, what are you—?"

"Hello, *Dianne*. Or should I call you, *Dee?*"

To Danielle's surprise, Nathalie simply stepped aside and said, "Come in."

Danielle stepped into the small but beautiful cottage. A stone fireplace with a rustic stone chimney sat in the center with an old fashioned wood-burning stove and kitchen to one side, and a living room with knotty hardwood flooring you stepped down into, to the left.

"It is Dee, isn't it? At least that's the nickname Kristina Buchanan called you, instead of using your real name—*Dianne*. Is that why you ripped the sublet agreement out of my hands? Because you realized it had your real name on it?"

Nathalie sat down and crossed her arms and legs. "As a matter of fact, yes."

Danielle walked up to her and put her fuming face in front of Nathalie's. "Look me in the eye and lie to me again, just like you lied when I asked you if you knew Kristina Buchanan!"

Nathalie was stern in her response. "I wasn't aware I was under oath when you asked me. I just thought it was a casual question, since you were in my home on a personal basis, not an official one."

"Well, consider this an official visit." Danielle gripped her gun again, bringing attention to the fact it indeed was. "Now let me ask you again. How did you know Kristina Buchanan?"

"I know my rights, and I know I don't have to talk to you," Nathalie said fiercely. Then she uncrossed her arms and her eyes softened as she looked at Danielle and said, "But I will."

"It must have been last night that they slept together," Melissa said to Lilly. "I knew Nathalie was going away—she said she was hitching a ride with a friend and not taking her car. I just assumed she was going to her cottage, but she must have gone to Cape Breton with Danielle."

Lilly's eyes were fixed on Melissa's in disbelief. "Surely to God she didn't take Nathalie with her on official police business."

"Yes, I knew Kristina," Nathalie admitted.

"You more than knew her. You were—" Danielle envisioned Nathalie in bed with Kristina Buchanan, making love to her. She wanted to slam her fist against something. "You were sleeping with her and you were very upset when you figured out she was just using you!"

Nathalie stood up, exhibiting a fearlessness most would not under the circumstances. "I am *not* going to discuss this with you. If this is an official visit, then I want another officer."

Had this been any other suspect, Danielle would have ended the "interview" and arranged for another member to conduct it. But under these circumstances, the fact that Danielle had slept with Nathalie, had taken her to Cape Breton with her, and that her evidence had disappeared while Nathalie was there...

"Where are the dolly and blanket?" Danielle demanded to know.

"I don't know."

"Tell me where they are!"

"I've told you I don't know!" Nathalie shouted back. "I didn't take them!"

Danielle was amazed at Nathalie's apparent acting skills. "You tell me what you did with my evidence, or I swear to God—"

"Fuck you!" Nathalie shot out of her chair, enraged. "I'm not going to stand here and let you accuse me of theft—"

"Theft? Theft is the least of your crimes! You're a murderer!"

"That woman cop knows about the *Special K* Lucy was getting for us," Maurice said to one of his associates.

"Lucy? But that was ages ago. I wouldn't worry about that." Then Maurice's associate thought about it. "But you're right, though. That could start the ball rolling on them watching you."

"I'm scared they might do a raid."

"When did that cop find out about the *K*?"

"Yesterday."

"Okay, well worst case scenario, if they do decide to do a bust, I can tell you they'll need at least a couple weeks to organize it. One good thing about the police, my friend, is that they're like the government. They can't do anything until a whole bunch of paperwork is done and the higher-ups approve it. I'll tell you one thing though, you'd be wise to get rid of everything you've got, and then cool it for a while. Like six months or even a year."

"That's what I was thinking too," Maurice said. "I'll tell everybody to give me absolutely everything they have, and I'll send one last shipment. That way none of us will have anything on hand in case we get raided."

"Are you out of your mind?" Nathalie cried out.

"Where were you the night she was killed?" Danielle's voice was even louder than Nathalie's.

"I was here! By myself! Just like I'd been every night since—" Nathalie's voice began to break, but she didn't cry. "After..." Nathalie thrust herself out of her chair and clenched her fists. "I was a goddamned prisoner in my own home because of her. I stopped going anywhere because I was so terrified of running into her. I lived in fear all the time, after—"

"After what, Nathalie?"

Nathalie gripped the back of another chair as though to steady herself, but didn't answer Danielle.

"I asked you a question, Nathalie. Now tell me, after what?"

Nathalie sat down again and answered quietly. "You wouldn't understand."

"Try me," Danielle said crossly.

Nathalie now spoke with great sorrow in her voice. "Kristina was the only person I told everything to. *Everything.* I had told Kristina some..." Nathalie's face tensed as though she were experiencing physical pain. "...extremely personal things. And she used that information to hurt me. Severely." Nathalie took a very deep breath.

"What did she do?"

Nathalie choked back tears and whispered, "She slaughtered me."

"There's something I should probably tell you about Nathalie," Melissa told Lilly. "She's my friend and all, but..." Melissa leaned forward and pressed her knees together.

Melissa looked so concerned, it alarmed Lilly. "What is it?"

Melissa seemed very reluctant to answer that question.

"You have to tell me, Melissa."

Melissa paused, then said, "She's got problems. Serious ones."

"What kinds of problems?"

"She seems to drift in and out of reality. Sees and hears things that aren't really there."

"Are you telling me she's got a mental illness?"

Melissa pressed her lips together.

"Is Nathalie schizophrenic, Melissa?"

Melissa looked straight into Lilly's eyes. "Yes, she is."

"Nathalie, why did you lie to me when I asked you if you knew Kristina Buchanan? If you had nothing to do with it—"

"Because I didn't want to talk about her, Danielle. I *couldn't*. Meeting her was one of the worst things that ever happened in my life—and believe me, there was lots of competition for that. I just wanted to forget she ever existed."

"But you knew I was investigating her murder, and you pretended you had no clue who she was, when you not only knew her but..." Danielle felt sick as she completed her sentence. "...you were her lover."

"I wasn't her lover when she was killed, Danielle. I hadn't been for months. And I was nowhere near Halifax when she was killed. I was here. Those last few months she was alive, I lived in such fear of running into her or anybody she associated with, that I bought this place and spent most of my time here."

Danielle had never felt so torn in all her life. When she looked into Nathalie's eyes, she *believed* her. But her heart was feeling one thing, and her head was telling her something else.

Nathalie had lied to her about knowing Kristina Buchanan. Evidence that might have revealed Kristina Buchanan's killer went missing, and Nathalie could very easily be the one who took that missing evidence. Nathalie also had a motive for killing Kristina. Her strong emotional reactions more than a year and a half after her death were proof of that. Nathalie also had access to, and intimate knowledge of, the murder weapon: ketamine hydrochloride. And, she had no alibi or real proof that she wasn't in Halifax County when the killing took place. If this were a trial, all there would be left to address, would be the message carved on Buchanan's face.

Danielle glanced at the painting that was now turned, facing the wall. Danielle walked over to it and turned it around.

"Don't!" Nathalie pleaded.

But Danielle ignored Nathalie…and was now staring at a horrific scene that filled her sight.

"She was doing very well when she was taking her medications," Melissa told Lilly, "but she hasn't taken them for months now, and I'm very concerned. She's getting very delusional and dangerous— *again.*"

The painting titled *The Slayer* was of a large, beautiful, red rose, with just the flower itself set against a sunny background of blue skies. But just below the flower were clouds that were white on the surface but grew dark and menacing underneath. From above, the very thick clouds shrouded the disturbing, hellish scene below.

Below those clouds, on thorns along the rose stem, were the impaled bodies of men and women, some with blood oozing out of them, others with tears flowing from their faces. All of them, in agonizing pain. Their blood and tears dropped into a heart-shaped pond that the rose grew out of, a pond that was a bloody mixture of their suffering.

As disturbing as all that was, what disturbed Danielle even more was the snake that curled itself around the rose stem, in the same position as the snake on a medical staff—the symbol commonly used to represent nurses—except this snake was in the perfect shape of a large letter "S".

"I don't have absolute proof yet, but I know enough to believe she killed her former lover," Melissa continued telling Lilly.

"Who's her former lover?" Lilly asked.

"Kristina Buchanan," Melissa replied.

"Get out of my house! Get out of my house right now!"

Nathalie kept yelling at Danielle to get out, but Danielle wasn't budging. She swiftly swept her handcuffs out of their case and grabbed Nathalie's arm.

Not expecting much resistance, Danielle was unprepared for Nathalie slipping her leg under Danielle's and tripping her to the floor. Before Danielle even landed, Nathalie pounced on her and reached for Danielle's gun...

Lilly sat at extreme attention across from Melissa. "I want you to tell me absolutely everything you know."

Danielle's hand gripped Nathalie's wrist as Nathalie's hand grasped the gun. For a small woman, Nathalie had incredible strength. She yanked the gun from Danielle's holster, and even though Danielle's equally strong hand was now on hers, Nathalie swung as hard as she could before releasing. The gun landed about ten feet away.

"My God," Lilly lamented, after Melissa filled her in. "That would explain why nothing would have shown up on a criminal records check. If she was sixteen when she killed her sister, and found not criminally responsible due to mental illness, she would have served just a few years in a forensics unit before being released."

"I don't understand, Lilly. How can they let a murderer out after just a few years, and not even give them a criminal record?"

"If someone is found not criminally responsible for a crime, they are considered not to have committed that crime. Basically, the person didn't commit the crime, the illness did."

"Are you fucking serious? That's like saying, 'I didn't rob that store, the devil inside me did.'"

"You don't know how many times that defense has been tried."

"And people get away with it?" Melissa asked incredulously.

"No. But no defense lawyer has yet been able to prove the existence of the devil. Unlike mental illness, which has not only been proven, but physicians willing to testify to a defendant's mental illness—real or fabricated—are a dime a dozen these days."

Nathalie couldn't sustain her resistance against Danielle's strength for more than a few seconds, so Danielle easily gained dominance. She flipped Nathalie over and pinned her back to the floor. Her lower legs gripped Nathalie's upper thighs making it impossible for her to move. Danielle's longer body then lowered itself over Nathalie, and Danielle pressed Nathalie's arms to the floor. Nathalie stared deeply into Danielle's eyes. They were filled with disdain.

Lilly was worried, but even more so after what Melissa said next.

"She was doing well when she was under the care of a psychiatrist, but she stopped going a few months ago, and she threw out all of her medications too. If Danielle is with Nathalie, she could be in serious trouble."

Lilly grabbed the phone and called Danielle, but there was no answer at her apartment, and her cell phone was either off or in an area with no reception.

Danielle could not stop staring at the brown sunbursts in Nathalie's dark green eyes. Her mind was telling her to arrest Nathalie, but she couldn't break her gaze, and she couldn't stop herself from wanting to believe in Nathalie's innocence. So badly.

"You said you were talking to Nathalie tonight?" Lilly asked Melissa.
"Yes, at her apartment."
Lilly phoned Nathalie's apartment, but got no answer. "I'm going to drive to Maynard Street. I need to know Danielle's okay."

"I didn't kill Kristina, Danielle. I swear." Nathalie's eyes sought the depths of Danielle's crystal blue eyes. Danielle felt them penetrate so deeply...that they entered her soul.
Danielle lowered her body until her entire weight rested on top of Nathalie. Danielle felt Nathalie's breasts under hers, and Nathalie's cheek against hers too. Those touches sent such a flood of endorphins through Danielle's entire being, that her grip on Nathalie's wrists loosened...
Nathalie slowly moved her arms down, along Danielle, to the sides of her back, until they rounded her and held Danielle in an embrace. Nathalie began to cry...and Danielle did too.

Melissa and Lilly were in separate vehicles, but they both drove to Maynard Street. Both apartments looked lifeless, and both vehicles were missing. Lilly called Danielle's cell again, but a recorded message still reported that it was either off or out of the reception area. She rang Nathalie's cottage.

Nathalie's phone was ringing, but she made no attempt to answer it. She and Danielle were obviously preoccupied...they were now making love on the hardwood floor.

"Nathalie gave me a key to her apartment so I could check on Chai when she was away," Melissa said to Lilly. "We could go in and check on things."

"We can't, Melissa."

"Why not? It's not like we'd be breaking in. I have a key that she gave me." Melissa held up a shiny, new key.

"We can't enter her premises without permission."

Melissa's face soured. "Why not?"

Lilly raised her hands in exasperation. She wasn't sure if it was at Melissa, or at the judicial system. "We just can't, okay?"

Melissa appeared frozen for a few seconds, then said, "Fine." Her resentful tone resonated into her next sentence. "Stay here if you want, or go home." Melissa walked toward the entrance of Nathalie's building. "Since there's no crime on checking on a friend when you've got a key, I'm going up."

Only three seconds passed before Lilly said, "Wait for me."

Nathalie and Danielle made their way from the floor to Nathalie's bed. Their lovemaking was again filled with passion, and a need for each other.

But a different type of need this time. A need not only for comforting and consoling, but for reassurances that the reality of their situation didn't really exist.

But of course it did.

As much as they both tried to pretend that the nightmare of Kristina Buchanan and her murder never happened...

After they made love they both lay there...

Knowing...

That the harsh reality they had to face...

Was still there.

Melissa and Lilly looked around Nathalie's apartment. Everything seemed in order, though Melissa seemed disappointed when she walked over to a bookcase shelf and saw it was empty.

"I've got a headache," Melissa said abruptly. "Nathalie keeps some Ibuprofen in her bedside table. Just give me a sec to go get one."

Almost two minutes passed before Lilly walked into the bedroom and asked, "What's taking you so long?"

Melissa pulled on a drawer. "It's stuck. I can't—" Melissa yanked hard on a drawer and a yellow, padded envelope fell to the floor. Melissa turned the drawer around, inspected its back side, and said to Lilly, "Looks like this envelope was taped to the back of the drawer. Should we open it, or should we call the police?"

"What makes you think whatever's in there is worth calling the police over? Maybe it's her will. Or the key to her safe deposit box."

"Or maybe it's a murder weapon," Melissa snapped.

Lilly eyed Melissa. "Even if it is, we can't call the police. We're here without Nathalie's knowledge or consent, remember? Even if we found a knife in there with Nathalie's fingerprints and blood all over it, it wouldn't be admissible in court because it was obtained without a warrant."

Melissa stood and placed her hands on her hips. "Are you shitting me?"

"Welcome to my world."

Melissa seemed to be contemplating matters for a moment, then said to Lilly, "Well, I'm looking at what's inside. I at least want to know if my friend is a murderer." Melissa tore open the envelope and dropped its contents onto the bed. "Wow. Thirty-six emeralds."

"How did you learn of Kristina's death?" Danielle asked, as Nathalie lay in her arms.

"On the news."

"How did you feel when you heard about it?"

Danielle felt wet droplets land on her bare shoulder as Nathalie said in a low voice, "I was relieved."

Lilly stared at Melissa, not the bracelet. "We didn't come here to rummage through Nathalie's personal belongings, Melissa. We came in to look around just to see if anything was amiss. There's nothing in here to indicate any type of struggle or foul play, so we need to leave. I shouldn't have entered these premises in the first place."

"That woman put me through hell, Danielle." Nathalie released herself from Danielle's embrace and sat up. "I used to think, if I ever woke up one day and discovered I was a child again, I would kill myself because I would never want to relive my childhood. But I swear to God, I would relive it ten times over if it meant I would be spared ever having crossed paths with that woman."

"You had a bad childhood?" Danielle asked with concern.

Nathalie lifted her left shoulder and dropped it again. "Me and a few million other kids around the world. So I guess you could say I had an average childhood." She attempted to make light of it, but her words were permeated with sorrow. "I just made the mistake of telling Kristina about it."

"What's the painting about, Nathalie? *The Slayer.*"

Nathalie took a deep breath before replying. "*The Slayer* is Kristina." Nathalie brought her legs up, wrapped her arms around them, then rested her cheek on her knees. "Some people are serial killers, Kristina was a serial slayer. She didn't kill her victims, but she slaughtered their hearts and souls and left them empty, gutted shells. She didn't finish them off and end their suffering like a serial killer would. She enjoyed taunting and driving the knife in over and over."

Danielle knew there was massive symbolism throughout the painting, and wanted Nathalie to explain it all. "The rose is beautiful, but underneath…"

"The rose is the initial beauty and charm that entices people in. All they see is the beautiful rose, not the evil that lurks beneath. They lean in close because they're attracted to the rose, and that's when they get sucked into her vortex."

"That's all the darkness and suffering below?" Danielle asked.

"The people impaled on the thorns below are her numerous victims. The more victims she takes in, the more beautiful and healthier the rose gets, because it's her victims' blood and tears that provides her nutrients."

"Is that why the rose is growing out of a heart-shaped pond? It was created out of their blood and tears?"

"Yes."

"What about the snake?"

"The snake is the temptress. She will tell you whatever you want to hear—until she sinks her fangs into you, leaving you paralyzed and defenseless, while she slaughters you."

Danielle was dazzled by Nathalie's creative description, but disturbed by her use of the word "paralyzed". She needed to know more. "The way the snake curls around the rose's stem, it reminds me of a medical staff."

"Yes, the snake also represents Kristina's profession. Nurses are so revered as caregivers, as compassionate and caring people. But Kristina, she loved watching people suffer. It gave her a thrill. That's probably why she loved slasher movies so much. They were sickening to me, but she just loved them. The more she saw somebody suffer, the more of a thrill she got."

Danielle scrutinized Nathalie as she asked, "Why is the snake in the perfect shape of a letter 'S'?"

"I didn't cut the letter 'S' into her face, Danielle."

Danielle's stomach knotted in a half dozen twists. "How do you know about her face?"

Lilly was back at home. Although she was very worried, she knew Danielle would call her as soon as she got back to her apartment and got her message—if she ever did.

Lilly had spent the last hour weighing the risks—and probabilities—that something was *really* wrong. And the consequences of contacting police if nothing was.

Lilly ultimately decided she would wait until morning. If she hadn't heard from Danielle by then, she'd alert the cavalry.

"Melissa told me about her face, the night we had dinner at Lilly's," Nathalie told Danielle. "When she was driving me home." Nathalie looked off into the distance. "That haunted me, after that. I kept picturing Kristina's face with a letter 'S' carved into it." Nathalie traced a letter "S" with her finger. "I kept tracing the letter "S" over and over, wondering if she was dead or alive when it was done to her." Nathalie shuddered, then became very sorrowful. "I knew I wasn't the only one to have their heart slaughtered by Kristina, but I really thought I must have been her most successful slaying ever." Nathalie suppressed tears while her voice lowered several octaves. "Guess she must have hurt someone else even more than me."

Danielle didn't think anyone could have been more hurt by Kristina than Nathalie had been. Danielle could see the pain in Nathalie still, and not only in her face, but also in her speech and her demeanor. "No, Nathalie. Not more than you. She just finally hurt the wrong person, is all."

Very early Sunday morning, after watching a beautiful sunrise come over the beach while they held each other, Nathalie drove Danielle to her vehicle, then followed her back to the city. She hadn't told Danielle about Melissa's break-in—defending herself against murderous accusations had taken priority. Nathalie wasn't sure if Danielle truly believed her, but Danielle had pretended also that morning that their situation didn't exist.

As Danielle drove she felt sick to her stomach. The reality was, Nathalie could still very well be a murderer. Danielle needed more than ever now, to learn all she could about Lucy Miller.

Nathalie never put Chai outside when they were at the cottage. There were too many predators, and Nathalie feared her getting plucked by an eagle or killed by a coyote, so as soon as she arrived at the apartment, she let Chai out in the fenced-in back yard for some fresh air and exercise.

Danielle listened to Lilly's message when she got to her apartment. It was still early for a Sunday morning, but it sounded very urgent, so she called right away.

"Hi, Lilly. Everything okay?"

"Thank God! Are you all right?"

Danielle was still trying to wrap her head around everything. She didn't want to open up this can of worms right now, so she pretended everything was hunky dory. "Of course I am. Why wouldn't I be?"

"I've been worried sick about you."

"Why? You knew I was away."

"Were you with Nathalie last night?"

Danielle fell silent. She thought Lilly didn't know about her and Nathalie, and Danielle didn't know how to tell her about it—or how complicated it had become.

Lilly started to say something but got cut off when Danielle heard a blood-curdling scream come from upstairs.

"I have to go!" Danielle hung up the phone and flew up the stairs. She pounded on the door, shouting to Nathalie asking if she was all right.

When the door opened, Nathalie's face was deathly white, and she couldn't talk. All she could do was point to the open door that led to the balcony facing the back yard.

Danielle walked through it, and saw—hanging from the maple tree with a rope around its neck—Nathalie's cat, Chai.

✌ 47 ✍

"It's a stuffed cat, Nathalie! It isn't real! It's not chai!" Danielle was so relieved to discover this, but incredibly disturbed that someone would be so cruel as to do this to Nathalie. Danielle spied a similar cream colored form underneath a bush. "There she is!" Danielle pointed to Chai's location.

By the time Danielle was down from the tree with the rope and stuffed animal, Nathalie had Chai safely in her arms, cradling her.

"Do you know who would do this?" Danielle asked Nathalie.

"Melissa," Nathalie declared without hesitation. Nathalie then told Danielle how Melissa had basically broken into her apartment.

"I knew there was something sick about her, the second I met her," Danielle said. "You're going to sleep in my apartment tonight. And just to be safe, you should come right now."

"I'll need to bring a few things," Nathalie said.

"I'll help you bring some things down, but first we need to report this."

Danielle called Halifax Regional Police from her cell and two officers responded within minutes. They documented what Nathalie and Danielle had seen, and included Nathalie's statement about Melissa having copied Nathalie's key without her permission, and going through her personal belongings. They also took the rope and realistic looking cat with them.

As soon as they left, Danielle suggested Nathalie get her things. Wanting to help, Danielle followed Nathalie into the bedroom. When she entered, her face went as white as Nathalie's had earlier. For sitting on Nathalie's bed was the custom designed bracelet that could have only been removed from Kristina Buchanan's wrist...by her killer.

Lilly kept trying Danielle's number, but there was still no answer. She tried Nathalie's too, but got no answer there either.

"God, almighty," Lilly exclaimed as she slammed the phone down. She grabbed her jacket and ran out the door.

Before Nathalie could reach the phone she felt a handcuff snap around her wrist. "What—"

"Dianne Nathalie Boudreau, you're under arrest for the murder of Kristina Ann Buchanan."

"Danielle, you're making a mistake."

"I'm sorry, Nathalie. You have no idea how sorry I am."

When Danielle turned Nathalie around to put the second cuff on her arm, Nathalie saw the bracelet on her bed.

"That…"

Danielle turned Nathalie around so she could face her. "Finish your sentence, Nathalie. That what?"

"*Melissa*," Nathalie said with revulsion.

"Are you telling me Melissa planted that bracelet to frame you?" Danielle hoped and prayed.

Nathalie shook her head. "No." She paused, then said, "But she must be the one who pulled it out of its hiding place."

Danielle tensed so quickly, even her tear ducts clenched and would not allow the tears she felt to escape. She grabbed Nathalie's arm and demanded, "Where did you get the bracelet, Nathalie?"

Nathalie turned her head in the opposite direction of Danielle and didn't utter a word.

"Answer me, Nathalie." Danielle grabbed Nathalie's shoulders and turned them to force her to face her.

Nathalie remained stoic—until Danielle's eyes locked onto hers, and Nathalie succumbed. "At the funeral home. It was on her wrist and I took it."

Danielle had not only poured over photographs showing every single person who paid their respects and attended the funeral, but had also asked Gillian and Caroline if "Dee" had shown up. Danielle therefore knew for a fact that Nathalie hadn't gone to the funeral home. Plus, if she had, she'd have known Kristina had a closed casket. It was clear Nathalie didn't know about the closed casket, because she had not been there at all—and must have taken the bracelet off Kristina's wrist before dumping her body in the pond.

"You really did kill her, didn't you?"

Nathalie shook her head. "No, Danielle. I couldn't kill anyone. Not even someone I hated. I would just walk away, just like I did when Kristina—"

There was a loud pounding on Nathalie's door.

"Wait here," Danielle commanded.

"And where am I going to go? To a hacksaw specialist?"

Danielle approached the door and looked through the peephole but all she could see was a brown leather jacket. "Who is it?"

"Danielle? Is that you?"

"Lilly?"

"Yes, it's me. Let me in."

Great. Danielle had about ten seconds to decide whether or not to remove Nathalie's handcuffs.

Maurice Coultier and his associates were very busy indeed. They normally spent Sundays with their family—after all, very few of them knew how they really made their money. Other than Lucy, none of Maurice's family knew that his automotive body shop was just a front for his drug dealing. Some had questioned why he still worked for the rail station with such a successful business, but he explained it away by saying he was just five years away from retirement, so he might as well put in his time and collect his pension.

And while Maurice was not with his family this Sunday, no one thought anything of it since Lucy told them he'd gone fishing with his buddies. Fishing all right. The rod never left his truck as Maurice made his way from one location to another, picking up product he would stash under the train early next morning.

Danielle opened the door and let Lilly in. Nathalie was standing slightly behind Danielle, to her left.

"Hi," Lilly said apprehensively, as she stepped in.

"Hi," Nathalie replied. "I'd offer you a drink, but—" Nathalie lifted her arm, revealing she was handcuffed to Danielle.

"What's going on?"

"It seems I'm under arrest for murder," Nathalie quipped.

Danielle pulled Nathalie to the sofa and sat her down next to her.

"Danielle?" Lilly's face implored for an explanation.

Danielle rubbed her forehead. She stood back up, yanking Nathalie up with her also.

"Hey! You could give me some notice you know. You're taller than me, and these cuffs hurt like hell," Nathalie complained.

"I'm taking you to the bedroom."

"Oh, I'm so not in the mood for sex right now, Danielle. Think I'll take a rain cheque."

Danielle whipped her head around and clenched her fingers around Nathalie's shirt collar. "You think this is funny? You're about to be charged with murder, and you're cracking jokes?"

"I didn't kill anybody!" Nathalie screamed. "There, is that better? Is screaming my head off and pleading my innocence what you want instead? I tried that earlier, but you wouldn't listen!"

Danielle jerked on Nathalie's arm.

"Ow!" she yelped.

When they got to the bedroom, Danielle undid the handcuff from her wrist, then pulled Nathalie's arms behind her back and handcuffed them together. "Where's Chai's leash?"

"Don't hurt Chai!"

"I'm not going to hurt Chai. My God, what do you take me for?"

Tears seeped from Nathalie's eyes. "What are you taking *me* for?"

Danielle had to look away. Her heart was breaking, but she couldn't let her emotions stop her from doing her job. She went back to the living room and rooted through a basket labeled "Chai". Inside, she found a leash. She returned to the bedroom and clipped it to the handcuffs.

Danielle tried her best not to notice—or care. With as little emotion as possible, she said to Nathalie, "If you make a move for the bedroom window, this leash will tug, and I'll be here before you even make it to the edge of the bed."

Danielle went back to the living room, holding the end of the leash, then sat down.

"What the hell is going on, Danielle?"

It took Danielle twenty minutes to fill Lilly in. Then an extra five for Lilly to tell Danielle what she had learned.

"Are you taking her down to the station and charging her?" Lilly asked.

"I can lay the charge, Lilly, but you tell me. Would it stick, or would the Crown be forced to drop it?"

"Danielle, as you know, murder cases are tried under the provincial Crown and I'm federal, so I can't give you any official advice, but are you aware that if you charge anyone other than Lucy Miller right now, that Judge Harrington will not sign your warrant?"

Danielle shot Lilly a shocked look.

"Yes, the warrant you're supposed to spring on Lucy Miller at ten o'clock tomorrow morning."

"How do you know—"

"Oh, for Christ's sake, Danielle. Who do you think called your staff sergeant and told him you figured out Lucy Miller had been swiping ketamine? I stuck my neck out, and I bent over backwards to find someone in the provincial Crown office to persuade a supreme court judge to sign that warrant for you too, but Luis needed more time to organize the roll on Coultier. The bust is set to go at ten a.m. tomorrow morning, the exact same time you're supposed to be arresting Lucy Miller." Lilly pressed her hands together then looked intently at Danielle. "Our operation depends on you following through with picking up his wife tomorrow, Danielle."

"But what if Nathalie is the one who killed—"

"Danielle, you can't just *think* you know who killed Buchanan. You're going to need absolute proof before you lay your first murder charge. Embarrassing yourself is one thing, but you know if you're wrong, all hell will break loose. You know the press will run with it, and it'll be one more very embarrassing blunder for the RCMP. All you'll do for the rest of your career is write speeding tickets, and you know it."

"Don't you think I haven't thought about that already? I'd like nothing better than to be proven wrong in regards to Nathalie, but it just doesn't seem plausible, Lilly. Not with all this mounting evidence."

"Danielle, Melissa already knew that bracelet was in Nathalie's bedside table. She purposefully pretended to find it so I'd see it."

"How do you know that?"

"Because without even picking it up and counting, she knew exactly how many emeralds it contained. She's seen that bracelet before, Danielle. She might even be the one who planted it."

"She didn't plant it, Lilly." Danielle lowered her head and wiped a tear from one eye, then the other. "Nathalie admitted to taking it and hiding it in her beside table."

Lilly's eyes opened wide. "Where did she get the bracelet?"

"Oh, she tried to tell me some lame story about taking it off Buchanan's wrist at the funeral home, but that holds about as much water as a wire basket. No one saw her there, and it was a closed casket because of her face." Danielle's mouth took a downward turn and she looked like she was about to cry.

"Danielle, I don't know for sure that Nathalie didn't kill Buchanan, and what Melissa told me definitely points in her direction, but if Melissa's the one who pulled that stunt hanging a stuffed cat that looks like Chai from the tree, then she's out to get Nathalie. Why, I don't know. But the thing is, Danielle, aside from this Nathalie mess, you have another suspect you've convinced a judge to allow you to pick up tomorrow morning."

"But what if I let Nathalie go, I'm wrong about Lucy Miller, and Nathalie runs?"

"Danielle, do you really think Nathalie is a murderer?"

"I don't know, Lilly. I don't know what to think anymore."

"What does your gut tell you?"

Danielle closed her eyes, and tears formed in them. She felt like she was about to confess a terrible sin to a priest, and she worried what penance Lilly might give her for this confession. "I can't trust what my gut tells me, Lilly. Because I'm in love with her."

Lilly and Danielle were out in the hall talking. Danielle still held on to the leash, which was now attached to two additional leashes, so they could snake their way under Nathalie's apartment door, across the living room, and into Nathalie's bedroom, where she still sat, handcuffed.

"I know it's taking a risk, Danielle, but don't charge Nathalie—just yet, anyway. First thing tomorrow morning, get your hands on her medical records, see if she's ever been diagnosed or treated for schizophrenia or any type of mental illness. In the meantime, I'm going to pull every string I can, and see if I can access any sealed records. That'll at least tell us if Melissa was telling the truth or not. Nathalie doesn't have an alibi, but there's really no evidence linking her to Buchanan's murder either. Legally, Nathalie owns that bracelet, since she's the one who purchased it, and there's no way to prove that the bracelet Buchanan's friends saw on her wrist is the same one."

Danielle tried to sound hopeful, but she wasn't. "I'll get her medical records soon as I can, and I'll also try to find out how her sister died. Hopefully I'll have the information early enough so I can make a decision about the warrant for Lucy Miller before ten."

After Lilly left, Danielle brought Nathalie and Chai down to her apartment. Danielle had decided not to charge Nathalie. Just yet. But she wasn't comfortable removing the handcuffs and letting her go either, so Nathalie now sat in Danielle's apartment, with her hands cuffed together.

Nathalie didn't say a word. She hadn't since Danielle walked out of the bedroom with the other end of Chai's leash. Three hours had passed since then.

"Are you hungry? Do you have to go to the bathroom?"

Nathalie didn't reply.

"You're not talking to me?"

Nathalie stared forward.

"Nathalie, it was either this or take you down to the station and have you charged."

"The only reason you didn't, is because it would screw up the drug bust they're planning for ten tomorrow morning," Nathalie said bitterly.

Danielle looked at Nathalie with probing eyes.

"I'm not deaf, Danielle. I was in the bedroom tied to a leash, remember? And for the record, I do not have schizophrenia. If anybody's mentally ill, it's Melissa Lambert."

Danielle looked at Nathalie intently but didn't comment, which seemed to anger Nathalie even more.

"I could have you charged for kidnapping, you know! Do you realize that? I may not know much about police procedures but I doubt keeping somebody in handcuffs against their will in *your apartment* is in the procedures manual."

Danielle rested her head in her hands and closed her eyes. Her first—and probably last—special investigation had become a nightmare. One suspect threatened to have her charged with sexual harassment, and now a second suspect—that Danielle had slept with, no less—could have her charged with kidnapping and unlawful confinement. After all, Nathalie wasn't arrested or charged with any offenses, yet Danielle had her in handcuffs, and not at the police station, but forcibly confined in Danielle's apartment.

Yet as tempted as Danielle was to succumb to this extraordinary stress, she stayed in investigative mode and zeroed in on the problem at hand. "Where did you get the bracelet, Nathalie?"

Nathalie pursed her lips.

"I asked you a question," Danielle curtly reminded her.

"So? No matter what I tell you, you aren't going to believe me, so why should I bother answering?"

"Maybe if you tell me the truth."

"I've *been* telling you the truth!"

"Nathalie!" Danielle barked.

"Fine!" Nathalie barked back. "It was lying on top of her wrist—in the coffin. And I took it."

"Nathalie, the first problem with that story is that Kristina wasn't wearing the bracelet when her body was found. Gillian clearly remembers Kristina wearing it that night, but when her body was found, the bracelet was missing. It wasn't in her house, or in the pond, or anywhere in the park, and it was never found in any of her belongings, anywhere."

"Well, somebody must have put it in her coffin. I didn't."

"Okay, Nathalie. I'll play this little game with you. Why didn't anyone see you at the funeral home?"

"Because nobody was there."

Danielle rolled her eyes and shook her head.

"Remember the funeral director I took you to so you could locate your potential witness?"

"What about him?" Danielle asked indifferently.

"Well, he used to be one of my foster parents. When I found out where Kristina was being waked, I called him up and asked him for a favor." Nathalie lowered her head. "I sort of lied. I gave him the impression that Kristina and I were still dating when she died. I told him I wanted to say goodbye to her, but that her family didn't approve, so I wouldn't be welcome at the funeral. "

"Her funeral was here in Halifax, Nathalie, not Cape Breton," Danielle said with impatience.

"He called the funeral home here and arranged it with them. They let me in, ten o'clock at night, after it was closed. The funeral director took me into the room, to her casket." Nathalie swallowed, and her speech slowed. "I wanted to know if it was really her, so I opened the casket, but her head was all bandaged up."

Danielle gave careful consideration to what Nathalie was saying. It *sounded* convincing.

Danielle wasn't speaking to Nathalie, but said her thoughts out loud. "Her head would have been bandaged because of what was done to her face. They wouldn't have wanted her loved ones to see that."

"The bracelet was just lying there on top of her wrist. I know this might sound awful, but she didn't deserve that bracelet, so I didn't want her buried with it."

Danielle sat quietly, thinking. A few minutes later she asked Nathalie, "Kristina was waked for two days. Which evening were you there? Was there a viewing the next day?"

"No, her funeral was the next morning."

Danielle went to her briefcase and pulled some pages out of it.

"What's that?" Nathalie asked.

"It's a photocopy of the condolence book from the funeral home."

"You photocopied the condolence book? *Why?*"

"Because sometimes killers like to revisit their own handiwork. It's not uncommon for murderers to stand next to their victim's coffin with crocodile tears streaming down their face."

Danielle leafed through copies of the book. "According to this, Joe and Joyce Coultier didn't pay their respects. No surprise there. But Maurice Coultier was the second to last person to sign, right before a Restin Piecekay. I haven't come across that name anywhere else in the investigation. Very odd name, too."

"It's not a name," Nathalie clarified. "It stands for 'Rest in Peace, K.' It's me who wrote it."

Danielle now saw the creative message in the name. Very few people would have the creativity to come up with something like that. *Could Nathalie be telling the truth after all?*

Danielle probably shouldn't have verbalized her thoughts, but did. "So if Maurice signed the book just before you did, he might have been the one who put the bracelet on Kristina's wrist. And if that's the case, then Maurice must have been given the bracelet by whoever killed Kristina."

Nathalie's slouched shoulders straightened up and her eyes brightened. "Does this mean you're going to take these cuffs off me?"

Very early the next morning Danielle was pouring over Nathalie's medical records from the Halifax Health Authority. It had taken a *lot* of extra pushing to get them so quickly, but it paid off. The fact that the hospital is a twenty-four hour operation was definitely a help in this case.

Other than perhaps being somewhat clumsy—drilled through her finger, dropped a pot of boiling water on her foot, tripped on some stairs and broke an ankle—Nathalie was very healthy and had never been prescribed anything more than the occasional antibiotic.

Danielle then called the funeral home that handled Buchanan's arrangements. The funeral director confirmed he had indeed allowed Nathalie a private viewing after closing as a favor to another funeral director from Cape Breton. He couldn't confirm if Nathalie had gotten the bracelet off Buchanan's wrist or not, but he did confirm she had been alone in the room with the casket. He also verified that Kristina Buchanan's head had been bandaged just as Nathalie had described.

Danielle was still waiting on information from any sealed records Lilly might find, and Nathalie's medical records from Cape Breton, which covered Nathalie's birth to age fifteen, but Danielle doubted they'd be any different.

She was wrong.

"What are you so happy about? Got yourself a hot date?" One of the DNA techs asked Melissa Lambert.

"Let's just say, this cool cat is about to swallow one hot canary." Melissa then started dancing around her workstation.

Danielle had leafed through the first six years of Nathalie's medical records in a matter of seconds. There was hardly anything prior to starting school, then with each passing year the reports got worse. By the time she was on page twenty-four, she thought she was going to be sick.

Nathalie sat in her apartment at her electric piano, but she couldn't play. She stood up and walked over to the back window. The one curtain that was almost always drawn in order to block the view of a maple tree cast a dark shadow over half the living room. Nathalie inhaled deeply, then flung it open. She grabbed the window sash to steady herself and stared.

Tears predictably flowed. But it wasn't her sister or Kristina she was crying about this time. It was realizing that just like her sister—and Kristina—Danielle...would have to die.

Danielle had been a strong, confident child. Although the loss of her parents and brother had shattered her, she had managed to remain intact. Outwardly at least. Her grandmother hadn't been affectionate, but she did show Danielle much love and support in her own way. It taught Danielle that you can feel something but not necessarily show it.

That had helped Danielle when she joined the military, and her subsequent police training had furthered her skills of pushing through with the task at hand, no matter what she was feeling on the inside. Danielle had always been able to remain unaffected by whatever information came her way during an investigation, no matter how shocking or gruesome.

Until today.

The pages of a previously sealed file, couriered directly from the Department of Justice to Constable Danielle Renaud via instruction from the Public Prosecution Service, shook as though at the epicenter of an earthquake—until they dropped from Danielle's hands.

The splatter and pooling of turbulently shed tears carried ink off the surface, causing previously readable words from the trial involving Dianne Nathalie Boudreau to bleed off the page.

Danielle's body shook, trembled, and shivered, alternating through each as she struggled to keep her stomach from ejecting its contents.

She lost that struggle.

Lillian Marsh answered a frantic call from Sergeant Luis Carvery.

"My eyes and ears on Renaud's floor tell me she's had some sort of breakdown this morning. She's a total wreck," he told her.

"She received some extremely shocking news this morning, Luis. I'm used to terrible crimes, but even I was floored. Not just the how, but the who. She's really been shaken to the core, and rightly so."

"What are you talking about?"

"That's not important right now. Not for us, at least. Everything's a go, just as we planned."

"We're gonna need somebody else to execute the warrant if Renaud is in no shape—."

"Don't worry, Luis. I know Danielle. She won't let us down. No matter what, she'll still do her job. That, I can guarantee about her."

"Anybody from her unit has authority to execute the warrant now that it's signed. Why take a chance on Renaud if she might be falling apart?"

"For the exact same reasons you're taking a chance on me, Luis."

While Danielle had been tempted for the first time in her career to hit a bar for a few stiff drinks, she instead ran across the street and hit the pool where she swam till her arms were sore. She'd just stepped out of the shower at Citadel pool when her cell phone rang.

"Constable Renaud," she answered.

Staff Sergeant Kline was extremely stern. "Get to my office. *Now!*"

Nathalie didn't want to believe it was happening all over again, but it was. She wanted so badly to be able to stop herself, but she didn't know how. Would moving away help? But where would she go? And would it really matter? Danielle would be dead soon. Perhaps after she was, Nathalie's emotions would go dormant for a while. Maybe even die off altogether, and never return. That would be good. But what if she met someone new and the pattern repeated itself?

No, Nathalie knew that wouldn't happen. Nathalie knew Danielle would be the last, because she knew how much Danielle's death would devastate her. Even if she was the one who would be responsible for it.

Staff Sergeant John Kline sat across from Danielle with an extremely concerned look on his face.

"The Chief and Superintendent received a very disturbing email this morning, telling them you're sleeping with a woman suspected of murdering Kristina Buchanan. They both want you off the case effective immediately."

Danielle knew exactly who had sent that email. If Melissa wanted a war, she was going to get one. Danielle's priority was getting out of this quicksand first, then she'd deal with Melissa Lambert. But deal, she would. Melissa Lambert was about to meet her match and get what was coming to her.

"Did you hear what I said, Renaud? If that's true, then you're off the case," Staff Sergeant John Kline repeated. "Your private life is none of our business, and it seems awfully far-fetched to me that an officer of your caliber would jeopardize her career by doing something like that, but you do understand, we do have to look into it."

"Yes, I understand sir. Of course."

"The person who wrote the email was quite specific it was the Buchanan case, though they didn't name the suspect. As far as I'm aware, Lucy Miller is your only suspect at the moment. Is she your only suspect, or is there anyone else?"

"Lucy Miller is my only suspect at the moment, sir." Danielle knew her lie was absolutely necessary, so it rolled off her tongue with ease. After the case was solved, she would explain everything to Kline, and he would understand—she hoped.

"And are you sleeping with Lucy Miller?"

"No, sir. Absolutely not, sir."

Kline stared at Danielle so hard, she felt heat emanating from his eyes. After some hesitation he said, "All right then. Tech Crime is working on tracing the email. Of course it was sent anonymously, but we should know where it originated, very soon."

Danielle tried her best not to let her relief show. "Tell them to use VPN sniffers—and include QNX, Unix, and Linux based."

Staff Sergeant Kline's eyebrows lifted considerably. "I'd like to say I have a clue what—"

"Virtual private networks. It's an overlay that's used to mask a computer's IP address so it can surf the net or send email invisibly without being traced. I know Tech Crime already uses complex sniffers to detect VPN's in order to identify owners of computers containing child pornography, but they should also include non-

standard language-based OS sniffers. I wouldn't put it past—"
Danielle caught herself before saying Melissa Lambert's name. If she
mentioned it she'd have a lot more to explain and Danielle didn't
have time for that right now. "Just to make sure, they should do a
sweep of all platforms, is all I'm saying."

Kline gave Danielle a grim, steely look. He had no doubt caught
her near slip. He hesitated for what felt like forever, then placed his
hands flat on his desk and said, "Is there something you're not telling
me, Renaud?"

Danielle glanced at a clock on the wall and panic started
rumbling through her gut. It was 9:35 a.m. As it was, she would need
to hoof it to make it to Lucy Miller's house on time.

Kline followed her glance at the clock. He picked up the phone
and said to her, "I'll call Tech Crime. In the meantime…" He tapped
his watch. "You've got a warrant to serve."

Coordinating a drug bust in such a public place could be a nightmare.
But since the Halifax Rail station served only one route, from Halifax
to Montreal and back with a single departure daily in the early
afternoon, there weren't very many people inside the station, and the
regular bodies rushing about outside preparing the train for its
afternoon run made it easier for Carvery's team to get into position
without being noticed.

Maurice Coultier had just finished loading the remainder of his
shipment under a fourth rail car and was headed for the coffee
machine when the clock struck ten.

The look on Lucy Miller's face when her home was swarmed by
police officers and she was taken into custody was a combination of
shock and extreme concern. Danielle knew Lucy would be worried
about the safety of her infant son, so when Lucy was placed under
arrest, she was told he would be held in protective care until her legal
matters were resolved. It was a bargaining chip Danielle would be
depending on.

"We've got nothing. Absolutely nothing," Constable Blanchard
reported. "His body shop, house, grounds—it's all clean."

"Normally that would be really bad news, but I've got great news
for you," Sergeant Carvery told Blanchard. "This end just seized the

largest shipment of illicit drugs Halifax has ever seen. Four rail cars, stuffed with everything from ecstasy to Oxycontin, cocaine, hashish, and heroin. Looks like he decided to ship everything out on one last run. If we'd have waited till Friday," Sergeant Carvery reminded Blanchard, "we'd have been royally screwed."

Halifax Regional Police headquarters was a very busy place indeed. Maurice Coultier had been arrested at the train station and was sitting in a holding cell. His wife, Lucy, was strategically placed in a room where she would be visible when her husband was taken from his cell to interview room 'C'.

The look of fear on Maurice Coultier's face when he saw his wife told Danielle everything was going according to plan—so far.

"Where's my son?" Maurice beseeched. Only one of the officers escorting Maurice Coultier responded—by shoving him along.

Danielle received some crucial information as she was about to enter the room occupied by Maurice Coultier. As a result of that information, she gave an extremely important directive. She instructed two RCMP officers to pick up Dianne Nathalie Boudreau on Maynard Street.

"I'll tell you where your son is, as soon as you tell me who killed Kristina Buchanan," Danielle told Maurice Coultier.

"I have no idea who killed Kristina. Where's my son?"

"He's in protective custody. He'll be taken care of until the courts have a better idea of what will happen to his mother."

"Lucy had nothing to do with the drugs. She didn't know anything about it. It was all me, and only me."

"I don't believe you, Maurice, because I know Lucy cooked the books for you. She's very good at phantom number crunching. First she hid the fact that she was ordering extra ketamine at the clinic, then she finagled the books of your auto body shop to make it look like your profits from the drug running were coming from your business. She'll get a couple years just for that."

"I did the books, not Lucy. I swear to you, she had nothing to do with the drugs at all. Look, I'm willing to take full responsibility for the drugs, but that was all me. I'll tell you everything I did, but just let Lucy go. Our son needs his mother at least."

"Even if I believed you, Maurice—which I don't—but even if I did, it still wouldn't change a thing. I've got nothing to do with the drug bust. That's not why your wife's been arrested," Danielle said, dropping her next domino into place.

Maurice looked predictably confused. "What's she been arrested for, then?"

Ah, the Gods could not have timed it more perfectly. Just then, Joseph Coultier, Maurice's brother, walked past the see-through glass partition, not in handcuffs, but holding a coffee cup and chatting with a uniformed officer.

The two RCMP officers escorting Dianne Nathalie Boudreau were very quiet. They were following their orders to the letter, and had no time to waste.

"How much of a stretch do you think he'll get?" Sergeant Carvery asked Lillian Marsh.

"I'm hoping for at least seven years," Lilly replied. "That was quite the haul. First offense or not, just the amount and range of drugs he was distributing should get him that much."

"Yeah, this one will go down in the record books for sure. Cocaine, heroin and hashish off the ships at the container port, pharmaceutical drugs from illegal labs, and high potency pot from medicinal grow ops. It was perfect, when you think about it. Halifax being a seaport, and with so many universities and research labs, he had himself quite the network of suppliers. And how ingeniously simple, to just stash it all under the rail cars of a train that goes to Montreal every day."

"Thanks for the nod, by the way," Lilly said with a grateful smile.

"Hey, you earned it. If it wasn't for you, we wouldn't have gotten what we did. If we'd have waited like my team originally planned, it would have been too late. I just told your higher-ups the truth. You were instrumental in guiding us with your legal genius. They're impressed too. Word is you're probably going to be lead attorney on this one."

Lilly's smile broadened. "I was only aiming for redemption, but I'll take the icing on the cake too."

Danielle left one interview room and entered another. Joe Coultier sat, drinking his coffee.

"Is it true my brother's been arrested?"

"Yes, it is, Mr. Coultier."

"What's he been arrested for?"

Instead of answering Joe Coultier's question, Danielle placed a clear plastic bag on the table. It contained Kristina Buchanan's bracelet.

"Now how do you suppose your brother got a hold of this? Kristina was wearing it the night she was killed, but it wasn't on her wrist when her body was found. It wasn't in her house either. Do you have any ideas, Mr. Coultier?"

"How do you know that's Kristina's bracelet?"

"Oh, we know it's hers. The only thing we don't know, is how it got from Kristina's dead wrist to your brother's live hand."

"What's my brother been arrested for? If it's about Kristina, he's already been cleared."

Danielle continued to ignore Joe Coultier's questions. "Since Kristina's body was wheeled into the park, it didn't take much strength—even a small man like your brother could have done it."

"Look, just because he can push a dolly doesn't mean he's the one who did it. The cops already cleared him, so why did you arrest him?"

Danielle looked at her cell phone even though it wasn't vibrating or ringing. "Excuse me for a moment, Mr. Coultier. I'll be right back."

Getting the confirmation she needed to ensure that she was on the right track, Danielle exited interview room 'B' and entered room 'A'.

Lucy Miller was a nervous wreck.

"Do you understand clearly why you're here, Ms. Miller?" Danielle had waited for Lucy's lawyer to arrive before speaking with her.

"You're forcing me to tell you where I was the night Kristina was killed."

"Yes, well, I did try to ask you from the comfort of your own home, but you slammed the door in my face."

"I was at my sister's in Montreal," Lucy snarled. "She broke her leg, and I was there helping her out. There'd be lots of proof I was there that entire week."

Lucy's lawyer wasted no time. "My client has provided her alibi. Is she free to go now?"

Danielle had no intention of speeding up matters—just yet, at least. "We can hold her for twenty-four hours. We'll need time to verify her alibi, and I've got more questions for her."

"Twenty-four hours? But my son—he's breast fed."

"Your son will be fed, Lucy. He's in good hands. But if you're in a hurry to get out of here, then I suggest you be a lot more cooperative than you have been, and stop playing games with us."

"I'm not playing games. You asked me where I was the night Kristina was killed, and I told you. What more do you want?"

"What did you do with the extra Ketaset you ordered for yourself? And don't try to feed me that cockamamie story about getting it for a shelter."

Lucy Miller looked at her lawyer.

"Lucy, your husband is already going to miss your son's childhood. He's been under investigation for over a year, and they've got months of surveillance on him. It's up to you if you want your son to grow up without a mother as well. We can make you a deal, but you're going to have to give us something in return."

Lucy and her lawyer had a whispered conversation, then he said to Danielle, "She will answer your question if you don't charge her with any offenses relating to it."

Danielle knew the case against Lucy for selling ketamine wouldn't be strong enough to hold up in court almost two years after the fact anyway, so she agreed, then asked again, "What did you do with the Ketaset?"

"I gave it to Maurice. He turned it into powder, then sent it to Montreal."

"Did it all get sent to Montreal?"

"All except the last batch."

"What happened to the last batch?"

"It was stolen."

Danielle looked skeptical. "Really, now."

"That's the truth. Maurice kept it stored in his shed out back— the house he lived in before we got married—and it went missing from there."

"Do you know who stole it?"

"Don't know for sure, but I think it was Kristina."

"Did Kristina play a part in Maurice's drug running?"

"Not that I'm aware of."

"When did the Ketaset go missing?"

"About two weeks before Kristina died. Maurice asked me if I had taken it, but of course I hadn't. I tried to ask him about it a few days later, but he got really mad and told me to stop asking about it, so I figured it was Kristina who took it. He and I always fought over her, and usually if he got mad like that it had something to do with her, so I just let it go."

"How much was in the last batch that got stolen?"

"Twenty grams of powder."

"And you never ordered any extra Ketaset after that?"

"No. When Joe found out, he was livid. He told Maurice if I didn't stop, he'd report me. Maurice was scared of Joe. He said Joe wasn't just talking out of his hat, that he'd really do it, so I stopped."

"When did Joe talk to Maurice about it?"

"Um…the same night the ketamine went missing from Maurice's shed, actually."

Melissa Lambert was being escorted from the lab to a small meeting room by two armed security guards.

On one side of a long table sat her boss, his boss, and someone from their Human Resources Department, as well as Dianne Nathalie Boudreau and the two uniformed RCMP officers who had accompanied her.

Melissa's boss pressed the play button on Nathalie's digital recorder. Melissa heard her own voice telling Nathalie how she had gotten away with her corrupt money-making scheme at the hospital, and had blackmailed her former boss into giving her a good reference in order to gain employment at the RCMP crime lab.

Her boss also detailed how an anonymous email sent to the Chief of Halifax Regional Police and Superintendent of the RCMP's 'H' Division was traced to an RCMP computer—one that required her personal login I.D. and password to access.

While none of this warranted any criminal charges, it did however, provide grounds for immediate dismissal.

Melissa was stripped of her security pass cards and work identification, and was escorted out of the building.

❧ 50 ❧

Danielle didn't really have time to chat with Lilly, but she was ecstatic to report Melissa's firing. She also wanted to thank Lilly for successfully arguing during an emergency hearing that she be granted access to sealed records of the rape trial that ensued after Nathalie and her sister had been taken into protective custody. (As per Canadian law, the records had been sealed to protect Nathalie's identity since she was a minor when she was victimized.)

Danielle had never read anything so brutal and revolting in all her life. She had lost all composure when she read how Nathalie had been so violently raped when she was just eleven years old by a man who had purchased her for the evening from her own mother. Nathalie had required reconstructive surgery on her right breast and vagina, and had suffered three broken ribs during that particular rape. During the trial it had also been revealed it hadn't been the only rape Nathalie had endured, that the sexual assaults had started at age seven and had continued until she'd been taken into protective custody at age eleven.

"I know how hard it was for you to read all that," Lilly said to Danielle. "But at least you know now why she was so secretive. I've met a lot of victims, Danielle, and especially those whose lives are so traumatically disrupted, they only want to be known for who they are, their own accomplishments and skills, not for the abhorrent behavior of others."

"I'm so saddened by what she's been through, but I'm also so relieved. I really was starting to think I was in love with a murderer."

"You really are in love with her, aren't you?" Lilly stated, more than asked.

"Yes," Danielle admitted. "And I think she's in love with me too."

Lilly went surprisingly silent.

Danielle nervously asked, "Aren't you happy for us, Lilly?"

"Sure I am," Lilly replied.

But Danielle wasn't convinced, because Lilly sounded quite resentful when she said it.

After Nathalie left RCMP 'H' Division headquarters she went straight to her appointment with Beulah Hunt.

A few minutes into their session, Beulah was trying to change Nathalie's mind about something Nathalie was convinced of. "Danielle's not going to die, Nathalie."

"But every single person I've ever loved has ended up dead. If I let myself love Danielle she'll end up dying too, I know it."

"You can't live your life in isolation because you're afraid to lose someone, Nathalie."

"I can't risk allowing myself to love Danielle, Beulah. I just can't."

"But Nathalie, you already *do* love her."

Maurice Coultier was perspiring so much by the time Danielle returned, he looked like he'd gone for a swim. "What's my brother doing here?" he fearfully asked.

"He's here providing us with some information." Danielle opened the file folder she came in with, and pretended to be reading from it.

"What kind of information?"

"Pertaining to Kristina Buchanan's death," Danielle said nonchalantley as she continued scanning the contents of the file.

"Like what? What's he saying?"

Danielle readied herself for the most important interview of her career. She dropped the file, stood up and walked slowly around the table, looking much taller and more commanding from Maurice's seated position.

"Did your brother disapprove of every woman you ever went out with?"

Maurice started rubbing his knuckles and stared at them. He wouldn't look at Danielle, and he wouldn't reply.

"He got rid of Kristina, and now he's going to get rid of Lucy too."

That got Maurice's attention. "What are you talking about?"

"I'm talking about the fact that your older brother took Kristina away, and now he's going to take away your wife and son. With you and Lucy in jail, he'll raise your son as his own. He and his wife were never able to have children, were they?"

"Why would Lucy go to jail? She hasn't done anything wrong."

"We know the brand of ketamine used to killed Kristina was Ketaset, the same brand Lucy was swiping just before Kristina was killed."

"How do you know it's the same stuff?"

"Because Ketaset also contains a preservative called benzethonium chloride, Mr. Coultier. That preservative was also found in Kristina's tissues. So that, along with what your brother's telling us about Lucy right now…"

That last part wasn't exactly true. Danielle had instructed the officer to chat with Joseph Coultier strictly about hockey—and only hockey—until Danielle got back in there.

But Maurice didn't know that. "I want to make a deal. I'm not going to say another word until my lawyer gets here and we work out a deal," he announced.

Beulah spoke quietly as she said, "I know you loved your sister very much, Nathalie, and you loved your mother too. Regardless of her failures, she was still your mother, and I'm sure you still mourn her in your own way." Beulah made sure she had direct eye contact with Nathalie before she added, "I know you loved Kristina too."

Nathalie's only response was to lower her gaze.

"Danielle's not going to die because you love her, Nathalie. Chantal, your mother, Kristina…they all died for different rea—."

"I ended Chantal's life, and you know it."

Beulah studied Nathalie's reaction and came to a clear conclusion. "Nathalie, it's time you talked about how Chantal died."

"No way!" Lillian Marsh shouted at Constable Danielle Renaud in front of Sergeant Carvery and Staff Sergeant Kline. "Not a chance in hell, positively, absolutely not in this lifetime, am I going to drop the charges against Maurice Coultier! This is the largest drug bust in the history of Halifax, and he's going to serve his time for it."

"But it's my only shot at snaring Buchanan's killer," Danielle pleaded.

"That's your problem," Lilly caustically replied.

Danielle's gut reaction was to flare into a rage. As a matter of fact, if it hadn't been Lilly on the other side of that desk, she might have inappropriately lunged at the person behind it. But thanks to their friendship—albeit a little strained recently—she kept herself miraculously anchored to the task at hand.

"You might lose this case anyway, Lilly. Do you really have proof it was Maurice himself who put the drugs on the train? Maybe it was another mechanic."

"No! I will not budge on this, so stop wasting your time. You've already got some circumstantial evidence against Joseph Coultier, you'll have to build your case on that."

"Oh, for God's sake, Lilly. You know it would only take about thirty seconds for a half decent lawyer to render what we've got useless. We all know it's not enough. And he's not about to confess, so we need the only other person who knows to flip him over."

Lilly's eyes seared into Danielle. "You picked up a dolly and blanket in Cape Breton, didn't you? Isn't that why you went there?" Lilly broke her visual lock on Danielle and grabbed a folder from the right side of her desk. "You don't need Maurice Coultier to turn on his brother if you've got physical evidence."

Danielle glared at Lilly. Lilly *knew* she no longer had that evidence. Danielle had confessed to Lilly what had happened to it when she had Nathalie handcuffed—and tied to a cat leash—as she related the predicament she was in.

"Danielle, I've done my best for you, and that's all I can do."

"You mean, that's all you're *willing* to do. And you and I both know the *real* reason why."

The men gave each other knowing looks. This was no longer about work, and everyone in the room knew it.

Lilly rose from behind her desk and stood as imposing as possible. "Gentleman, please excuse Constable Renaud and I. She and I need to have a private talk so she can be reminded of her *restrictions* as a police officer *after* charges have been laid."

It took Nathalie a few minutes to prepare herself before telling Beulah the circumstances of her sister's death.

"Ten seconds after I told Chantal I couldn't let her sneak into my room, I changed my mind, but she'd already hung up on me. I wanted so badly to call her back and tell her I was sorry, that I'd rather take the chance and sneak her into my room than to let her be out there cold and hungry, but I didn't know how to reach her. I had no idea where she was calling from, or where she was. I was so upset, Beulah, I didn't sleep the entire night. I kept praying for her to call back, but she didn't. She was so angry with me when she hung up on me, I wasn't surprised she didn't call back." Nathalie closed her eyes, but it didn't stop the tears from escaping.

"What happened the next morning, Nathalie?" Beulah was so focused on keeping an eye on Nathalie, she had to remind herself to breathe.

Nathalie opened her eyes, though not fully, and spoke softly. "First thing I used to do when I woke up every morning was open the curtains. I always got up at exactly seven, but that morning…I felt like scum. I just hated myself for telling her she couldn't come stay in my room." Nathalie nibbled on her lip and swallowed several times. "I stayed in bed for a long time. It was almost eight-thirty when I finally opened the curtains. And that's when…" Nathalie was biting her lip so hard, it started to bleed.

"Tell me what you saw, Nathalie."

Nathalie's squeezed her hands together, but it failed to stop them from shaking.

"You need to tell me what you saw, Nathalie."

Nathalie squeezed her hands together even harder. "My sister, Chantal."

"Where was your sister, Nathalie?"

Nathalie closed her eyes as tightly as she could but it didn't stop the flow of tears.

"Breathe, Nathalie. Take a breath, then tell me where your sister was."

"She was…" Nathalie pressed her hands into her stomach, as though trying to stop herself from vomiting. "Hanging from the tree…with a rope around her neck."

Maurice Coultier looked like he'd aged years in a matter of hours.

"Do we have a deal or what?" he asked Danielle when she finally came back.

Danielle handed his lawyer details of the deal approved by the Crown prosecutor's office. The drug distribution charges against Maurice Coultier would be dropped if—and only if—he provided sufficient information leading to the arrest of Kristina Buchanan's killer.

Maurice Coultier's lawyer outlined their conditions. "His wife gets released immediately, and my client gets released as soon as he's provided you with the information he has."

Danielle explained the agreement. "As this states, the Crown will drop all charges stemming from the drug bust at the train station. We can't hold him on those charges if they're no longer there. As for his wife, we're willing to release her as soon as Maurice tells us what he knows. The faster he tells us, the faster she can go home and retrieve their son."

Maurice Coultier's lawyer looked at him and nodded his approval.

Nathalie had cried solidly for several minutes after telling Beulah about her sister's suicide. Then, she said, as if her speaking had not been interrupted by an expulsion of tears, "That's all I see now when I look at a maple tree. Chantal's dead body hanging by a noose around her neck."

Beulah closed her eyes briefly as she said, "I'm so sorry, Nathalie."

Nathalie didn't respond to the sentiment. She stared into space while she said, "I can't picture Chantal's face at all anymore without seeing her with black eyes, even though hers were blue."

"Why black eyes?" Beulah asked.

Nathalie swallowed. "The funeral director back home—he was one of my foster parents—he told me it was because she died with her eyes open." Nathalie swallowed again. "The last image my sister saw as her life faded, was my bedroom window. She knew I got up at seven every morning. I think she jumped at exactly that time, thinking I'd see her when I opened the curtains and save her. But I didn't. I think she died, staring at my bedroom window…waiting for me to save her."

Sergeant Carvery's veins were bulging out of his neck. "You dropped the charges? Have you lost your fucking mind? A year's worth of—"

"Luis, trust me. *Please.*"

"I can't believe this. If you want to throw your own career down the drain for good this time, you go right ahead, but you have no right—"

"If you'd just let me explain—"

"Do you know how many officers worked their tail off, for over a year—"

"Just listen to me!"

"Go to hell!" Sergeant Carvery flew out the door so fast, Lilly felt a breeze as he left.

Lilly sat down in her chair, tossed a pen onto her desk and said to the air, "Danielle, I pray to God you know what you're doing—for both our sakes."

"Nathalie, did you go into therapy after Chantal's suicide?" Beulah asked.

"Yes, for the next two and a half years, till I went to university."

"Were you able to forgive yourself by then?"

Nathalie's mouth quivered and some tears escaped. "Not fully."

"How did it affect you at university?"

"I tried to never think about it, to be honest. I buried my head in my studies, and I joined some sports teams. It helped."

"But you never allowed yourself to get close to anyone after Chantal's death, did you?"

"No," Nathalie admitted. "Not until…"

"Until you met Kristina Buchanan?"

Nathalie closed her eyes and nodded. "Yes."

Making sure Maurice Coultier was comfortable, Danielle began her carefully coordinated interrogation.

"Maurice, you didn't call Kristina on your cell phone that night, did you? You didn't have it on you because you forgot it in your brother's truck. Is that right?"

"No, I didn't call her," Maurice admitted. "I didn't notice until I went to call a cab the next morning that I didn't have my cell phone on me."

"Didn't the original investigators ask you about the call to Kristina from your cell?"

"They asked me what I called her for, and what we talked about, but I didn't even remember phoning. I didn't tell them I didn't remember. I figured I probably called her but didn't remember because I was drunk. They knew I was drunk too, so when I told them I couldn't remember the entire conversation, they didn't keep asking me about it. I didn't know the call had come from my cell though. I figured they meant from Gillian's house, so I didn't put two and two together until I found out I left my phone in Joe's truck, and that was only after I spoke to the police."

"When did Joe return your phone to you?"

"After he got back from work the next day. That's when he gave me the bracelet too. He thought I had bought it for Kristina, and wanted to give it back to me."

"Did he tell you how he got it?"

"He said he got it off her dead arm. I knew then he was the one who killed her."

"What did you do with the bracelet?"

"I didn't want the bracelet. I hadn't bought it for her. Even if I had, why would I hold on to something proving my own brother..." Maurice Coultier rubbed his eyes. "I wasn't going to go to the funeral home at all," Maurice said as he wiped tears off his face. "I couldn't face her family knowing Joe..." Maurice broke down crying.

Danielle allowed Maurice some time to let out some of his grief, then brought him back on track. "What did you do with the bracelet?" she asked.

Maurice tossed a tissue Danielle had handed him into the garbage, then said, "I went to the funeral home on the last night of her wake, just before they closed. I asked her mother if I could spend a minute alone with her to say goodbye, and she said okay. When I was alone I opened the casket, placed the bracelet across her wrist, then closed it again."

"Did Joe tell you what he did to her face?"

"He said if I didn't stop being a sissy he'd cut a letter 'S' into my face too."

"Maurice, this is very important. Did your brother, Joseph Coultier, tell you directly that he killed Kristina Buchanan?"

"Before he gave me the bracelet, he told me to put my hand out. He emptied a plastic baggie in my hand, and the bracelet fell out. I was looking at it close to see if it was Kristina's, and that's when he said, 'That's the bracelet Kristina was wearing when I killed her. I still had gloves on when I took it off her, and it's been in this plastic baggie since then, so my fingerprints aren't anywhere on it. If you're even thinking of going to the cops, the only fingerprints on it will be yours.'"

"Did he tell you how he killed her?"

"I asked him if she suffered. He said no, that he just sent her on a long trip to no return. I already figured it was him who took the drugs from my shed, so I asked him if he used them to kill her and he said yes."

"What were the drugs?"

"About twenty grams of ketamine powder and six pills."

"Six pills of what?"

"They were ketamine too. Just, on the street they'd be sold as ecstasy, but there was no ecstasy in them, just ketamine. I took some of the powder I made from the liquid, and put it in a presser. Made just six, to see how they would turn out."

Danielle now had what she needed to arrest Maurice's brother. An arrest did not guarantee a conviction, however. It was time for Danielle to put her last two dominos into place.

"Tell me about your relationship with Kristina," Beulah said to Nathalie.

"We first met when she brought her cat into my clinic. He'd gotten into a tussle with a porcupine—my guess is that the porcupine won." Nathalie produced a Mona Lisa smile which quickly dissolved. "The bill was more than she could afford, so I didn't charge her for my services, just the clinic's portion and the drugs at cost. Then after that, seems everywhere I went I kept running into her. We started hanging out."

"How soon before you started dating?"

"At first we just spent time together, canoeing, cooking, doing renovation or landscaping projects together, but it grew into a relationship. At least that's what I thought it was at the time." Nathalie played with the strap of her watch. "I had no idea I was just one of several. I consider myself such a good judge of character, but I was totally snowed." Nathalie shook her head. "My God, I can't believe how stupid and naïve I was. I spent so many years trusting no

one. No one, Beulah. And the first person I do end up trusting…"
Nathalie crossed her arms and shook her head again.

"What was it about her that made you trust her?"

"I've given that a lot of thought. I guess it all started with her
telling me she'd been molested by her grandfather when she was
young. Of course I empathized, but it was a lot more than that. I felt
a connection with her after that, which I'd never made with anyone
else, feeling that she would understand." Nathalie whispered her next
sentence. "That I could trust her."

"That's when you confided in her?"

"Not everything right away. But yes, eventually I told her
everything. And I think that's why I felt such a bond with her. I don't
know how to explain it, Beulah. The only word I can use to describe
what she came to mean to me, is 'family.' And you have *no idea* the
power that kind of bond had over me."

"Considering your past, Nathalie, feeling so bonded to someone
that they became family to you certainly would have been extremely
powerful."

"I realize now it's how she played me. She said that our meeting
was written in the stars, that she felt like she'd known me her entire
life. She looked me directly in the eyes once and said, 'I love you,
Dee. You're like my lover, my best friend, and my sister all rolled into
one.' And I foolishly believed her. I *believed* her. For the first time in
my life, Beulah, I trusted someone enough to tell them everything.
Everything. About my mother, the rapes, and Chantal. I opened myself
up and bared my heart and soul to her. I *trusted* her. Then she turned
around and—" Nathalie bit down hard on her bottom lip.

Danielle explained what she would be doing next to a very relieved
Maurice Coultier. "I'm going to go release your wife then let the
prosecutors know you gave us what we need. They'll be dropping the
drug distribution charges, and you should be able to join your wife
momentarily."

But Danielle didn't go see Lucy just yet. First she entered
interview room 'B' with four armed officers. "Mr. Joseph François
Coultier, you are under arrest for first degree murder in the death of
Kristina Ann Buchanan."

Beulah took a sip of water while Nathalie talked about her relationship with Kristina Buchanan.

"Looking back, I sensed Kristina had a deceitful nature early on, but I had major blinders on. Believe it or not, Beulah…" Nathalie lowered her face and her eyelashes dampened. "I'm ashamed to admit this, but…it really is the truth. I loved her. I really did."

"Most people have a combination of good and bad traits, Nathalie. I'm sure she had her good, loveable traits as well."

"So did Jeffrey Dahmer. I hear he often helped little old ladies cross the street, and he was a great guy to hundreds of people. He only *ate* seventeen of them."

"Glad to see your sense of humor is back," Beulah told Nathalie with a brief, appreciative smile.

"My point is, Beulah, I should have known better. I spent so many years being so cautious, trusting no one, telling no one. And the one person I do…" Nathalie seemed disgusted with herself.

"Nathalie, how did your relationship with Kristina end?"

Nathalie took a long, deep breath, then swallowed. "We'd been spending a lot of time together, and when we weren't together we were on the phone or sending each other messages all the time. Then one day out of the blue she drops off the face of the earth. I think a week later I got an email saying she decided to take some vacation. Anyway, to make a long story short, I found out she'd gone camping with another woman. Some cousin of one of her coworkers."

"So she cheated on you?"

"Kristina and I didn't have a real commitment—at least that was her defense after I found out. But she was right, we had never discussed dating exclusively. After almost a year though, I just naturally assumed we were. Especially since everything she said to me led me to believe we were." Nathalie rolled her eyes. "Another naivety on my part." Nathalie pinched the bottom of her chin. "Then, out of the blue again she calls me up as if two whole weeks hadn't gone by, and she wanted me to come over."

"Did you?"

"Yes, I did. I shouldn't have, but…I really mourned for those two weeks she dropped out of my life. I felt like I did after Chantal died, having a huge, cavernous hole inside me. I had missed her so much. Just little things, you know? Hearing about her day, going for a canoe ride, just hanging out.

"I was upset with her of course, but at the same time, I had missed her so much, I couldn't wait to see her. When I got there she acted like she hadn't shoved me in a drawer for two weeks. I was only there a couple of hours before she tried to lure me into bed for sex, saying nobody's ever topped what she and I had sexually."

"Did you have sex with her?"

"I did go to bed with her, but I wouldn't have sex with her. I couldn't. I needed to know that I meant more to her than just sex. I told her I loved her, but that I just wanted to be held that night. I put my arm around her, but she turned away from me and threw my arm off. She said if I couldn't touch her where she wanted me to, then I couldn't touch her at all." Nathalie's eyes welled up. "I thought I mattered to her, that she cared about me. But all she cared about, all I was to her…" Tears came down Nathalie's face. "Was just someone who could get her off."

Crown attorney Lillian Marsh and Sergeant Luis Carvery stood side-by-side at the police station. His hands were on his hips, hers were behind her back, tucked under her suit jacket, with her fingers crossed.

"Is everyone in position?" Danielle asked another plainclothes officer.

"Yes."

"Okay, let's go," Danielle said as she gave the signal to six officers in on what was about to go down.

Knowing Nathalie's past, Beulah was very aware of how devastating it would have been for her to come to the realization that someone she loved and trusted had just been using her for sex. It surely would have brought back the devastation of her mother's transactions: of Nathalie's body for whatever alcohol or cash anyone was willing to pay.

"That must have been very painful for you, Nathalie."

"It was. But that wasn't the worst of it. Yes, it hurt me, but I just sort of dusted myself off and tried to move on."

"But you weren't able to?"

"Maybe if she had let me." Nathalie rubbed the back of her neck. "At first she tried to charm me back into her bed. She actually thought telling me how great the sex was would work. But it wasn't just sex for me, and she knew it. She knew my past, and how much it took for me to give myself to someone.

"You should have seen the look on her face when I told her it was over. But you know, I don't think she was even hurt. I think it just bruised her ego. Maybe it was her extreme ego that made her do what she did, I don't know."

"What did she do, Nathalie?"

Nathalie took another deep breath. "When she finally figured out I was done with her, she turned on me like you wouldn't believe. She transformed from human to monster in no time flat. Although, I'd seen a glimpse of that monster before, so I should have known better.

"I had confided in her how I had a hard time watching anyone drink out of a beer bottle because this man had used a beer bottle to…break my hymen so he could rape me. Then the night I wouldn't have sex with her, she gets up out of bed, comes back a few minutes later with a bottle of beer, and sits there, grinning and taunting me with it. I asked her to please stop, but all she did was ridicule me and call me names. I think she was stoned out of her gourd at the time, but it's still no excuse. I got out of bed and left. And that was the last time I was ever at her house."

"But you did see her after that?"

"I saw her in the washroom of a movie theater soon after that, and she had the gall to tell me I looked good. I told her to get out of my sight."

Lucy Miller was told she was free to go, and was walking down the corridor when her husband and his lawyer emerged from interview room 'C'. She ran to Maurice and they hugged each other.

"They let me go," he said to her. "I told them what Joe did—to Kristina. They dropped the charges and let me go in return for my testimony against him."

"Joe killed Kristina?"

"Let's just go pick up Samuel. I'll tell you everything when we get home."

Danielle and the same four officers who accompanied her when she arrested his brother Joseph, approached Maurice.

"Joseph Maurice Coultier, you're under arrest for accessory after the fact to murder and obstruction of justice." As she informed Maurice of the charges, Danielle did the honors by slapping the cuffs back on him.

Sergeant Carvery stepped into place. "Furthermore, Mr. Joseph Maurice Coultier, you are also under arrest for the illegal processing of an illicit drug for the purposes of trafficking."

"But you dropped the charges—"

Lillian Marsh responded to Maurice Coultier's objection. "The Crown dropped the drug distribution charges stemming from the bust at the train station, Mr. Coultier, but we didn't say we wouldn't charge you with any new offences. It might not be illegal to be in possession of liquid ketamine, but it is illegal to turn it into powder or pill form. That should get you an extra three to five years on top of the fifteen you'll get for accessory after the fact and obstruction. That's about thirteen years more than you would have gotten with just the drug distribution charges."

Maurice looked at his lawyer. "Why are you just standing there? Do something!"

His lawyer's face said it all. In awe of the brilliant blindside, all he could do was admit, "There's nothing I can do."

"Take him away," Staff Sergeant Kline instructed.

Beulah Hunt's training had taught her that narcissists don't take well to rejection, so she asked Nathalie to confirm what she suspected. "Is that when Kristina turned on you? When you rejected her attempt to charm you back into her life with a compliment?"

"She turned on me all right. First I started getting nasty emails, and notes dropped in my mail box. Even people I didn't know or hadn't met before were sending me messages through Facebook."

"What were the messages about?"

Nathalie shook her head dismissively. "Just trash, basically. I only read a few words of one or two before closing my Facebook account. I don't know if that was Kristina's goal, or if she had just wanted to hurt me with her viciousness, don't really know because I didn't stick around on Facebook to find out."

"So that ended your online socializing. What about offline?"

"Pretty much the same thing. Didn't matter if I went to a bar or to a soccer game, it seems somebody she was dating was just dying to say something to me. Never mind that they shouldn't have had a clue who I was, since we'd never met. But it was pretty obvious Kristina was pointing me out somehow, doing some mouthing off, and using her network of bedmates to humiliate me."

"What were they saying to you?"

"She was telling everybody I was emotionally unstable." Nathalie crossed her arms and looked at her feet. "I was a very strong, smart, and amazing woman while I was willing to have sex with her and lavish her with money and gifts, but the minute she realized I wasn't going to let her use me anymore, I was suddenly unstable and a mental case."

"You're neither of those, Nathalie. She was just saying those things as a way of punishing you for cutting her off."

"But why punish me, Beulah? *Why*? I'd understand if I had done something to her, but I hadn't. I never did one single, hurtful thing to her. All I did was refuse to let myself be used. And for that, she paints a bull's eye on me, and sends it out to all her..." Nathalie flung her hand in the air. "She told everybody she could, everything she could, and twisted it all to boot. She knew she was someone I used to love and *trust*. She didn't have to turn on me like she did, Beulah. She didn't have to—"

Nathalie's face fell into her hands. When she lifted it back up she looked anguished.

"I just wanted to cut my losses and move on after I realized she'd just been using me. Yes, I was hurt. Yes, I mourned. The loss of what I thought the relationship was, and the person I thought Kristina to be. But it wasn't enough for her that I was already devastated by having the deepest romantic relationship I'd ever had, unveiled as a worthless sham.

"She had no right to con me for my trust and...my body. But even after doing that, if she'd have just let me be. But instead, she hurt me even more...on purpose." Nathalie shed a few tears, then said, "That's what hurt me so much, Beulah. It wasn't the things she was saying or doing even, it was the fact that she was *choosing* to do things to hurt me *on purpose*, and that it brought her pleasure to do it."

Beulah recalled the sadistic nature of Nathalie's last rape, which had been documented at trial. "Is that what triggered your nightmares again? Kristina taking pleasure in causing you pain?"

Nathalie nodded. "One day I was walking in the park near my house where she knew I took walks. I noticed two women lying on the grass staring at me. It was only when I got really close that I realized it was Kristina—with another woman. When she saw I noticed her she grinned from ear to ear then wrapped herself around the woman and whispered something to her. They both laughed hysterically and were looking straight at me while they did it."

"How did you react?" Beulah asked.

"As much as it hurt me that she would ridicule me to someone else like that, I didn't react to it. It was that..." Nathalie allowed some of her pent-up sorrow to escape by allowing a few tears to flow. "She *grinned*. Not just *any* grin. The *exact same* grin..." Nathalie rubbed her forehead. "One of the last things I'd told her about was...that last rape. How he had grinned from ear to ear while...he was ripping me apart and breaking my ribs and..." Nathalie placed her arms across her breasts as if trying to protect them. "While he was on top of me...doing that...he pinched my right nipple with his nails...so hard that he severed part of it." Nathalie winced.

Beulah had read Nathalie's medical records, which detailed how she had required reconstructive surgery on her right breast and vagina, and had suffered three broken ribs during that particular rape. But as trained in emotional trauma as Beulah was, it had not prepared her for the photographs that still existed in those files, though Beulah did not comment on this. It was more important for Nathalie to continue uninterrupted.

"I had told her how he had grinned while he watched me suffer. How the more painful it was, the sicker his grin got. I told her I couldn't understand cruelty. I couldn't understand how another human being could know they were hurting someone else so much and take such pleasure in it that they'd grin from ear to ear while they were doing it.

"It wasn't even seeing her with another woman that hurt me. I knew what she was like. I knew she'd have somebody else lined up before I was even gone. It was the fact that she—someone I had allowed myself to *love*...and *trust*—was taking *such pleasure* in making me suffer. It really gave her a thrill to see me hurting. Just like that sadistic..." Nathalie choked up.

Beulah didn't want Nathalie reliving that last awful childhood rape, so she brought Nathalie back to the incident at the park. "What did you do when you saw her grinning at you like that? Did you say anything to her?"

Nathalie inhaled and exhaled before speaking. "No, I didn't say a word to her. I just kept walking forward. I don't know how, but I did. By the time I reached the edge of the park though, I started throwing up.

"I don't even remember getting home. That part's just a blur. But the second I got inside I started throwing up again. Then when I had nothing left to throw up I curled up in a ball on my bed and trembled like a heroin addict."

Beulah wasn't surprised by such intense physical reactions to emotional trauma. "How long did that last?"

"I wanted to go to sleep so badly and just never wake up. But I didn't have any sleeping pills or anything like that. I never liked taking medications. All I had was some Gravol I kept on hand for friends when we'd go sailing, so I took two of those to try knock myself out so I couldn't think or feel—at least for a little while.

"But then that's when..." Nathalie rubbed her forehead. "That horrendous recurring nightmare began."

"Which nightmare is that?"

"It was about the last time I was raped. Except, I could *feel* it, Beulah. I could feel the tearing of my flesh, the crushing of my ribs, the blood pouring down me. I felt it all again as if it were happening for real all over again. The pain was so excruciating, I can't even tell you. But the biggest difference, the *worst* part of it..." Nathalie closed her eyes, crossed her arms over her breasts, and began to slowly rock herself. "When I looked up at the person doing that to me, the person who was getting such a thrill out of watching me suffer..."

Beulah moved the waste basket closer to Nathalie because she looked like she might throw up.

"It was the same sick grin, but, the face it was painted on...was Kristina's."

After Maurice Coultier was taken away and everyone else had dispersed, Staff Sergeant Kline asked Danielle, "Why'd you want to give him time to see his wife and hug her? Take pity on the guy?"

"Not at all, Staff. I just didn't want him to forget what it felt like to hold his wife one last time. For the next twenty years, that last taste of freedom will play over in his mind. That's more of a punishment than three squares and an hour's yard exercise each day."

Beulah leaned forward in her chair. "Nathalie, what Kristina did to you is called bullying. It may not have occurred in a school yard, but it was the same thing. She targeted you, attacked your vulnerabilities, and was relentless. Like all bullies, she even rallied others and set it up so they could continue the bullying for her when she herself wasn't around to do it."

The sorrow in Nathalie's face intensified. "It made me feel so worthless, Beulah. I couldn't figure out what was so wrong with me that people I loved, Kristina and my own mother, couldn't see me as a human being with human feelings and a human heart. I was just...an *object* to them. An object for them to use up, chew up, and spit out in the garbage when they were done with me. Which was bad enough, but then to *want* to hurt me on purpose even more?"

Beulah knew all too well the serious and harmful effects bullying could have on a person—especially someone who already suffered and struggled to understand repeated acts of cruelty. Beulah was also well aware that having loved ones who took their own lives dramatically increased the risk of suicide. Those two factors, Kristina's bullying and her sister's suicide, could have proven lethal for Nathalie.

"Did you think of committing suicide, Nathalie?"

Nathalie used a tissue to dry the tears that were now flowing. "Yes."

"Did you attempt it?" Beulah asked softly.

Nathalie took a very deep breath then replied, "I came so close to doing it, Beulah. It took every single bit of strength left in me not to go through with it. And considering how very little strength I had left after what Kristina put me through, to say that I was fragile and at great risk of going through with it, is an understatement.

"Kristina really pushed me to the very brink of suicide. I found myself standing at that edge without any strength left to turn back from it. I knew all it would take was for her to propel one more breath in my direction and..." Nathalie choked back tears. "It would have finished me off."

"But you didn't go through with it."

"I didn't die, no. But I had to stop living in order to save my life. After all the...bullying—the nightmares she triggered after the park incident especially—I lived in such terrible fear of running into her, of...what would happen to me if I did.

"I stopped going out. Not just to events, or for walks in the park, or movies. I couldn't even go to the grocery store or do anything at all because I was too terrified of running into her—or anybody in her circle. I was alive, Beulah, but I wasn't living. I was a prisoner in my own home because I lived in absolute terror of running into her after that."

"Did you consider moving?"

"Yes, but Kristina had bragged how this woman had moved to Vancouver because she'd fallen in love with her. I didn't want to give

Kristina the satisfaction of having two women to brag about having done that."

"But you let her drive you into seclusion."

"I had no choice, Beulah. It was either that, or risk—really, really, risk—my life ending because of her. I had no emotional strength left, Beulah. Not a single atom of it. After every other thing she'd done to me, seeing her grinning at me like that in the park…the unyielding nightmares she caused…" Nathalie closed her eyes. "…completed her decimation of me."

Beulah watched Nathalie as she pulled another tissue from its box and wiped her tears with it.

"You know, I thought I'd paid my dues. I thought I would at least be spared in adulthood for what I'd endured during childhood. But to find myself…after everything that happened…

"To think I had found love, but instead just ended up another…" Despite her effort to hold back tears, Nathalie could only finish her sentence after a few fell over her cheeks again. "Just another victim of the serial slayer named Kristina Buchanan."

❧ 53 ❧

Beulah sat as comfortably as she could in her chair.

"Nathalie, you had a very painful childhood and tremendous challenges to overcome, but don't you think the adage is true? 'What doesn't kill you, makes you stronger.'"

"No, I don't," Nathalie said with conviction. "I firmly believe that what doesn't kill you, leaves you damaged."

"Nathalie, you're not damaged, you're scarred. And you've been working on healing those scars in the healthiest manner possible."

Nathalie didn't respond, just sat there, looking pensive.

"Nathalie, did you ever think about hurting Kristina? About getting revenge against her?"

"Of course not. I'm not like that."

"No, you're not. It's the damaged people who cause harm to others, Nathalie. People like Kristina and your mother who avoid their own issues by turning to drugs or alcohol, who not only have no conscience or remorse about how they treat others but attempt to avert responsibility for their own hurtful and damaging behavior by using ridicule to re-victimize the person they've hurt.

"You didn't take your pain and anger out on others, Nathalie. And God knows you suffered enough, it would be understandable if you had. But *you didn't*. You used your creativity to help you cope with your pain instead."

Nathalie didn't verbalize a response, but she looked at Beulah as though thinking about what Beulah said.

"Nathalie, how many animals have you treated for little or no money? How many holidays did you spend volunteering? Despite everything that's happened to you, you've remained a very kind and compassionate individual."

"Of course I am. It's not their fault that other people did things to hurt me."

Beulah sighed after what seemed like a year and a half of holding her breath. "Exactly my point, Nathalie. People who are truly damaged, who refuse to work on healing themselves, take it out on others. But you didn't do that. And you didn't run away from your issues by picking up a joint, or popping pills, or drinking your sorrows."

"But do you know how many times I've wanted to get drunk, or bash somebody's face in? I've wanted to so badly sometimes."

"But you didn't, Nathalie. Because you're a lot stronger than that."

"Yeah, so strong I almost killed myself over some scum—" Nathalie shook her head instead of completing her sentence.

"Nathalie, it took enormous strength to stay in school and to continue getting high marks after your sister's suicide, but you did it."

"Only because I knew it was my one shot at a decent life."

"But you did it, Nathalie. You finished high school, got your scholarships to university, and reached your goal of becoming a veterinarian. You should be very proud of yourself for doing that entirely on your own, without any support. You're a very strong person, Nathalie. You couldn't have survived all that adversity if you weren't."

"I might have had some strength back then, when I had such important goals to reach, but meeting Kristina…by the time she was done with me, I had nothing left."

"But Nathalie, you recognized you had nothing left. That's why you left the city isn't it? And put things in place to protect yourself from any further harm from her? Yes, you retreated, but it was so you could give yourself a chance to heal, and to build your strength back."

"I didn't fully realize that's what I was doing, but I guess you're right. I traded in my SUV for a car she wouldn't recognize. I sold my house too, and bought a building with three flats in it so I could rent out two of them and stay in one, making it a lot easier for me to be gone from the city for long periods of time.

"I quit my job at the clinic and bought a cottage in the Valley. I started volunteering at a shelter there, and spent most of my time at the cottage. I started feeling safe there, a sense of—I wouldn't say *peace*—but at least a reprieve. The nightmares settled down. Then a few months after that, I found out she'd been killed."

"How did you feel when you found out?"

"Honestly? I know this sounds awful to say, Beulah, but…I was so relieved I didn't have to live in fear of her anymore."

"One of your best hits was with a song called, 'I Live in Fear' wasn't it?"

"Yes, that song was written about her. Many of them were."

"Nathalie, you took an extremely painful period of your life and used your talent and creativity to turn it into something positive."

"No, nothing positive came out of that."

"Nathalie, you can't tell me that the success of those songs hasn't changed your life for the better."

Nathalie traced her chin with her fingertips. "If I never earned another penny again in my lifetime, I'd still be financially secure for the rest of my life," she admitted.

"Well, then, something good came out of all that. I know it was a terribly high price to pay, but—"

"This is the honest to God's truth, Beulah. Even if I made a billion dollars from those songs, I would give every single penny back if it meant I had *never, ever* laid eyes on Kristina Buchanan."

❧ 54 ❧

Just two weeks after being incarcerated, Joseph Coultier wanted to make a deal.

"Guess dealing runs in the family," Lilly said to Danielle, after telling her of Joe Coultier's request.

"What's he want?" Danielle asked.

"It appears Mr. Tough Guy isn't so tough when it comes to imprisonment. Says he's willing to tell us exactly how he killed Buchanan and answer any questions if the Crown will reduce the charge to second degree with possibility of early parole."

"But it wasn't second degree. He had it planned ahead of time, and that's premeditated murder in the first degree."

"The Crown is well aware of that, Danielle. But aren't you interested in hearing what he has to say?"

"Of course I am. But not if it means—"

"He'll get the mandatory life sentence for first degree with absolutely no chance of early parole, Danielle—if you play him right. I'll be honest with you. The case as it stands right now might not have a reasonable likelihood of conviction if he has an excellent defense team. The only evidence you have right now is purely circumstantial, and I could see a good shark destroying his brother's testimony against him, leaving you with nothing.

"The prosecution might not have any intention of even entertaining the idea of a plea bargain, but he doesn't know that. Just play along. Even if you tell him the Crown won't consider a plea until after he's talked, I think he's so desperate to get out of that jail cell for a few hours he'd agree to it. Then all you have to do is play him like a violin while he's enjoying some decent coffee. They get served crap while they're awaiting trial for a reason, you know," Lilly said as she winked.

Beulah Hunt smiled at Nathalie as she told her, "I'm so incredibly happy for you, Nathalie. You deserve this newfound happiness, you know that, don't you?"

"Yes, I do. We both do. We're both so very happy to have found each other." Nathalie's soft smile turned humorous. "Even if it was a little complicated getting there."

"And the nightmares?"

"Haven't had a single one in weeks. I know it took me a long time to be able to talk about the things that were troubling me, but when I did, I got rid of them. Therapy isn't the most pleasant thing in the world, but it really does work—if you have a great therapist, that is." Nathalie smiled gratefully at Beulah. "Thank you."

"I seem to recall a very astute client telling me quite recently that therapy was like feeling sick to your stomach. The more you ignore it and try to fight it, the more nauseous you get, but as soon as you deal with it, you throw it all up and it's gone."

Nathalie laughed. "I think I used the term crap, but I like your version better."

Joseph Coultier was seated in a very comfortable chair sipping a large coffee from his favorite coffee shop when Danielle asked him her first question.

"You're the one who stole the ketamine powder from your brother's shed, aren't you?"

"Yep."

"Did you steal the ketamine because you were planning on using it to kill Kristina Buchanan?"

"No, I stole it to teach Maurice a lesson. I went over there to tell him what Lucy was doing, and that he'd better put a stop to it. He was in the shed when I went over to talk to him, and I could see he was really nervous and standing in the same spot. Maurice never had much of a backbone, so I could tell he was hiding something, which is why I went back later that night and broke into the shed. I found that the floor boards he'd been standing on were loose. I lifted them up and found the drugs. I didn't want him getting caught up in that racket, so I took them."

"Did you know he was distributing drugs using the train?"

"Had no idea. If I'd have known, I'd have kicked his ass from here to Sunday, and he knows it."

"When did you decide to kill Kristina?"

"Just that night, when she called me."

Danielle didn't believe that. Joseph Coultier was no doubt saying this to avoid a first degree murder conviction, which requires premeditation. "You stole the ketamine two weeks before she was killed. If you only took the ketamine to teach your brother a lesson, why didn't you just get rid of it? Why did you still have it two weeks later when you decided to kill Kristina?"

"When I got the drugs home, *Special K* was written on the package. At the time I thought it was stuff he was planning on giving to Kristina, because he used to call her that sometimes, say she was his special K. I didn't know at the time it was ketamine. I thought it was cocaine, actually. I'm not sure why I kept it. Something just told me it might come in handy, and it did."

"When did you learn it was ketamine?"

"A few days after I took the drugs I went to Dieppe to visit some relatives, and after they went to bed I used their computer to look up Ketaset and cocaine."

"Why those two?"

"Because Ketaset is what Shelly said Lucy was selling, and I thought what I had was cocaine. Right away it said Ketaset was a brand of ketamine and that some people called it *Special K.* When I read how easy it was to turn it into powder and there was a market for it on the streets, it wasn't too hard to put two and two together. But I didn't know then that Maurice was stupid enough to get into selling drugs for himself, so I thought he must be doing it for Kristina."

"Is that why you decided to kill her?"

"When she called me that night, she was a real cunt, barking at me to come get Maurice or else, so I figured I'd give her what was a long time coming to her." He flashed a grin that quickly faded. "But I didn't plan it," he added emphatically. "I didn't know until she called me that night that I was going to kill her then."

Danielle wondered if Joe Coultier was aware that taking just hours or minutes to plot someone's murder was just as premeditated in the eyes of the law as taking weeks or months. "What made you decide to kill her that night?"

"Like I said, she was a real cunt when she called, so I decided then to give her what was a long time coming."

"What did you do when you hung up?"

"I got my gloves and the drugs, and took two straws with me." Joe Coultier looked at Danielle as though delivering a cheesy pickup line. "Using a straw was really smart of me, wasn't it?"

If Coultier thought Danielle was going to reward his murderous actions with praise, he was sorely mistaken. But she also wanted him to keep talking, so she didn't say what she really wanted to. "You already had the drugs, gloves, and straws in the truck when you picked up Maurice and Gillian from Kristina's house?"

"Yeah."

"How did you know the drugs would kill her?"

"I wasn't a hundred percent sure if it would be enough to kill her, but I thought it should be. I figured she would at least pass out and it would be easy for me to strangle her if I had to, but I didn't have to. The drugs were enough after all."

"Was there just powdered ketamine, or did you bring anything else?"

"Taped to the bag of the powder was a small plastic bag with six pills in it. I brought those too."

"What kind of pills?"

"Just plain white pills, no marking on them."

"Did you ask Maurice to borrow his cell phone, or did he forget it in your truck?"

"Neither. When they were getting out, I slipped the phone in my pocket. Both of them were already half baked so they didn't notice."

"And you took the phone because…?"

"Because I wanted the bitch to think Maurice was asking me to drop some stuff off to her."

"Who are you referring to when you say, 'bitch'?" Danielle knew of course, but she was starting to think like a prosecutor—and heeding Sergeant Carvery's earlier advice of ensuring her net had no holes in it.

"Who do you think I'm referring to?" Joe looked at Danielle as though thinking she was a little slow. "Kristina. Buchanan. Remember her?"

Danielle ignored Joe Coultier's sarcasm. "What did you say to Kristina when you called her?"

"I told her Maurice asked me to deliver something to her, and was it okay if I dropped it off. She asked me what it was. I told her I couldn't tell her over the phone, but that it was something she would definitely want. She kept asking me questions like, 'is it green' and things like that. She kept asking questions till I finally told her it was cocaine."

"But she knew you didn't like her. Why would she trust you?"

"Because she was a druggie! She'd have taken it from Satan himself if he'd have offered it to her."

"How much of it did you give her? When you handed it to her, I mean."

"Before I left home I put a small amount in a baggie and put a straw in with it. I just took a guess how much from what I saw on TV and in movies. I put the rest of it in my inside jacket pocket so she wouldn't see it."

"What did she do with the baggie of stuff you handed her?"

"What do you think she did with it? She sucked it up her nose, is what she did with it. Soon as I gave it to her. She didn't even ask me anything about it, where Maurice got it, or why I was dropping it off. She just grabbed it and sucked it up her nose right away."

"Did she notice it wasn't cocaine?"

"I don't think so. She said it was an awful head rush and smiled, so I figured she liked it."

"What happened next?"

"I just sat there talking to her, making conversation, then all of a sudden she says she thinks she's going to be sick. I tell her I'll get her some Gravol. I go to her kitchen, get a glass of water, put four of the *Special K* pills in it, stir it up with my finger, then hand her the glass of water and the two other ketamine pills to swallow." Joseph Coultier laughed. "Dumb bitch."

"She didn't notice the water tasted bitter?"

"After she gulped it down she did, but it was too late then, it was already in her stomach."

"Did she realize you had put something in the glass of water?"

"I don't know if she did or not. Almost right away she started moving really funny, like her body was made of Jell-O or something. She tried to make her way over to the couch, but she couldn't really walk by herself. I pretty much had to drag her."

"How long did you wait before you started blowing the ketamine into her?"

"About twenty minutes. She was so out of it by then, she couldn't even lift her arms to try stop me."

"How long did it take for her to die?" Danielle didn't show the slightest emotion when she asked this question, but she couldn't help but wonder if Kristina Buchanan was aware of what was happening to her, and Danielle found that possibility very disturbing.

"By the time I was finished blowing it all into her, she looked dead to me. Just to be sure though, I taped everything up."

"What did you tape up?"

"Her nose, mouth, and ears."

Taping the nose and mouth was obvious to Danielle. But from the beginning, investigators were stumped as to why her ears were taped over. "Why her ears?"

"I wasn't sure if any oxygen—just enough to keep her alive, you know—could get to her brain through her ears or not, so I figured, why take the chance."

Danielle did her best to hide her reaction as she asked for clarification, "You put duct tape on her ears..." Danielle was trying so hard not to sound condescending—or to roar laughing. "...so no oxygen could get to her brain?"

"Yeah."

Danielle wondered if Kline and two of the prosecutors, who were behind the one-way mirror watching, were either laughing or picking their jaws up off the floor. Danielle moved along quickly because she knew if she didn't, she'd start laughing for sure. "Where'd you get the duct tape and the dolly?"

"Her basement. Got the blanket off her bed."

"Why didn't we find your fingerprints anywhere?"

Joe smiled, displaying great pride in himself. "I wore my leather gloves when I walked in, so there was none on the door knob. Once I was in the house, I made sure not to touch anything. Only thing I did touch was the water glass I handed her. I used my sleeve to open the tap and cupboard. I wiped the glass down afterwards too, but just to be sure, I took it with me. I threw it out the window over a bridge on my way to the park. By the time the pills hit her, I had my gloves back on, so there were no prints on anything else."

"Where exactly did you throw the glass? We'll have to confirm your story by locating it before we can discuss any deals." Danielle hoped Coultier hadn't noticed she didn't say "offer" any deals.

"It was near Five Island Lake, but if you take me out there, I'll show you exactly where. Don't know if it'll still be there, but it might be. The bridge goes over a swamp."

"Let's get back to that night. She's lying on the sofa, she's dead. You've placed duct tape on her nose, mouth, and...ears. You went and got a blanket from her bedroom, and a dolly from her basement. What did you do next?"

"I put the blanket on the floor and rolled her in it. That's when I noticed a real nice bracelet on her wrist. Looked really expensive, so I figured Maurice gave it to her. I got a baggie from her kitchen and put the bracelet in it. Then I cleaned up. Took the glass and straws and put them in my coat pocket. Just looked around, made sure I didn't leave anything behind. I saw her wallet on the counter and put it in her back pocket. And man, what a mess that was. You know, she friggin' shit her pants."

Danielle didn't feel Joe needed—or deserved—an explanation as to why, so she didn't comment. She simply asked her next question. "Why did you put her wallet in her pocket?"

"I wanted to make sure they reported her dead right away. I wanted Maurice to know she was dead as a door nail and never coming back."

"What did you do next?"

"I put the dolly in the truck, then went back and got her."

"You didn't use the dolly to take her to the truck?"

"No, her stairs going from her door to the driveway were too steep. It was easier for me to carry her. I only used the dolly once I got to the park."

"Her house had motion activated lights outside. Did they not come on when you carried her to the truck?"

"Yeah, they did, but I wasn't scared. Her house was surrounded by trees and they were full of leaves. The leaves hadn't fallen yet."

Danielle had visually inspected the exterior of Buchanan's home when she first got the case. There were no leaves on the trees yet at the time, and this allowed neighbors and vehicles that drove or walked past to partially see the house. But Joseph was right. In the fall, the house, nestled among trees, was hidden from view.

"Why did you dump her body in the heart-shaped pond at Hemlock Ravine?"

"Even before I knew how or when I was going to kill Kristina, I knew where I would dump her ass when I did. She was always leading Maurice on, saying that's where they'd get married one day."

"You dumped her there as a message to your brother?"

"I sure did," Joe declared.

"Did you leave your brother—or anyone else—any other messages?"

Joe Coultier grinned. "Oh, yeah. All the way I was driving to the park, I kept thinking about what a sissy my brother was. How I had to get rid of the garbage in his life because he didn't have the balls to unhook the leash she had on him. I kept telling him he should have a big letter 'S' on his forehead because he was such a sissy. When I got to the pond, it dawned on me. I'd show him what the difference between a man and a sissy was. She never looked so good as when I was done with her face, I tell ya."

"Was the duct tape on her face when you cut it?" Danielle needed to tie Joseph's statement to the circumstantial evidence.

"No, I took it off first. I knew she was dead for sure by then, so I tore the duct tape off and cut her face."

"What did you use to cut her face with?"

"My Swiss army knife. Threw that over the bridge too."

"The same bridge?"

"Yeah."

"Okay, we'll look for that too. What did you do with the dolly?" Danielle also wanted to be sure Tucker Hill's story correlated with what Joseph would say.

"I knew I couldn't throw that off the bridge, and my fingerprints weren't on it, so I wasn't worried about it. Just threw her and the blanket and dolly all into the pond."

"What did you do next?"

"Just walked to my truck and drove home."

"And nobody saw you during any of this?"

"Nope, not a soul around."

"Was your wife awake when you got home?"

"No, she always takes a sleeping pill at night. She was asleep when I got back."

"Did you do anything else when you got home?"

"Nope, went right to bed. Slept like a baby, too."

I bet you did, Danielle thought to herself. "What did Maurice say when you gave him the bracelet and told him you killed Kristina?"

"He started to cry, but when I told him to act like a man or I'd kick his balls and really give him something to cry about, he stopped."

"Is there anything else you have to add, Mr. Coultier?"

"Like I told you earlier, I didn't plan on killing her till that night, so that's not first degree murder. I was told I'd only get ten or fifteen years for second degree, and be eligible for parole in seven or eight."

"Mr. Coultier, you might think you're so much smarter than your younger brother, but one thing I can tell you that you both have in common, is thinking you can talk yourselves out of hot water, when all you're doing is spilling the pot over hot coals. By the time the steam clears, you've figured out too late that your goose is already cooked."

∽ 55 ∾

A few days after media reported Joseph Coultier's trial date for first degree murder in the death of Kristina Buchanan, Danielle received a letter addressed to her attention in care of Halifax Regional Police. The letter read:

> *Dear Officer Renaud,*
> *I'm sorry I had to steal the dolly and blanket back. I felt I had no choice. After you left I called a buddy of mine and he told me you'd find my hair and skin cells on that blanket and probably arrest me for that woman's murder. He's the one who drove me to the bed and breakfast to see if that's where you were staying.*
> *I couldn't believe my luck when I saw your car there and the door was unlocked. I didn't even have to smash the glass to get it. I burned the blanket and the dolly is at the bottom of Bass Lake. If you need it you'll find it there.*
> *Yours truly,*
> *Tucker C. Hill*

Staff Sergeant John Kline was hosting a dinner party at his home. In attendance were RCMP and HRP officers of various ranks, including Constable Douglas Blanchard, Sergeant Luis Carvery, Crown attorney Lillian Marsh, and their guest of honor, Constable Danielle Renaud.

"Everyone, I am so proud to introduce to you the newest, *permanent* member of the Special Investigations and Major Crimes Unit, Constable Danielle Renaud."

After much applause and an embarrassing speech she was forced to make, Danielle snuck off to a quiet corner to be with Nathalie. They weren't together very long, however, when John Kline's wife came over with a glass of wine for each of them.

"You have a very beautiful home, Mrs. Kline," Danielle complimented.

"Thank you. Call me Heidi, please."

"You have so many beautiful paintings," Nathalie observed.

"Yes, I collect paintings from local artists. I bought one just recently at the Healing Hearts' silent auction. It's my absolute favorite. Would you like to see it?"

"Yes, we'd love to," Nathalie said for both of them.

Heidi guided them to another room. She beamed as she pointed to a painting titled, *The Slayer.* "I just *love* this painting," she said.

"You do?" Nathalie opened her eyes wide at Danielle's.

"Yes, it reminds me of my husband. I used to worry about him, being a police officer. But week after week after fighting crime, he'd come home with a smile on his face and a beautiful red rose in his hand. In twenty-four years he's never missed a week.

"That beautiful rose in the painting is my John. All that darkness and everything below the rose is the evil he fights every day at work. It doesn't say who painted it. Whoever did it didn't sign their name, but they're obviously very talented."

Danielle slipped an arm around Nathalie's waist and pulled her close. "Yes, I agree. Extremely talented." Danielle squeezed Nathalie hard and smiled.

When they were alone again later, Danielle said to Nathalie, "You didn't tell me you were donating the painting."

"That's why I had it off the wall. I decided to donate it, but I really didn't think anybody would buy it, so I included a large financial contribution with it. Actually, all the money I got back from the bracelet. I took it back to Fire Wonders so they could extract the emeralds and melt down the gold." Nathalie smiled. "They actually paid me more for the emeralds and gold than I paid to have the bracelet made in the first place. It seems commodity prices have skyrocketed in the past two years."

Danielle pulled Nathalie closer and kissed her forehead. "That money's going to benefit a lot of women and children, sweetheart."

"I can't believe she feels joy when she looks at that painting," Nathalie said. "If she only knew how much pain inspired it."

"Well, you know, the stinkiest manure can grow the tastiest mushrooms. It's all about what you do with the shit that gets thrown at you. And considering your songs are all over the radio, I think you did a pretty darned good job of dealing with that shit, my sweetness."

"Mademoiselle! What language!"

Danielle grinned. "So how many tongue lashings do I get for that?" Danielle asked, as she pressed her face into Nathalie's neck and nuzzled while Nathalie giggled.

Lilly was standing solo in the center of a large grass circle confined by slim, skinned, spruce logs weaved in such a way that they made the barrier they created look picturesque.

Danielle was standing behind Nathalie and had her arms wrapped around her as they stood near the barrier amongst an enthusiastic crowd of spectators.

"Oh my God, that woman looks like a piece of art," Danielle heard one spectator say. And though Danielle didn't respond, she agreed.

Lilly's straight, long hair was divided into two braids, one on each side, with thin, teal blue rope creating a pattern down the braids with intricately beaded decorations tying them off at the end. She wore a matching beaded necklace, and the same beaded pattern and colors were strategically placed on her wrists, the bottom of her dress, and her boots.

Her dress was cinched at the waist by the same type of thin rope that was in her hair, except it was weaved in a mesmerizing pattern that created a belt. Lilly's tall body not only displayed the dress as a beautiful canvas, but the way her body filled that canvas made her a living, breathtaking sculpture.

Lilly stood motionless until the drums started. When they did, she moved her body first in slow, calculated steps. Then, as the chanters married their voices with the drumming, she brought more power and speed to her movements.

The rhythmic clatter of the mussel shells attached to her dress was so in time with the drumming and chanting, it sounded like an additional instrument. To Nathalie it was one of the most impressive, primal musical performances she'd ever heard.

The visual of the dance was just as impressive. Not only was Lilly's costume—and the way she moved in it—stunning, but the power that came from her movements, in perfect harmony with the drums and chanting, stirred such profound emotions that it brought tears to many eyes.

When the dance was over, Nathalie said, "Oh my God, she is such an amazing dancer."

"Yes, she's as amazing as a dancer as she is an attorney—and a friend."

Nathalie took Danielle's hand, brought it to her mouth and kissed it, then said, "Not many friendships would survive such circumstances and challenges, but I knew yours would. You two will be friends till you're in your nineties, using your canes like javelins, seeing who can throw the farthest." Nathalie laughed heartily.

"I love it when you laugh. It makes my heart sing," Danielle told Nathalie.

"Well, aren't you becoming the poet. Rubbing off on you, am I?"

Danielle squeezed Nathalie. "You're more than rubbing off on me. Even when we're apart I carry you inside me, and it makes me so happy." Danielle kissed Nathalie's cheek.

After Lilly finished her dance, she joined Danielle and Nathalie in the outdoor eating area for some salmon pie. They sat at one of the more private picnic tables, closer to the densely forested perimeter of the powwow.

After she tossed her used napkin onto her empty plate, Lilly asked Nathalie, "I've been meaning to ask you, how did you ever manage to record Melissa admitting to what she did that led to her firing?"

"The funny thing about that is, every time we went out to dinner or drinks, I'd secretly turn on my recorder in case she let anything slip about having killed Kristina, but she never did. I guess because she hadn't killed Kristina after all."

"What made you think Melissa might have had anything to do with Kristina's murder in the first place?"

"I only found out about Melissa's run-in with Kristina the last time I was at Kristina's. I already knew at that point that I needed to cut ties with Kristina. I did wonder if Melissa might try to get back at Kristina, but at the same time, I really needed to get away from her, so I thought, Kristina's an adult, let her take care of herself." Nathalie lowered her head. "I didn't warn her about Melissa, and later I felt so guilty about that. Especially after I found out Kristina had been murdered, because I thought Melissa might have been the one who killed her."

"What was their run-in?" Lilly asked.

"Melissa used to work at the hospital lab where her job was to run routine blood work. If I remember this correctly, Melissa was performing an extra blood test she wasn't supposed to, looking for matches to people who were desperately looking for organs—mostly kidneys. When she found a match, she was given a financial bonus for providing the individual's personal information. The people whose blood she tested and came up as matches, had no idea. They were just approached by somebody waving a lot of money in front of them, asking them to willingly submit to a blood test. Of course it always turned out to be a perfect match because Melissa had already done the testing. It seems from there, private sales were negotiated."

"Wow," Lilly uttered.

"I always knew Melissa was super smart," Nathalie said. "And I also knew she had a certain lack of morality. She had no qualms doing whatever she wanted. She never considered the consequences or felt any remorse either, and that's why after I got to know her for a few months that I started keeping my distance from her."

"But you became friends again," Lilly reminded Nathalie.

"I only became friends with her again after I found out Kristina had been murdered. She was my prime suspect. I didn't know for sure though, and I thought if I went to the police they'd be more interested in my relationship with Kristina than Melissa. I knew I hadn't killed Kristina, and I knew I was in the Valley when it happened, but I realized I couldn't prove it.

"It wasn't so much that they'd suspect me, it's that I knew they'd question me up the ying-yang, and I was afraid that talking about Kristina would bring everything back and spur the nightmares even more. I felt way too fragile for that at the time." Nathalie shrugged. "So right or wrong, I decided to do my own little investigation. It might not have led me to Kristina's killer, but it led me to Danielle." Nathalie then let out a chuckle. "In a weird, complicated way."

Danielle wrapped her arms around Nathalie. "Honey, as much as I love and adore you, and think you're one of the smartest women on the planet, I think you'd best stick to veterinary work and music, and leave the detective work to me."

"Hey, don't forget, Danielle. It's Nathalie who came up with the evidence that led to Melissa's firing. You can't dispute a recorded confession. I think that was an ingenious sting operation if you ask me."

"Thanks for the vote of confidence, Lilly, but it was just a coincidence. When we got back from Cape Breton I was so upset Danielle found out I'd been lying to her about my real name and my involvement with Kristina. I figured no amount of explaining would excuse it, and I thought she'd hate me for the rest of her life."

Danielle squeezed Nathalie and said, "Never."

"I was lying on my sofa in the dark feeling like crap when I heard someone insert a key into my door. The only weapon I had was the syringe I'd used on the cat that had been hit by the car. It wasn't much protection, but I thought, if anything's going to happen to me I should record it and leave as many clues as I can. The recorder was sitting on the coffee table, and when I heard the key in the door, I just reached over and pressed the record button."

"I would have loved to have seen the look on her face when Melissa heard that play in front of her superiors," Danielle remarked.

"It was priceless," Nathalie said. "I don't think anybody's ever put one over on Melissa."

"Well, she met her match, didn't she?" Danielle nudged Nathalie with her shoulder.

"Hey, you're the genius. You're the one who figured out it was Maurice's brother who killed Kristina. Too bad you hadn't figured it out a few days *earlier*. I would have preferred my first experience with handcuffs to be a lot more pleasurable."

All three laughed.

"What was the first thing that made you suspect Joe, Danielle?" Lilly asked.

"At first it was just a sense that I needed to take a closer look at him, but the very first thing was probably the phone call from Maurice's cell phone to Kristina's house that night. Maurice said he just told her they made it to Gillian's apartment safely and then hung up, but the call had lasted seven minutes. That prompted me to check the cell phone tower that transmitted the call. It turned out to be in Timberlea, just outside Halifax on the way to Hubley, where Kristina lived. And since Gillian had used Maurice's cell to call her sister, I knew he had his phone on him when he was in Joe's truck.

"Then, when I was talking to Joe in the interview room, I mentioned that it wouldn't have taken much strength to wheel Kristina's body into the park. That's when he drove the nail into his own coffin without even realizing. He said that just because his brother could push a dolly, didn't mean he was the one who did it. I never mentioned a dolly. It could have been a wagon, or a shopping cart even, but he knew it was a dolly."

"But that wasn't a whole lot of proof," Nathalie said. "He could have said it was just an assumption on his part. A good lawyer might have—"

"But I had the *best* lawyer ever on my side." Danielle smiled at Lilly, then directed the rest of her response at Nathalie. "Lilly told me what I needed for a rock solid case. After my interview with Joe

Coultier, I was able to provide the Crown with evidence linking him directly to the murder. We found the drinking glass that matched her set, and the knife that cut the letter 'S' into her face, in the swamp he told us he threw them in."

"He pled guilty, then?" Nathalie asked.

It was Lilly who answered Nathalie's question. "No, even with his confession and the evidence, his lawyers will take it to trial. He'll get convicted, but they'll try to get him a reduced sentence."

"Could he get one?" Nathalie asked with concern.

"With all the incriminating evidence we got from him because of Lilly's legal advice, and with her as lead attorney? He'll be lucky if he gets out after twenty-five years," Danielle proudly announced. "You are going to take the job, aren't you? I know you enjoy being a federal prosecutor, but if you join the provincial Public Prosecution Service you'll have more interesting cases."

"I'm thinking about it. I was more relieved than happy when my boss offered me the lead on the drug case against Maurice Coultier, because I didn't know if they'd let me try another drug case ever again, but I must admit I was thrilled when I got an offer to join the provincial Crown and be lead prosecutor at Joseph Coultier's murder trial."

"Here's to Lilly," Nathalie said as she raised her glass. She touched hers to Lilly's, then Danielle's. "Here's to both of you. The Clever Constable and the Ardent Attorney, Halifax's best crime-fighting duo.

"Lilly, you could easily turn your Crown attorney's robe into a cape, and Danielle, I've got some living room curtains I don't need anymore that I could use to make you one."

The joke with a serious connotation—Nathalie was finally able to enjoy the view of her back yard—reminded Danielle of the cruel stunt Melissa Lambert had pulled, hanging a stuffed cat that looked like Chai, from Nathalie's tree. "I was never so glad to hear of someone getting fired," she said.

"You and me both," Lilly agreed. "Can't believe I let that woman into my house."

Danielle wondered if "house" was an allegory for "bed". Lilly never clarified whether she and Melissa had slept together or not, but Danielle decided it didn't matter, that if Lilly had, it was her private business.

"Looks like she's moved away," Danielle said. "Both her home phone and cell have been disconnected, and she was seen moving out."

"Knowing Melissa like I do," Nathalie said, "she'll probably finagle her way into a job in another province, or the States maybe, but at least we'll never see her again, that's all I care about."

"Here, here," all three said as they raised and clinked their glasses together.

Lilly, Danielle, and Nathalie were clearly enjoying each other's company and having a very good time. They had no reason not to be as relaxed as they were. After all, they had no idea that one of them was being captured into view by the scope of a high powered rifle. And that the eyes peering through that scope…belonged to Melissa Lambert.

About the Author

Nadine was born and raised in Restigouche County, which borders Québec, in north eastern New Brunswick, Canada.

Though French is her mother tongue, she learned English at a very young age and received much of her education in English.

She moved to Halifax, Nova Scotia, to pursue her education in Computer and Analytical Science, and quickly fell in love with the city. She has called it home ever since.

When Nadine isn't writing she's most likely outside enjoying nature (usually on or near the water), gardening, or indulging in her other passions: creating music and cooking.

Photo by Shelley Nagle.

A Note From Nadine

Having readers who enjoy and recommend my books is the best reward I could have for the work I put into them.

Thank you for reading, and should you have any comments or questions, I would love to hear from you.

I may be emailed at *nadine@nadinelapierre.com* or you may join me on Facebook: *www.facebook.com/nadinelapierre*

Verity and the Virgin Queen is the sequel to *The Slayer* and picks up right where *The Slayer* left off. To learn more, visit *www.nadinelapierre.com*

Made in the USA
Lexington, KY
14 May 2012